A.M. RILEY

Derailed

A Hobbs & Stirling Mystery

Copyright © 2024 by A.M. Riley

All rights reserved. No part of this publication may be reproduced, stored or transmitted in any form or by any means, electronic, mechanical, photocopying, recording, scanning, or otherwise without written permission from the publisher. It is illegal to copy this book, post it to a website, or distribute it by any other means without permission.

This novel is entirely a work of fiction. The names, characters and incidents portrayed in it are the work of the author's imagination. Any resemblance to actual persons, living or dead, events or localities is entirely coincidental.

A.M. Riley asserts the moral right to be identified as the author of this work.

Designations used by companies to distinguish their products are often claimed as trademarks. All brand names and product names used in this book and on its cover are trade names, service marks, trademarks and registered trademarks of their respective owners. The publishers and the book are not associated with any product or vendor mentioned in this book. None of the companies referenced within the book have endorsed the book.

Trigger warnings: this story contains themes of an adult nature and is not recommended for those under the age of 16. It contains occasional uses of strong language, in context, references to smoking, drug and alcohol use as well as violence and depictions of death. References to the behaviour of British and Thai government officials are fictional in nature.

First edition

*This book was professionally typeset on Reedsy.
Find out more at reedsy.com*

For my children, Austin and Abigail.

This book is proof that you can do anything if you believe in yourself.

As your grandad used to say,

'Have faith in yourself. I have faith in you.'

Love, Dad x

Contents

Chapter 1	1
Chapter 2	14
Chapter 3	19
Chapter 4	29
Chapter 5	38
Chapter 6	50
Chapter 7	59
Chapter 8	67
Chapter 9	77
Chapter 10	84
Chapter 11	92
Chapter 12	103
Chapter 13	120
Chapter 14	129
Chapter 15	143
Chapter 16	156
Chapter 17	166
Chapter 18	174
Chapter 19	191
Chapter 20	209
Chapter 21	221
Chapter 22	229
Chapter 23	246
Chapter 24	258

Chapter 25	271
Chapter 26	282
Chapter 27	296
Chapter 28	306
Chapter 29	314
Chapter 30	325
Epilogue	334
Author's Note	341

Chapter 1

Frank Hobbs emerged from the exit of Vauxhall tube station, yanking up the collar on his long dark winter coat. The vehicles that lined the streets still sported a thin layer of frost which shimmered with the soft light of the headlights of buses and black cabs carrying commuters through the Lambeth dawn.

Hunched over in protest at the icy breeze which stung his cheeks, and ruing his recent decision to shave his full beard into a more stylish goatee, he stepped into the frozen street. He hurried under the monstrous twin stainless-steel cantilevers of Vauxhall Bus Station which stretched skywards like a bizarre tuning fork. After narrowly avoiding being flattened by a signature London bus and its signature less-than-cheerful driver, he turned right towards the railway and the tunnel which ran beneath it.

Dimly lit and daubed in uninspiring graffiti, the pedestrian path that stretched through the tunnel could be viewed as downright menacing to a lone out-of-town visitor trying to find their stop for a night bus home but Frank Hobbs was unphased by the short walk through the darkness for two reasons: firstly, this was his daily morning commute and had been for the last five years, since the National Missing

Persons Unit was absorbed into the National Crime Agency, and secondly, Frank Hobbs was an imposing figure himself. At over six feet tall and seemingly half as wide, the sight of him in his dark winter coat, silhouetted against the orange glow of the tunnel lights, his condensed breath or cigarette smoke rising in tendrils above him, would make even the bravest soul think about crossing the road to avoid a close encounter. So, he made the journey every morning without a care, other than the biting cold which enveloped him on frigid December mornings such as this one.

Reaching the end of the tunnel without incident, Hobbs turned left and crossed a small street, putting in a half-hearted run as he mistimed his dart in front of an early-morning courier who had slowed to let him cross. He continued straight, into Goding Street and, as normal, found himself parallel to the famous Vauxhall Arches - an eclectic mix of businesses nestled in the arched spaces under the railway line. Hip eating establishments, luxury motorcycle showrooms and boutique theatres vied for attention with bars, nightclubs and spas servicing the vibrant LGBT community of Central London.

The sky was beginning to lighten to the east, across the river, behind the Tate Britain and the City of Westminster. Trains click-clacked on the rails overhead with the rhythmic cadence of an ancient metronome as he headed diagonally across Vauxhall Pleasure Gardens. He had always thought it an odd choice of name for a park so close to a string of gay bars and he smiled to himself once more as he passed the sign at the entrance to the park.

Travelling through the park was a less-direct route to his place of work, yet he still preferred to take it. London, and

CHAPTER 1

particularly Vauxhall Cross, was a noisy and dirty place. The city's few green spaces acted as small oases for the almost 9 million inhabitants that called London home and Hobbs himself enjoyed his brief stroll among the towering oak trees each morning. If he wasn't in a rush, he would often feed the birds from a bag of bird seed that he kept in his inside coat pocket. On occasion, a hungry or inquisitive grey squirrel scurried down from its resting place and Hobbs was willing to indulge its curiosity.

Today, however, there was no time for such luxuries as Hobbs and his partner were scheduled for a meeting with the head of the Missing Persons department. Hobbs had woken that morning to find a message on his phone about an important meeting first thing. He had inquired into the nature of the meeting but was simply told it was 'important' and that he 'better not be late getting his bloody bacon butty.'

Hobbs mimicked the threat under his breath as he walked into the Tea House Theatre Café. A small brass bell rang out in protest as it was rudely jostled by the opening door which Hobbs closed quickly behind him to keep out the icy draft that had followed him in uninvited. It was still early and the cafe wasn't busy. An older gentleman sat in one corner with a steaming cup of tea, his head buried in a broadsheet newspaper. A mid-30s black gentleman, sat in a smart pin-striped suit, sipped at his coffee while he scrolled lazily through his E-Mails. Neither of the men looked up when Hobbs entered.

Behind the counter, a young barista busied. She wore her bleach blonde hair in a short pixie style with a severe undercut. It was covered by a small black beanie rolled up so far it covered just the top of her head. Her ears were pierced in multiple places, along with her nose and the area between her chin and lower lip which Hobbs didn't remember the name of. He wasn't sure if he'd ever known the name, in fact. Below rolled up white sleeves, she sported a colourful half-sleeve tattoo which comprised of various elements: playing cards, roses, musical notes and a few images which he recognised as being from one of the many Harry Potter movies that his own girls so adored. She looked up from her work as Hobbs approached the counter, wiping her hands on her brown industrial-style apron.

"Morning, Frank. The usual?" she asked with a warm, sleepy smile.

"Yes, please, Iris," replied Hobbs, rubbing his large, weathered hands together and blowing into them, half to actually warm them and half as a conversation starter about the weather.

"Chilly one this morning. Two degrees it says on my phone," he said at the end of a long, exaggerated out-breath.

"Mine said minus one when I got up this morning. Should warm up later on, though. Might be a nice sunny day. You never know," replied Iris, as she grabbed Hobbs' bacon from a hot plate on the counter and placed it carefully into a floury white bap.

Hobbs had never really understood the national obsession with conversing with strangers about the weather. He guessed it was the only thing that anyone really had in common at any point in time - something that connected them, something to talk about to fill the void of silence between two people who don't know each other well enough to ask about work, family or their most recent holiday. He wished he had more to talk about with Iris each morning, but it was clear they were very different people. They both had tattoos - there was that. But his were faded symbols of a bygone era of his life: Frank Hobbs the London cabby and part-time boxing trainer. Boxing trainer sounded better than failed professional boxer, he thought. The new Frank Hobbs was different; he wore a suit to work, albeit refusing to wear a tie, and spent the majority of his day at a desk, poring over CCTV or police reports, sipping rubbish instant coffee and dreaming of his next bacon sandwich.

Iris squirted a generous blob of HP sauce onto Hobbs' butty, dropped it into a brown paper bag and placed it on the counter before turning round and attending to Hobbs' coffee: black, with a double shot. Hobbs paid for his breakfast with a tap of his card and dropped a pound coin into the tip jar. He thanked Iris, jammed his bacon butty package into his coat pocket and continued his commute.

His coffee was too hot to drink at that moment but did a wonderful job of warming his hands as he walked the final hundred metres of his journey - down Vauxhall Walk, right into Tinworth Street and finally into Citadel Place to the entrance of Spring Gardens - the London headquarters of the National Crime Agency.

It had been a little over five years since the UK Missing Persons Bureau was absorbed into the NCA from its original home within the Metropolitan Police and renamed the UK Missing Persons Unit. Hobbs had been present through the whole transition and was widely regarded as a piece of the furniture among both the old guard and the new fish that came through the doors of Spring Gardens each year.

Hobbs' office was on the third floor of the rather nondescript building which was a stone's throw from the iconic

River Thames that meandered lazily through Central London.

Hobbs proffered his ID badge to a bleary-eyed security guard who gave it a perfunctory glance and buzzed him through the heavy-duty black metal gates. He buzzed himself in the front door of Spring Gardens and climbed the stairs to his office. One more buzzed card and he flopped into his office chair, simultaneously firing up his PC and taking a first swig of his now cool-enough-to-drink coffee.

On a flat-screen television in the corner of the office, the BBC's Nadia Kapoor was doing a round-up of the morning news. EU leaders had recently endorsed the long-awaited Brexit withdrawal agreement, a labour MP had come out in the House of Commons as HIV+ and something else about a satellite and national defence. None of the stories particularly grabbed Hobbs' attention so he quickly turned instead to the guilty pleasure of the bacon butty in his coat pocket.

As Hobbs bit hungrily into his breakfast bap, he heard the familiar buzz of the office security door and the tell-tale sound of high heels on the dated linoleum flooring. He glanced at the clock in the corner of his computer screen: 8:00 A.M. - on the dot.

"Morning, Debs," he called, without looking over his shoulder to see who had entered behind him. He didn't need to. He knew exactly who it was. There was only ever one person who buzzed in at exactly eight every morning and that was Debra Stirling.

"Morning, Frankie," she replied cheerfully, slipping off her long, woollen maroon scarf and draping it over her own chair. "Bloody freezing out there this morning."

"You can say that again," Hobbs replied, through a mouthful of his breakfast "What do you think Harding wants with us?

CHAPTER 1

She said it was important."

"No idea. She thinks everything's important. Anything in the news this morning?"

Hobbs swivelled around on his chair, cradling his hot coffee in two hands. "Nothing much. The usual crap about Brexit and something about a Labour MP who got HIV from falling in a young man's lap in Clapham Common."

"Frank!" exclaimed Stirling trying her best to hide the smirk faintly appearing on her bright red lips. "It's 2018. You can't be saying those kinds of things, especially as a public servant," she added with feigned admonishment.

"Well, I'll stop saying those kinds of things when they stop doing those kinds of things," Hobbs retorted with a boyish grin and Stirling finally afforded him a wry smile.

The picture on the TV cut to a backdrop of a river straddled confidently by an iron-framed trestle bridge. Stirling and Hobbs looked on. The thick but dry foliage around the river indicated that the setting was tropical, probably south-east Asian. A middle-aged correspondent with greying hair and glasses raised his microphone to speak. Stirling recognised him as the South East Asia correspondent for the BBC but couldn't muster up his name. The red banner at the bottom of the screen eventually identified him as Edward Hines. He began his report with an earnest tone.

"I'm here in Kanchanaburi. A sleepy railway town in the west of the Kingdom of Thailand, famed only for its small cameo in the Second World War as the home of the Bridge over the River Kwai. But tonight, all eyes are on Kanchanaburi as the fifteen-year-old daughter of Richard Patterson, the British Ambassador to Thailand, has gone missing aboard a routine train journey from the country's

capital Bangkok to partake in the annual River Kwai Light and Sound Festival. Details are still emerging, but sources confirm young Ella Patterson boarded the train with her father yesterday afternoon but failed to disembark as planned at the River Kwai Bridge station. Local police have completed a thorough search of the train and surrounding area but have thus far found no trace of the teenager. They are understandably concerned for Ella's safety but remain confident that she will be found in the very near future. Meanwhile, the Foreign and Commonwealth Office in London has confirmed that they will be supporting the Royal Thai Police with assistance from the United Kingdom but would not yet comment on what form that might take."

"Poor lass," said Stirling, once the programme had cut back to Nadia Kapoor. "I doubt they have much of a missing persons unit over there."

"Aye," agreed Frank, "They're notoriously bloody useless… and corrupt, by all accounts."

"Have you been out there then? Thailand?" Stirling asked.

Hobbs replied, "Once, when I was younger. Must have been twenty years ago now. I studied *Muay Thai* - that's Thai boxing - out there for a few months at a camp in *Foo-ket*. I didn't last long to be honest. Bloody hard bastards those Thai fighters. They're brought up on it. The only way out of poverty for some of 'em. They start at five years old kicking the whatsit out of a banana tree and by six, they're kicking the whatsit out of each other in professional fights. Hands, feet, knees and elbows – the lot. They call it *The Art of Eight Limbs.* You can imagine what they're like when they get to 18 or 20 - bloody killing machines. Boxing is one thing, but Muay Thai is a whole different kettle of fish."

CHAPTER 1

Frank noticed Stirling losing interest and quickly brought his rough documentary on the origins of Thai boxing to an end. "Never got out to the River Kwai, though. Shame that, because I do like my history."

Stirling glanced at her watch. "Come on, Frankie. Its ten past - time to see Captain Hard Arse. Oh, and it's pronounced *poo-ket*, not *foo-ket*, by the way." Hobbs looked indignant but decided he didn't have time to argue and conceded the point, making a mental note of the correct pronunciation.

"Alright, Smart Arse. Let's see what she's got to say this time," he replied, rising to his feet with the obligatory moan of a man nearing five decades on this earth.

Stirling knocked twice and strutted confidently into the central office - a glass cube with metal blinds which could be raised and lowered based on the confidentiality of the conversations taking place inside. Her short red curls bounced lazily on the collar of her navy business suit. Hobbs followed reluctantly behind with his trade-mark nonchalant swagger which incidentally curried no favour with his hard-nosed boss.

Yvonne Harding looked up from her computer and removed her glasses to better see the two detectives. Her West-Indian eyes were dark and intense and at that moment were boring into Hobbs and Stirling as they stood in the doorway like a couple of naughty schoolchildren at the door of the head teacher's office.

Yvonne Harding was an imposing superior. Her dark Jamaican skin glowed at the ridge of her high cheek bones. Her hair was collected atop her head in a neat network of braids, interwoven with an off-white thread. One could tell at one time she had certainly been beautiful, but now her age was betrayed by the wiry white hairs which stuck out at jaunty angles from her temples like the wayward springs of an old mattress. Deep furrows of crow's feet stretched outwards from the corners of her eyes; signs of a double life lived playing in the island sun as a child and now behind a desk in a high-stress position as Head of the UK National Missing Persons Unit.

Debra Stirling couldn't decide if she envied her or admired her. Yvonne Harding was the polar opposite of her. Harding was dark where Stirling was pale. Harding had a dark intense gaze, where Stirling's green eyes glinted with intelligence and a glimmer of Celtic playfulness. Harding was tall and rather stocky where Stirling was shorter and less defined. Yvonne Harding embodied the *power woman* persona, but Stirling was forced to augment her outward appearance with high heels, business suits and bright lipstick. They had one thing in common, though. They were both incredibly good at their jobs and had risen from the bottom to their current positions on merit alone.

"Well, don't stand there like a couple of lemons. Come in and take a seat. You're late. Have you been at those bacon butties again, Frank?" Harding asked, again with those deeply inquiring eyes.

"Sorry, Ma'am," Stirling interjected, as they both sat down on the other side of Harding's desk. "We were just watching the news there about the missing lass in Thailand."

"Ah, yes. About that," began Harding. "How do you like Thai food, Frank?"

Both of their faces suddenly and simultaneously dropped.

"Well, erm…" spluttered Hobbs, as the realisation of what was coming next came tumbling to the forefront of his mind.

CHAPTER 1

"It's not bad. A bit spicy for me, Ma'am. Truth be told."

"Well, you're going to be getting a lot of it – both of you," began Harding in her usual authoritarian tone. "As you've seen this morning, we've got a misper in Thailand." (*Misper* was a commonly-used abbreviation for *missing person* in the NMPU). "Now, of course, this wouldn't normally be our jurisdiction, but she's a British national and she's the daughter of a high-ranking diplomat, so that changes things. I had a call last night from Jenny Bateman the Director-General of the FCDO (Foreign, Commonwealth and Development Office) for the Indo-Pacific region." Hobbs and Stirling exchanged a furtive glance but sustained their attention. Harding continued, "She says they're duty bound to send some sort of assistance. Now, bearing in mind that this is a 15-year-old girl, it's more than likely that she's just buggered off in some futile act of teenage rebellion. Having said that, if that's not the case, then the Thai police are actually going to need our assistance. They're bloody useless, by all accounts."

Frank risked a sideways glance at Stirling to say, *"I told you so."* but Stirling didn't take the bait and kept her gaze fixed on Harding.

"Anyway," Harding continued. "they need a couple of our officers to pop over there, keep an eye on the local search efforts, reassure the great British public that we're doing all we can to assist distressed British nationals overseas. I thought you two would be the perfect choice."

"I'm honoured that you thought of us, Ma'am," began Hobbs with insincere deference. "But, I'm not sure my wife would be too happy, what with it being Christmas in a few weeks."

Harding's riposte was swift and clearly pre-prepared. "You'll only be gone a week and I've already spoken to Eileen.

She's also very concerned for the young girl's safety and is packing you a bag as we speak." Frank sat back in his seat, mollified. "I also called your home number, Stirling, to see if there was anyone who could prepare your things but got no answer. Still on your own, I gather?"

"Yes, Ma'am," replied Stirling, choosing not to add, *"Not that it's any of your business".*

"Right," exclaimed Harding, clapping her hands and rubbing them together.

She was enjoying this, Stirling thought.

"Your flight leaves at just after one this afternoon. I don't need to tell you that the first 48 hours of a missing persons investigation are the most crucial. The poor mite has been missing for 12 hours already and it's a 13-hour flight to Bangkok. So, you better get your skates on. She might even be found by the time you get there."

Stirling and Hobbs both groaned inwardly.

"I've got all the information in the file here," Harding continued, passing a beige foolscap folder to Hobbs. "Frank, you can have a look over it and check online for anything else that is coming out of Thailand. Debra, you head on home and do your packing. We'll send Frank here in a taxi to pick you up at 9:30. That should give you time to find someone to look after the cat. I'm assuming you've got a cat - you single 30-something females normally do."

Stirling rolled her eyes and nodded her head in silent confirmation. Harding was definitely enjoying this.

"Right, well, chop-chop then. Celia has all your flight information. You can grab it on your way out. We managed to get you on BA, non-stop from Heathrow. Unfortunately, Jonny Taxpayer couldn't spring for business class, but I'm told the fish and rice in economy class is lovely."

Yvonne Harding stretched a disingenuous smile across her thin lips which signalled the end of the decidedly one-sided conversation.

"Very good, Ma'am," acquiesced Stirling and Hobbs in unison before turning on their heels and heading back into the office with a hefty sigh. It was going to be a very long day indeed.

Chapter 2

Hobbs shifted uncomfortably in his seat and tapped aimlessly at the in-flight entertainment system. To his left, in the aisle seat, Stirling attempted to doze, her eyes covered with a sleep mask emblazoned with the colours of British Airways. Seven hours into the flight and 35,000 feet in the air, the pair were halfway to their destination: the bustling metropolis of Bangkok.

Hobbs hated flying long haul. He wasn't built to be crammed into a tiny seat for half a day at a time and he hated the boredom. He liked to be kept busy, following up leads, checking CCTV, interviewing eyewitnesses, not cooped-up in a giant flying bean can with nothing to do but watch cinema blockbusters on a 6-inch screen using headphones which sounded like they'd been pulled from the river the night before.

"Debs, pssst!" he whispered sharply. Stirling turned away towards the aisle and Hobbs swore he could see her rolling her eyes underneath her sleep mask. "Debs, you awake?" he tried again.

"What is it, Frank?" replied Stirling with a purposeful sigh.

"You reckon this lass will have been found by the time we get there, like the Gaffer said?"

CHAPTER 2

"I don't know," replied Stirling, pulling her sleep mask up onto her forehead and turning to sit straight in her seat. "We don't know much about her. You've seen the file. The information is scant to say the least. You'd think they'd have given us all they had if they really do want us to assist them in their enquiries."

"I'm sure the local cops aren't thrilled to have us over there stepping on their toes, though. I certainly wouldn't fancy a couple of busybodies showing up during one of my investigations," replied Hobbs.

"Well, neither would I, but they must want her found, surely. Maybe they're also thinking she'll turn up hungover after a night on the town with her mates."

Hobbs frowned."Yeah, maybe. It just doesn't sit right with me. Anyway, there's a decent amount on the father, Richard Patterson. British Ambassador to Thailand - been in post for donkey's years, since 2001, apparently. He was in Manila, for four years before Thailand and Singapore for three before that. Before his long and distinguished career with the diplomatic service, he studied at King's College, Wimbledon and studied International Relations at Cambridge. A highbrow diplomat through-and-through, by the looks of it. No previous marriages that the Embassy knows about and just the one daughter. He's had sole custody of Ella since 2009 after a messy divorce with her mother - a Thai national." Hobbs stumbled over the pronunciation of the name. "Anchalee Jitpracharoen."

"Where is her mother now?" interjected Stirling.

"It doesn't say. It just says she's living abroad."

"Great. Well that's a piece of information that should definitely be in the file," sighed Stirling. "Make a note, would you, to find that information out as soon as we arrive?"

"Roger, Roger," replied Hobbs, scribbling the note in handwriting that could only ever be read by himself and, on occasion, his partner.

"And we need to try to find out if she has any regular contact with her mother, or when she last spoke to her," added Stirling.

"Last…contact," repeated Hobbs, writing his note and ending it with a large question mark.

Stirling replaced her sleep mask and turned once again into the aisle, signalling the end of the short mid-air conversation. Hobbs clicked his pen and placed it back in his pocket. He shoved the file roughly back in his bag and pushed it once again under the seat in front of him.

"Night, Frank. Try to get some sleep. It'll be morning when we arrive and you'll be fit for nothing, especially if you haven't had your bacon butty."

Hobbs himself closed his eyes and pulled his navy blanket up around his neck. After a few minutes of trying in vain to fall asleep, he reached into his bag once again to pull out the file on Ella Patterson. He slipped out a small photograph of Ella that was paper clipped to the inside cover of a Manila folder and stared into the face of the girl they had been tasked to find.

She was undoubtedly pretty, a seemingly perfect meeting of east and west. Her skin was a golden tan colour that glowed next to a beaming smile of shining white teeth and full lips. Her long hair, lighter than is usual in South East Asia, was streaked with blonde and partially covered by a straw boater hat that was part of the ceremonial uniform of the international school she attended in the northern suburbs of Bangkok. She had not the wide, somewhat-squished nose that is common in many areas of Thailand, but instead was blessed with a long prominent ridge that was ever so slightly turned up at the end. Hobbs figured her nose must have come from her father. But it was the eyes that were the most striking aspect of her appearance. Staring back at Hobbs from the photograph were a pair of dazzling hazel-green eyes – almost unheard of among people with Asian ancestry.

During the time at the station, waiting for Stirling to pack her bags, Hobbs had performed numerous Google searches on Ella Patterson. It seemed that Ella was a minor Internet celebrity. Search results showed she had over 35,000 followers on Instagram, @ellybelly2003, and almost double that on Facebook. Hobbs didn't have an Instagram account but had access to the Facebook account that he shared with his wife. He scrolled curiously through Ella's public Facebook feed which consisted mostly of pictures of her at various eating and drinking establishments throughout what appeared to be downtown Bangkok. Who knew that a 15-year-old's selfie with a Krispy Kreme doughnut or Starbucks iced coffee would garner quite so much attention online?

Hobbs experienced a momentary feeling of contempt but quickly brushed it off, deciding he was only feeling envious.

Finally, for the first time since take-off, Hobbs began to feel tired and thought he better make the most of it. He carefully replaced the photograph back into the file and put everything back under the seat in front of him. Within minutes, he had drifted into a light, fitful sleep and began to dream.

In the dream, he was in an ageing train carriage with painted wooden walls the colour of duck eggs, walking in a narrow aisle between hard wooden bench seats. The photograph of Ella Patterson, that he had held just moments ago, drifted and twisted in front of his face as if suspended in a breeze. He reached out his hand multiple times to snatch it, but it perpetually slipped from his grasp and finally ended up face down on the train carriage floor. He stooped down to retrieve it, but it skittered away on the breeze once more.

When he finally caught up with the photo and turned it over, the pretty high-schooler from his memory was nowhere to be seen, replaced instead by a grotesque figure laying prone in a twisted position in a filthy industrial skip. The blonde streaks in her hair were replaced with dark, rivers of dried blood. The dazzling green eyes were now portrayed as black pits, writhing with maggots, feasting on the dead girl's face. As Hobbs stared at the unfathomable scene in front of him, the corpse's head suddenly snapped towards him and he was jolted violently awake.

He gasped a huge inward breath as he checked his surroundings, momentarily confused by the similarity of the train carriage and the aircraft cabin. He swung his head backwards and forwards, looking for any sign of the macabre scene he had just witnessed. To his profound relief, he found himself safely back in his seat and surrounded by rows of slumbering passengers. Stirling remained in the seat next to him, snoring peacefully. His hammering heart began to slow gradually as he wiped away the cool sweat which had formed in beads on his forehead and temples. His mind wandered to the dream which he had just escaped. He leaned back in his chair, with a long exhale and, though he was not a religious man, he hoped to God that Ella would be found by the time they landed.

Chapter 3

Upon collecting their bags from the luggage carousel at Suvarnabhumi International Airport, Hobbs and Stirling made their way through customs, opting for the green channel labelled N*othing to Declare*. "I have nothing to declare except my genius!" Stirling quipped gleefully, quoting the late great Oscar Wilde, and bounced energetically towards the arrivals hall with all the energy of someone who had just had seven hours of uninterrupted sleep. Hobbs trudged in the same direction with all the energy of someone who clearly hadn't.

Stirling scanned the waiting crowd, looking for the arrival sign from the British Embassy that they were expecting. The crowd was a healthy mix of bored looking drivers, excited family members eager to be reunited with their loved ones, and representatives from a host of different hotels and golf resorts. She quickly discounted any signs bearing the words *hotel* or *resort* and any that looked home-made. She watched as couples kissed and families embraced. She wondered when she would find someone who would be waiting excitedly for her at the airport.

Finally, she saw their names written neatly in capital letters on an official-looking board bearing the name and logo of the British Embassy, Bangkok. The board was being held lackadaisically by one of the bored-looking drivers but next to him, looking around eagerly, was a woman who appeared to be in her mid-thirties with long, curly hair that hung in rivulets down past her slender shoulders. She appeared to be of mixed-race, possibly Middle Eastern and European. Her tan skin was smooth and unblemished other than a smattering of dark freckles which danced across her high cheekbones and over the arch of a slightly hooked nose.

Stirling offered a small wave to catch her attention and she waved back with a friendly smile. Stirling and Hobbs rounded the barrier and brought their pull-along bags to a standstill in front of the pair.

"Welcome to Thailand!" the woman exclaimed, holding out her hand, first to Stirling and then to Hobbs. "I'm Stella. Stella Ismael," she continued. "I'm the Deputy Ambassador here in Bangkok, and this is Loong Pon our trusted driver at the embassy. He'll be driving you down to Kanchanaburi this morning. It's a pleasure to have you both. I'm terribly sorry to bring you all the way out here, but we really could use your help."

Her appearance may have been exotic, but her accent was very typically British.

"Thank you, Stella," replied Stirling with deference. "I'm Debra. Debra Stirling. And this is my partner, Frank Hobbs."

"Hi, Frank," said Stella with a genuine smile. "How was your flight? It's terribly long, isn't it?"

"That it is," replied Frank. "But it was fine, thank you. We're just eager to get going and find our misper as soon as possible."

"Of course, you are. How silly of me. Well, let's get going, shall we? Here, Frank, if you pass your bag to Pon and I'll take yours, Debra, we'll be on our way. The van is parked just outside the exit doors. There are some perks to working at the embassy, after all."

Hobbs and Stirling followed the pair towards the exit. As soon as the doors opened, they were hit by a wall of tropical heat and humidity that first slapped them hard in the face and then travelled deep down into their lungs, stinging their nostrils and warming them deep in their chests.

"Phwooar!" exclaimed Hobbs, wincing at the extreme change in temperature. "You forget how hot it is here. It's like a bloody steam room!"

Stella chuckled. "You won't believe me, but this is actually the cool season. It gets a lot hotter than this in the summer… and more humid."

"More humid?" asked Stirling incredulously. "My hair is going to be a nightmare in this! You didn't tell me about that, Frank."

"Not something I really have to worry about," he said rubbing his thinning, grey hair. "Low maintenance is the style I go for."

Stella chuckled again and said, "Don't worry, I can recommend you some hair products that work wonders. We curly-haired goddesses have to stick together."

"Thank goodness for that," replied Stirling, trying without success to flatten down her mass of red curls which looked like it was trying to escape from the top of her head.

The group stopped at the kerb next to a white Toyota Alphard with blacked out windows. There was no sign of the British Embassy logo anywhere on the vehicle. The automatic doors opened to reveal four large comfortable seats upholstered in brown leather. Stella gestured for the detectives to get in as Loong Pon heaved their luggage into the generous boot space. Stella climbed into the front passenger seat and they all fastened their seatbelts as the driver returned and blasted the air conditioning to a frigid temperature.

Hobbs and Stirling both breathed a sigh of relief as the cool air washed over their weary faces and they relaxed into the soft leather seats. As the driver pulled away, Hobbs was reminded that they drove on the same side of the road as they did in the UK.

"Right, that's better," began Stella. "Unfortunately, I won't be able to accompany you down to Kanchanaburi as I have to fill in for Richard at the Rotary Club Winter Gala this evening. Rotten luck. However, we have a young Thai police constable who speaks excellent English who we've roped into looking after you while you're with us. He's a terribly nice fellow and a good copper. He's a Kanchanaburi local but went to secondary school and university in Kent. He works out of Pahon Yothin Police Station here in Bangkok now, so you'll pick him up after you've dropped me off downtown and then you'll be on your way out west. Does that sound OK?"

"That sounds fine, Stella." replied Stirling. "Thank you for picking us up at least. It's always nice to see a friendly face on the other side of the barrier."

"How long of a drive is it?" asked Hobbs.

"Oh, not too long," Stella replied. "A couple of hours, I think Richard said. He does it often. He's somewhat of a history buff. He attends the festival every year as well as a memorial service around Remembrance Sunday and another coming up next week. That's once you get out of Bangkok, of course, which can take a while. The traffic can be brutal. Thank God for air conditioning and comfy seats."

CHAPTER 3

"Which festival is it, again?" asked Hobbs, curiously.

"The River Kwai Light and Sound Festival, or something along those lines. They have a full-on production with actors, pyrotechnics and the like. They tell the story of the allied troops during World War II who fought and were imprisoned there by the Japanese occupiers. Most of them were forced to build what's now called *The Death Railway* between Thailand and Burma. Many of them died. Terribly sad. Richard obviously knows much more about it than I do. He'll undoubtedly fill you in. He loves talking about it to just about anyone who will listen. His grandfather was there, I believe."

Stirling interjected, "I'm not so sure about that. I would have thought he'd be worried sick about his daughter's disappearance. There will hardly be time for war stories."

"Oh, why yes, of course," replied Stella, slightly abashed. "After she's found, I mean. I'm sure it won't be too long. You know what teenaged girls are like, especially those who belong to single fathers."

"Has she a history of running away, or rebellion then, do you know?" Stirling asked, reaching into her inside pocket for her trusty notebook and pen.

"No, not that I'm aware of, but just in general, you know?" Richard thinks she's probably just turned her phone off so she can have a good old party with friends and worry her old man to death at the same time."

The word *death* pricked suddenly at Hobbs and he was momentarily transported back inside the ageing train carriage of his mid-air dream, staring once more at the macabre image of a deceased Ella. He shook his head sharply which was noticed by Stirling.

"Are you OK, Frank?" she asked.

"What? Oh, yeah. I'm fine. Just tired, that's all. I don't sleep well on planes. Look at the size of me." he replied, feigning a yawn.

"Well, it'll be the best part of an hour to the embassy, even on the elevated express way. So, you might as well try and get forty winks," said Stella. "The seats in here are a bit more comfy than British Airways economy class."

Both Hobbs and Stirling didn't need to be told twice and both quickly found the recliner lever of their seats. Almost as soon as their weary heads hit the headrest, they both fell into an exhausted sleep.

* * *

The two missing persons detectives were woken by the open door alarm of the Toyota Alphard as Stella Ismael alighted outside the British Embassy on South Sathorn Road. They watched as she dashed across the pavement and into the AIA building foyer.

The driver, who Stella had introduced as Loong Pon, twisted his shoulder to hand two business cards and a hand written note on British Embassy stationery back to Hobbs and Stirling in the rear of the vehicle. The business cards belonged to Stella Ismael and Richard Patterson and the note was from Stella. It read:

I didn't want to wake you. You've had a long journey and it's not over yet. Richard is awaiting your arrival in Kanchanaburi. London says you're the best, but please do call or E-Mail me if there's anything I can help with. We're all desperate to have Ella

CHAPTER 3

back safe and sound. Speak soon. Stella.

Stirling passed the letter to Hobbs to read and watched as the vehicle moved slowly down the busy road in the heart of the commercial district of downtown Bangkok. Motorcycles whizzed past the van on either side, sharing the road with meter-taxis in a plethora of different colours: some green and yellow, some bright blue, purple or pink. Huge bundles of sprawling electricity and phone cables snaked down either side of the road and met in a maelstrom of wires, junction boxes and electrical tape at every corner. Hordes of locals, some in smart business suits, some in shorts, t-shirts and flip-flops, milled this way and that, crossing the large pedestrian crossings in front of an army of motorcycle taxi drivers jostling for position at the front of the pack in their colourful numbered vests. The elevated trains of Bangkok's mass transit system - officially called the BTS but locally named the Skytrain - shuttled commuters and shoppers backwards and forwards above the gridlocked traffic below.

This setting continued for more than half an hour as they battled their way through the bustling streets of Bangkok and its notorious traffic. Finally, they pulled off the main road and into a small car park which had a sign saying *Pahon Yothin Police Station* in English and the same, presumably, in Thai script above it.

The driver, Loong Pon, parked the van in a bay marked *Visitors,* opened his door and said cheerfully in broken English,"I come back five minute. You wait me here, OK?" Stirling and Hobbs nodded their approval and the driver made his way across the car park to the police station.

When their driver returned, he was accompanied by a

young male police officer who strode confidently across the car park. He wore the official uniform of the Royal Thai Police which was light brown, almost grey, in colour and skin-tight. A length of bright red piping ran over his shoulder from under the armpit and the insignia on his epaulettes identified him as a police constable. On the lapels of his heavily starched collar were pinned the twin silver badges of the Royal Thai Police emblem that also adorned many of the vehicles parked in the vicinity. His black leather shoes were polished to an impressive shine and he moved towards their vehicle with his peaked police cap tucked neatly under one arm which carried a black leather briefcase. Over the opposite shoulder he carried a small rucksack, presumably containing the belongings he needed for his trip west accompanying Hobbs and Stirling. He nodded courteously as the driver spoke to him in an animated fashion, no doubt illuminating the young police constable with his theories regarding the disappearance of young Ella Patterson.

The pair parted as they walked to opposite sides of the vehicle. They both climbed into the vehicle and the police officer turned, bringing his hands together in front of his face to form the traditional Thai greeting of the *wai*, before offering his outstretched hand first to Hobbs and then to Stirling as he introduced himself.

He spoke in accented but fluent English. "Good morning, Detectives. I am Police Constable Sittichai Boonchanalert, but you can call me Chai. Most people use their nicknames here as their real names can be quite long."

"You can say that again," replied Hobbs. "I'm Detective Frank Hobbs. You can call me Frank. This is my partner, Debra Stirling."

CHAPTER 3

"You can call me Debra, or Debs."

"Frank and Debra. Got it. Welcome to Thailand. It is my pleasure to assist you in this investigation."

Frank spoke first. "Thank you, Chai. It's a pleasure to meet you and we're very lucky to have you. Neither Debra nor I speak any Thai, so it would be very difficult for us to conduct our enquiries without your help."

"Yes, it's wonderful to have you with us," Stirling chimed in. "We're sorry to take you away from your family. We hope Ella will be found very soon and you won't be away with us too long."

"Oh, never mind. It is my duty. Also, I am single so no need to worry about my family."

Debra blushed. She had not meant it in that way but now she had noticed that Chai was indeed fairly good-looking. He looked to be mid-twenties, possibly 25 or 26, slim, that much was evident from his overly-tight uniform, and seemingly tall for a Thai. His dark hair was cut in the style compulsory for all Thai police officers since the previous year. Officially called the '904' cut, it was colloquially known on the force as the 'khaaw saam daan' or 'white on three sides'. On the back and sides, the hair was cropped impossibly short with the top left a little longer, similar to the buzz-cut of the US Marine Corps.

Chai turned to face forwards as the van pulled out of the police station and back onto the main road. Stirling was limited to the view of his eyes in the vanity mirror of the sun visor which he had just pulled down to shield his eyes from the fierce morning sun. His eyes were dark, like 99% of the Thai population, and kind, almost playful, which was in direct contrast to the outward appearance that he projected as a conscientious young police officer.

Debra's eyes caught his as he looked into the back to speak to the detectives once again and she lowered them immediately.

"It will take a few hours to get to Kanchanaburi and there isn't much to look at. I think you can get some sleep. I can wake you just before we arrive in Kanchanaburi, then you can see the town as we drive through," he suggested.

"Good idea," replied Hobbs with an exaggerated yawn. "I'm knackered."

Chai gave a puzzled look in the mirror as if he didn't understand Hobbs' slang, but Hobbs was too tired to explain. They both once again settled back into the comfort of their seats and took the chance to get some more much-needed rest.

Chapter 4

As promised, Chai had woken the detectives as they were coming into Kanchanaburi town and, after a brief pit stop at their hotel for a shower and a change of clothes, they were now on their way towards the bridge of epic war movie fame.

Kanchanaburi town was much like any other provincial capital in Thailand. Tentacular developments followed the large main roads which forged their way across the plains of Central Thailand. Three or four lane highways were separated by wide, green medians decorated with topiaries and other tropical flora as well as ornate street lights which illuminated the road at regular intervals. In Kanchanaburi, said street lights took the form of large golden Koi carp, leaping skywards from the invisible river below. Shophouses of up to four storeys and varying colours lined the roads housing a wide range of small businesses. Hardware shops, motorcycle repair shops and pharmacies shared the roadside with an abundance of 7-11 convenience stores and local banks.

As the detectives travelled farther into the town and closer to the bridge, the roads narrowed and businesses became more touristic. The aforementioned local staples were replaced with guest houses, bars, restaurants and massage shops all catering to the 7 million or more western tourists who visited the sleepy riverside town each year. In honour of these visitors, the local streets were named after countries from which they hail: England Road and New Zealand Alley featured as well as roads named after India, Korea, Malaysia and Taiwan.

After a while, Hobbs and Stirling realised that their van had not moved for several minutes in the staunch traffic generated by the start of the upcoming festivities. Private cars, taxis and the ubiquitous tuk-tuks all sat motionless, honking their horns and spewing exhaust gases into the humid air.

"I think it might be quicker to walk," said Chai, defeated. "It's not far from here."

"Righto," replied Hobbs as he grabbed his bag and waited for the automatic door to open. "Thank you, Driver."

"Yes, *khob khun kaa*," Stirling said shyly to the driver as she hopped out of the passenger side of the van. "That means *thank you* by the way, Frankie."

"Got ourselves a walking, talking phrase-book here, Constable Chai," replied Frank.

They all laughed as they gathered their belongings and picked their way between car bumpers, trying not to get run over by the motorcycles which weaved purposefully around them. At last, they reached the safety of the pavement and began to follow the gathering crowd towards the bridge.

In front of the bridge was a large open area, now filled with hundreds of colourful market stalls selling a plethora of handicrafts, clothing and street food to the baying horde of festival-goers.

Stirling cupped her hand to her mouth to be heard over the

hubbub. "That looks like the press tent over there," she said, pointing in the direction of a tent on the other side of the square. "Stella called this afternoon while we were at the hotel and left a message saying that we will meet the Ambassador there. She said that he'll be opening the festival this evening, as he does every year. Why on earth he still wants to do those duties while his daughter is missing is beyond me."

"And me," replied Hobbs. "I guess we'll find out soon enough."

They picked their way through the crowd to a large orange gazebo marked *PRESS AND MEDIA*. A trio of local photographers moved quickly out of the way, seeing Chai in full uniform escorting a couple of foreign visitors.

Inside the tent, a couple of dozen people from various media agencies busied testing cameras, flashes and extension cords. At the back was the small delegation from what they assumed was the British Embassy, all crowded around a large fan which was also spraying a fine mist of water vapour. In the centre of the group was a tall, lean man in what appeared to be his late fifties. His grey hair was parted at the side and a pair of thin-rimmed spectacles perched precariously on the bridge of a long, hooked nose. Dressed in a beige linen suit with a dark red tie, the man was undoubtedly Richard Patterson. Though, for a man who had spent the best part of his career in South East Asia, he hadn't seemed to have acclimatised to the heat. Despite the large fan, he was sweating profusely around his collar and was wiping his forehead with a silk handkerchief when he noticed the detectives and their police escort enter the tent.

Richard Patterson excused himself and pushed his way politely through the crowd, affording himself one last wipe of his forehead before stuffing the drenched material into his trouser pocket and shaking the hands of the three visitors.

"Welcome, welcome. You must be the bulls over from London. Hobbs and Stirling, if I'm not mistaken."

"That's right, Mr Ambassador," replied Stirling. "I'm Debra Stirling. This is my partner, Frank Hobbs and this is our trusty interpreter, Chai. I won't try to pronounce his surname, from Bangkok."

"Wonderful, wonderful," began Patterson. "I trust he is taking good care of you, along with our man, Pon and, of course, the lovely Stella - my deputy. I just wish they hadn't dragged you halfway across the world like this, and so close to Christmas. Indeed. I tried to tell Jenny that it simply wasn't necessary, but she wasn't having any of it. Protocol, she said. So, I do apologise."

"It's no problem at all, Mr Ambassador," replied Hobbs. "We're here to do everything we can to help find your daughter, Sir, and we'll leave no stone unturned in the process."

"Of course, of course," began the ambassador again. Stirling noticed he had an interesting habit of repeating the first word of all his sentences and wondered if it was a trick to sounding more diplomatic. "I just fear it will all be for nought. You know what teenaged daughters are like. Maybe you've got one or two of your own." Hobbs nodded in confirmation. "They're full of rebellion at this age and will do all they can to get one over on their poor old dads. I'm sure she'll turn up soon with a flat phone battery, wondering what all the fuss is about."

"Well, we sincerely hope so, Mr Ambassador. But, in the meantime, we'd like to sit down with you and go over

CHAPTER 4

everything about your journey here on the train and anything which might be of value in the days, weeks or months leading up to it," continued Hobbs.

"Yes, yes. Certainly. As soon as my duties here are done, I'll be all yours. I know a great restaurant - right on the river. You can hear the fish frolicking beneath you. They do a wonderful whole fish, fried in garlic. It's simply unmissable. How about I get Stella to text you the address and I'll meet you there? Save us trying to find each other in this chaos."

Hobbs and Stirling exchanged a sideways glance but nodded in silent agreement.

"Excellent, excellent. Well, I'm awfully sorry but I must dash. I'm due to open the festival in a few minutes. Thank you, Detectives. Again, I'm sorry you've been dragged all the way over here. I'm sure you'll be back on the plane to Heathrow in no time. Maddie, do give these good people tickets for the show. It would be a shame for them to come all this way and miss out. Bye for now, Detectives."

And with that, he was gone, disappearing into the throng of locals, wiping the sweat from the back of his neck with his small entourage in tow. The blonde girl in the group, presumably Maddie, handed over three tickets and followed dutifully, but not before offering an apologetic shrug.

* * *

An hour later, Hobbs, Stirling and Chai found themselves sitting in a section of seating overlooking the famous bridge and river below. Hundreds of plastic seats had been arranged in rows and covered with white nylon seat covers. Laid out in front of them was a host of theatrical scenery arranged on pontoons floating in the river. The scene resembled that of a dock from the Second World War. There were boxes of munitions, khaki-coloured barrels and guards stations flying the imperial flag of Japan with its bright red rising sun motif. Huge spotlights anchored on the bridge itself and on the floating stage oscillated, lighting up the twilight in yellows, blues and reds. A lone local man stood centre-stage playing a rendition of the *River Kwai March*, now known almost exclusively as *Hitler Has Only Got One Ball* on an ageing fiddle while the actors manoeuvred into their starting positions. The detectives deduced that they must have missed Richard Patterson's grand opening as they ambled around the small settlement of clothing and food stalls.

"This is bloody surreal," moaned Hobbs folding his arms in distaste. "We should be out searching for this young girl and instead we're sat here waiting for His Lordship to finish playing Winston Bloody Churchill."

"I know, Frank. It's frustrating," replied Stirling with a sigh. "But, there's really not much else we can do. Nobody else seems to have much information to go on and *His Lordship*, as you so aptly put it, is otherwise engaged. So, we may as well sit tight and figure out what we're going to be asking him later on."

Chai entered into the conversation. "The Ambassador doesn't seem too worried."

"That's what's weird, Chai mate." replied Hobbs, gruffly. "He seems a bit too unconcerned, doesn't he? Apart from the fact he's been here donkey's years and he's still sweating like a pig at market, of course."

Stirling chuckled. "You can talk. Have you seen yourself lately?"

CHAPTER 4

Hobbs looked down at his linen shirt which was beginning to cling to his chest and raised his arms to check his armpits which sported large unsightly sweat patches brought about by the stifling tropical humidity.

"Fair point," he replied, abashed. "but my point is that nobody here seems too bothered about Ella's disappearance. The general consensus seems to be that she's going to reappear in a few hours with a hangover and her tail between her legs, but I'm not so sure. With kids who have never gone missing before, there's always the chance that something more sinister is at play."

Stirling turned to Chai, on her right, and asked, "Do we know whether Ella has run away before? Gone missing for a few days, or hours even?"

"I'm sorry, Debs. We don't have that information yet," Chai replied, shaking his head.

"Well, this is precisely why we need to speak to Patterson," lamented Stirling.

Hobbs shook his head roughly. "I'm going to get a beer. Does anyone else want one?"

"Yeah, go on then," shrugged Stirling.

"No, thank you," Chai respectfully declined.

As Hobbs weaved his way through the seating towards the concession stands, the spotlights lowered and there was a ripple of applause for the fiddler who took a low bow and trotted off the makeshift stage.

As a chorus of drums and strings began, a chain gang of western actors appeared on the dock in well-worn allied uniforms, many shirtless, brandishing large pick axes and sledge-hammers. A contingent of presumably Thai actors, playing Japanese Imperial soldiers followed them onto the dock. They were attired in their typical beige uniforms with long brown boots, brown leather belts and peaked caps with the trademark hanging fabric that protected them from the harsh sun of the Pacific theatre of war. They pointed long rifles at the allied prisoners of war, which they also used to ram into the back of the presumed leader of the POWs once they had him surrounded.

Stirling rolled her eyes as Hobbs returned carrying two ice cold cans of Leo beer. They clinked their drinks together and before they could start any kind of professional conversation, an overly-dramatic, and wholly unnecessary, sword battle ensued between a Japanese officer and the leader of the POWs as music thundered from massive speakers on either side of them.

The noisy spectacle continued for a further thirty minutes with gratuitous gunfire, pyrotechnics and seemingly dangerous stunts as Japanese soldiers fell aflame into the river and rockets streaked across the river to impact with the bridge. At one point, a scale model of a P-51 Mustang fighter traversed the river on a wire and flew low over the dock, strafing the wretched Japanese soldiers below. The final act saw a genuine steam engine crossing the bridge, adorned with Japanese imperial flags before a barrage of pyrotechnic explosions rocked the bridge and destroyed it, signalling the victory for the allied forces.

Cue *The River Kwai March* again and a whole host of flag waving before the sky erupted once more, not with gunfire this time, but with a firework display that lit up the night sky, to the delight of the crowd of onlookers.

* * *

CHAPTER 4

Stirling, Hobbs and Chai waited a few minutes while they finished off their drinks and waited for the majority of the audience to filter away from their seats towards the pop-up market stalls. Chai led them through the throng of locals and tourists towards a side street where their ride was waiting.

Hobbs checked his phone and, to the Ambassador's credit, there was indeed a text from Stella Ismael with the address for the restaurant in English and Thai. It ended with a message from Stella: *'I recommend the sea bass - Stella.'*

Hobbs shook his head and passed the phone to Chai who showed the glowing LCD screen to the driver, Loong Pon. He squinted to read the address and nodded before handing the phone back over his shoulder to Hobbs.

"Right, I've had enough of people recommending the bloody fish. Let's go and do some actual detective work, shall we?" said Hobbs, dropping his phone into his breast pocket.

Stirling replied, "Yes, let's."

Chapter 5

Hobbs and Stirling arrived to find Richard Patterson sitting alone at a table on the riverfront. Chai had made his excuses and headed to the police accommodation in town to get an early night, knowing his interpreting skills wouldn't be required that evening, but not before exchanging telephone numbers with Stirling who would pass Chai's number on to Hobbs.

The restaurant was as the Ambassador had described it. It sat directly on the banks of the river with a good portion of the dining area extending over the river itself. The floor consisted of long wooden planks with gaps between them large enough to see the water below. A simple wooden balustrade prevented the diners from falling headlong into the river during their main course. Large wooden tables in a rustic style were flanked by two parallel rows of colourful plastic chairs with seat covers not dissimilar to those at the festival earlier.

Richard Patterson sat with his right arm rested on the balustrade, a glass of what looked like local lager with ice dangled precariously from his hand over the river below. He clearly hadn't returned to his hotel to change, but had removed his tie which hung loosely over the back of his

CHAPTER 5

chair along with his linen suit jacket. He appeared to have been there a while, as three large empty beer bottles sat on a black metal service table behind him, while a half empty one stood on the dinner table. He looked rather dishevelled as he watched absent-mindedly a pair of dragonflies that flew in twists and turns over the surface of the water.

The restaurant wasn't particularly busy, in spite of the ambassador's rave review, and a member of the waiting staff was available to show them to their table. Patterson spotted the pair approach and stood up, wiping the condensation from his beer glass onto the front of his creased linen trousers before he shook their hands.

"Good evening, good evening," he began in his typical double-barrelled style. "Come, sit down. You must be starving." Patterson called over the waitress who came with a large, plastic covered menu. "Can I get you good people a drink?" he asked, flipping open the menu and turning it in their direction.

"I'll have whatever you're having, Sir," replied Hobbs.

"And the same for me," agreed Stirling, as they both took their seats. Patterson spoke to the waitress in Thai, gesturing with one hand at the open beer on the table and holding up two fingers on the other.

"What would you like to eat?" he asked.

Stirling replied, "Oh, we're game to try anything, Mr Patterson. Why don't you go ahead and order for us? I wouldn't know what's what and we've got a lot to talk about."

Patterson proceeded to order what looked like enough food to feed a small army before closing the menu and handing it back to the waitress who dipped her head and hurried back towards the kitchen at the rear.

"Right, let's get down to business, shall we?" said Patterson, taking a long draw of his lager. Both detectives fished their notebooks from their pockets; Hobbs opening his up to a page of pre-prepared questions and Stirling to a blank page to begin writing the answers and anything else of interest given away by the interviewee.

This was the way they always worked. Hobbs was an expert at putting people at ease. He was a people person. A no-nonsense, friendly sort of bloke - at least outwardly. He had a face that people trusted, in spite of his size, and a voice to match. He had a way of getting people to talk, one way or another.

Stirling, on the other hand, was somewhat of a social outsider. With a Master's degree in psychology from St. Andrews, her interest in people was purely academic. What she lacked in bedside manner, she made up for with her sharp intellect and the ability to read what a person didn't say rather than what they did.

So, they began, with Hobbs asking the questions and Stirling doing the silent analysis of the high-brow diplomat and father.

"Right, Mr Patterson. I'm sure you've been over all this with the Thai police, but it's obviously difficult for us to get a lot of the details, given the language barrier. So, if you don't mind, we'll start at the beginning. When was it that you realised that Ella was missing?"

"As soon as I got off the train near the bridge, I suppose. Ella had wanted to get off in town at the main station. She'd organised to meet one of her friends who has a condominium here - without consulting me, of course. We'd argued about it earlier in the journey. She'd never once wanted to come down here with me, in all the years I've been doing this. So, naturally, I wanted her to accompany me to the bridge and attend the festival. That's what she said she wanted to do. I really didn't understand the change of plan. Anyway, we had a few crossed words, nothing major, but she stomped off down the train in a strop and I didn't see her again."

The words seemed to hang ominously in the air over the dinner table for a palpable moment.

"I see," continued Hobbs. "Is it a regular occurrence, the arguments?"

"No, not at all. Well, no more than a usual father-teenaged daughter relationship. She's very into her social media nonsense, which I have zero interest in. That causes some tension, but that's about it."

"Gotcha. And this friend? Have you got a name for her? An address, maybe?"

"Address? No. I'm afraid not. I'm sure her name is Ploy. They're in the same year at school. Pretty little thing. Good family, I've heard. Very big in the golf scene. Father has shares in one of the courses around here, hence the condo. He shouldn't be too hard to track down."

Stirling scribbled down the details, angling her notebook towards herself out of habit.

"OK. So, what did you do when you realised she hadn't got off at your station? Did you alert the authorities straight away?"

"No, no. I just assumed she'd sneaked off the train in town to go and spend time with her friend. I tried calling her mobile but it was switched off. I was a bit worried, of course, but I was pushed for time with the opening of the first night of the festival, so I couldn't hang around. I didn't have any contact information for her friend. There wasn't much I could do. Ella knew the name of the hotel I am staying at, so I just assumed she would turn up there later that night. But, she didn't, of course - which is why you're here."

Patterson took another swig of his beer which was being watered down at an alarming rate by the added ice. Meanwhile, the waitress reappeared with two large bottles of cold beer covered in a misty film of condensation and a small plastic bucket of ice with a flimsy white plastic handle and a pair of tiny steel tongs. The waitress proceeded to place a large ice cube into each of the empty glasses and one more into Patterson's, before opening one of the new bottles of beer in one skilful movement and pouring it in equal measures into all three of the glasses.

"Never had ice in my beer before," remarked Hobbs lifting his glass. "But, when in Rome."

"Yes, it takes a bit of getting used to but your beer would be warm in ten minutes without it and it helps you avoid the hangover the next day," replied Patterson, also raising his glass.

"Well, that sounds alright to me," interjected Stirling and they all clinked their glasses together.

"To Ella," said Patterson wiping his eyes with the back of his hand. "May she be found safe and well…and soon. I know I must have appeared a bit unperturbed earlier, but I have somewhat of an appearance to keep up in front of the locals. Stiff upper lip and all that. I hope you understand."

Hobbs and Stirling both nodded in recognition and took a long refreshing draw on their ice cold drinks as the food began to arrive.

Stirling was right. There *was* enough food to feed a small

army and the small army seemed to be the string of waitresses who emerged from the kitchen carrying the vast array of dishes to their table and waiting stomachs.

There was a long plate upon which was the garlic fried fish that Patterson had recommended. To accompany that, a half pineapple, hollowed out and stuffed with fried rice, peppered with chunks of fresh pineapple, a salad of young papaya loaded with bright red chillies, a plate of grilled pork neck with a dish of spicy tamarind sauce, and a huge platter of deep orange prawns singed from their time on the grill, served with a violent looking green chilli sauce. The food just kept coming, and before long, the entire table was filled with a veritable feast of seafood, salads and different grilled or deep fried meats.

The three of them feasted hungrily. The food was an eclectic mix of all the right flavours and in perfect balance. Sweet, savoury, sour and salty featured in almost every dish and the detectives almost forgot why they were there in the first instance.

"This is wonderful food, Ambassador, and so much of it," explained Stirling, wiping her mouth on a napkin as demurely as she could and taking another sip of her beer. "Do you mind if we continue with our questions, while we eat? It seems such a shame but it really is important."

"Of course, of course. Fire away. I'm willing to do anything that is asked of me to find my little girl, including interrupting this fine supper."

Hobbs continued, perfectly timing mouthfuls of food after each question he asked. "So, what have you heard from the local police? What efforts have been made so far in locating Ella?"

Stirling put down her cutlery and readied her notebook and pen.

"Well, they did a full search of the train but it didn't bear anything particularly fruitful, I'm afraid. They interviewed a few staff from the train. There isn't a manifest or anything like that, so they couldn't interview any passengers. I heard they asked in a press conference for any passengers to come forward but I haven't heard anything that's come from the appeal. There was a staff member; a porter, I think. He said that he saw a girl whom he thinks was Ella, looking upset and heading towards the back of the train. They did a search of the rear of the train, but only found a few cigarette butts and a couple of beer cans. Nothing much to go on."

"Where is that evidence now?"

"I've no idea. I assume the police have them. But, knowing that lot, they could have just thrown them away. They get a pretty bad rap here, the boys in brown."

"The boys in brown?"

"Yes, that's what the ex-pat community calls them - because of their uniforms." Hobbs remembered the light brown colour of Chai's uniform and the moniker suddenly made sense.

Hobbs said to Stirling, "Make a note to follow up with Chai about that evidence, Debs. It could be significant."

Stirling nodded in confirmation but said nothing. She was watching their interviewee as Hobbs was speaking. Looking for clues; tell-tale signs that people don't know they're giving off - a nose touch here, a lip-lick there - unconscious body language which all helps to build a picture of the stranger sitting on the other side of the interview table, or in this case, dinner table.

So far, Patterson was still troubling her. Her first impressions had found him callous and uninterested in his daughter's disappearance. But, behind closed doors, he had started to open up to the detectives and show some cracks in his outward persona of stoicism and besides, she had been doing this job long enough to see the vast spectrum of reactions to a loved one going missing which ran from nonchalance to outright hysteria. Everyone is different and relationships are complicated. It's seldom as clean-cut as it seems in the movies.

Hobbs continued with his questioning. "Where is the train now, Richard?"

"Oh, the police impounded it briefly at *Hua Lamphong*, the main station in Bangkok, but once they'd done their forensics it was released back into service."

"Not ideal," replied Hobbs as Stirling made a note. "You mentioned that you had an argument. Do you remember what time that was?"

"I'm not sure of the time, but it was just after the train left Nakhon Pathom. I remember distinctly because I could see the Chedi out of the window."

"The Chedi? Sorry. As you know, we don't exactly have the local knowledge."

"Sorry, the Phra Pathom Chedi. It's a huge Buddhist stupa, the largest Buddhist monument in the world, in fact. You can see it from the train. So, the last time I saw Ella on the train was as we were passing it."

"I see," replied Hobbs, nodding in recognition. "So, we have Ella somehow leaving the train at some point between Nakhon..." Hobbs paused.

"...Pathom" Stirling chimed in, reading from her notes.

"Nakhon Pathom, right, excuse me, and the River Kwai

station. Is that right?" continued Hobbs.

"That sounds right, yes."

"And we have witnesses saying that they saw Ella walking towards the rear of the train, which is where the beer cans and cigarette butts were found. Does your daughter smoke, Ambassador?"

"No. Gosh, no."

Stirling chimed in for the first time, "Are you sure about that? I smoked on-and-off through my teenage years and my parents never found out. I asked them about it years later and they had no idea."

"Well, as far as I know she doesn't smoke. But, I guess you don't know what you don't know," replied Patterson through a mouthful of fish and fried rice.

"We'd like to ask about Ella's mother," started Hobbs, opening his briefcase to take out the folder and finding the name of Ella's mother. "Anchalee Jitpracharoen. I know I'm not pronouncing that correctly."

"Yes, that's right. Her nickname is Anne. The Thai are generally known by a mono-syllabic nickname which is a lot easier to pronounce than their official name. Official names are reserved for documents and the like. Most people don't even know their friends' official names."

"I see. The two of you are divorced. Is that right?"

"That's correct, yes."

"Amicably?"

"Not really, I'm sorry to say. We had not been terribly happy for a long time but the marriage started going downhill when we moved back to Thailand from the Philippines. That was in late 2001. We had Ella in 2003 and that seemed to help. Brought us together a bit, you know? But, as soon as Ella started at nursery, her mother started to get back into the drinking and gambling. A remnant of her former life, before she met me."

Stirling noticed an almost imperceptible flush rising in the ambassador's cheeks."What former life might that be, Mr Patterson?" she probed.

"Well, I'm rather ashamed to admit - and please don't go shouting this around, it certainly isn't common knowledge - but my ex-wife, Ella's mother, was a woman of questionable morals, as they might have said a long time ago. I believe sex worker is the PC phrase these days."

"I see," replied Hobbs, nodding his head. "Well, there's no judgement here, Ambassador, and thank you for being honest with us. If we are going to build a picture of Ella's whereabouts, we need to know as much information as possible."

"Yes, yes." replied the ambassador, visibly relieved. He continued. "She knocked that all on the head when we began seeing each other, of course. But, you know what they say. You can take the girl out of the bar, but you can't take the bar out of the girl. At least, in my experience. Anyway, as soon as she got back to Bangkok, she hooked up with some of her old friends, and some new ones, and got back into the community, so to speak. She'd spend most of the day in a gambling den. You can imagine, bringing in a senior diplomat's salary and having all our expenses paid, we managed to amass quite a large chunk of savings from our time in Manila and Singapore. Well, most of that was gambled away without my knowledge. So, not only was she a gambler, but a bloody useless one, apparently."

Patterson took a long draw of his drink, finishing the glass and topping himself up from one of the open bottles in the centre of the table.

"I'm sorry to hear that, Sir," said Hobbs, before also taking a sip of his own drink. "Do you know where your ex-wife is now?"

"Denmark, somewhere. I heard from a mutual friend that she'd taken to online dating and ended up marrying a Danish chap. I heard she's doing much better over there. But, that's all I know, I'm afraid. We don't talk any more."

"And when was the last time Ella saw her mother?"

"In the summer. She spends a month or so every year in Denmark. I never go with her, though. Thai Airways have a wonderful chaperone programme. So, I drop her off at the airport in Bangkok and her mother picks her up in Copenhagen. My secretary makes all the arrangements. I know it might seem a bit callous but I'm a very busy man and we really haven't had the best relationship, Anne and I, since I was granted custody."

Stirling noticed what appeared to be a tinge of regret in Patterson as he explained the arrangement he had made with his ex-wife and the breakdown of their relationship. He lowered his head and ran his fingers through his hair, around the back of his neck, bringing them together in front of his face in a pensive pose.

"Again, we're not here to judge." replied Hobbs, placatingly.

"Thank you, Detectives," sighed Patterson as he regained his composure. "Can we take a break and eat some of this lovely food before it goes cold?"

"Of course," replied Hobbs, symbolically closing the file on Ella Patterson and picking up his forgotten cutlery.

For the next 45 minutes, the trio ate and drank and

CHAPTER 5

exchanged small-talk across the table. A few more bottles of cold Singha lager were brought full to the table and taken away empty. Before long, even the two detectives had relaxed to the point that they had themselves almost forgotten that a vulnerable teenaged girl was missing.

The culture had begun to take hold of the two British detectives already. It was getting late and the cicadas and crickets on the riverbank were now in full song. Hobbs checked his watch and saw that it was past eleven.

"We should make a move," said Hobbs with a genuine almighty yawn. "It's been a very long day and I think we have what we need from you for now."

"Of course, of course," replied the ambassador, getting to his feet and wiping his moist brow with his handkerchief. "I really do appreciate all you are doing in the search for our Ella."

"It's our duty and our pleasure to help, Mr Ambassador," replied Stirling, also rising to her feet. "I only hope that Ella will be found safe and sound very soon and we can enjoy the rest of our trip knowing that she's safely back with her family and friends."

"Good night, Ambassador," said Hobbs, shaking Patterson's hand.

"Good night, Frank. Safe journey back to your hotel. Where are you staying by the way?"

"It's more of a guest house than a hotel, but it's got a nice little pool. Pong Phen, I think it's called. Or, Pen Phong. Something like that."

"Ah, Pong Phen, I know it well. Perfect," said Patterson, with a smile. "Perfect."

Chapter 6

The hotel rented by the British Government to accommodate the two guest detectives was far from luxurious but entirely comfortable. Chosen for its proximity; it was situated roughly equidistant between the bridge, where they were to meet Richard Patterson, the police station and the railway station - all key locations in their search for young Ella Patterson. Situated down a small lane, or *soi*, just off the main road heading down to the bridge, was Pong Phen Guest house. A cluster of small one-room bungalows ran alongside a small, but perfectly clean, bright blue swimming pool. On the other side of the pool was the car park and guest house restaurant - a modest, open-air establishment filled with a few heavy wooden tables and bench seating. A small bar served local beers and a selection of common cocktails and mixed drinks. Pictures and messages from former guests covered the walls along with a plethora of flags and maps from all over the world. On the far side of the pool was a small patio with steps that ran down to a short promenade on the river bank.

Hobbs and Stirling were accommodated in adjacent bungalows, each with their own small veranda overlooking the pool where one could enjoy a cigarette with the morning paper

CHAPTER 6

or one last drink before retiring to bed. Each bungalow was decorated in the same way. Blue patterned tiles covered the floor of the bedroom. The walls were painted a soft yellow tone and adorned with oil paintings of typical Thai scenes surrounded by rustic bamboo frames. The bed, a small double, covered in cotton sheets and a thin silk blanket plenty thick enough for the tropical heat, was flanked by two simple side tables. A small wet room lay off the main room, again tiled in blue, with basic amenities. Both rooms were air-conditioned and contained a small ceiling fan which whirred perpetually above their heads to circulate the humid air.

It was 6 A.M. and the sun was already peeking nosily through the gap in the curtains of Stirling's room. She turned over to escape the coming morning and wrapped herself tightly in the thin silk sheet as the temperature in the room had plummeted to below 20 degrees due to the rather heavy-duty air conditioning. Her head felt heavy and her mind hazy - no doubt a sign of jet lag starting to set in.

On the side table to her right, her phone buzzed. A detective's phone can rarely be ignored, so she reluctantly rolled over to answer it. The conversation was brief but the message relayed was loud and clear.

Stirling jumped up from her bed and hastily rummaged in her yet to be unpacked suitcase for some clean clothes. She pulled a simple white tank top over head and slipped into a pair of olive green shorts. Hopping as she pulled at the back of a pair of black sling-back sandals, she pulled open the wooden door and rounded the small wooden fence that separated her bungalow from Hobbs'.

She banged heavily on the door to his bungalow and shouted, "Hobbs! Hobbs! Wake up! Open the door!"

She banged again at the door. She could feel the cold air-conditioned draft flowing over her exposed toes. Inside the room she heard a groan and some lumbering footsteps. A few moments later, Hobbs appeared at the crack of the door, squinting in the bright morning sun.

The conversation was even more brief than the phone conversation she had just had with Chai: "They've found a body."

* * *

By the time Hobbs had got dressed and quickly smoked a cigarette, Chai was sitting in a police pick-up truck in the car park of Pong Phen. Stirling was in the restaurant grabbing three cups of coffee to-go and leaving their room keys at reception. Hobbs was leaning against one of the tall palm trees that stood on the edges of the car park, making use of the free Wi-Fi and checking his E-Mails. Dressed in a white linen shirt over a grey vest, beige cargo shorts and Jesus sandals, he was now much better attired for what was destined to be another scorching day in western Thailand.

The pick-up was standard police issue: a Toyota Hilux 4-door, painted in a dark maroon with white doors and a set of red emergency lights fixed on top. The flat bed at the rear was open and empty, save for a spare tyre and a couple of orange traffic cones. The door featured the same police emblem they had seen yesterday morning in Bangkok: a maroon patterned circle with a mandala-like pattern, bisected by a traditional Siamese short sword. At the centre, almost hidden amongst the pattern was the image of a *yak* - a mythical giant of Thai folklore and the Hindu Ramayana.

CHAPTER 6

Stirling, carrying the three coffees on a takeaway tray, clambered into the cramped rear section and Hobbs joined Chai in the front. They both thanked Stirling for the coffee and Chai pulled away up the soi. The roads were clear other than a few local peddlers pushing their wares in steel carts close to the gutter.

"Right, Chai mate. Where was this body found then?" asked Hobbs after a swig of his coffee.

"She was found in a paddy field, just off the main railway line," Chai replied.

"She? It's a female then. Is it our misper? Our missing girl?"

"They don't know for sure. The police only just received the call. They called me as soon as they heard. There's been no formal identification yet. The body, especially the face, has been damaged." Chai spoke matter-of-factly as he negotiated a busy junction which appeared to have no working traffic lights.

"Approximate age?" asked Stirling.

"Not sure. All we know is she's female."

"Could definitely be Ella, though," remarked Stirling, sadly. "Female found close to the railway line, damage to the body, particularly the face. That's consistent with a fall from a moving train," she said, to nobody in particular.

"You're not wrong, Debs," replied Hobbs, anyway. "Let's hope for her sake and her father's sake it's not, though. As much as I'd like to get out of this sweat box in time for Christmas, I'd prefer to find Ella safe and well."

"Wouldn't we all, Frank?"

After around ten minutes, Chai turned a corner and they found themselves on a concrete road running parallel to the main railway line going out of Kanchanaburi towards Nakhon

Pathom and eventually Bangkok. A short while later, they crossed the tracks at a level crossing with not a hint of a safety barrier and continued to follow the train tracks on the opposite side of the railway line. Ahead, in the distance, they could see a congregation of emergency service vehicles: two or three pick-ups similar to their current vehicle, a handful of police motorbikes and an ambulance. That was in addition to a few civilian motorcycles which must have belonged to the small crowd of intrigued locals gathered to gawp at the unfolding spectacle. A few uniformed officers were making a half-hearted attempt to keep the civilians back far enough that the body was out of public view.

Hobbs, Stirling and Chai pulled up at the side of the road and exited the pick-up. The heat hit them hard once more and they noticed that there was very little shade anywhere around them. Many of the locals were sporting large woven hats of pale colours which covered their heads and shoulders completely. They were also, the detectives noted, all in long sleeves and long trousers. This seemed illogical, but these people were clearly farmers who worked all day in the scorching heat, so they must have known something that they didn't.

The trio approached the scene. Chai spoke briefly to the uniformed officers and, as he was also in uniform, they were waved through, but only as far as what appeared to be a senior officer talking on a radio through the window of another police pick-up truck. He placed a firm hand on Hobbs' chest as he tried to walk past. This stopped all three of them in their tracks.

Chai saluted the senior officer who, by the looks of his uniform, had to be a captain or higher in rank. He had on the same brown uniform as Chai but his chest was filled with medals and badges of all shapes and colours. His rotund pot-belly was being kept barely under wraps by a few overstretched buttons. Upon closer inspection, three silver stars on his epaulettes identified him as a captain, as Hobbs had suspected.

Chai spoke to the Captain in Thai and although Hobbs and Stirling could not understand what was being said, they could tell that Chai was addressing the Captain with a high degree of deference.

He turned to speak to them. "Detective Hobbs, Detective Stirling, this is Captain Anupong. He's in charge here and unfortunately, he says he can not allow you to see the body. He says that here you are mere civilians and therefore have the same rights as everyone else. You'll be permitted to look at photographs but I'm afraid you'll have to wait in the car."

Captain Anupong watched, with a smug look upon his face, as Chai interpreted his message to the two detectives. Captain Anupong was an older male, in his early-fifties, Stirling surmised. He was short, between 5'3" and 5'4". His hair was shaved into the compulsory '904' cut, but unlike Chai, the top of his hair was thinning and was streaked with grey. Both his eyebrows and his eyes were dark and looked even darker with the prominent bags under his eyes. His broad nose looked like it had been squashed by one too many punches to the face and that was exactly what Hobbs wanted to do at that precise moment in time.

Hobbs spoke through gritted teeth. "With the greatest respect, Captain, Sir. We are here to help - here to help at the request of the British Embassy. As you know, the daughter of the British Ambassador, Richard Patterson, is currently missing and we are assisting with the investigation. We have reason to believe that the body here could belong to his daughter. It's vital to our investigation that we're able to view the body, Sir."

Chai dutifully interpreted Hobbs' plea into Thai for the Captain and nodded courteously as he gave his response. "He said that while he is aware of your investigation, the investigation remains the responsibility of the Royal Thai Police and he was informed that you are here on purely a consultant basis. He will allow me to approach the body and take pictures for your reference which I am permitted to show you at any time."

Anupong said something else to Chai and gestured towards their vehicle once more before walking away towards the small group of officers dealing with the newly found cadaver."He said you're welcome to wait here with the rest of the civilians, but you Europeans will probably be more comfortable in the air-conditioning."

"What a prick," said Stirling, distastefully, in a rare utterance of foul language.

"You can say that again," replied Hobbs as he turned to walk back towards the pick-up, kicking up a cloud of red dust as he went.

Stirling turned to Chai and handed him a heavy Nikon SLR camera with a pancake lens. "Here, Chai," she sighed. "Take this and get as many photos as you can before they kick you out. I have a feeling it won't be long before they do. Anupong wasn't exactly welcoming. Oh, and try and get a look at her eyes."

Stirling then weaved through the growing crowd of locals and slumped down into the driver's seat of the pick-up to get a better look at what was going on.

"Can you believe this shit, Debs?" said Hobbs, visibly seething. "That idiot is shutting us out and in the mean time it seem he couldn't organise a piss up in a brewery. Did you see the mess down there? No forensics tent. No cordon. No forensic suits. Constables trampling all over the scene. It's a wonder they catch anyone at all."

Stirling just watched as Chai made his way carefully along the edge of the rice field towards the body. Before long he came face-to-face with the grisly scene.

The body was laying face down, semi-submerged in the shallow water of the rice field at the bottom of an embankment which rose steeply to the train tracks above. There was significant damage to the knees, elbows and other areas which were not covered by the young girl's clothes. She was clad in a torn halter-neck top - black with a red and blue floral print - and a pair of brown shorts which had not taken any damage but were wet and soiled in the rear. One of the girl's strappy white sandals was still on her right foot, but the other was missing. At least two of her toes on her left foot stuck out at a grotesque angle and were almost detached. Chai noticed the missing sandal laying half way up the embankment. Chai also noticed the girl's left arm was broken and both the ulna and radius were protruding through the skin. Two of the girl's finger nails on the same hand were missing and the others were damaged and filled with dark grit. Chai walked around to the other side of the body, snapping pictures as he went - the macabre images saving to the camera's SD card, but also being seared indelibly into the memory of the young police constable.

The girl's face was partly obscured by the lank, damp hair

which clung to her face like the roots of a long-dead tree. The face was heavily bruised on one side but as another officer moved her head, Chai could see that the other side was almost gone, leaving an exposed jawbone and the gleaming white of her cheekbone, which before now had never seen the light of day.

Chai heaved and turned away from the body to recover his composure. Even in his work as a police officer in Bangkok, one of the largest metropolises in South East Asia, he had never come across a body this badly damaged. He wanted to walk away there and then. He wanted to get in his truck and drive non-stop back to Bangkok but he knew, in spite of the lack of a face with which to identify her, this was undoubtedly the horribly mangled body of the missing Ella Patterson and he knew that he had to do all he could to find out what had happened to her.

As his final act, remembering the last thing that Stirling had said to him, Chai swung the camera over his shoulder and bent down beside the corpse. He first raised his hands in front of his face in a *wai* and then gently and respectfully, using his thumb and index finger, opened one of the eyes of the dead girl. Staring back at him from beyond the abyss was a heavily bloodshot but unmistakeably hazel-green eye.

Chapter 7

Hobbs and Stirling watched helplessly as Chai reappeared from the crowd of onlookers which was growing steadily larger by the minute. He stopped for a few minutes to talk to a pair of uniformed policemen and then made his way back to the vehicle, climbing in and removing his hat. He took a long drink from a bottle of water and let out an extended sigh.

Stirling asked, "Are you alright, Chai?" Chai nodded as he took another gulp of water.

"Is it our girl, Chai? Is it Ella?"

"We can't be sure yet, but I think so. She has green eyes. She fits the description. Here, take a look," replied Chai, handing back the camera to Stirling and running his fingers through his thinly-cropped hair.

Stirling powered the camera on and switched to playback mode as Hobbs shifted in his seat to get a better view. As soon as the first pictures appeared on the small LCD screen, he wished he hadn't. Hobbs closed his eyes for a moment and shook his head in disbelief.

"Bloody hell," he swore, as he was temporarily reminded of the nightmare he had experienced mid-flight on the way over from London. This time, there were no maggots writhing at her face, of course, but there were some eerie similarities all the same, like the twisted position of her body and the dark streaks of blood running through her hair. It was suddenly all a little too much and he was forced to look away.

Stirling continued to flick through the pictures. Some of them were wide-angle shots which showed the body in-situ. Some of them were close-ups showing important details. All of them made tough viewing. Chai had done a good job of documenting the appalling scene.

"How long has she been there? And why wasn't she found earlier?" asked Stirling, not taking her eyes off the pictures in front of her.

Chai replied, "Well, we think since the evening that she went missing. The body is at the bottom of a steep, like a hill, or something like that. I don't think anybody could see her from the train."

"An embankment," said Hobbs, helping Chai with his English vocabulary.

"Right, at the bottom of the embankment."

"OK," said Stirling. "But, that doesn't explain why she wasn't found until this morning. Who found her and why did it take so long? Surely the farmers would have found her first thing the next morning?"

Chai shook his head. "No, no. The second rice has been planted already. It won't be ready for harvest until March. The farmers dig some channels to flood the fields with water and then they have nothing to do until harvest time. Most of the time, they will try to find some other work, so they don't get bored and spend all their money sitting around drinking whisky."

Hobbs nodded along pensively to the mini-lesson in Thai

CHAPTER 7

agriculture. "So, who found the body then, if nobody goes into the fields for months on end?"

"The family who own the land have a daughter - eight years old, or something like that. She was chasing field mice early this morning and found it."

"Jesus," remarked Hobbs.

"Yeah, so she ran to tell her parents and they called the police."

Stirling finally powered off the camera. "She's going to be scarred for life, poor little thing. What about personal possessions? Wallet? Phone?"

"Nothing on the body, they said," replied Chai.

Stirling frowned. "Nothing? No phone? That doesn't make sense. Our girl was a social media addict. She never went anywhere without her phone. Did they search the surrounding area? It might have been thrown clear. I saw her shoe was halfway up the embankment."

"They're still searching but they didn't find anything yet."

"Hmm," Stirling frowned again. "Right, no point in us being here any longer. Let's get going. There's a space for us at the station in town, right, Chai? Chai nodded in confirmation. "Frank, you take another look through those photos and see if there are any distinguishing marks on the body that we could match up with her social media pictures. I want to make sure this is definitely our misper. The whole phone thing has got me questioning it."

Frank was not particularly keen to look over the pictures again, but not wanting to expose his weak stomach, he reluctantly powered on the camera and began clicking through the close-ups that Chai had taken.

"There," he said after a couple of minutes. "On the shoulder;

some kind of tattoo by the looks of it." He zoomed in closer using the physical button. "Looks like some kind of a heart shape." He passed the camera to Stirling for a second opinion. "What do you think?"

Stirling screwed up her eyes for a better look. "I think you're right." She passed the camera back. "I'm just bringing up her Instagram. Signal isn't very good out here."

Stirling brought up Ella Patterson's Instagram feed, scrolling upwards with her index finger through a huge collection of images and short videos. The amount of likes and comments on each one was staggering; literally thousands of likes and hundreds of comments. She scrolled past scores of pictures of Ella with different friends, eating and drinking at different restaurants, trying on clothes in the changing rooms of different high-street fashion stores. Finally, she came upon a picture which almost whizzed by. She tapped the screen and zoomed in for a closer look. The picture was of Ella, pool-side, in a swimsuit that her father certainly wouldn't have approved of. On her left shoulder, was seemingly a small tattoo. Stirling zoomed in further to see a small heart-shaped tattoo made up of delicate wildflowers in tones of lilacs and lavenders.

"Got it!" Stirling exclaimed, triumphant. "Take a look at that, Frankie. Looks like a match to me."

Hobbs took the phone from Stirling and put them side-by-side to compare them.

"Yep, that's our girl, alright," he said glumly.

Suddenly, Stirling didn't feel so triumphant after all.

Chai pulled away slowly in a long sweeping arc and the chaotic scene they had just witnessed began to shrink in the rear-view mirror. They accelerated down the road, leaving

CHAPTER 7

behind them a large crowd of locals, a small group of cagey police officers and one dead ambassador's daughter.

* * *

It was a silent and sombre drive back from the scene. Hobbs couldn't help but feel that they had failed. It was their job to find missing people. It was their job to reunite people with their loved ones as soon as possible. To find a missing person dead was the worst case scenario for a member of the Missing Persons Unit and it was evidently showing on his face.

Stirling broke the uncomfortable silence. "Don't beat yourself up, Frank. The poor girl was most likely dead before we even arrived in the country. Before we even heard her name on the TV back at Spring Gardens. Bless her."

"Yeah, I know, Debs," Hobbs replied. "but it doesn't make it any easier, does it? A girl is dead - same age as my Millie. I feel for her mum and dad. It's going to be such as shock. Which reminds me, does her mum even know she was missing, Chai?"

"Not sure yet. We'll know more when we get back to the station," Chai replied, staring morosely at the road ahead.

"She's in Denmark, right?"

"Right."

"Surely she must have heard something on the news?"

"Maybe."

Clearly Chai was not in the mood for extended conversation, Hobbs thought to himself. To be fair to him, he had just witnessed a pretty gruesome scene. Hobbs had seen his fair share himself. It never got any easier. Some cases really got to you - kept you up at night, gave you nightmares, even. Hobbs thought back to his dream on the plane. Was it some sort of premonition? Did he know from the beginning that Ella Patterson was dead, even before they touched down in the Kingdom, or was it something from his past, bubbling up into the present, blurring the lines between the dream world and the real world?

Stirling brought him back to reality. "There's a chance she still might not know," she began. "It made the news in the UK and Thailand, of course, but she's in Denmark and has been for some time, it seems. Think about it. If the daughter of the French Ambassador to Senegal went missing in Senegal, would it make the news in the UK? I doubt it, to be honest."

Frank nodded his head in understanding. "But, surely she keeps up with the news from back home? Has Thai friends in Denmark? Surely someone must have seen it on the Thai news and contacted her," he replied, pensively.

"Well, I guess we'll find out soon enough. What happens with the body now, Chai? Stirling asked.

"The body will be taken to the local morgue. The police will ask Mr Patterson to come and identify the body then they'll probably do an autopsy to find a cause of death.

"Probably?" asked Stirling, with a tilt of her head.

"Yes, they don't always do an autopsy, if the cause of death is clear, like this one. But, because she is a foreigner and an important foreigner, they will probably do one. Also, they will hope to find some trace of drugs or alcohol so they can blame the victim, not the safety standard of the railway."

"Oh, wow," exclaimed Stirling. "That's not very respectful of the dead."

"No, it's not, but the police and the railway are both owned and operated by the state, same as the schools, the hospitals and the immigration offices. If anything looks bad for one, it looks bad for all of them. So, there's a lot of things that don't get reported, or just go away.

"*Swept under the carpet* is how we say it in English," interjected Hobbs briefly.

"Right, swept under the carpet."

"But all of those entities are there to help people, aren't they?" posed Stirling, idealistically.

"Yeah, but *T.I.T*," replied Chai with a shrug.

"T.I.T?" asked Stirling. Chai's eyes met Stirling's once again in the rear-view mirror.

"*This. Is. Thailand*. This isn't the UK, or any other developed country. It may not look like it, but Thailand is still a third-world country. It's all smiles and *wais* on the tourist posters but deep down all the people at the top care about is money. Money, money, money. They don't care about the people. They just lie and cheat their way to the top. I had a good life in England. Good education. Good job. But I feel bad for the people at home. That's why I came back. That's why I became a police officer. I wanted to make a difference - fight for change. Show people that not everybody in the police force is bad. But I can't even do that. I tried to say 'no' to taking bribes - I couldn't. The guy above me needs the bribe money from me to pay the guy above him, who needs it to pay the guy above him, and on and on it goes, all the way to the top. The money trickles up in Thailand not down. Every day, millions of Baht goes from the pockets of ordinary Thai people into the bank accounts of a few corrupt assholes. They drive around in their fancy cars and eat at their fancy restaurants while the man on the street has to make do with boiled rice and fish sauce. It makes me sick."

Neither Hobbs nor Stirling knew quite what to say in response to Chai's emotive illumination of systemic corruption within the Thai police. It had stunned them both into silence and also given them an insight into their new companion. Hobbs knew, undoubtedly, that his was a young man who could be trusted, a straight shooter, more so than anyone they had met on their trip so far. There was no reason to wonder which side Chai would be on in a battle with Anupong or anyone else. If push came to shove, Hobbs knew that Chai would go to bat for them and he would go to bat for Ella, too.

Chapter 8

After a break at the hotel to eat a late breakfast or early lunch, Chai drove Hobbs and Stirling to the main police station in the centre of Kanchanaburi: a wide, four-storey concrete building of unimaginative architecture from the 1970s. The incident room at Kanchanaburi Police Station was equally unremarkable. It was furnished in Spartan fashion. Several blue plastic chairs were arranged around a large wooden table in the centre of the room. The table was covered in thick, see-through plastic which protected a series of maps detailing the local area and the borderlands with neighbouring Burma, or Myanmar, as it is now referred to at the behest of the ruling junta government. A variety of whiteboards and cork pinboards adorned the other nicotine-stained walls along with an assortment of posters in the Thai language that seemed to be condemning illicit drugs, drink driving and human trafficking, among other things. Large ceiling fans rotated and oscillated above the team of Thai police men and women who busied to and fro with their paperwork.

Hobbs and Stirling sat on one corner of the table - Hobbs reading through the case notes and Stirling typing up a list of questions to ask the Thai authorities on a government-issue laptop. Chai entered the room carrying two coffees in flimsy plastic cups which he handed to the two detectives. They thanked him, had a taste of the coffee and then wished they hadn't. It was unbearably sweet and appeared to have been made using condensed milk.

Stirling said to Hobbs, "I've just had a reply from Harding in London. I emailed her earlier to update her. She sends her condolences and asked us to hang around until our original flight time to support the Ambassador and help out in any way that we can."

"I'm surprised by that," replied Hobbs. "I thought she would have had us on the first flight back to save Johnny Taxpayer a few bob in expenses."

"Well, maybe she's not as much of a hard arse as we thought, Frank. I think you've got to put on an act when you're in one of those positions. Command respect from those below you in the food chain, you know?"

"There's other ways to earn respect though, Debs. She may be a pain, but she was *and is* a bloody good detective. There's no need to be such a smart arse all the time."

"Do I detect a hint of a compliment for our esteemed superior there, Detective Hobbs?" Stirling chuckled.

"Yeah, yeah. Just don't tell her I said that. Alright?"

Chai returned with his own cup of coffee and sat down, sipping happily before addressing the two detectives. "So, the body is now at the morgue and they are preparing it for the identification. Mr Patterson is on his way."

"Poor bloke. It won't be easy for him. He must have been expecting her to turn up any minute," remarked Hobbs sympathetically, leaning back in the flimsy plastic chair and then thinking better of it as the legs began to buckle slightly under him.

"What about her mother?" asked Stirling. "Has she been tracked down?"

"Yes, actually. She has been in contact with the British Embassy in Bangkok. Her Thai friend saw something on the local news and contacted her on Facebook. She knows that Ella was missing and we've found a body, but Mr Patterson has agreed to call her after formal identification."

"Well, at least she knows," sighed Stirling.

Chai continued, "There isn't an available autopsy slot until tomorrow, but they've rushed through the blood work. As I said, they were probably hoping to find alcohol or drugs in the victim's system - which they did."

Hobbs and Stirling looked at each other.

"What did they find then?" asked Hobbs, sitting forward in his seat now.

"Alcohol, but only in trace amounts. She definitely wasn't drunk. But they also found evidence of cannabis and methamphetamine."

"Meth?!" exclaimed Stirling with shock turning to look at Hobbs who was also sitting with raised eyebrows.

"Yes, in Thai we call it *yaa-baa*, *yaa* in Thai means *medicine* or *drug*, *baa* means *crazy*. *Yaa-baa* roughly translates as *crazy medicine*. It's a big problem in Thailand," said Chai pointing to one of the posters on the wall that showed two dishevelled young Asian men crouched together heating a small pink pill on some foil and inhaling the rising vapour.

"Where does it come from and why how did it end up in the bloodstream of a 15-year-old girl?" asked Hobbs, incredulously.

"Most of it is produced across the border in Burma by the

military wing of the Wa State ethnic minority. It's a mixture of meth amphetamine and caffeine. It was legal until around 1970. It was sold to long-distance drivers to keep them awake. It's illegal now, but the government did talk a few years about decriminalising it."

"Decriminalising meth? That's a new one," snorted Hobbs.

"They probably just want to legalise it and tax it," replied Chai. "I'm sure you'll see that with cannabis soon. They just want the tax and tourist dollars. They say Bangkok will be the Amsterdam of the East."

"I thought they executed drug dealers here?" remarked Hobbs.

"Yes, they do. They had the *War on Drugs* here too in the early 2000s. I was just a kid but they say they killed thousands of drug dealers and traffickers. No arrests, no trials, just killings in the street. This year, we seized over 500 million tablets of yaa-baa, more than double last year." Now, the government thinks the war on drugs is lost, so they may as well make some money off it."

"None of that explains why this *yaa-baa* ended up in our girl's system, though," Hobbs chimed in.

"She must have been given it," said Stirling, half to herself. "She's a clean-cut, fancy boarding school student. No history of drugs - not even tobacco, according to her father. She's not the type to be using this type of drug."

"Right," replied Chai. "It's a *lo-so* drug - that's *low society*. Ella was definitely *hi-so*. It's cheap, too: 80-100 Baht, less than two pounds, per hit. It's still popular among truck drivers, but also taxi drivers and bar girls - anyone working long hours or night shifts that needs to stay awake."

Stirling was in full-flow now. "So, if we think she was given

CHAPTER 8

it, who gave it to her? They found beer cans and cigarette butts at the rear of the train. That explains the alcohol in her system. I guarantee they'll find Ella's DNA on those and presumably whoever gave her the meth. So, we're looking for someone with access to this drug, maybe with connections to long-distance transport, taxis or prostitution. Most probably male, young, good looking enough to strike up a conversation with Ella and good enough at English to maintain it."

Hobbs was always impressed at the speed that Stirling was able to join the dots.

"Most young people around here don't speak good English, but the Burmese do - one of the better things left over from their time under British rule," said Chai.

Hobbs interjected, "So, we need to get a DNA profile off those beer cans and fag butts, but what are we going to do with it? I don't even know if they have a DNA database here and even if they do, if there's no match, what do we do? We can't go door-to-door looking for young, good-looking Burmese fellas."

"We can check the Burmese migrant camps. There's one around 90 minutes from here - Ban Tham Hin." Chai pointed to a star on one of the maps permanently spread out on the table. "It's just across the provincial border in Ratchaburi province. There's over four thousand refugees living there. It's a closed camp, so people aren't supposed to come and go from the camp but many have relatives outside the camp so the rules are only loosely enforced. It's possible our man came from there."

"Well, we're glad you've got the local knowledge, Chai mate," said Hobbs, clapping him roughly on the back. Hobbs continued, "If we're quick, we could get there this afternoon and start questioning people based on Debs' profile."

"Let me pass this on to Captain Anupong. Excuse me."

Chai got up and left the room to relay the messages from the British detectives. A few minutes later he returned looking rather glum. Hobbs and Stirling got up from their seats.

"I spoke to Anupong. He said they have already sent the DNA from the beer cans and cigarette butts to Bangkok for analysis but he won't let anyone approach the camp before the results come back. He's on good terms with the *Palat*, the governor, of the camp and he doesn't want to mess with that."

Hobbs and Stirling returned to their seats, dejected.

"When do they think the results will be back?" asked Stirling.

"Tomorrow morning, hopefully, but we can't be sure. They run on *Thai Time*, unfortunately."

"Shit," swore Hobbs, slamming his huge fist down onto the table and turning a few heads of the police staff nearby. "He could have done a runner to Bangkok, back to Burma or be half-way to America by the time we get there!"

"Anupong also said to remind you that you are here as consultants, not as police officers and definitely not murder detectives."

Hobbs gritted his teeth and shook his head. "That Anupong is a real…". A look of raised eyebrows from Stirling stopped him mid-sentence. "…tricky customer," he said, regaining his composure.

"So what can we do now?" asked Stirling to Chai.

"Anupong said that Mr Patterson is arriving at the morgue soon and he has asked that you accompany him to the identification."

"Of course," replied Stirling, standing up and pushing her

chair under the table. "The poor man must be devastated."

"Sounds more like Anupong is trying to get rid of us," muttered Hobbs, getting to his feet and mopping up the sickly sweet coffee that he spilled through his recent outburst. "We may not be murder detectives, but that isn't going to stop us doing everything we can to find out what happened to that young lass."

"Come on, Frankie," whispered Stirling, placing her slender hand gently on Hobbs' huge back. "Let's go and see Ella."

* * *

Hobbs and Stirling waited impatiently in the waiting room of the Kanchanaburi morgue. The room was not air conditioned and was cooled only by a pair of wall fans which buzzed noisily from side to side. Hobbs fanned himself with a dog-eared magazine he found in a rack beside him as beads of sweat rolled down the back of his neck. Stirling looked similarly uncomfortable, her pale skin taking on an even more pallid tone in the oppressive heat.

Hobbs felt a mixture of relief and apprehension as the lean figure of Richard Patterson appeared through the frosted glass of the waiting room door. He greeted the receptionist, an older lady with greying hair and kind eyes, with a low *wai* and made his way slowly across the room to the waiting detectives. Hobbs and Stirling rose from their seats and lowered their heads in respect.

"Frank, Debra, thank you both for coming," Patterson began, shaking both their hands in a less-formal two-handed grip. "I didn't really know who else to call on. Stella is tied up with things at the Embassy and, well, you know, it's nice to have someone who speaks your language at times like this, I suppose."

Stirling forced a muted smile. "Not at all, Mr Ambassador. We're here to help," she replied, as Patterson reluctantly released his grip. The receptionist spoke in hushed tones to Patterson and gestured towards a corridor to the left of the reception desk.

Patterson heaved a heavy sigh and said, "Let's get this over with, shall we?" They walked slowly down the corridor, following the receptionist, and stopped at a room with a bilingual sign that read: IDENTIFICATION SUITE. The receptionist opened the door and gestured for them to go inside.

The name *suite* was terribly misleading. The room was small and suffocating. It was also depressingly sterile and tiled floor-to-ceiling in white tiles held together with yellowing grout. Bolted to the floor were four grey moulded plastic chairs, similar to those one might find at a bus station. Just in front of the chairs, about a metre or so away, was a low, wide viewing window which allowed the visitors to see into another small room. This one was also tiled all in white with a solitary brilliant white light hanging low on a long cord from the ceiling. There was a metal door on the right-hand wall with a small viewing window in the centre. The receptionist pushed a button on the wall of the identification suite next to the window and a buzzer sound was heard in the adjacent room. A few moments later, the door opened and a battered metal trolley was pushed slowly into the room on the other side of the glass.

Patterson took a sharp inward breath as he saw the profile of a young female body covered by a long white sheet. The mortician was a short man, dressed in classic baby blue scrubs. Small intelligent eyes peered out over a pair of thick-rimmed glasses. A surgical mask covered the remainder of his face and a few tufts of grey hair stuck out at jaunty angles from under his surgical cap. He nodded to Patterson as if asking if he was ready and Patterson nodded morosely back. The mortician then slowly and respectfully pulled back the sheet and folded it gently half-way down the dead girl's chest, just under the armpit line.

After an initial glance, both Hobbs and Stirling folded their hands in front of them and looked down. Patterson looked on at the body of his only daughter. The mortician had done a good job of tidying her up. The body on the trolley looked strikingly different to the grisly photographs Hobbs and Stirling had viewed earlier in the day. The mortician had placed her on the trolley so as to show the undamaged side of her face. Her hair was washed and combed and no longer streaked with blood. She looked peaceful, beautiful, in fact.

Patterson's bottom lip quivered as he nodded confirmation first to the mortician and then to the receptionist who then handed him a piece of paper attached to a clipboard to sign. He signed the paper and handed it back with the pen as the mortician nodded respectfully and proceeded to re-cover the body before wheeling it back out of the room. The solitary lightbulb in the room behind the glass went out and plunged the room into darkness.

Patterson wiped at his eyes with the back of his hand as he had done before at the restaurant at the river, but held himself together, stoically as ever. The receptionist opened the door and they all filed out of the identification suite and down the corridor to the waiting room once more.

There was an awkward silence as the three were left standing in the waiting room which was eventually broken by Stirling.

"Are you alright, Sir? she asked, sympathetically.

"Yes, yes. Thank you, both of you. I appreciate you being here. Now, I really must be going. I need to call Ella's mother and begin making arrangements to return to London with Ella," replied Patterson, his voice cracking slightly as he mentioned his late daughter's name.

"Of course, if there's anything we can do, please don't hesitate to ask," said Stirling, extending her hand to shake Patterson's.

"We'll do our best to find out what happened to your daughter, Mr Patterson," said Hobbs, offering his own hand to the Ambassador.

Patterson shook his hand firmly. "Thank you, Frank. Though, I don't think there's much to it. A tragic accident - God's way of punishing me, it seems. Goodbye, Detectives. Have a safe flight back to London."

And with that, he was gone again, with another trademark wipe of the back of his neck with his trusty handkerchief.

Chapter 9

Upon leaving the morgue, Hobbs and Stirling checked their phones and both had a message from Chai in full caps:

CCTV HAS COME BACK. SOME INTERESTING STUFF. I WILL PICK YOU UP ASAP. CHAI

Loong Pon and his comfy air-conditioned van had been called back to Richard Patterson's hotel to take him back to Bangkok, but the police issue Toyota pickup was waiting for them dutifully at the kerb with Chai at the wheel. Hobbs and Stirling climbed in.

Chai greeted them with the customary *wai* and asked, "How did it go?"

"As well as can be expected," replied Stirling. "The body is definitely Ella, although I think we knew that already. Patterson left pretty quickly."

"Yes, I saw the van pick him up," noted Chai

"How about this CCTV then, Chai mate? What have we got?" asked Hobbs, excitedly.

Chai pulled a small tablet from his leather briefcase and turned on the screen. The footage was already on the screen.

He pressed *play* and a grainy CCTV clip sprang into motion.

The footage was dated the day Ella disappeared and was from what looked like a fixed CCTV camera at a train station. From the left of the picture strode what appeared to be an Asian man carrying a flat tray, perpendicular to his body that was hanging from some kind of string tied around the back of his neck. He walked purposely towards the train and boarded near the rear. The image was of very poor quality but Hobbs and Stirling spent a good deal of their working day in London watching CCTV footage, so there was a lot more they could tell from a grainy video than the average person.

"What are we looking at, Chai? Where is this footage from?" asked Hobbs, taking the tablet from Chai and allowing him to pull away in the pickup.

"This is a video from the platform at Nong Pladuk train station. It's the station between Nakhon Pathom and Kanchanaburi. It's a smaller station so a lot of the illegal hawkers get on here instead of the larger stations at Bangkok or Nakhon Pathom. The station master gets a small kick-back from the hawkers to let them on the trains, so he knows the regular hawkers well. He said he didn't recognise this guy. Never seen him before."

"Interesting," remarked Stirling, taking notes in her trusty notebook as Chai weaved through the afternoon traffic.

"Take a look at the next two videos," continued Chai. "The next video is from the platform at Kanchanaburi. You see someone who looks similar getting off the train, it looks like he still has most of his goods to sell."

"Is that unusual?" asked Hobbs.

"Maybe, maybe not. People don't always buy a lot from the hawkers. But what's unusual is that he got off at Kanchanaburi. The station master at Kanchanaburi said most hawkers stay on the train until the final stop at Nam Tok then ride it back the other way to get the best chance of selling their stuff."

"Do we have anything from outside the station at Kanchanaburi?"

"Take a look at the third video."

Hobbs swiped again to check the third video. The footage was clearer than that of the train station, but the figure was much further away.

"Where is this from?" asked Stirling.

"This is from a 7-11 outside the station," replied Chai.

The footage showed what appeared to be the same man exiting the train station, dumping his hawker tray on top of a rubbish bin and leaving on the back of a motorcycle.

"Who's he leaving with there?" asked Hobbs.

"He left on the back of a *win mosai,* a motorcycle taxi. We tracked down the driver. He wasn't very willing to talk, but a few hundred Baht changed his mind. He said that he took the guy to the place where the vans to the migrant camp leave from."

"BINGO!" exclaimed Hobbs, rewatching the footage again.

"Did you figure all this out while we were at the morgue?" asked Stirling, clearly impressed.

"Well, the footage came in just after you left and the station is close by, so I just came down to speak to the taxi drivers."

"See, Frank? Not *all* the Thai police are useless." said Stirling giving Chai a pat on the back from the rear seat.

"Yeah, nice one, Chai mate. Good old fashioned detective work that." agreed Frank, handing the tablet back to Stirling to take a closer look.

Stirling swiped back to the first video which had the man walking directly across the shot from left to right.

"Those train carriages - how long are they, Chai?" asked Stirling, without looking up from the tablet.

Chai hesitated. "I'm not sure, why?"

"Can you find out? Call the station master? He might know."

"Umm, yes, hang on."

At the next traffic light, Chai took out his mobile phone and flicked through his call history until he found a phone number and dialled it. He had a brief conversation with the person on the other end, presumably the station master at one of the stations, whom he thanked and then hung up.

"He said all the passenger carriages are 25 metres long," he relayed to Stirling.

Hobbs smiled as he saw Stirling's brain whirring while rewatching the footage over and over again before she said aloud, "Right, this guy takes 36 steps to cover the length of one train carriage." She took out her mobile phone, opened the calculator app and began to punch in numbers. "That means that he covers around 69 centimetres with each stride. If we divide that by 0.415 for a male, that puts him at around 166 centimetres tall, give or take a few centimetres, of course."

"What's that in old money?" asked Frank. "5 foot 5?"

"Exactly. Well done, Frank. That maths O-Level is coming in handy, I see," joked Stirling, clearly pleased with herself.

Hobbs didn't take the bait. "Ha-de-ha-ha, Brainbox. Well, we can add that to the profile then. Asian male, slim, between 165 and 170cm tall. Do you still think he's good looking, Debs? Mr Grainy? Or can't you tell from that footage?

"If we could tell that from the footage, we wouldn't need a DNA test, Frank, but let's face it, Ella was a beautiful girl

CHAPTER 9

and clearly valued good looks, from all her Instagram posts. I can't see her chatting to just anyone on that train, even if he did have beer and cigarettes to share. I still believe we're looking for a good-looking young man, no older than 30, who speaks at least good conversational English."

"Right, Chai mate," said Hobbs, placing the tablet back in the briefcase. "What are we waiting for? Let's get over to that camp and round up some suspects. Let's catch the bastard who did this to our Ella."

Stirling interjected, "He might not have done anything, Frank. It still could be an accident and he just happened to be there with her."

"No way, Debs. This Harry Hawker is dodgy as they come. Why wouldn't he just call for help, if it was an accident? Why did he jump off at the next stop and make a run for it?"

"Maybe he was in shock. He's just seen a girl fall from a train, probably to her death," offered Stirling, playing Devil's advocate, which was always a good idea when surmising about possible motives and suspects.

"You saw in the third video - he dumped all his wares. I'm sure these hawkers don't earn much. They can't afford to be dumping that stuff. What do you reckon, Chai? You think a real hawker would just dump their stuff like that?"

"No way," replied Chai, as he pulled into the car park of Kanchanaburi police station. "Those people are some of the poorest. If they lose their stock one day, they don't eat the next. We need to look into this guy."

"Right, let's get in there and pass all this on to Anupong. Maybe he'll change his mind about raiding the migrant camp today, at least round up some suspects who fit the profile and get them tested. We can look for matches tomorrow when the DNA comes back from Bangkok."

"You two stay here in the air-con. I'll go and see what I can do."

Chai left the vehicle with the keys in the ignition and the air-conditioning on full blast. He stopped to put on his police cap before entering the building. Hobbs and Stirling passed the time looking over and over again at the CCTV evidence that had been collected by the Thai police. It was indeed of poor quality but had turned up a good quality lead into the disappearance and possible murder of Ella Patterson.

Chai reappeared around 15 minutes later and Stirling could tell from his body language that the outcome wasn't going to be positive. He opened the car door and slumped into the driver's seat with a sigh.

"No luck?" asked Stirling.

"Sorry, guys., Anupong won't change his mind. He said they need to look for a match on the national database before looking anywhere else. He said he has enough trouble with the migrants without accusing them of murder without any evidence."

"Without any evidence?!" Hobbs shouted, angrily. "This is the best lead we've had so far. We've got a suspicious person leaving the scene of a crime, or accident, whatever you want to call it, in a big hurry. That's probable cause for an investigation, in anyone's book. What is this guy's problem, for God's sake? I should be in there giving him a piece of my mind, or a bloody right hook."

"I'm sorry, Frank. We all want to get out there, but we can't do it without Anupong's permission," replied Chai.

"Chai's right," sided Stirling. "We're on thin ice with the Captain as it is. If we piss him off any more, he might just send us home and then we'll never find out what happened to Ella."

Hobbs was passionate, but he wasn't stupid. He knew when a battle wasn't worth fighting. Although he was visibly seething, after a while, he began to calm but continued to shake his head, looking down into the footwell of the pickup and absent-mindedly sliding his wedding ring on and off his finger.

"Alright, alright," conceded Frank, pulling his seatbelt across his barrel chest. "Let's get out of here, then. I need a drink."

Chapter 10

Hobbs began to calm down further once he had a cold beverage in his hand sat in the open air bar-cum-restaurant-cum-reception of Pong Phen Guesthouse. Being open to the elements, he was also allowed to smoke, which served to placate him even further. Stirling, who had headed back to her room to freshen up, reappeared in the restaurant and ordered herself a gin & tonic before sliding along the bench seating to face Hobbs. Hobbs, out of respect, stubbed out his cigarette in an adjacent plant pot and blew the remaining smoke away in the opposite direction. It was past 6 P.M. and almost fully dark. The chorus of insects was in full swing.

"How are you feeling now, Frank?" Stirling asked, genuinely.

Hobbs sighed. "A bit better now I've got a cold drink in me, Debs. I'm sorry for causing a scene back there but that kind of stuff just makes my blood boil."

"Don't worry about it, Frank. I get it. I really do. It's really frustrating to have your wings clipped like this."

"Exactly. If we were back home, we'd be making far more progress."

"But, we're not back home, Frankie. You heard what Chai

CHAPTER 10

said: This is Thailand. Things run differently around here. We made good progress today. Don't lose sight of that."

"*You* made good progress, Debs. I reckon that profile you've made is spot on," said Hobbs, taking a long draw from his glass of beer.

"Come on, Frank. It's a team effort. You've been great and Chai, of course," replied Stirling.

"Yeah, he's done well for a young lad, hasn't he? Just shows you what you can do with a good head on your shoulders and an axe to grind. Not much of a team effort from the other boys in brown though, is it?"

"No, it's not. It's very odd. They, especially Anupong, are pretty set on rubber stamping this as an accident. They don't seem bothered at all that her purse, and especially her phone, are missing."

"Right. They have all seen the CCTV footage as well. That Harry Hawker is definitely dodgy. Whether he is a Burmese migrant or not remains to be seen, though."

"Chai seemed pretty confident about that."

"Yeah, but he was just basing that on your profile and the fact that this guy must have spoken good English. We can't rule out a Thai local being able to speak good English. Look at Chai, for example."

Stirling shrugged. "Good point." A waitress arrived with her drink and set it down on a bamboo coaster.

"Well, hopefully we'll soon find out when we finally get over to the camp. I reckon we get in to the station early doors tomorrow. The DNA results might come in overnight and we don't want to miss anyone leaving the camp in the morning."

"Chai said it was a closed camp or something though, didn't he? People aren't allowed in or out?"

"People aren't allowed to do a lot of things in this country, Debs, but it seems like you can do what you want as long as you've got money to grease a palm or two."

"Mmm, seems that way, doesn't it?"

Stirling had barely taken a sip of her drink and Hobbs was only half-way through his when another two drinks were plonked down on the table in front of them. Stirling looked up, puzzled, ready to explain to the waitress that they hadn't ordered another round but instead saw a very rotund western man looming over them but smiling broadly.

"Do you mind if I join you folks?" he said with a broad American accent. Both detectives were taken aback momentarily. Hobbs found himself in the rare situation of being lost for words.

Stirling spoke first. "Umm, sorry, we're sort of having a work discussion."

"Right," nodded the stranger, his generous jowls wobbling slightly with the movement. "I couldn't help but overhear some of your conversation, being on the table at the back there. You're right not to trust the boys in brown, though, I will tell you that for free." Hobbs and Stirling looked at each other, not quite knowing how to handle the situation. The stranger took the initial absence of rejection as an invitation and clumsily slid onto the bench seat next to Stirling. "The name's Larry Dean, pleased to meet both of y'all," he said, offering a large sweaty paw first to Hobbs and then to Stirling after quickly wiping it on his large beige shorts. "I'm with the Post," he continued, raising his glass to toast the two detectives.

"Sorry," began Stirling, raising her own glass, still a little bemused. "The Post?"

CHAPTER 10

"The Bangkok Post. The newspaper?"

"Oh, right, sorry. We're not expats, I'm afraid. We've only been here for…well, I'm not entirely sure how many days or hours it's been. Anyway, sorry, I'm Debra."

"Debra Stirling, right? And this is your partner Frank Hobbs. Am I right? Of course I'm right," chuckled Dean smashing his beer glass roughly into Hobbs'. "We've been following the story up in Bangkok but ya know if you want to get the real story, ya gotta get boots on the ground." Stirling noticed he had a very different pronunciation of the English name of the Thai capital, putting the emphasis on the first syllable 'Bang', rather than the second syllable 'kok', as is customary in the UK.

It had been a long day and the arrival of the stereotypically loud-mouthed American reporter was not an entirely welcome one. Hobbs did notice, though, that he no longer held the title of sweatiest man in the hotel as he noticed an ever-present film of sweat that covered the face, arms and any other part of exposed skin of their new, albeit uninvited, drinking buddy. As well as the unnecessarily large beige shorts, Larry Dean wore a quite obnoxious floral print shirt which was bordering on Hawaiian in its style and a fading blue baseball cap with the crest of a North American sports team that Hobbs didn't recognise. A pair of what looked like non-prescription reading glasses, the kind you might buy at a service station out of necessity, hung from his shirt pocket. Hobbs didn't dare take a glance at what he might be wearing on his feet.

Larry Dean took a long drink of his beer, taking off his hat and hanging it on the back of his chair, exposing a shock of surprisingly thick brown hair. Hobbs felt a pang of envy but quickly dismissed it.

"I bet you're getting nowhere fast with the boys in brown, huh?" he asked, knowingly. "I've been in country for over twenty years and I can count on one hand how many times people have spoken about those guys in a positive light."

Stirling could tell that Hobbs was none too happy at the arrival of the American reporter, especially with him sidling up next to her on the, thankfully, stout wooden bench. Hobbs had always protected Stirling, ever since they had become partners. The support had come in various forms; sometimes dealing with lecherous drunks in the local pub around the corner from work and sometimes genuinely protecting her from physical harm when they asked a few too many questions on rough council estates in South London. She sensed that Hobbs was getting close to telling Larry Dean to sling his hook but she decided that they could use all the local knowledge they could get.

Hobbs visibly relaxed as Stirling began to take control of the conversation.

"What kind of things do they get up to then, Larry, the Thai police?"

"Oh, you name it, Sweetheart, they're into it," replied Dean, ready to launch into a speech he had clearly made more than once. Hobbs glowered at how he had addressed Stirling, but she shot him a glance and he was placated. Dean continued, "Corruption, extortion, protection rackets, scapegoating, police brutality - it's all in a day's work for those guys. Oh, they protect and serve alright - but only themselves. It's a wonder the locals haven't launched a revolution already."

"Well, we did hear about some of that from our local police liaison," interjected Hobbs. "He's a local lad but studied in Britain. He's not a huge fan of them either."

CHAPTER 10

Dean wagged a sausage finger at the detectives. "Word of advice. I'd be careful trusting anyone in the Thai police. They may say all the right things, but in my experience, they're all rotten. You might think you've found a good one, but just be careful this guy's not leading you up the garden path, as you Brits might say.'"

Hobbs nodded. He considered himself a good judge of character; it was a big part of what he did, but that was back home in the UK, not here on the other side of the world. Hobbs had a creeping realisation that he might be getting out of his depth, something that he hadn't felt for a very long time.

"You just wait," continued Dean. "If they can't frame this thing as an accident, those guys will start pointing the finger at the Burmese. Hell, it's not even subtle any more. If one more young Burmese guy gets scapegoated, they're going to start eating grass in those camps." Hobbs and Stirling exchanged an uneasy glance. "They did it down on Koh Tao a few years ago, with the murder of those British backpackers. You must have heard about it. Ain't no way those poor Burmese bastards did what they said they did. The British guy was big, six feet tall and getting on for 200 pounds, for Pete's sake. Neither of those boys could have been a hundred pounds wringing wet. Everyone on that island knows they didn't do it, but they are in jail for it all the same."

Stirling had taken out her notepad and was busy scribbling notes as Dean told more stories of police corruption and brutality and both men supped greedily on their cold drinks. She felt like she had to take what he was saying with a pinch of salt, being a reporter, but the stories were opening her eyes and offering a new perspective on what had been happening since they arrived. He was bang on so far. But how much of their conversation had he heard? Did he have sources inside the police station at Kanchanaburi? She doubted that, but she also knew what reporters were like and decided she couldn't rule it out. The police had indeed initially tried to frame it as an accident, then they had gone straight to the conclusion that the man on the train had to be Burmese. Had it been Chai that had come to that conclusion, or her? She was finding it difficult to remember, to focus even. She was still jet-lagged, she thought. She didn't even know what day it was. Was Chai really just like all the rest? He'd given that speech in the car that seemed genuine enough, but was it all an act? She had been attracted to him initially. Was that clouding her judgement? Did they plant him there knowing that she would react that way? Was she being played? She suddenly felt embarrassed and stupid. She picked up her gin & tonic and drained half the glass in one go. She stood up and took another long gulp, leaving the glass empty but the second glass completely untouched.

"I'm sorry, Gentlemen," she yawned. "I'm going to have to hit the sack. It's been a long day and I think I'm still jet-lagged. You two feel free to stay, but I'm going to get an early night."

Hobbs replied, "No, no, Debs. You're right. I think an early night would do me good, too. It was good to meet you, Larry, sorry to leave you as Billy No-Mates."

"Nah, you're good," replied Dean, sliding over Stirling's surplus gin & tonic for himself. "I'm used to it. You guys go ahead and get some shut-eye." Dean reached into his breast pocket. "Here's my card. You guys call me if you need anything - off the record, of course."

Hobbs chuckled as he took Dean's business card and flipped it over to see his contact details in Thai script as well as

English. "If there's one thing I've learned about reporters, it's that there's no such thing as *off the record.*"

Dean laughed heartily. "You're a smart guy, Frank. I like that. Nothing gets past you, huh?"

Hobbs tipped the business card towards Dean in a mini-salute. "Let's hope not."

Chapter 11

The journey to Ban Tham Hin camp began early. Hobbs and Stirling had met Chai at the police station at 7 A.M. and by 7.30, they had received the go ahead to accompany the local police to the camp. After around an hour, the paved roads ended and the journey continued on dirt roads that wove their way between low mountains covered in dense green foliage. The going was slow but the police issue pickup was up to the task and at least it provided some beautiful scenery for the first time in the trip.

Half an hour later and a whole lot dustier, the pickup pulled up with around four others and a black boxy police paddy-wagon, in front of the Ban Tham Hin Refugee Camp. Nestled between several forested mountains was a sprawl of temporary dwellings that climbed haphazardly up the sides of the valley. Almost exclusively made of bamboo with plastic sheeting as roofs, the houses were packed impossibly close together, leaving just enough space for people to move around in narrow congested walkways which couldn't really be called streets. A couple of the police vehicles were parked very deliberately across the entrance, presumably to stop any residents trying to escape when they saw the police arrive. Four or five uniformed police officers stood leaning against their vehicles, some smoking, some scrolling idly through their social media feeds.

Hobbs and Stirling followed Chai and a few other more senior officers into the camp and towards the main administration building. The group's arrival was met with consternation on the faces of the adult residents but with genuine curiosity from the many children who came out of their dwellings or peered through open windows at the surprise visitors. Despite being the closest camp to Bangkok, Ban Tham Hin received the fewest visitors, particularly foreign ones. Residents there lived hard, quite desperate lives, relying on very basic rations for survival. Rice, split peas, salt and cooking oil were given out every two weeks to the residents but everything else had to be grown by hand with basic tools.

Three teenaged girls watched from a bamboo veranda, pointing and giggling through covered mouths as Hobbs and Stirling approached. They were dressed in western clothing but it was definitely not new. Their shorts were more holes than material and their t-shirts and vests were covered in small tears and stains. Their skin, hair and eyes were dark but they had a playful sparkle in their eyes. Considering their situation, they seemed to be rather happy. On their cheeks and foreheads was daubed a paste of white powder which seemed to be common among many of the children who were now following them down the crowded main thoroughfare of the camp. None of the houses on the street had electricity or running water. Sneaking a peek inside the dwellings, Hobbs could see that many had a dirt floor bar a few which were furnished with some recycled plastic sheeting or scraps of old linoleum.

At the administration building, the senior Thai officers spoke to the officials, handing over documents which were begrudgingly signed. The officials called over three or four teenaged boys presumably to spread the word about the DNA testing.

"They're calling together all males aged from 16-30 for mandatory testing," relayed Chai. "The local governor, the *Palat,* isn't too happy about it. They said the last mass re-settlement was a couple of weeks ago, mostly to America, but nobody has left the camp since then. So, they think we're wasting our time…and his."

"Well, we'll see about that," said Hobbs, sceptically.

Over the next hour or so, more and more male inhabitants arrived at the administration building to be tested. The administrators had set up three small folding tables upon which were set thousands of individually-packaged swabs. One-by-one, the willing testees opened their mouths and three police workers diligently swabbed the inside of their cheeks for twenty seconds before breaking off the end of the swab into a small plastic vial marked with the testees name, registration number and date of birth. A few men were visibly unwilling to participate in the testing, for reasons unbeknown to Hobbs and Stirling, but were forcibly marched down and took the tests, anyway. Chai made a note of their names and registration numbers for future reference.

All the time, Hobbs and Stirling watched from a pair of plastic seats which the administrators had placed out for them. They were in range of a large fan which had been wheeled out and plugged in at the front of the administration building. The administration building seemed to be one of the only buildings with electricity, along with the infirmary and the maternity suite. A few inquisitive children came periodically to practise their English and ask some questions: *What is your name? Where do you come from? Can you speak Burmese?*

Also watching the rather mundane spectacle were the majority of the women and older children in the camp, including the three teenaged girls that had caught Stirling's eye when they arrived. By now, she assumed, they all knew the reason for their visit to the camp and were probably theorising about which men, if any, might fit the profile of the person the police were looking for.

"You know what, Frank? I think I'm going to have a chat with those young ladies over there. You sit tight and keep a look out for anyone who might fit our profile," said Stirling. Hobbs grunted in approval as Stirling rose from her seat and went to find an interpreter to help her communicate.

After a few minutes, Stirling had roped in one of the young English teachers from the school to help her and they both walked over to the veranda where the three girls had been overseeing the testing for the past hour.

"Hi, Girls," Stirling began, stopping every couple of sentences for her interpreter to translate. "I wonder if you could help me. We're looking for someone who might be able to help us with our investigation. A girl died a few days ago. She was probably around your age. This person might have some information to help us find out what happened. Do you think you could help?" The girls nodded in agreement and Stirling continued. "This man we're looking for, he's probably young. He definitely speaks English. We think that he is able to leave the camp and we think he is probably quite good looking." The girls giggled to each other when the final sentence was translated. They exchanged a few words, possibly names, between them and giggled some more, one slapping another on the shoulder playfully for reasons Stirling didn't understand. "Can you think of anyone who fits that description that you haven't seen here today?" The interpreter translated again and the three young women conversed again, putting up fingers as they hypothesised.

"They have some names. Do you have a notebook? I could write them down for you." asked the young English teacher.

"Yes, yes, of course," replied Stirling, taking out her trusty notepad and ballpoint pen and handing it over. The teacher listened to the girls as they relayed a list of names. It took a little time and a few attempts, presumably as the girls struggled to spell the names in English letters. After a minute or so, the teacher handed Stirling back her notebook which now contained the names of three men who the girls had identified as fitting the profile.

"Thank you, Girls," said Stirling, bowing her head slightly in thanks. She wasn't sure if that was a custom in Burmese culture, but it felt right in that moment.

"You're welcome," replied one of the girls in heavily accented English before they all burst into fits of teenage laughter once again. They all waved good bye and Stirling thanked her interpreter, the young English teacher. She tried to give her a red one-hundred Baht note for her services but she politely refused before hurrying back into the school.

Stirling crossed the main street, squeezing between the men lining up to submit their DNA samples for testing. She took her seat once again beside Hobbs who was beginning to drift off due to the stifling heat and boredom of the whole affair.

"You're not going to catch any criminals with your eyes closed, Frank," she quipped.

"I'm just resting my eyes," he replied. "What did you get from the Burmese girl band over there?"

"I managed to get a list of people who fit our profile that they didn't see line up today. If the results from today come back negative, I don't fancy that bumpy ride to come all the way back to interview them."

"Good idea, Debs. I knew there was a reason I brought you along."

After some time, the line of testees was almost exhausted and the crowd of curious onlookers was beginning to dissipate as the sun rose higher in the sky and the temperature began to climb. Fifteen minutes later, the last sample had been taken and the police began to pack up their equipment. Some lugged the boxes down the main thoroughfare while others spoke to the administrators and got more paperwork signed. Chai motioned to Hobbs and Stirling that it was time to go. Stirling handed the piece of paper with the names on it to him and explained who they were as they all made their way back through the maze of makeshift houses towards the entrance to the camp. A stray football from a nearby football game came Hobbs' way and after a few touches he kicked it back to the waving children. He called one of the boys over and dipped his hand into his pocket to retrieve a handful of change, mostly five and ten Baht coins, which he handed over to the boys and gestured for him to share with his friends. The young boy jumped for joy and hurried off to show his friends, eventually sharing out his horde to the delight of his team-mates.

After a few minutes, the group reached the entrance to the camp and began loading up and heading out. All had gone peacefully and the armoured paddy-wagon turned out to be surplus to requirements. Hobbs and Stirling got into their pickup and Chai blasted the air conditioning before pulling away, leaving a cloud of orange dust behind them.

Stirling relaxed back into her seat and took a swig of water from a bottle in the seat pocket in front of her. The DNA sampling was a success and had gone off without a hitch, but she still felt uneasy. The majority of people there seemed kind and happy people, even though they were living in some of the worst conditions she had ever seen. Part of what Larry Dean, the loud-mouthed reporter from the previous night, had said had stuck with her and even caused her to lose some sleep. Were the police out to railroad a Burmese national just to maintain a positive light on Thailand for the tourists? She wanted to run it by Frank at that moment but what Dean had said about Chai also had her rattled and suddenly she wasn't so sure he could be trusted either. She decided to keep her mouth shut, at least until she could talk to Frank alone, out of earshot of Chai and especially in-your-face newspaper reporters. After a long couple of hours in the sun, the bumps of the dirt road beneath them actually served to relax Stirling and before long she felt her eyelids grow heavier and heavier until she couldn't fight it any more and drifted off to sleep.

* * *

Stirling was woken by a gentle nudge on the shoulder from Hobbs after they had come to a stop in the car park of Pong Phen Guest House.

"Wakey, wakey, rise and shine," said Hobbs turning in the front seat to face the rear of the vehicle. "We're back at the hotel. Chai reckons it's going to take a while for those DNA samples to be tested. We probably won't get them back until tomorrow at the very earliest, even if they're being rushed through, so it's best to make the most of some time to rest."

"Yeah, OK," mumbled Stirling, sleepily. She gathered her possessions and climbed out of the vehicle into the hot, dusty car park.

"I'll call you if I hear anything," called Chai from the driver's seat.

"Yep, OK, Chai mate. You make sure you get some rest, too. Bye now," replied Hobbs with a wave, as Chai pulled out of the car park and drove casually back up the soi. "I don't know about you, Debs, but that pool is calling my name."

"Yeah, maybe in a bit," replied Stirling. "I think I need to wake up a bit first. Maybe I'll grab a coffee from the bar. I'll meet you poolside."

Hobbs lumbered off to his room to get changed and Stirling ordered her coffee at the bar, asking the waitress to bring it to her room when it was ready. She walked along the path next to the pool until she came to the patio outside her bungalow. She took her laptop computer out of her bag and then plonked the bag down roughly on the solid wood table. She opened up her laptop and connected to the hotel Wi-Fi before logging in to her E-Mail account. She heard a loud splash and then saw a large dark shape approaching her from the depths of the pool. Hobbs emerged from the water with another large splash and blew out his cheeks, sending droplets of water flying over the side of the pool and onto the extremities of Stirling's patio.

"Frank!" groaned Stirling, shaking off her sandals and clapping them together to be rid of the splashed water.

"Sorry, Debs, you should get in. The water's lovely."

"Yeah, I might do later." Stirling focused on her computer screen.

"Right. What's wrong with you, then?" asked Hobbs, leaning on the side of the pool, letting the water take the brunt of his weight.

"Nothing. I'm fine."

"Come on, Debs. Give me some credit. I am a detective, after all. It's kind of my job to know when people aren't telling the truth. You've been acting weird all day. Come on. Spit it out."

"What do you think of Chai?"

"Chai? What do you mean? Ohhh, I get it. I know what *you* think of him. I think you'd like to get to know our new friend a lot better."

"I'm serious, Frank. Do you think we can trust him?"

Hobbs was taken aback momentarily. "I mean. Yeah. I think so. Don't you?"

"I don't know. It was just what that reporter, Dean, was saying last night. Maybe we *are* being led down the garden path by the police and Chai is a part of that."

"Come on, Debs. You should know better than to trust a reporter, especially a bloody yank."

"I know, I know, but doesn't it all seem a bit easy to you? It's playing out just like he said it would. Police try and peg it as an accident and blame the victim. When they can't do that, we're pointed straight towards a camp of Burmese refugees. The camp was bloody marked on the map before we even got there. Chai was the one who pointed it out. Maybe he has been in on it the whole time, giving us this sob story about wanting to change the world. They found him pretty quickly, didn't they? A Kanchanaburi local who happens to speak great English. It's just all a bit too convenient for me."

"I think you might be reading too much into it, mate. I've

spoken to a lot of people from a lot of walks of life in my time and Chai seems pretty genuine to me. Don't forget that Captain Arse-pong, or whatever his name is, didn't want us anywhere near the camp in the beginning. Surely, if they wanted to pin this on some poor Burmese fella, they'd have marched down there as soon as they could, before public opinion started to turn. That's what Larry was saying last night. They tend to drag their heels until the public start kicking up a fuss wanting answers and then, when they haven't got any, they invent some and pin it on an immigrant. That's their M.O., I think."

Stirling sighed and closed the lid of her laptop. "Yeah, maybe."

"Look, all I'm saying is let's just keep an open mind. See what the DNA test results come back like and go from there. To be honest, I'm surprised we're allowed anywhere near this thing any more. Let's face it, it's not a Missing Persons inquiry any more."

The waitress appeared with Stirling's coffee and a welcome segue from the topic that had been bothering her all day.

"Come on. Come and have a dip. It'll do you good," said Hobbs, leaning back in the water and trying in vain to float. "I even promise not to splash you."

"Alright, alright," acquiesced Stirling, begrudgingly. She finished her coffee and felt a bit brighter. Maybe it was the caffeine, or maybe it was the reassurance from Hobbs about the investigation so far, but Stirling felt she could let her hair down, at least for a while.

She grabbed her things and stepped into her bungalow to change. She changed quickly into a simple black one-piece swimsuit and hastily applied some sunscreen to her pale skin before venturing outside. She slipped into the pool via the steps at one end. The water felt icy cold as it rose steadily up her legs and towards her groin, so she decided to take the plunge and submerge herself fully. The cool water enveloped her as her whole body disappeared beneath the shimmering surface of the pool. She evacuated all the air from her lungs before pushing herself back up and standing up straight in the water, gasping for air.

The experience felt strangely cathartic as she stood in the centre of the pool with her arms outstretched, floating gently on the surface. Frank was right; things were out of their control for the moment. The best thing she could do now was to relax, and that's what she was going to do. She took Hobbs' lead and leaned back into the water, letting it take her weight. It was as if her worries were melting away as she looked up into the bright blue sky above her. A solitary white cloud drifted across her field of vision and she thought of Ella once more. She made a promise to herself, and to the solitary cloud, that whatever happened, she would find out what had happened here so Ella could finally be at peace.

Chapter 12

Hobbs and Stirling spent the rest of the afternoon in and out of the pool, trying to escape the tropical heat which was at its peak in the early afternoon. Hobbs alternated between wallowing in the pool and reading a chapter or two from his true crime book that he had picked up at the airport in London. Every so often, a member of staff would walk by and he would order a cold beer, adding it to his room tab. Stirling did much the same but interspersed her swimming with reading work E-Mails and doing crosswords online. Hobbs did manage to persuade her to join him in some day-drinking, saying that drinking alone was for sad old men. So, Stirling indulged in a few late afternoon gin & tonics and really felt herself begin to unwind. She kept reassuring herself that there really wasn't anything else she could do at the moment each time before she ordered another drink.

The sun was beginning to set over the river and the evening sky began to darken and disappear in a canvas of dark oranges and purples. Hobbs checked the skin on his hands and saw it had shrivelled to a prune-like texture, signalling that it was probably time to get out of the pool. He hauled his over-sized frame out of the water and wrapped himself loosely in a towel.

"Must be nearly dinner time, Debs. I saw a pizza place down the road. I know it's not Thai food, but do you want to check it out?" asked Hobbs, hopefully.

"Yeah, go on then. I think a bit of comfort food will do us both good, actually," replied Stirling as her stomach began to rumble at the thought.

"Righto, I'll just jump in the shower then and we'll grab a tuk-tuk," replied Hobbs towelling roughly what was left of his greying hair.

Stirling collected her valuables as she replied, "Alright, I'll see you at the bar in about twenty minutes then," and headed inside her bungalow to shower and change for dinner.

* * *

Hobbs and Stirling entered the pizzeria and were asked to remove their shoes. They had heard this was common in temples and local people's homes but this was the first time they had done so at a restaurant. They didn't mind, though, and slipped off their flip-flops, placing them in a small wooden pigeon hole by the door. The restaurant was decorated rustically mostly in wood - which seemed to be the general style in the area - with around five or six large wooden tables with chairs and some smaller ones outside designed for one or two people. Towards the back was a *fusball* table, occupied by what seemed to be a pair of young brothers, and a large bookshelf stocked with mostly Western novels. They decided to sit on one of the smaller tables near the street and were soon greeted by the Western owner. He was a tall long-haired gentleman who spoke with a European accent when he gave them a warm welcome and a run down of the specials, listed on a free-standing chalk board by the entrance. The owner took their food and drink order and disappeared into the back, reappearing a few minutes later with a small bottle of cold local beer in a foam koozie for Hobbs and a large glass of red wine for Stirling.

"Here's to expense accounts," said Hobbs, holding up his bottle with a grin.

Stirling raised her wine glass to cheers his bottle. "Pizza and wine courtesy of Johnny Taxpayer," she replied.

"I hope it's better than the fish from B.A. Economy Class," quipped Hobbs, taking a swig from his bottle.

"Anything is better than that - and Harding had the nerve to say it was decent!"

"Can't trust her farther than you can throw her. How is the moody cow, anyway? What's going on back in London? I saw you checking your mail earlier."

"Oh, nothing too interesting. They found that girl- Latitia or Lequetia, whatever her name was, from Moss Hill. You were right; she had run off with that northern lad again. He's a bad influence that one. I've tried telling her mother, but she doesn't seem to be able to talk sense into her. They found her in a chicken shop by the station in Oldham in the end, safe and sound bar a few needle marks."

"Good news. Any ending where they turn up alive is a good one in my books."

"Cheers to *that*," exclaimed Stirling and they brought their drinks together for a second time. "That reminds me, I never asked you how you got into this game. You said you used to be a cabby and a boxing coach. That's a bit of a jump into Missing Persons, isn't it? If you don't mind my asking?"

"Yeah, I guess it is. It's a bit of a long story, really."

"Well, the sign said hand-made pizzas so they'll probably be a while, if you're comfortable sharing - the story, that is, not the pizza - I know you'll smash a whole one to yourself."

Hobbs chuckled. "Well, you're right about that, and you're right about me being a former cabby and boxing trainer. I was pretty good at both, to be fair. I was never the best boxer, but I did pretty well with the training. We had quite a few good fighters pass through our gym throughout the years. It was a haven for a lot of them; a chance to get off the streets and stay out of trouble. Most of them didn't have what it takes to make it professionally, but I reckon it kept a good amount of them out of prison and a couple out of the morgue. There was this one lad, though. Ali Haider was his name. He was a refugee kid from Afghanistan, fled the Taliban insurgency in 2002 after his father and his brother were killed. Anyway, he was the business. I mean, this kid was dynamite. Tall, rangy, and bugger me, he was fast. It was like he was born to box. He just strolled into the gym one day and started going at the speed ball. The whole gym just stopped and stared at him. My jaw was on the floor, Debs."

"Sounds like a lucky find," replied Stirling with interest.

"Bloody right he was," replied Hobbs, becoming more animated as the memories came flooding back. "He didn't speak much English at that point, but we managed to communicate that he should come back tomorrow and he did. He kept coming and eventually we asked his mum if we could train him properly. She wasn't particularly happy about it - said that they had run away from violence - but eventually she agreed to let us train the lad. We trained him every single day for nine months and by then he was a machine, the best we'd ever seen. We had him his first professional fight lined up

CHAPTER 12

and he was champing at the bit. He wanted to make money and take care of his mum. Then, one day he just stops coming. A couple of days go by and we start to get a bit worried. We get a phone call from his mum and she's bloody frantic - says he hasn't come home for two nights, phone was going to voicemail and nobody had seen or heard from him. She's pleading with me on the phone. *Please, Mr Frank. Please find my boy, Mr Frank. He's all I've got left, Mr Frank."*

"So, what did you do?"

"Well, I couldn't say no, could I? I was a cabby so I knew the local area pretty well - the council estate he lived on and a few of the places where the kids liked to hang out. So, I started asking around. Didn't get very far to begin with, of course. You know as well as I do that people on those estates don't like to talk to strangers much."

"You can say that again," agreed Stirling. "but you generally find one person who's willing to in exchange for a few quid."

"Exactly. So that person happened to be this little street urchin on a BMX. Fat little bastard, looked like he lived on frozen pizza and chips. I caught him slinging some bags for a local crew. So, I pretend that I'm an undercover cop and will let him off with a warning if he gives me some information on a kid I'm looking for. The kid's too stupid, or scared, to ask for ID or anything like that, so he rolls over and tells me everything I want to know. He says that Ali had been working the corners for a while, trying to make money for his mum. Nobody messed with him because a video had been going around on Whatsapp of him beating seven shades out of a couple of numpties from a rival crew. Word on the street was that he misplaced a few bags the week before and nobody had heard from him since."

"Shit," exclaimed Stirling, taking a large gulp of her wine. "So what happened next?"

"Well, I did some more digging, spoke with the kids at the gym, that kind of thing. They're talking about this rival gang from another estate and how Ali had stolen from them to pay back the debt he owed to the Moss Hill crew. Well, my stomach just dropped, hearing that. I knew something was up, so I jumped in my cab to get over there and then I get a call from one of my cabby mates. He says they've found a body over on the wasteland by the flyover."

"Oh, no," said Stirling covering her mouth with her hands.

"Yeah, so I race over there and there's already a crowd. Police are ushering people back. His mother's there, just straight-up wailing, like you see them do in the war documentaries - just bloody awful. That's when I see his body, dumped in a skip. I know it's him because he's got on the trainers that I bought him the month before, when the contract came through for his first fight. But it didn't look like him. He was so pale. The life had been drained from him. His shirt just covered in... like a cascade of dark, dark blood. Single stab wound to the heart they said. Wouldn't have suffered they said. Didn't make it any easier, though. Not for me and certainly not for his poor mother." Hobbs stopped and took a long drink from his bottle of beer, finishing it and placing it back on the table deliberately.

"I'm so sorry, Frank. I had no idea it was such a sad story. So, that's what got you into Missing Persons then?"

Hobbs recovered his composure before answering, "Yeah. I just looked at his mother and my heart just bled for her. I was a new father back then. Maddie was a year old and Eileen wasn't long pregnant with Millie. I couldn't imagine losing either of them. It wasn't long after that I signed up with the Bureau."

"Well, I'm glad you did, Frank, and there's a bunch of mums and dads out there who are glad you did, too. The work you've done over the years has brought countless children, young and old, back to their parents." Stirling placed a slender hand gently on to Hobbs' rough bear paw. "You should be very proud of yourself, Frank. You're a great detective."

Hobbs took Stirling's hand in his and squeezed it gently. "Thanks Debs, but I think you've had too many G&T's."

"That be as it may, but it doesn't change the fact," replied Stirling with a comforting smile.

"So, what brought you to this moment in time then?" asked Hobbs, relaxing back into his chair. "Sitting here conflabbing with a worn out old boy in a pizzeria in Thailand, of all places."

"You wouldn't believe me, if I told you, Frank," replied Stirling in earnest.

"Can't be any weirder than my story, can it?"

"I guess not. Well, I finished my undergraduate in International Relations at St. Andrew's in 2004."

"International Relations? Same as the Ambassador, eh? Don't tell me you used to be in the diplomatic core, too."

"No, not quiet, but I finished top of my class and I was cherry-picked to work for the British government in Iraq."

"Iraq? in 2004? Like, Second Gulf War Iraq?" asked Hobbs, incredulously.

"The very same. See? I told you you wouldn't believe me."

Hobbs chuckled to himself. "It's not that I don't believe you, it's just surprising, that's all. Not to be rude, but why did they choose you?"

"Well, it probably had something to do with my academic

results and the fact that I spoke Arabic."

"Woah, woah, woah," blurted out Hobbs, shaking his hands in a *slow down* fashion. "*You* speak Arabic? You're pulling my leg now."

Stirling laughed. "I'm not! I promise. Not fluent, of course, but decent enough. I had an Egyptian boyfriend at university."

"Well, bugger me sideways. You're just full of surprises today, aren't you?"

"I guess so. So, I went to Basra in the winter of 2004 to join *Operation Telic*. The British had already secured the city the previous year but were dealing with insurgency on a pretty major scale. I worked on a team whose job it was to increase stability, build positive relationships with different factions in Basra and the surrounding countryside."

"Was it dangerous at that time?"

"For me, not particularly. There was the odd mortar strike, but nothing major. I wasn't on the front line, of course, but for the lads who went out on patrol it definitely was. I lost count of the amount of boys who came back injured or worse. A few were victims of ambushes or crowd control that, well, got out of control, but most fell foul of I.E.D.s, home-made road-side bombs, that kind of thing. There were even some friendly-fire incidents, which were always hard for everyone."

"That must be awful," commented Hobbs, sympathetically.

"It was. There was always a commotion in camp when that kind of thing happened. I watched them come in and…well, let's just say those are the kind of things that nobody should ever have to see. I didn't last long, to be honest. I was there the best part of a year, but in the end, the carnage just got too much for me and I didn't feel like I was making a difference. The insurgents kept it up, day in day out. We just weren't welcome there. So, I came home with my tail between my legs, just in time to enrol in a Master's programme in the autumn of 2005. I joined the Bureau not too long after graduating."

"Well, well, well, our own Debra Stirling the war hero, who'd have thought it?"

"Oh, I'm no hero, that's for sure. We all had to muck in, of course, but when the going gets tough, Debra Stirling gets going, I'm afraid."

"That's bollocks, Debs. You and I have been through some pretty hairy situations back home. You've never been one to back down."

The conversation was interrupted by the welcome arrival of their pizzas - a large pepperoni for Hobbs and a more sophisticated prosciutto and rocket for Stirling. Hobbs was indeed ready to inhale his pizza all to himself, but did eventually agree to exchange a slice with Stirling, as long as he could take the 'green shit' off.

The pair ate and drank too much for the next few hours. Other tables came and went, but the two detectives remained, drinking heartily with a kind of British stoicism thankfully uninterrupted by intrusive journalists. The passing traffic gradually thinned out from a steady thoroughfare of pickups, motorcycles and *songthaews* - the modified pickup trucks with two rows of covered seating - to the odd lone motorcycle, to almost nothing. The adjacent and opposite shops and restaurants had all closed for the evening and Hobbs and Stirling found themselves the final customers.

"I guess we better make a move," hiccuped Hobbs, finishing the last dregs of his bottle of lager. Stirling had finished drinking some time ago and a few drops of red wine remained in the bottom of her wine glass.

"Waste not, want not," exclaimed Hobbs as he picked up Stirling's glass and upturned it, draining the last remnants of their evening into his waiting mouth.

"Frank!" exclaimed Stirling, giggling, "I can't take you anywhere!"

Hobbs paid the bill in cash and thanked the owner before staggering into the empty street.

"Doesn't look like there's any tuk-tuks about, Debs. We must have lost track of time. What is the time anyway?" asked Hobbs, squinting hard at the watch on his left wrist. "I haven't got my glasses on."

"Come here, you old git," replied Stirling, grabbing his wrist and taking note of the time. "It's quarter to midnight."

"Quarter to midnight? Looks like we're walking home, Debs. Do you promise to protect me, seeing as you were in the Gulf War and all that?" Hobbs joked with a snigger.

"I think you'll be alright, you big oaf," replied Stirling as they began walking in a zigzag fashion down the side of the road in the direction of their accommodation.

Around half of the way to their destination, Hobbs heard the engine note of an approaching motor vehicle and turned to see if they might be rescued by a passing tuk-tuk or motorcycle taxi. He was disappointed not to see a tuk-tuk but did see two motorcycles coming towards them from the direction whence they had just come. Hobbs was just about to flag them down when he noticed they both had a rider and pillion passenger. The pillion passenger on the first bike was brandishing something that looked like a large stick or club. In his drunken state, he couldn't put together the information that he was receiving and he was too late to stop the inevitable. The pillion passenger swung the innocuous looking weapon

CHAPTER 12

in a shallow arc finally connecting with the top of Stirling's head. The heavy blow sent her sprawling to the floor in a cloud of dust, illuminated by the headlight of the second motorcycle which was also carrying two men. The attacker on the first motorcycle swung again, this time at Hobbs but luckily, even in his drunken state, he was able to duck out of the way at the last moment. He heard the faint whoosh of the weapon as it sped past his head. He heard a shout of "Go home!" from one of the men on the second motorcycle as it went to speed past him. Instinctively, Hobbs kicked out at the vehicle coming past him and connected squarely with the faring surrounding the seat. There was a crunch as the plastic buckled and the motorcycle wobbled then slid out from underneath the rider and passenger, sending the two riders sliding down the concrete road. Hearing the commotion behind them, the first motorcycle rider slowed and swung round to return to the scene of the crash. The two stricken riders were beginning to get to their feet. They were both wearing full face motorcycle helmets with dark visors, so Hobbs had no idea what they looked like. Other than that, though, they weren't wearing any protective equipment, just T-shirts and ripped jeans, so both of them sported visible injuries on their knees and elbows from the crash. The taller of the two men was limping noticeably and after a few steps, he gave up and sat down in the middle of the road. The shorter of the two men, probably the driver, was less severely injured and started towards Hobbs.

Any hint of drunkenness from Hobbs had now evaporated as the adrenaline coursed through his veins and into his brain. He looked back at Stirling who was still laying prone, unconscious on the road-side as the assailant edged closer, shouting what he assumed to be obscenities at him. The other motorcycle arrived and the other two assailants jumped off. The driver went to attend to his friend sitting in the middle of the road, but the passenger started to run in Hobbs' direction, carrying the wooden club that had just rendered Stirling unconscious.

Hobbs was a big man and with his boxing background, he knew he could hold his own against most untrained opponents, but there were two men here, soon to be three and one of them was armed, albeit with a less than lethal weapon. He steadied himself as the first attacker lunged at him throwing a wild jumping kick in his direction. Hobbs took a half step backwards and caught the foot of his attacker, throwing him off balance and sending him sprawling to the dirt. The attacker rallied quickly though and was on Hobbs again, this time throwing a poorly timed punch to the face. Hobbs expertly blocked the blow with his guard and countered with a swift right hook which landed, as intended, right in the man's liver. Hobbs watched in slow-motion as the attacker's legs crumpled beneath him and he clutched at his abdomen in delayed shock. He hit the floor with a thump and his head snapped back, connecting with the kerb at the side of the road and, rendering him unconscious, despite his helmet. The second assailant, witnessing the swift dispatch of his partner, slowed from a run to a walk as his confidence faltered. The third man was now joining the fray and the fourth had propped himself up holding on to the handlebars of the first motorcycle and was shouting to his compatriots.

The two men faced off against Hobbs, who was now breathing heavily, poised, ready for action. Just as the two men were about to engage Hobbs there was a tirade of

CHAPTER 12

screaming and shouting from somewhere across the street and some kind of projectile flew through the air between them and smashed into the ground, shattering and sending liquid splashing in all directions. This was followed by a second and a third. Both Hobbs and his attackers covered their heads and watched as glass bottles containing what smelled like petrol were hurled one after the other in their direction from behind a short wall of old tyres in front of the small motorcycle repair shop across the road. Behind the wall, Hobbs saw a slight local lady with long dark hair, clad in pyjamas and flip-flops. She picked up bottle after bottle of petrol from a black metal rack and continued hurling them like unlit Molotov cocktails towards the fracas that had begun in front of her home and workplace. Finally, a man, presumably her husband, emerged bare-chested from the shop and raised a snub-nosed revolver in the air. He fired one shot into the night sky over the road and then lowered the barrel towards the two attackers facing Hobbs. He shouted again and again the words, "*Ork pai! Ork pai!*" Both Hobbs and the attackers were frozen in place, dumbfounded by the actions of the husband and wife team. The man fired a second shot, this time not in the air, but not directly at anyone in particular. At this, the attackers turned and fled, including the previously unconscious attacker who had been brought back to consciousness by the gunfire. In an almost comical fashion, they picked up their fallen motorcycle and threw their fallen comrade roughly across the back of the seat before hopping on and accelerating away with a screech of burning rubber.

After watching the motorcycles disappear from view, Hobbs' thoughts immediately jumped to Stirling who remained stricken by the side of the road. He rushed over to her side, kneeling in the dusty earth, and gently rolled her over onto her back. A small amount of dark blood has messed her unruly red curls at the back of her head. Her already pale complexion had taken on an ashen grey and her eyes were closed. Hobbs slapped her gently, repeatedly, on her lightly freckled cheek. He called her name at the same time, looking for any kind of response. He didn't get any.

"Debs, Debs. Can you hear me? It's Frank. Come on, Debs," he called, trying in vain to keep the panic from his voice as it rose from his stomach. He cocked his head sideways, placing his ear above her nose and mouth and looking down over her chest. To his profound relief, he watched her chest rising, almost imperceptibly and tiny shallow breaths from her nose lingered on his ear.

"Oh, thank God for that," he exclaimed, rocking back on his heels and running his hands through his hair. He called over to the other side of the road. "Help! Please, help!" The brave woman who had come to his aid just moments before with her makeshift projectiles came running across the street with a pile of towels and bottles of water. She knelt by the side of Stirling, lifted her head slightly and slid a folded towel underneath. She soaked another smaller towel in water from one of the bottles, folded it and placed it on Stirling's brow. Her shirtless husband followed soon after, rushing over with a small first aid kit, his revolver shoved roughly in his belt. Clearly, he thought they might not be out of danger yet.

Hobbs scrabbled for his phone in his pocket and fumbled over the buttons on the touchscreen as he searched for Chai's number. The husband had now unpackaged a small menthol inhaler which he was waving gently under Stirling's nose in a bid to rouse her back to consciousness. After a few seconds, Stirling's eyelids began to flit and then, groggily, she opened one bleary eye and then the other. Hobbs could see she was having trouble focusing as she blinked and moved her dazzling, but now bloodshot, green eyes from side-to-side. Hobbs swore roughly as the dial tone continued in his ear. Finally, after what seemed like an age, Chai picked up the phone. "Hallohh," he answered, sleepily.

"Chai? Can you hear me? You need to come quickly. We were attacked on our way home. Debs is hurt," blurted Hobbs.

"Frank? Is that you? What's happened?"

"No time to explain, Chai. Just get down here, please, mate. We're on the main road, not far from the hotel." Frank looked around for any landmarks. "We're next to a motorcycle repair shop and a school, a primary school, I think. Just get down here and bring an ambulance."

"OK, Frank. Just calm down. I'm on my way, OK? I'll be there in ten minutes, OK?"

"OK, OK, thanks, Chai. Just hurry, OK. Thanks. Bye. Bye."

Hobbs hung up and returned his attention to Stirling who was now sitting up at the side of the road, to the objection of her two local carers and rescuers.

"Jesus, Debs. Are you alright? You had us worried there for a minute. I thought we'd lost you."

"Yeah, I'm OK. My head hurts though," winced Stirling as the local lady dabbed at the wound on the back of her head with antiseptic.

"What happened?" asked Stirling, screwing up her eyes in pain.

"We got jumped by some local thugs on motorcycles. They clubbed you over the head and then swung round to have a go at me. If it weren't for these two brave people, I think I might have ended up in a worse state than you."

"Khob kun kaa," said Stirling to her rescuers, thanking them.

"Mai bpen rai, mai bpen rai," repeated the wife, dismissively.

"Chuay gan," said the husband in Thai, motioning back and forth between them with an upturned palm and then in English, "Never mind. We help each other."

A few minutes later, the scene was illuminated by flashing red lights as Chai appeared in his police pickup truck with another officer whom Hobbs didn't recognise, followed by a small ambulance that looked rather like a converted minibus. Stirling was helped up by Chai and the other officer to sit on the open tailgate of the pickup, her legs dangling in the cooler night air. After a brief conversation with Stirling to make sure she was OK, Chai stood with the husband and wife and they told the story of what had happened while he made notes in his notebook.

When he had finished, he came back to Hobbs who was now sitting next to Stirling on the tailgate, smoking a cigarette while paramedics tended to the wound on the back of Stirling's head.

"I spoke to the couple here. They told me what happened, but they didn't see the start and they didn't see what happened to Debra. They got an idea of the make, model and registration of one bike and a partial registration of the other," informed Chai.

Hobbs relayed his part of the story: "Two motorbikes. Two men on each. Rough and ready types, tattoos, at least one had long hair, but they all had full helmets on so I couldn't tell you what they looked like. Debs here got whacked on the back of the head with a club or stick or something. She was out cold for a while. Gave us quite a scare."

CHAPTER 12

"OK. I'll put it all in the report and I'll get some officers down here tomorrow to check for any CCTV, see if we can further ID the bikes. The medics said they're going to take you to the hospital now, Debs. They're going to keep you there tonight for observation and if everything is OK, you can leave tomorrow but you need to take it easy for a few days because of the head injury."

"Thanks for coming out in the middle of the night, Chai," said Stirling, leaning her head on Hobbs' comforting shoulder. "and please say thank you to these guys who saved us. We tried but there's a bit of a language barrier. Can we offer them some kind of reward?"

"I can ask them. Hang on," he replied. Chai walked over to the couple who were talking with his colleague. He returned quickly.

"They won't accept any reward. They said they just wanted to help. They'll get their good karma when the time is right."

"So there are good people in this country after all," commented Hobbs as he helped the medics transfer Stirling into the ambulance."

"Of course. In fact, 99% of the Thai people are good-hearted, kind people. It's just the few bad guys who ruin it for everyone," lamented Chai.

Hobbs thanked the local couple again and told Stirling he would see her in the morning.

"Any chance of a ride back to the hotel, Chai? he asked. "Don't really fancy walking home on my own any more."

Chapter 13

Frank Hobbs woke early the following morning and travelled the few kilometres to Synphaet Kanchanaburi Hospital with Chai in the pick-up. They arrived at the hospital around 8 A.M. and visiting hours had only just begun. Chai spoke to a pretty nurse at reception to enquire on the whereabouts of the female *farang* (the loose, and sometimes considered impolite, translation for 'foreigner' in Thai) police officer who had been brought in the night before. She checked their credentials and invited them to follow her. She had long, dark hair which was bunched up in a large bun and netted under a traditional heavily starched nurses' cap. She was dressed all in white, in yet another impossibly tight uniform and Hobbs tried in vain to avert his eyes as they followed her down the antiseptic looking corridors of the hospital. Hobbs wondered to himself about the Thai obsession with skin-tight uniforms, but decided in this case he would allow it.

The nurse smiled kindly but professionally as she showed them the door to Stirling's room before performing a deferential *wai* and heading back to her station. Chai gestured for Hobbs to go first and he knocked softly on the door before pushing it open. Stirling was sat upright on the hospital bed dressed in her standard-issue blue hospital gown with her laptop open on the portable tray table which hovered over her bed. On the table was a half-eaten breakfast of what looked like rice porridge and fruit.

"Hiya, Debs," greeted Hobbs with a compassionate smile. "How are you feeling? Are you *working*?" He shot her a disapproving look before leaning over and planting a gentle peck on her forehead.

"Who me? Nooo," she replied with a wry smile. "I'm just catching up on E-Mails. Checking where I might want to go on my next adventure."

"You need to rest, young lady. Concussions are no joke," rebuked Hobbs before perching on the edge of the hospital bed.

Chai placed a hand on Stirling's shoulder. "I'm glad you're OK," he said and then took a seat on a visitors chair in the corner of the room. The room was small but private - in direct contrast with the majority of government hospitals in Thailand. There was a large window on the wall behind the bed and next to the chair in which Chai was sitting and a small, private bathroom in the opposite corner.

"Thanks, Chai," replied Stirling, with a smile. "I'm glad you were there to pick up the pieces."

Chai opened up a file which he had taken from his ever-present briefcase. "I've been going over the witness statements from the couple at the motorcycle repair shop. It turns out the plates are fake and not registered to anyone, but they have been used in other petty crimes and assaults around Kanchanaburi and Ratchaburi on at least two other occasions. So, we know the group that attacked you have some links to organised crime in the area."

"Organised crime, eh? That fits. They looked like hired local muscle to me. Nefarious types. Long hair, tattoos - not the kind of tight fancy uniforms you lot seem to wear," offered Hobbs.

"You mean like the nurses here at the hospital, Frank?" asked Stirling.

"I mean, in general, like. Look at Chai, he looks like he's wearing a bloody wetsuit sometimes!" retorted Hobbs and they all laughed, causing Stirling to wince in some pain. The wound at the back of her head was covered by a large pad of gauze and attached with a single bandage wrapped around her head and under her chin. Other than that, Debra Stirling looked to have recovered well, considering she had been the victim of a violent assault just hours earlier. Her eyes were no longer bloodshot and colour had begun to return to her cheeks.

"So what do you think they wanted with us?" asked Hobbs, changing the subject back to the topic at hand.

"Well, it looks like someone's getting anxious that we're getting a bit too close to the truth," speculated Stirling, closing her laptop and laying it down beside her. "Don't you think, Chai?"

Chai looked over the documents once more. "Well, those bikes have been used in a few different incidents. Let me see. There was a gold shop robbery in Ratchaburi in March of this year, an armed robbery at a traffic light in Kanchanaburi of a wealthy businessman in August and another incident in Ratchaburi where they were trying to scare some people into paying some debts. I don't know the word in English."

"Intimidation, probably," replied Hobbs, pouring himself a glass of water from a jug on the bedside table.

CHAPTER 13

"Right, intimidation. So it could be any one of those things, or more."

"But, I had my bag on my shoulder facing the road," interjected Stirling. "If it was a robbery, surely they would have just grabbed that?"

"Right," agreed Hobbs. "Also, I am pretty sure one of them shouted *'Go home!'* after you were hit, Debs."

"Really?" frowned Stirling, trying to remember some of the events of the previous evening.

"Well, you wouldn't remember, would you? You were unconscious at that point," replied Hobbs, matter-of-factly.

Stirling's hand subconsciously rose to the back of her head and the bandage covering her wound. "Well, that's got to be it, hasn't it? These thugs, or others riding the same bikes, have a documented history of intimidation and violent crime. They were sending a message. There's more to Ella's death than meets the eye and they want us gone before we figure out what it is."

"You could be right," conceded Chai.

"Of course she's bloody right, Chai mate," huffed Hobbs. "She's a bloody genius, our Debra. Finished top of the class, cherry-picked by the government to go to a war-zone straight from university. It's no mystery that she's up and about solving crimes a few hours after being bashed over the noggin with a bit of wood."

Hobbs' complimentary rant about his partner was interrupted by the ringing of Chai's mobile phone and he excused himself to answer it, stepping outside into the hall and closing the door behind him.

"Are you sure you're OK, Debs?" asked Hobbs, taking her pale hand in his giant paw. "I know you want to show the old

British stiff upper lip and all that, but if you need anything, you just let me know, alright?"

"I'm fine, Frank. Thanks for the concern. The doctor said I won't be able to leave until at least 24 hours after the concussion, so it looks like I'll be here another night. You and Chai will have to hold down the fort until I get back. You just make sure you keep me in the loop."

"We will, Debs. Don't worry. It looks like that massive brain of yours is still firing on all cylinders. Well, at least half."

Stirling chuckled."Thanks, Frankie."

At that moment, Chai re-entered the room with an excited smile beginning to curl on his narrow lips.

"What are you so happy about?" asked Hobbs.

"That was the Station," Chai replied enigmatically.

"And?"

"None of the DNA samples taken at the camp came back as a match for the DNA from the beer cans and cigarettes."

"Shit," swore Hobbs as Stirling shook her head in disappointment. "So, what are you smiling about then?"

Chai walked over to his briefcase and took out a small piece of paper. "Debs, do you remember these three names that you got from the girls at the camp? Well, two of them are already in America - they went with the last batch of relocations a few weeks ago - but this one," gestured Chai pointing to the middle name on the list. "Win Nyan Bo. This one is still here, in Bangkok. He works on and off in a gay bar on Silom Soi 4. It's the most well-known gay street in Bangkok; especially for foreigners. I got my colleagues at Pahon Yothin to check in on him. They found him working in the bar, swimming around in a giant fish tank in his underwear."

Hobbs and Stirling looked at Chai and then at each other,

CHAPTER 13

speechless for a moment. Stirling was the first to speak as Hobbs still tried to process the image of a young Burmese man swimming around in a fish tank in his underpants for the pleasure of foreign tourists.

"Ummm, wow," she stuttered. "Did they bring him in? Take a DNA sample?"

"Yes, I told them to," replied Chai, showing a flash of pride. "They swabbed him and sent it off to the lab as an express request. We should get a result this morning. If it comes back as a match, my boss said he will organise for some constables to drive him down to Kanchanaburi this afternoon."

Hobbs was now on his feet. "Bloody hell, Chai mate. That's brilliant. Great work. Really, great work." He strode across the room and shook Chai's hand roughly and patted him excitedly on the shoulder.

"It's good team work, Frank," replied Chai smoothing down his uniform. "The names came from Debs. She's the one we should be thanking."

Stirling blushed at the compliment. "I just thought if we're looking for good-looking men, who better to ask than a few of the pretty girls. Call it women's intuition."

"I'll call it whatever you bloody like, Debs, if that DNA comes back as a match. That means we've got the bastard that killed Ella." Hobbs was elated, but amid all the excitement, he saw that Stirling suddenly looked weary and was subconsciously touching her wound again. "Right, well that's bloody good news, Chai. How about we let Debra here get some rest? What do you think, Debs?"

"Yeah, I'm sorry, I wish I could do more. I think that's a good idea, though. You just keep me updated about the suspect, won't you? What was his name again, Chai?

125

Chai glanced at the paper once more with the three names. "Win Nyan Bo is his name, but here in Thailand he goes by his nickname *Win*."

"Win?" replied Hobbs with a staunch look appearing on his face. "That's something he's not going to be doing. Not on my watch."

* * *

Chai had dropped Hobbs back at the hotel to rest while they waited for the result of the DNA test to come through. Hobbs was relieved. It finally looked like they were going to get to the bottom of what had happened to poor Ella Patterson. As he absent-mindedly scanned through the backlog of E-Mails that had piled up in his work inbox, he reflected on the work he had done as a missing persons detective. Stirling was right, he had brought countless children back to their parents after what must have been fraught and harrowing times for them. He had also brought countless fathers and mothers back to children and pupils back to their classmates and teachers. There was a definite buzz to seeing the faces of the relatives when they see their loved one standing there on the doorstep, or the sound of pure unbridled relief down the telephone line when he had uttered the words 'We've found him' or 'She's safe'. Despite all that, though, it was still the failures that lingered in the back of his mind: people who he hadn't brought back, people who to this day had never been found, or had turned up dead - like Ali or Ella. As he sipped his coffee sitting on the wooden terrace overlooking the pool, he couldn't decide what was worse, knowing your loved one had passed on, or living with that tiny shred of hope that they would one day come back to you, but really knowing in your heart of hearts that in all probability they wouldn't.

Hobbs noticed that the sun was now high in the sky and the surrounding flora no longer cast their long shadows across the hotel grounds. He guessed it must be around noon. He checked the clock on his laptop: just after 1 P.M. He thought of his wife and daughters back at home in London. It would be early morning there, maybe around 6 A.M. He thought about calling but decided against it. He wanted to give Eileen some good news. He wanted to say that they'd caught the man responsible for Ella's death and he would be back soon to do some Christmas shopping. He went over the scenario in his head. In his head, Eileen was proud of him, she told him what a wonderful job he and Stirling had done under the circumstances, being so far from home and in a strange country. He decided he wouldn't call until that was genuinely the case. He went to put away his phone when the screen lit up quickly with a message notification. The message was from Chai and in his trademark full CAPS. Hobbs squinted to read it:

HI FRANK. DIDN'T WANT TO CALL IN CASE YOU WERE SLEEPING. DNA IS A MATCH. BANGKOK POLICE BRINGING WIN TO KANCH NOW. I WILL PICK YOU UP AT 4. - CHAI

Hobbs brought his fist down on the table with enough force to spill his coffee. "YES!" he exclaimed loudly in excitement to nobody in particular. "Now, we're getting somewhere!" He went to dial Stirling's number, but again decided against it, thinking about what Chai had said in his message about not wanting to wake him, so he too wrote out a hasty message to his partner:

Debs, the DNA is a match! The boys in brown from Bangkok are bringing our man here for questioning. Just keeping you in the loop. Do not even think about checking out of there early! Will keep you updated. Get some rest. Big day tomorrow. Frank

Chapter 14

At just after 4 P.M., Frank Hobbs clambered into the pickup that was parked in the car park of Pong Phen Guesthouse. Chai greeted him with the customary *wai* and Hobbs gave him an awkward fist bump in return. Chai reached into his briefcase and took out the small tablet with which he received most of the information about his cases. After powering it on and opening the Gallery application, he handed it over to Hobbs who had just finished wrestling with his seatbelt buckle.

Staring out of the screen at Hobbs was the face of a young Asian man in the form of a recent police mug shot.

"Is this our man, then?" Hobbs asked, taking in all the features of the man who was their new, and only, suspect in the disappearance and subsequent murder, or manslaughter, of young Ella Patterson.

"Yep," replied Chai as he reversed out of the parking space and then pulled away. "Win Nyan Bo - *Win* for short."

Most of the Burmese nationals that Hobbs had so far come across had been of a lighter skin colour than many of their Thai counterparts, but this young man's complexion was darker in tone. It complemented his thick dark hair which was somewhat longer than normal and held back with a simple black plastic hairband. His left ear was pierced with a large black circular piercing - one of those that can be replaced with increasingly larger ones to make an ever increasing hole in one's earlobe. His dark brown eyes stared back at Hobbs, revealing an air of stoicism, or perhaps indignance. With a prominent brow, angular cheekbones and good general symmetry, Hobbs supposed he could be considered handsome. Swiping once to the left, Hobbs now saw a full body shot of Win, the measure behind him put his height at around 165 centimetres. Stirling had been almost spot on in her estimation. Her intellect never failed to impress him.

Dressed in bleached black denim jeans, complete with torn knees and a jet-black *Ramones* T-shirt, he was every inch the teenaged girl's dream, Hobbs thought. He would have put money on the lad playing guitar, too. His left forearm bore some kind of fading tattoo; a pair of swallows, or swifts, perhaps. In profile, Hobbs could tell that although small in stature, he was in reasonably good shape. The slightly rolled-up sleeves of his T-shirt exposed small but toned biceps - no doubt a hit with his ageing European gentlemen customers at the bar.

Hobbs swiped back to his head and shoulders mug shot once more. His appearance suggested more edgy indie bar tender than cold-blooded killer, but Hobbs knew from experience that one should never judge a person solely on their outward appearance.

"What is he saying so far?" probed Hobbs, pinching two fingers to zoom in on different parts of the two pictures.

"Nothing, so far," replied Chai, keeping his eyes on the road and the myriad of hazards presenting themselves in front of him. "They are still processing him at the station. They'll start interviewing him soon."

"Let me guess, we won't be allowed to interview him."

"Not yet, or maybe not ever. I don't know, Frank. You know what Anupong is like. He's already getting problems from the Palat at the camp. He is letting us watch the interviews from the observation room, though."

"Really? Well, that's a start. We can work on Captain Arsepong later. What language does this guy speak anyway?"

"His native language is the Karen dialect, but he speaks quite good Thai and a bit of English - probably just enough to talk to customers in the bar."

"Right, I'm getting outsmarted by a murdering homosexual prostitute now. Brilliant. Stirling would love that," grumbled Hobbs.

Chai chuckled, "Don't feel bad, Frank. People learn languages because they need to, not because they want to. You grew up speaking English. Everyone else is trying to learn English. You're lucky."

"Yeah, I suppose so. I still think we need to talk to this guy, especially if he speaks a bit of English. Maybe we can get Debs to work her feminine charms on the Captain," said Hobbs, hopefully.

"I think he won't be able to resist," replied Chai quickly.

"Ahhh, so you've noticed her feminine charms then, have you? I thought I saw you admiring my partner once or twice," poked Hobbs, playfully.

Chai smiled but didn't look away from the road as he navigated yet another busy junction, bustling with other trucks, motorcycles, tuk-tuks and bicycles; none of which seemed to be paying even the remotest attention to the traffic lights which hung on low cables over the street.

"Shouldn't you be giving this lot a ticket, Constable Chai?" asked Hobbs, changing the subject to save his new colleague's blushes.

"There isn't enough time in the day, Frank. Anyway, it seems to work, in a strange way. Everyone gets to where they are going," mused Chai, as he finally pulled into the car park of Kanchanaburi Police Station. They both unbuckled their seatbelts and collected their things before alighting the vehicle and heading across the car park, squinting in the late-afternoon sun.

"There aren't enough hours in the day," said Hobbs as they neared the main doors.

"What?" replied Chai, puzzled.

"In English, we say 'There aren't enough hours in the day', not 'There isn't enough time in the day'," offered Hobbs, holding open the door for Chai.

"Thank you, Teacher," replied Chai, entering the building before Hobbs. "See, you are good at languages, after all."

* * *

The CCTV room at Kanchanaburi Police Station was nothing like the movies. There was no bank of monitors connected to cameras offering multiple camera angles of the interviewee. In fact, there was just one small 28 inch monitor which looked like it had seen better days. Covered in dust and remnants of old sticky notes, the monitor showed a basic, but clear enough, image of the inside of the main interview room which, like the majority of interview rooms, was sparsely furnished with just a simple table and chairs. Upon the table was an ancient-looking recording device with a large red light, showing it

CHAPTER 14

was yet to be recording.

Hobbs and Chai sat on a couple of well-worn office chairs, both with their arms folded across their chests, both blowing at the surface of a sickly sweet instant coffee from the vending machine in the corridor, both silently surveying the scene being beamed into the small room.

Win Nyan Bo sat motionless in his seat, other than the rapid tapping of his right foot which hammered away rhythmically next to the front leg of his chair, betraying his anxiety at the situation he now found himself in. Clad in a baggy, faded orange shirt and shorts and simple black rubber sandals, his body language portrayed a young man who appeared a shadow of his former confident self from the mugshots that Hobbs had viewed on the way over. His hands were shackled loosely in front of him and rested in his lap as he stared morosely at the table in front of him.

From the door behind him, entered a duo of Thai police detectives that Hobbs vaguely recognised from around the station but had not yet been introduced to. One of them he was confident he had seen talking to Anupong at the scene of Ella's body. This man was tall and also bore the 904 haircut which identified him as a member of the police force, but wore no other uniform. Instead he was dressed in blue jeans and a simple white T-shirt. The other detective was shorter and wore a pair of black combats and a similar white T-shirt, but over that he wore a sleeveless vest with the word POLICE in white on the back and its Thai translation underneath. He too sported the 904 haircut but was due a trim.

The two detectives took their seats opposite the suspect and busied with files. There was no lawyer or any kind of representation for Win Nyan Bo whose foot was now moving a mile a minute under the table. The taller of the two detectives pressed a button on the recording device and a long buzzing noise sounded for around five seconds to signal the start of the interview.

The audio wasn't the clearest and Chai strained to hear as the two detectives began their interrogation. Chai informed Hobbs that the taller of the two Thai investigators was named Panit, and a Sergeant in rank and the shorter was *Prachuab*, a Lance Corporal.

The questions began in Thai and Chai interpreted. "They asked him what he knew about the *luk kreung* girl - the half-Thai half-western girl."

At first, Win said nothing. He stared back at the investigators with a blank look on his face; not a look of defiance, nor a look of trepidation, just a blank look that made it seem like the feed had paused momentarily. Hobbs wondered whether Win could understand Thai at all. He also wondered how Thai investigators conducted their interviews. Did they go with the *softly-softly-catchy-monkey* approach? Did they have a *good-cop, bad-cop* routine? Hobbs' musings were rudely interrupted and his questions answered as Panit reached across the table and in one swift movement slammed Win's head into the table in front of him.

"Bloody hell!" exclaimed Hobbs, taken aback at the brutal opening scene of the drama. A wound opened up across the bridge of the interviewee's nose and a rivulet of thick crimson began to wind down his nose and drop in small puddles on the table. "Is that normal?!" he asked Chai, incredulously.

"Not really, I've never seen it in Bangkok, but I don't do many interviews. This is Kanchanaburi, though, it's like the Wild West out here."

CHAPTER 14

Win tried in vain to stem the bleeding from his nose with the sleeve of his jumpsuit as the questions continued and Chai did his best to interpret for Hobbs.

"They asked him about the girl again. He said he didn't know the girl. He met her on the train. She bought a couple of beers from him and some cigarettes. She said she had an argument with her dad and needed someone to talk to and asked him to join her for a beer, so he did."

"OK, that checks out. He probably knows his DNA is on those beer cans. He seems like a smart kid," replied Hobbs, making notes in his notebook to share with Stirling later.

"They're asking him what he knows about what happened to the girl," continued Chai, holding a pair of headphones tightly to his ears. Win responded but before he could tell Hobbs what he had heard, Win's head was again slammed unceremoniously into the table. This time, a small cut appeared on his left cheek. He tried in vain to stop the bleeding, but with cuffed hands, all he could do was dab ineffectually at the wounds with his sleeve once more.

"Let me guess," began Hobbs. "He said he didn't know?"

"Right," replied Chai, shaking his head. It was a difficult scene to watch. "He initially said he had no idea but it looks like he's beginning to change his mind."

"I wonder why," said Hobbs, facetiously. "What's he saying now?"

"He's saying that it was an accident. He gave her some drugs - probably the yaa-baa - and she started acting all crazy and then fell from the train. He thought he would get in trouble, he panicked and got off the train at the next stop."

Win Nyan Bo was weeping now, head down, a pool of bloodied tears forming on the table in front of him as he no doubt contemplated his actions and his future before speaking to the investigators once more.

Chai interpreted, "He said he's sorry. He didn't mean for anything to happen. He knows he should have tried to get help but he knew he would go to prison for giving her the drugs. He has to support his family in Burma. He is the only one with a job right now."

The suspect began to weep again as the two Thai investigators conferred together in hushed tones before both standing and exiting the room, leaving Win alone in the room with his fate.

"Jesus. This gets more tragic by the minute," lamented Hobbs, placing his pencil down on the open page of his notebook.

"Do you believe him then?" asked Chai.

"You don't?" retorted Hobbs, frowning. "He seems pretty genuine to me. Doesn't he to you?"

"Well, he seems genuine, but don't forget he dumped all of the stuff he was selling, including his tray after he got off the train. That stuff is expensive for a guy like him. He says he is the only earner in his family. That's what doesn't make sense to me."

"He said he panicked, though. People do strange things when they're in shock, don't they?"

"Maybe you're right, but that doesn't explain why we haven't found her phone or bag."

"Right. Do you think he took it?"

"Police in Bangkok searched his accommodation at the bar. They didn't find it."

"Maybe he sold it?"

"Maybe, we could check here in Kanchanaburi at all the

second-hand phone stalls but he could have taken it to Bangkok. There's no way we could check all those."

"Damn it," lamented Hobbs. "But, to be honest, even if he did steal her phone, that doesn't prove it was anything other than an accident, does it? All it does is add an extra charge to his rap-sheet. What is he looking at? Jail time? How long?"

"Methamphetamine is still what they call a Schedule 1 drug, the same as cocaine and heroin, but as he wasn't producing it or smuggling it, he will go to jail for 1-5 years and have to pay a fine. I think it's between 20 and 100 thousand Baht - something like that. He won't be able to pay the fine, so his sentence will be extended. He's probably looking at a two-year prison sentence. With good behaviour, he could be out in a year, especially with a Royal Pardon."

"A Royal Pardon? What's that?"

"So, twice a year, once in July and once in December, some prisoners will receive a pardon from His Majesty the King. They may have their sentences reduced or be freed from prison if they have served many years already."

"Interesting. What's the reason for that?"

"Thailand's prisons are full. They're more than full, actually. They're overflowing. Most of the prisoners go to jail on drugs charges. They need to make room for new inmates every year. The rapists and murderers don't have a chance at a Royal Pardon, though. Everyone has to make an application, explain why they think they should be released. The rapists and murderers get rejected every time."

At that moment, two junior officers entered the room and grabbed Win Nyan Bo roughly from behind. They rudely pushed and shoved him towards the door before closing it behind them. Hobbs wondered whether this was how they treated all their suspects, or whether this treatment was exclusively for foreign nationals.

* * *

Hobbs pondered the events of the interview that afternoon as they crawled through the rush hour traffic that flowed like treacle through the centre of Kanchanaburi. The journey should have taken around ten minutes, but it was after 25 minutes that they finally pulled into the car park of the hospital where Stirling was recuperating.

The duo entered the hospital and, remembering where Stirling's ward was, didn't bother with checking in at reception. They negotiated the maze of sterile hallways and staircases until they found Stirling's ward. Hobbs knocked gently on the door and slipped inside.

They found Stirling in much the same position as before: sitting upright in bed, with her work laptop open. A blue glow from the screen splashed over her pale face making her appear almost ghostly in the dying light of the evening.

"Do you ever stop?" asked Hobbs, half-jokingly.

"What? I was just checking my lottery numbers," replied Stirling, closing the lid of her computer and laying it down beside her.

"Right..." replied Hobbs "... and my New Year's Resolution is to give up alcohol. I am a detective, remember? Give me some credit."

"Speaking of which," said Stirling, steering the focus of the conversation away from herself. "How did the interview go?"

"You mean, apart from the boys in brown beating the shit out of their suspect at every opportunity?"

CHAPTER 14

"What?!" exclaimed Stirling, pushing herself even more upright in bed.

"Yeah, they roughed him up pretty bad. In front of the cameras, even. They didn't seem to care. Smashed his face into the table...twice. Blood everywhere. It wasn't particularly nice viewing, to be honest."

"Is that normal?" asked Stirling, turning to Chai.

"Umm, no, not really. Not in Bangkok, anyway," he replied.

"That's exactly what I asked, Debs. Anyway, he claimed he had no idea what happened to her. Then changed his tune pretty quickly after, well, being assaulted. He admits giving her the drugs and spending some time with her, but maintains that she fell accidentally and he panicked. Hence, not notifying the authorities and fleeing the scene."

"Sounds like you can't really blame him, if that's how the police treat their witnesses and/or suspects," replied Stirling with a frown.

"We're not all like that," interjected Chai, somewhat defensively.

"Oh, gosh, no. I know, Chai. From what we've seen, you do an excellent job. What do you think? Do you believe this Win kid?"

"I'm not sure," replied the young constable. "Like I said to Frank, the thing that I don't understand is why he dumped all his wares and tray outside the station. Also, the phone. If it was an accident, like he said, her bag and phone should have been found near the body."

"Exactly, Ella was heavily into her social media. There's zero chance she wouldn't have her phone on her," agreed Stirling. "Do you think the Thai detectives believed him?"

"I don't think so. I think they will push him again. They

will want to push the blame onto him and not the railway, like we talked about before."

"That's right," replied Hobbs. "I remember you saying about that. Chai reckons that if they do believe him and he's just charged with the drugs offences, he could only spend a couple of years in prison, or less."

"He'll probably be pretty happy with that - especially if there's more to this than he is telling us," added Stirling.

The conversation was interrupted by the shrill ringtone of Chai's work mobile in his breast pocket. He took out the device and checked the incoming number.

"It's the station. Excuse me," he offered and once again stepped out of the room to take the call. He was gone a few minutes and Hobbs and Stirling could see him talking in an animated fashion through the frosted glass of the window of the ward door. When he returned, he had a look on his face that was somewhere between excited and anxious.

"They're charging Win with manslaughter," he stated simply.

"What?!" Exclaimed Hobbs, in surprise. "Do they have the evidence for that?"

"I don't know. They might be trying to scare him into telling the truth. Manslaughter carries a maximum prison sentence of 15 years, but Win fled the scene so they can add *Escaping Punishment* which is another five years. He could go to prison for 20 years. It looks like it worked because Win is freaking out, going crazy, screaming the place down. He says he has information, but he'll only speak to the two foreign detectives. He must have heard about you two on the news."

Stirling was shocked. "Oh, my God," she stumbled. "We get to interview him? When? Will Anupong even let us? Is

CHAPTER 14

anything he says to us even admissible in court?"

"Anupong said no, of course," replied Chai, answering one of Stirling's plethora of questions.

"Wanker!" blurted Hobbs, instinctively.

"But…" continued, Chai. "The Palat from the refugee camp has stepped in and is threatening to get Amnesty International involved. I guess they are not such good friends as Anupong thought. So, you're allowed one interview. 15 minutes and it's got to be tonight."

"Tonight?! exclaimed Stirling. "But, we can't do it tonight. I'm not getting discharged until tomorrow morning."

"I'm sorry, Debs. Those are the Captain's orders. It's tonight, or never. No negotiations. Anyway, Frank and I can handle it. You need to get your rest."

Stirling tossed back the corner of her bedclothes and jumped out of bed. "Bugger that," she exclaimed. "There's no way I'm missing this."

"Debs, what are you playing at?" asked Hobbs, as he watched Stirling start to collect her things from the chair in the corner of the room.

"What does it look like? I'm getting out of here," she replied, matter-of-factly.

"But, you heard the Doc - you need to stay here another night to be on the safe side."

"Oh, bugger off, Frank. You know as well as I do that if the roles were reversed, you would be climbing out the window on a rope made of bedsheets. Now, are you two going to be gentlemen and turn around while I get changed or do I have to give you both an eyeful?"

Hobbs and Chai looked at each other for a moment and both dutifully turned to face the door. Although he didn't agree with her decision, Hobbs couldn't help but crack a wry smile at the display of Celtic passion from his partner that was unfolding behind their backs.

"Ladies and Gentlemen," he began with a grin. "Debra Stirling is back."

Chapter 15

The trio had devised a simple plan for Debra Stirling's premature discharge from the hospital. Hobbs and Chai would go first, with Hobbs on the phone to Stirling as they walked a corridor or corner ahead of her at all times. Stirling would follow a little behind, waiting for Hobbs' periodic all clear signals down the telephone line. They were primarily looking for any of the nurses that had been tending to Stirling during her hospital stay. There were only two and Stirling had given them a rough description of both. One was the duty supervisor; she was an older lady and wore a slightly different uniform, which would be easy to spot. The second was a very short and larger lady whom Hobbs was also confident he would be able to identify.

So, the two lookouts set off down the sterile hallways once again, turning right out of Stirling's room and down a short corridor which ended at a left-hand turn and a door marked STAFF ONLY. They rounded the corner and sounded off an *all clear* to Stirling who began to follow at a short distance. She had a small bag, which Hobbs had picked up for her, containing her laptop, her phone charger and a few other essentials. She did her best to conceal the bag under a jacket so that nobody would suspect she was discharging herself.

Hobbs and Chai continued down the next corridor. Hobbs was just about to sound the *all clear* when he noticed a short, round nurse wearing too much makeup coming towards them from the other end of the corridor.

He quickly barked a short warning into his mobile: "Big Bogey at 12 o'clock, closing fast. Take evasive action."

"Roger," replied Stirling immediately, checking her surroundings for a temporary hiding place. She spied a blue cloth folding screen with wheels maybe five metres or so in front of her in the corridor and made a quick dash behind it. Through the gaps in the material, she watched as the familiar character waddled quickly up the corridor towards Stirling and her hiding place. She quickly pressed the mute button on her mobile phone. A brief moment of adrenaline bubbled up from her stomach as she watched the dumpy nurse pass her by, seemingly oblivious. However, all of a sudden the nurse stopped in her tracks, just a couple of metres in front of Stirling. The feeling in her stomach turned to panic and her face flushed hot. The nurse fumbled in her pocket for her phone and finally held it to her ear. Stirling could not, of course, understand the conversation, but it seemed urgent. The nurse ended her call and set off again down the hall in an urgent manner. Stirling wondered whether her absence had been noticed and quickly broke cover, half walking-half running down the corridor. She unmuted her phone and spoke in hushed tones to her partner. "How are we doing, Frankie?"

"All clear down to reception. Not much we can do there. You'll just have to put your head down and hope for the best. We'll bring the car around," replied Hobbs, pragmatically.

"Roger that, see you soon," replied Stirling, ending the call

CHAPTER 15

but keeping her phone in hand. She rounded the last corner and made her way purposefully down the final corridor to reception. Nobody seemed to give her a second glance.

At last, she was at the reception. She paused for a moment to take in the situation. Thankfully, it was busy and most people seemed preoccupied with what they were doing. Those in the waiting area sat with their heads down, glued to the screens of their mobile devices, as is the slightly depressing norm in many parts of the world. Stirling made her way across the reception area, trying her best to walk confidently but at the same time not draw attention to herself. Halfway across the hall, she risked a look over her shoulder to check that she wasn't being pursued. Nothing. Nobody behind her. She looked forward again, just in time to see the wheelchair being wheeled quickly across her path by a hospital porter. The wheelchair was empty but Stirling still had to swerve to avoid clattering into it and doing herself a mischief. In that split second, she managed to avoid the hard steel of the wheelchair but instead found herself colliding with the porter. The collision was minor, but it was enough to knock her off balance and dislodge her bag from her shoulder. She picked up her bag and apologised quietly to the porter who was also offering an apology in the form of a high *wai*.

The accident had drawn unwanted attention and Stirling was keen to make a quick exit. She turned quickly and headed towards the large glass exit doors in front of her. *Almost there*, she thought to herself.

"Excuse me," came a female voice from behind her in accented English. A chill went up her spine. She'd been rumbled. She continued walking, pretending she hadn't heard.

"Excuse me, Madam," came the voice again, this time closer to her, as if it were breathing down her neck.

"Madam," came the voice again and Stirling felt a hand on her shoulder. *So close*, she thought. *So close*. She turned round to see one of the receptionists from the hospital standing in front of her.

"You dropped this," she smiled, holding out a hair brush. A wave of relief flooded over Stirling, so intense she felt like she might cry.

"Oh, goodness. Thank you. That's very kind of you," she gushed, taking the hairbrush and stuffing it quickly back into her bag.

"You're welcome. Bye bye," said the receptionist and she waved as Stirling exited through the automatic doors and out into the tropical heat once more.

Stirling recognised the police pickup that Chai had been driving and hurried towards it, trying not to bring any more unnecessary attention to herself. She opened the passenger door on the left-hand side and clambered in, quickly pulling the door shut in one smooth motion.

"Step on it, Chai. Let's get out of here," she said, slumping back in her seat. Chai pulled away from the hospital entrance and Hobbs looked back at Stirling from the front passenger seat.

"You alright, Debs?" he asked with concern. "We saw some kind of hubbub at the exit doors there. We thought you might have got rumbled."

"So, did I. It's fine. It was just a lady giving me by brush that I dropped. Don't worry about it. Bloody hell, this has been an eventful trip."

"I think it's going to get even more so after this interview.

CHAPTER 15

Are you going to be OK to do it, Debs? You look a bit pale."

"That's just my Scottish blood. I'm fine."

"If you say so."

Stirling fumbled in her bag for her wristwatch and put it on, noting the time. It was a little after 6.30 P.M. and the evening light was fading.

"What time is the interview, Chai?" asked Stirling.

"Whenever we are ready. We should be there in 20 or 30 minutes," replied Chai.

"OK. Did he say what he wants to talk to us about?"

"No, he refused to say anything unless it was to you two. Hopefully, he has calmed down a bit by the time we get there."

"Curiouser and curiouser," mused Hobbs from the front seat, to nobody in particular.

"Sounds like he knows more than he is saying," proffered Stirling. "Run it past me again. What has he admitted to so far?"

"Nothing apart from supplying her with drugs," answered Hobbs.

"So, he said her death was an accident, right?"

"Right. But, he might change his tune this evening."

"Sounds like he wants an interview where he won't be physically assaulted."

"Or he doesn't trust the boys in brown with what he wants to tell them."

"Or both. I guess we'll know soon enough."

Chai interjected, "The interview will be off the record, because you don't have any jurisdiction here. But, you're supposed to tell Anupong about anything he says."

"So, whatever he says can't be used in evidence?" asked Stirling.

"Right," answered Hobbs. "But, it also means we don't have to tell Anupong everything we hear, if we don't want to."

"Do you think that's wise, Frank?" asked Stirling. "You know what he is like."

"Yeah, I know what he is like," replied Hobbs, quickly. "He's a snake, and a dangerous one, judging by the behaviour of his team."

Stirling frowned and said, "I don't know, Frank. We could be playing a dangerous game. We don't want to end up on the wrong side of the police as well as the criminals."

Hobbs pondered for a moment before replying, "Look, let's hear what the kid has to say first, yeah? Then, we can decide what, if anything, we're going to pass on to Anupong and his thugs. Alright?"

"Alright, Frank."

The rest of the journey passed quickly as they all wondered to themselves what was going to happen when they finally had their audience with Win Nyan Bo, the Burmese migrant charged with the manslaughter of the young and beautiful Ella Patterson.

As they pulled into the car park of Kanchanaburi Police Station, they could see the unmistakable figure of Captain Anupong silhouetted against the light emitted from the main entrance. They parked quickly and crossed the car park to be met with the formidable gaze of the police captain. Chai greeted his superior with a high *wai* and Hobbs and Stirling managed to bow their heads slightly with insincere deference.

"15 minutes," began Anupong in a rare utterance of the English language. "No record. No video. You tell me everything. Understand?"

"Krup!" replied Chai in acquiescence, clicking his heels

together and saluting with a stiff movement of his arm.

"Yes, Captain," replied Hobbs and Stirling, in unison.

"Go," said Anupong, gesturing roughly inside the station.

They moved quickly through the station, ignoring the looks from the station staff that greeted them as they rounded each corner of the nicotine-stained corridors. Chai, in the lead, reached the interview room first. He knocked on the door and then opened it, allowing Hobbs and Stirling to enter in front of him. Sitting with his back to the door was Win Nyan Bo. His wrists cuffed, as before, but this time, his ankles were also chained to a small iron ring screwed into the cement floor. Hobbs and Stirling took their seats opposite the suspect and Chai stood dutifully to attention by the door.

Win looked awful. The wounds he had sustained earlier during his first interview had now dried up but were still open and untreated. He had new bruises under each eye and, as he moved in his chair, he winced. Hobbs, as a result of his boxing background, recognised this as a sign of potential broken ribs.

Win looked up with bloodshot eyes at the two British detectives sat across from him. "Thank you for coming," he said in heavily accented English and brought his hands together in a gesture similar to the *wai*.

Stirling began, "I'm Debra Stirling and this is Frank Hobbs. We are Missing Persons detectives from London and we are trying to find out what happened to Ella Patterson." Stirling wasn't sure how much of what she said Win had understood.

"I know. I see you on TV before," he replied in broken, but comprehensible English.

"Good," replied Stirling simply, opening up her notepad and letting Hobbs take over the lion's share of the interview, as per their normal strategy."

"Why did you want to speak to us, Win?" asked Hobbs, shuffling his chair forwards and leaning in towards the suspect.

"I don't wanna speak to those guys. They not police, they mafia, like soldiers in my country," Win replied, with venom. Stirling could tell he was angry. Angry at the way the police had treated him, but maybe angry about something else. "I wanna tell you the truth, but I think if I tell them, the truth never come out, you know?"

Hobbs nodded. "I understand. So what is the truth? What happened? Tell us right from the beginning, the start. Try not to leave anything out."

Win's shoulders slumped and he hung his head in shame at what he knew he had to say. "I killed her. I killed that girl. It wasn't an accident. I killed her, for money," Win said as he began to weep once again.

"For money?" asked Hobbs. "Who paid you? Why don't you start from the beginning?"

"OK," replied Win, brushing away his tears with his sleeve. "I get a message on my phone. I don't know the number. This guy tell me he looking for good-looking guy for a job. Good money. He tell me to meet him at karaoke bar. Near to camp. I tell him I already have job in bar in Bangkok. He tell me that this job much more money. I think this not so good but I want the money, so I go out of the camp and go to karaoke bar."

"I thought people weren't allowed to go in and out of the camp," remarked Hobbs.

"Can. If you have money, no problem. Just give some money to Palat, you can come and go no problem," replied Win, who

CHAPTER 15

seemed surprised at Hobbs' naivety.

"I see. So, you went to the karaoke bar to meet the guy. Did he tell you his name? What happened?"

"He not tell me his name but I talk with him there. He tell me he has a job. One day, one job. He will give me 200,000 Baht but I have to kill a girl. I tell him no way. Can not. You know? I tell him I will go to jail. He tell me no problem. If police catch me, I will go to jail only two year and he help me get me out in one year, maybe less than one year. He show me a paper, like a letter, in Thai language. He said just be good guy in jail, give this paper to the jail and the King will let me go in one year."

"So, you agreed?"

"No, Mister. That is a lot of money but I don't want to kill anybody. I told him I no want. He said he pay me double. 400,000 Baht. Mister, you no understand. 400,000 is more than 12,000 American dollars. I can build a house for my mum and dad. I can start a business. I can have a life."

"But you have to take a life," interrupted Hobbs, holding Win in a fierce gaze.

"I know, Mister. I'm sorry." Win once more began to weep and raised his hands in an apologetic *wai* gesture. "I'm so sorry. Forgive me," he blubbed.

"I'm not here to give you forgiveness, Win. That's not my job. Now, tell me what happened next," demanded Hobbs, acutely aware of the time limit that Anupong had imposed on the interview.

Win regained his composure. "I say yes to the job. To kill the girl. He said he will text me more detail later and he give me 10,000 Baht. So I know he is serious, you know? Then I went back to the camp. Next day, he send me details, where to buy the stuff to sell, where to pick up the yaa baa and the day, train station, something like that. He tell me everything, what station get on the train, what station get off."

"OK. Tell my friend where this karaoke bar is," said Hobbs gruffly. Win explained in Thai where the karaoke bar was located and Chai wrote down notes in his notebook. Stirling was busy making notes in her own notebook. Chai gave Hobbs a thumbs up and he continued.

"Do you know why this man wanted Ella dead?"

"No," replied Win softly. "He never tell me. I never ask."

"OK. What did he look like?"

"He is Thai guy. Maybe 40 something year old. Little bit tall. Little bit handsome. Black hair, black eyes. Little bit of beard. He wearing nice clothes - like Lacoste shirt, or something."

"Could you help an artist to draw a picture of him?" asked Hobbs.

"Yes, I think so."

"OK. We've not got much time left, Win. Can you tell me how you killed her?"

Win let out a long sigh and his voice cracked as he spoke, "After I give her the drugs, she is acting so crazy, dancing, singing. So I dance with her a little bit and then…and then I hit her head on the side of the train. Very hard, like this." Win motioned with his hand across his body in a forceful, swift motion. Hobbs imagined that hand grabbing a drugged up Ella by the face and slamming her head into the side of the train. He shook his head and looked over to Stirling who he could tell was also sickened by what she was hearing. "Then I see she is not dead. Her eyes like this." Win recreated Ella's eyes as they flickered and rolled back in her head. "Then she fell down and I push her off the train." He lowered his head

CHAPTER 15

once more and all four in the room sat in a moment of silence as they absorbed the gruesome details of Ella Patterson's demise.

Stirling put down her pen and she too lowered her head as she imagined Ella's limp body falling from the train, tumbling, crashing against the heavy metal machinery and the rails below. Rolling like a rag doll, arms and legs flailing in a cloud of dust before sliding down the grass embankment and coming to rest face down in a flooded rice field. She put her head in her hands and focused on her breathing. She didn't know if she wanted to be sick or to beat the living daylights out of the man in front of her whom had just confessed in grisly detail to the most heinous crime.

Before she could come to any decision, the door to the interview room was shoved abruptly open and two uniformed officers entered. One secured Win's hands in front of him while the other uncoupled the ankle shackles from the iron ring in the floor to which they were tethered. The shorter of the two grabbed Win roughly by the back of the neck and pushed him out of the door and the taller reached back to slam the door behind them.

Hobbs let out a long sigh and ran his hand over his face and goatee beard. Chai left his post and came to sit down in the seat that was occupied by Win just previously.

"Jesus, Debs. What have we got ourselves into?" lamented Hobbs, sitting back in his chair. "Our Missing Persons investigation has just become a murder for hire investigation. This lad, although he is a murdering bastard, has been hung out to dry by this mystery man. There he is, thinking he's going to be out of prison and back to Burma in a year's time, meanwhile the Thai justice system is looking to throw the book at him and put him behind bars for 20 years."

Stirling was only half-listening. She was already thinking about the next step of the investigation. "Do you know where this karaoke bar is, Chai?"

"I think we can find it, yes."

"I don't know why I asked about the sketch artist. Anupong isn't going to let us near him again. I don't think we can tell him about any of this either. It looks like he's looking for an open and shut case and wants to nail this kid to the wall. Burmese migrant, acted alone. Case closed," said Hobbs with fully unveiled cynicism."

"So what do we tell Anupong?" asked Chai.

Stirling thought for a moment and then said, "Let's just say that he was pleading with us to help him get the manslaughter charge dropped. It was an accident and nobody believes him. Blah, blah, blah. Something like that."

"He won't believe that, Debs," retorted Hobbs.

"I know he won't, but we can't tell him what Win really told us and we've got to tell him something. There's a chance that Anupong already knows what happened to Ella but he definitely knows that there's more to this than drug experimentation gone wrong. That's why he's trying to bring this to a swift conclusion."

"Right, that's settled then. Chai, you find out how to get to that karaoke bar and make sure you have Win's mugshot on your tablet. Debs and I will go and spin this story to Captain Arsepong."

Stirling smirked. It really was no time for jokes, considering what they had just heard and where the investigation was going, but Hobbs always had a knack for making a difficult situation a little more manageable. A little joke here, a shoulder to cry on there. It all made Hobbs a great partner and she could think of no-one else that she would rather be spiralling down a Thai rabbit hole with.

Captain Anupong was not impressed with what Hobbs and Stirling reported to him. It was obvious that he didn't believe them, but there was very little he could do about it. With a disgusted look on his little pug face, he shooed them out of the station with a gesture Stirling might use with her cat. She didn't mind, though, as she regarded him with exactly the same level of respect. Chai returned to the lobby and Anupong shot him a look of similar contempt. Chai responded with a comically exaggerated salute and followed the two British detectives out into the night.

Chapter 16

After a quick roadside dinner of *khao man gai* - the Thai version of Hainanese Chicken Rice - Hobbs, Stirling and Chai were on their way to the location of the karaoke bar that Win claimed he had met the man who had hired him to kill Ella. Chai had stopped briefly outside the police accommodation to change out of his uniform and returned in civilian clothing - a pair of blue jeans, a grey T-shirt and white running shoes. Hobbs wore a plaid shirt open over a white vest, with beige shorts and his Jesus sandals, while Stirling was wearing a simple dress that hovered just above the knee and black sling-backs. After a few minutes, they were leaving the built-up centre of Kanchanaburi. The buildings at the side of the road became fewer and farther between, along with the street lights and other road users. Before long, the street lights disappeared altogether and they found themselves travelling parallel to a steep-sided canal filled with dark, murky water. Only the moonlight and the light from the pickup's head lights reflected off the surface and the road ahead. Every so often, they would pass a small dwelling; some were made from concrete cinder blocks, some were mere ramshackle shacks of rusting corrugated iron and disused advertisement boards. Stray dogs kicked up dust as they ran towards the approaching vehicles, barking madly for no apparent reason and then being left behind in the bright red tail-lights. A few other vehicles, mostly pickups and motorcycles, shared the road with them. The majority of them turned off the road and tackled steep slopes down to properties at the bottom of the embankment.

In the distance, a low hum of rhythmic music penetrated the night air and a bright glow of neon appeared on the horizon, just off the side of the road. A minute or so later, they pulled off the main road and into the vacant area in front of the karaoke bar, kicking up a large cloud of brown dust from the unsurfaced parking area. A number of motorcycles were parked in haphazard fashion to the left of the door of the establishment. The entire building was made of bamboo and the roof was palm-thatched like that of a backyard tiki bar. The door itself had no hinges and had to be lifted into place and secured with a piece of ageing metal wire. Fairy lights of multiple colours were strung across the face of the hut and a large neon sign saying KARAOKE in English and Thai was attached above the entranceway. A contraption of neon tubes of different colours, akin to a windmill, was spinning slowly in the corner of the lot, advertising the location of the bar for miles around.

The trio exited their vehicle and stepped inside. The interior of the bar was no more ostentatious than the outside. Thin and faded sheets of linoleum with a blue and white fleur-de-lis pattern covered most of the floor, save the multiple areas where it had been torn up to reveal the dusty earth beneath. The hut was predominantly one large room with a raised stage on a back wall with backstage area behind it. To the right was a small bar with three large drinks fridges stocked full with large bottles of beer, two large chests of ice and a pile of boxes containing bottles of whiskey of different brands. In the corner, near the door, was a small cashier's booth that wasn't manned at that moment.

The rest of the area was taken up with clusters of rickety wooden tables. Thick plastic tablecloths had been nailed to each one and each was surrounded by three to four of the ubiquitous flimsy plastic chairs. One of the tables was occupied by a group of young males, drinking Leo beer from glasses with ice and showing videos to each other on their mobile phones. Another table was occupied by a group of older men, indulging in a bottle of Regency brandy, complemented by bottles of Chang soda water and Coca-Cola. Both tables had huge buckets of ice in the centre.

On the stage, a young woman with impossibly long false eyelashes and far too much makeup warbled along to a Thai karaoke song while dressed in a skimpy neon-orange bikini and high heels. Attached to her bikini was a large white badge on which the number 23 was printed. Other girls, similarly dressed but in different coloured bikinis, waited in the wings for their turn to sing, idly scrolling through their Facebook timelines.

A hostess in a skintight Singha beer dress with long black hair and bright red lipstick showed the group to a table close to the stage. The music was obnoxiously loud but Chai managed to order some drinks while Hobbs and Stirling took their seats. The hostess returned with a large bottle of Singha beer, three glasses and again, a huge bucket of ice. She poured their drinks and then scuttled away to the table of older men who were clamouring for her service.

Although Chai was not in his police uniform, it was still

difficult for the trio to really blend in. Both of the other tables stole curious glances at them but nobody seemed too bothered by their presence. After a few minutes, one of the more worse-for-wear members of the older male group stumbled over to their table to say hello and ask where they were from. He welcomed them and made a toast before weaving back to his table and a round of back-slaps and laughter from his friends.

The song that had been playing came to an end and Miss Orange Bikini tottered off the stage to be replaced by the next singer, another young local lady, this time in a bright blue bikini of a similar style. A new song began but it sounded to Hobbs very much like the previous one. The young lady began singing and received a more enthusiastic round of applause from the audience as it appeared she could actually sing a note or two. She was very pretty, too, Stirling noticed. She looked young - very young in fact - and seemed to be a local favourite, judging by the hearty reception of the resident customers.

The hostess in the Singha beer dress came around again. This time with a bucket of artificial roses and garlands made of real Thai bank notes. There were some made of 20 Baht notes, some made of 100 Baht notes and one even made from 1000 Baht notes. Chai explained to the uninitiated British detectives that they were for sale and could be given to the singers as tips. Hobbs and Stirling respectfully declined but noticed Chai reaching for his wallet to buy one of the garlands. He paid the hostess 200 Baht and took a garland made of ten green 20 Baht notes from the waitress. Hobbs grinned as he took a mouthful of his beer and Stirling frowned with confusion. She hadn't taken Chai for the type to be tipping karaoke girls.

As the current song came to an end, Chai rose from his seat

with his garland. The singer in the blue bikini, or #16, came to the front of the stage and stooped so he could place the garland around her neck. He whispered something in her ear and she gave a courteous *wai* of appreciation before heading back to her dressing room behind the stage. Chai returned to his seat with a smug look on his face.

"What was all that about?" asked Stirling, slightly annoyed at the pang of jealousy she felt rushing to her cheeks.

"Well, we're not going to get anyone here talking without splashing some cash. That's what you westerners call it, right?"

"But why her? Why not one of the waitresses?" asked Hobbs, curiously.

"She's pretty, she's popular and she can actually sing, which means she is probably a regular. If Win really did meet our mystery man in here, there's a good chance she saw him," replied Chai, with quiet confidence. "I asked her to come and have a drink with me when she's finished her set."

"Good thinking, Batman," replied Hobbs, impressed by Chai's smarts in the field. "I knew there was a reason we brought you along."

The three detectives finished their drinks and ordered a few more bottles. The beer was cold but the temperature inside the karaoke hut was stifling, in spite of the time of day. The only respite when the oscillating fans cooled the sweat on the back of their necks for a fleeting moment before continuing on their way. They watched and listened to more quite terrible karaoke renditions of Thai pop music and classic Western music. Hobbs even started to enjoy himself as he watched a young Thai lady belt out *Hotel California* by *The Eagles* and, strangely, *Zombie* by *The Cranberries.*

CHAPTER 16

"I don't think any of these girls were born when these songs came out," said Hobbs flippantly to Stirling.

"They definitely weren't and I think that's the problem," she replied, with a perturbed look. "Half of these girls don't even look 18 to me. What do you think, Chai?"

"I agree. Some of these girls are definitely underage. A lot of them aren't Thai, either. You can tell by the way they pronounce some of the words."

"Burmese?" asked Hobbs.

"Definitely. Probably illegal migrants. It's quite common." replied Chai, matter-of-factly.

"So, shouldn't you lot be doing something about that?"

"The Immigration Police, yes. But, I'm sure the owner has paid her monthly tea money to the police. They probably come in for a drink sometimes."

The ease at which Chai spoke about the systemic corruption in his country and profession made Stirling uneasy. Here were government officials quite openly taking bribes to allow owners to employ not only illegal migrants, but underage ones. Stirling was pretty sure that it wasn't just singing going on behind the scenes, either. She shook her head and took a long gulp of her drink.

Just then, the singer in the blue bikini, that Chai had generously tipped five or six songs earlier, appeared from backstage and pulled a chair up to their table. She greeted them all politely with a *wai* and sat down, shuffling herself up close to Chai and smiling broadly. A sickly looking drink, bright orange in colour and with a long curly straw, was placed in front of her which she picked up and began to sip seductively. She gazed into Chai's eyes in a playful manner and put a flirtatious hand on his thigh.

Chai wasted no time and immediately took out the tablet on which was saved the mug shot of Win Nyan Bo. The music was still obnoxiously loud and Hobbs and Stirling couldn't hear, let alone understand, what was being said but it seemed that he was asking her if she had seen the man in the picture. To their satisfaction, she was nodding and pointing to one of the tables in the corner which were more dimly lit than theirs in front of the stage. Chai swiped left and right on the pictures, zooming in to make sure. She nodded again. This was good news but then they watched as she began to shake her head.

The exchange didn't last long and the young lady finished her drink quickly. Chai handed her a red 100 baht note, which she accepted with another *wai* and a cute curtsy before tottering away back stage once more.

Chai leaned over to make himself heard over the music, "She said she saw Win here, but only once. She said he was at that table in the corner with another older guy who she has seen a few times, but she doesn't know his name or anything else about him. She said they didn't seem like they were friends. It looked like they were arguing."

Hobbs shouted back, not at all worried about being heard over the music, "So, Win was telling the truth about the meeting, but we still don't know who the man is who hired him."

"No," replied Chai. "But, I'm pretty sure the *Mama-San* will know him if he's been here a few times before."

"The *Mama-San?*" queried Stirling, unfamiliar with the term.

"The lady who manages the bar and looks after the girls." Chai pointed to an older lady who had appeared behind the cashier's desk and was rifling through what looked like a stack of drinks bills. "That looks like her over there. I'll go talk to her."

Hobbs and Stirling watched as Chai worked his local magic once more. From the outset, it didn't look too promising. They watched as he showed the Mama-San the pictures on his tablet and she shook her head repeatedly. Chai gestured to the stage, no doubt telling her about what #16 had told him about her sighting of Win and the mystery man arguing that night. However, the Mama-San remained indignant.

Finally, after some back and forth between them, the expression on her face began to transition, first from indignance to anger, then to resignation, as she seemingly came to terms with what Chai was telling her. After a few minutes and some hushed words, Chai returned to the table, looking pleased with himself.

"Come on, let's go," he said, downing the last of his beer. "I'll tell you what she said when we're in the car. I don't think we're very welcome here any more."

Hobbs took out his wallet and placed a purple 500 Baht note on the table as he quaffed down the last of his beer. Stirling couldn't quite stomach the last of her watery lager and followed Chai out of the karaoke hut and into the night as the Mama-San and cashier shot them all unquestionably dirty looks.

"Come on then," coaxed Hobbs as they all settled back into the vehicle. "What did she say and how did you get her to talk?"

Chai replied, "Well, at first she didn't want to talk. People in her business normally don't want to talk to the police. They know they're either in trouble or it's going to cost them some money, or both. She denied knowing Mystery Man or that he'd been here a few times."

"So what did you say to her to change her mind?" enquired Stirling.

"I told her that everyone knows she employs underage Burmese girls to sing in her bar and that if she didn't tell me what she knows, then she can expect a raid in the next few days."

"Nice one, Chai," remarked Hobbs. "So who is he, then?"

"His name is Pee Mhee. He's part owner of a large club in the north of Bangkok. He sometimes takes some of her prettier girls to dance in his club - for a price, of course."

"Pee Mhee?" asked Hobbs with an incredulous look on his face. "You're just making these names up now."

Chai chuckled, "It's a normal name for us, but I guess it sounds strange to you guys. *'Pee* means *older brother or sister* and *mhee* means *bear*."

Hobbs chuckled himself this time, "So, he's *Brother Bear*, then. That's a lot easier."

Stirling brought the conversation back to the business at hand. "So this Brother Bear, did the Mama-San know what he was talking to Win about?"

"No, she said she didn't. But, she also said she didn't know him at first. So, we don't really know if she's telling the truth on that," replied Chai, as the pick-up's engine roared to life and he reversed in a short arc across the dusty forecourt of the bamboo hut.

"I don't think it matters, does it?" asked Hobbs. "Yeah, she's employing underage illegal migrants, but it doesn't look like she's involved in the murder. We just need to track down Brother Bear in Bangkok and bring him in for questioning."

CHAPTER 16

"How far away is this club from your station in Bangkok, Chai?" asked Stirling as she fastened her seatbelt and Chai accelerated up the dimly-lit road alongside the canal.

"Not far at all. She said the club was one of those on the Kaset-Nawamin Road. It's a 15 or 20-minute drive, without any traffic. It's inside our area of operations."

Stirling was buoyed by the news. "So, your colleagues there should be able to track him down?"

"I think so. I'll give them a call in the morning. Hopefully, we'll be able to pay him a visit tomorrow evening."

"Brilliant," chirped Hobbs. "I've always wanted to go clubbing in Bangkok."

Chapter 17

Chai had dropped Hobbs and Stirling back to their hotel the previous evening and the pair had retired straight to bed. They had only been in country for four nights, but it had felt to both of them like a mini-lifetime.

The lady at reception mentioned to Stirling upon her return that a nurse from the hospital had called earlier in the evening. The receptionist had said that she hadn't seen Stirling since the previous evening, and that had been true. There were no further calls after that and Stirling felt a strange flush of pride at her daring escape. She thought back to the bizarre light-and-sound show they had seen a couple of nights earlier. In her mind, she made a comical comparison of her hospital escape with those of the Allied POWs that may have escaped from the clutches of their Japanese captors.

She still felt an occasional fiery pain or a dull ache from the back of her head but with the clumsy use of two mirrors in her hotel bathroom, she was able to see her wound was healing nicely. She undressed, tossing her clothes haphazardly across the floor of her hotel room and stepped into the shower.

The water was warm, even before the water heater had begun to work, and quickly the small shower room filled with a heady steam. After a night in hospital and all the excitement

CHAPTER 17

of the previous days, the water felt as if it was cleansing her in more than just a superficial way. She stood motionless as the warm water flooded over her. Her mess of red curls, which until now had stuck out in a mess of humidity and stress, was now slicked over the back of her head and the nape of her neck. She threw her head back and let the warm water fall in a cascade over her weary face and chest. She hadn't expected the shower to feel so good. She hadn't realised how heavy the events of the last few days had weighed on her until her shower had begun to almost peel them off in layers. She afforded herself a few more seconds. She breathed in the heavy, moisture-filled air and exhaled in long, purposeful out-breaths.

All of a sudden, as she began to mentally recall all of the events that had come to pass over the last few days, her resolve teetered as if on a knife edge. Her long out-breaths became raggedy as her bottom-lip trembled. The water, which had felt so warm and relaxing just moments earlier, now felt cold and unwelcome on her skin. Her knees suddenly felt weak and she slumped to the floor of the shower. The layers of stress had indeed been peeled off but now she felt suddenly insecure and wholly alone. She sat, naked on the shower floor, clutching her legs to her chest, rocking gently back and forth. She began to sob gently, but her hopeless tears were lost in the rivulets of water which still streamed down over her vulnerable form. She noticed this immediately and it dawned on her the futility of her actions. She covered her face with the palms of her hand and breathed deeply. She ran her fingers through her hair and forced herself to her feet.

She had survived, she thought to herself. She was still alive and she still had a job to do. She would head to Bangkok tomorrow and hopefully she would find the man who had hired Win to kill Ella. She was going deeper down the rabbit-hole; she knew that. But, she had no choice. She was alive and Ella was not. She had promised to do everything in her power to find out what had happened to Ella and that was what she had to do.

She turned off the water with a turn of a squeaky handle and half-heartedly towelled herself dry before wrapping her hair up in the towel and collecting it atop her head. Avoiding seeing her own naked image in the bathroom mirror, she crossed the room and took a smaller towel from the corner of the bed and placed it over her pillow. She unwrapped her tousled hair from its restraints and tossed it onto the floor before slipping between the sheets. The freshly washed sheets felt wonderful against her skin and she closed her eyes to enjoy the feeling. Almost instantly, her eyelids felt so heavy that she felt as if they couldn't be opened even if she tried and within a minute she had drifted off into a much-needed slumber.

* * *

Hobbs, instead of heading straight to bed, had sat on the terrace at the front of his bungalow to smoke a cigarette. The ever-present chorus of cicadas hummed rhythmically all around. A pair of small pipistrelle bats took it in turns to dive in long arcs over the swimming pool which was illuminated by its underwater lights. They twisted and turned, lightly skimming the surface of the water with each dive but never going under. Hobbs was transfixed by the display, trying in vain to get a good look at them but they flew too

CHAPTER 17

quickly through the hazy night air. Just as he thought they were coming into focus, they were gone again. As he sat in contemplation, smoke rising from the lit cigarette that he held between two fingers of his right hand, he likened the situation to that of his current investigation. Every time the facts seemed to come into focus, something would happen to derail their efforts and they would be on the run again. They had been lucky so far with the evidence. Chai had done some solid police work and his local knowledge was really paying off. Debs had been spot-on, as usual, but he noticed that the attack a couple of nights earlier had left her shaken. He wondered if he should check in on her and briefly contemplated giving her door a knock. He decided against it, however. Stirling was tough, he thought to himself, or was she? He was previously unaware of her time in the army - that had surprised him - and he was even more surprised to hear that she had left prematurely. Stirling had always presented herself with somewhat of a power-woman persona, but it hadn't occurred to him that this might have been a facade of sorts; a defence mechanism to gain an edge in a male-dominated profession. He thought again about whether he should check in on his partner, but as he craned his neck over to take a look at her bungalow, he noticed that all the lights were off and all he could hear was the low hum of the external unit of her air conditioner.

Hobbs' thoughts turned to his family once more. During the day, with all the excitement and intrigue of a murder investigation, it was easy to keep his family far from his mind. But, sitting alone of an evening, Hobbs mind wandered to his wife and his two daughters. He had tried desperately not to draw comparisons between his own daughters and poor

Ella Patterson, but at times it was impossible. They were of a similar age. They were also popular at school - maybe not so popular as Ella, but popular all the same. He thought of Richard Patterson, Ella's father. How must he be feeling now? He tried to summon up how he would feel if one of his children had been brutally murdered for money, but he couldn't. It was unfathomable to him, yet it had happened. It had happened to Richard Patterson and it could happen to him. The thought churned his stomach and he took a long, calming draw on his cigarette, tilting his head back to exhale the smoke into the air in a vain attempt at catharsis.

Hobbs' thoughts then turned to Ella's mother. They hadn't seen or heard anything from her yet. Did she even know Ella was dead? Ella's mother and father didn't have a harmonious relationship but surely they could put their differences aside to grieve the loss of their child together? Patterson had mentioned that his secretary was in touch with her once a year to arrange Ella's visits to Denmark to see her mother. Hobbs made a mental note to check with Stella whether Richard had made contact with Ella's mother since returning to Bangkok.

Hobbs began to think about his own wife, Eileen. There weren't many times that they had been apart during their 20 years of marriage. There had been the odd overnight stay up in Manchester, Birmingham or Leeds while Hobbs had been following up leads in a case, but he thought that this was probably the longest they had been apart, and definitely the farthest. He had made a promise to himself earlier in the week that he wasn't going to contact her until he had caught the man responsible for Ella's death but he had an overwhelming urge to talk to his wife. For one thing, he missed her, but she was also a great listener. Hobbs often thought she would have made a good investigator herself. Although Hobbs was never able to discuss direct details of most of his cases, he was able to give an idea about the cases he was working on and Eileen almost always came up with an idea on how to move forward or a fresh perspective that he hadn't thought of.

Hobbs pulled out his mobile phone and checked the time. It was late there, but the 8-hour time difference between Thailand and the UK would make it early afternoon for her.

He punched in his wife's number preceded by the country code 0044 and hit CALL. The phone rang for an unusually long time and Hobbs thought for a moment that he might have the entered the wrong code.

After nine or ten rings, he was just about to hang up when a hesitant voice answered:

"Hello? Who's this?"

"Eileen?"

"Yeah. Is that you, Frank?"

"Yeah, it's me. How are you, Babe?"

"Oh, Frank. Sorry, you know what I'm like with unknown numbers. I'm alright, Hun. How are you? We've missed you. Even the girls keep asking when you're going to be back, which isn't like them."

"I'm fine, Babe. Don't worry about me. Investigation is going well. Has there been anything on the news over there? I haven't had much of a chance to check the BBC."

"Umm, not much, Hun. Other than that they had found a body. They said they were waiting for confirmation on whether it was her. Is it her, Frank? Can you say?

"I shouldn't, but…yeah, it's her."

"Oh, Frank. I'm so sorry. That poor girl, not much older

than the girls."

"I know. That's why I'm calling. I miss the girls, and you, of course. Tell them I called, won't you?"

"Of course I will. Do you know what happened?"

"Some of it. We're working on it. Let's just say it wasn't an accident."

"Oh, God, Frank. That's terrible."

"Yeah, it is. But, we're going to find out what happened, Debs and I."

"I know you will, Hun. You two are the best we've got. That's why you're over there."

"Thanks, Babe. I better go. This call is probably costing a fortune. Christmas is coming and I won't have any mullah to buy the girls' presents with, otherwise."

"OK, Frank. You just catch the bastard. Alright? Whatever it takes. Don't even think about coming back until you do. Do you hear me?"

"Even if it means missing Christmas?"

"Even if it means missing Christmas."

"OK, Boss. I'll call you soon. Love ya."

"Love you, too. Bye."

"Bye."

Hobbs hung up and placed the phone gently down on the table next to him, as if he were handling his wife rather than an inanimate telecommunication device. He took one final draw on his cigarette and stubbed it out neatly in a coconut shell ashtray provided by the guest house. It was an effort for him to rise from his chair, not merely because of his growing years, but he also felt the weight of expectation on his shoulders. He felt gravely determined once again. He had the orders from the Boss at home and he knew exactly what he had to

CHAPTER 17

do. He remembered Eileen's words as he opened the door to his bungalow:

Just catch the bastard.

Chapter 18

The journey from Kanchanaburi to Bangkok passed by without incident and they arrived in Bangkok a little after three in the afternoon. They spoke little along the way as they all mused introspectively about what lay in store for them that evening in the nation's capital. Stirling had exchanged a few messages with Stella Ismail from the Embassy along the way and, hearing their plan to raid the nightclub, Stella had quickly arranged two rooms at the Centara Grand hotel at Central Ladprao nearby to Pahon Yothin Police Station, courtesy of Richard Patterson and the British Embassy. Whatever happened, Stirling thought, they would get a decent night's sleep afterwards.

Chai had got word that a briefing would be organised at seven that evening, so it gave them some welcomed time to relax. Chai dropped them at the hotel lobby and said he would pick them up again at six-thirty. Hobbs and Stirling didn't need telling twice to take the opportunity to relax in the relative luxury of the Bangkok hotel provided to them. Stirling took advantage of one of the spa packages while Hobbs decided his time would be better spent with a beer overlooking Chatuchak Park and taking an afternoon nap in the comfort of his room.

CHAPTER 18

At just after six-thirty, as promised, Chai returned to the hotel lobby to pick them up and they crawled the six kilometres to the police station in just under 20 minutes. The new elevated rail above Pahon Yothin road had done little to ease the endemic traffic situation which seemed to snarl even more as the sun went down over the sprawling urban metropolis of Bangkok.

They arrived to the station at just before seven and were waved through by the supervisor on desk who exchanged a polite greeting with Chai as they hurried past. The incident room at the station looked very similar to that of the station in Kanchanaburi: nicotine stained walls of a bygone era where smoking was allowed within the walls of the station, covered in pin boards and white boards containing information about various ongoing cases. Hobbs groaned inwardly at the sight of the ubiquitous plastic chairs which were both uncomfortable and probably unfit to take his weight.

Chai introduced Hobbs and Stirling to the team, first in English, with a few officers who obviously understood some English, nodding and smiling towards the pair, and then in Thai which garnered courteous nods and *wais* from the remainder of the task force. The majority of the group were in uniform, save for three or four men who wore plain-clothes and were presumably detectives. One such man, a man who appeared to be in his late 30s, with short spiky hair and a small goatee beard, addressed the room, seemingly in charge.

Chai translated in real time, at a whisper, as the ranking officer, named Pawin, explained what would happen during the operation that evening. He pointed to a location on a map on one of the boards which was in the north of Bangkok and evidently quite close to the location of the station that was pinned on the map. Chai explained that the sting would be taking place at a nightclub called *Forum* which was located on the Kaset-Nawamin Road and part-owned by their suspect, Pee Mhee or *Brother Bear* as he was referred to for the sake of Hobbs and Stirling. Pawin went on to explain that tonight was the fifth anniversary of the club and there was a high likelihood that Brother Bear would be there.

He began to walk the team through a brief plan, using a crudely drawn map of the club to make himself clear. Pawin and another plain clothes officer named Tong would enter the club first and make a positive ID on the suspect. They would then radio back to the uniformed officers to enter and make the arrest. Chai was to form part of the arresting team. Hobbs and Stirling were ordered to hang back at the entrance with two more officers and a further two officers would guard the fire escape at the rear of the building.

The plan seemed solid enough. The intelligence the Thai police had garnered suggested that Brother Bear wasn't particularly dangerous and wasn't known to carry weapons on a regular basis. The team seemed confident that the sting would go by without incident and that they would soon have the suspect back at the station for questioning. It was difficult for Hobbs and Stirling not to share in their confidence as they watched the police officers slap each other on the back jovially as they headed out of the incident room.

The team made their way through the station and into the car park where they separated into different vehicles. The plain-clothes officers got into an unmarked and unremarkable blue Honda Civic while the uniformed officers piled into the back of a black paddy wagon emblazoned with the word POLICE in large white letters. Hobbs and Stirling joined

CHAPTER 18

Chai in their usual pick-up truck and the convoy rolled out of the gates and onto the streets of Bangkok once more.

***

Hobbs and Stirling watched as the blue Honda Civic entered the car park of *Forum* but the two marked police vehicles, including their own, pulled up at the side of the road around 50 metres from the entrance to the car park.

From their vantage point, Hobbs and Stirling could see that the club was a one-story building painted all in black which took up a large footprint of the lot. The front facade of the club was the only part that showed any colour and this was decorated in a gaudy neoclassical style. White faux pillars cast from concrete to mimic the style of a Roman state building held up a large triangular centrepiece upon which was inscribed the name of the club. The lettering was also in the style of ancient Rome with the 'u' in *Forum* resembling a 'v' to spell the name FORVM in large neon red letters.

There was a long red carpet that stretched from the entrance down a set of steps and around a fountain in the style of the Trevi Fountain of Rome itself. A small row of luxury cars - a bright orange Lamborghini Murcielago, a sleek red Ferrari 488 and a pearlescent green Nissan GT-R were parked on the diagonal to the left of the main entrance, attracting the envy and attention of many a customer.

The trio watched from their pick-up as Pawin and Tong - the plain-clothes officers - sauntered past the gaudy fountain and up the red carpet towards the entrance to the club. Hobbs noticed that they were acting as if they were under the influence, slapping each other on the back and laughing heartily. They showed their civilian ID cards to the security guards and entered the club without incident.

Hobbs, Stirling and Chai were instructed that they would be able to enter the club once the plain clothes detectives had gained entry and deemed it safe. Chai had changed into a more inconspicuous pair of jeans and a plain black T-shirt. After a minute or so, the radio crackled and a voice, presumably Pawin's, gave the all clear for them to enter.

They were all keen to get inside the club and finally, potentially, get a look at Brother Bear, who was now their prime suspect in their Missing Persons turned murder-for-hire investigation. Both Hobbs and Stirling had to check their pace and their step as they traversed the gravel car park with its numerous pot holes.

Thin, elderly gentlemen in pseudo security uniforms directed traffic with their torches, whistles and what looked to Hobbs like mini-lightsabers; the kind that might be used to guide in a fighter jet onto an aircraft carrier. There were no aircraft here though, in spite of the aircraft hangar-like dimensions of the nightclub, only the row of imported luxury cars to the left and the row of unassuming 125cc motorcycles to the right.

'Thailand: the land of contrasts,' Hobbs thought to himself as he surveyed both groups of vehicles. The rich and the poor living together all over the capital, Bangkok, in a symbiotic, or possibly parasitic relationship. Hordes of servants on minimum wage, or less, catered to the every whim of the super-rich up and down this road of nightclubs, restaurants and car showrooms, and this was one of thousands. The average men and women of Thailand toiled relentlessly while the rich partied and frolicked. Such is the way all over the

world but it just seemed so obvious in the *Land of Smiles.*

Hobbs' internal musings fizzled out as they mounted the steps up to the entrance of the nightclub. After a quick passport check and a welcome from a line of scantily-clad female staff, the trio were granted access through a large, heavy door that gradually exposed them to the near-deafening sounds of obnoxious techno music.

The inside of the club was vast; a sea of hundreds of high tables and stools took up the centre of the club, surrounded by a semi-circular band of pockets of deep red sofas and armchairs with squat tables. The colossal stage took up almost the entire back wall of the club. It was tiered in different places with taller podiums at the corners where more scantily-clad performers danced in rhythmic fashion with feigned excitement spread across their pretty faces.

The sofa areas, presumably reserved for VIPs, were occupied by small groups of generally older local men in sharp suits and shiny shoes. A small army of waitresses in skin-tight beer branded dresses catered to them, pouring drinks, adding ice and replacing full ashtrays while a seemingly different strata of girls, dressed in faux-Roman brilliant white togas, sat next to the customers or on their knees, rubbing thighs and giggling as they shouted over the thumping music. A further group of male employees, dressed in all black, buzzed busily between the tables and kitchens, carrying a plethora of different Thai dishes to both the VIP areas and the tall tables in the centre.

"A well oiled machine," shouted Hobbs to Stirling over the din. Stirling shrugged, seemingly unimpressed. They took up positions at a tall table, just inside the door and scanned the crowd for the two plain-clothes members of the Royal Thai

Police. After a few seconds, Stirling pointed surreptitiously to an area on the far left of the tall tables, where Pawin and Tong had set up, ordering themselves what appeared to be a squat bottle of Regency brandy.

Hobbs watched as they stole furtive glances towards a roped-off area of the VIP area which sat to the left of the stage, next to where the performers exited. A large group of younger-looking males sat with multiple bottles of whisky and a few bottles of champagne in tall ice buckets on the periphery. A large silver balloon in the shape of the number 5 fluttered back and forth in the air conditioning just behind their sofa.

It couldn't be more obvious that the group in the roped-off area where the owners and shareholders of the club, celebrating the 5th anniversary. Undoubtedly, one of these men was their quarry, Brother Bear. The trio watched as the Thai detectives seemed to check images on their phones before Pawin put a finger to his ear and the distorted message was relayed to Chai and the waiting uniformed officers.

"POSITIVE ID - MOVE TO APPREHEND."

Outside, the black paddy wagon, packed with uniformed officers, lurched into motion and screeched across the club car park, unhindered by the wide smattering of pot holes. The vehicle came to an abrupt stop and the officers swarmed out. Some moved quickly to the rear exit of the building, while others took the red carpeted stairs two at a time to quickly gain access to the building. Shocked onlookers took one or two steps back as the officers went about their business and soon a line of six or seven uniformed officers passed Hobbs, Stirling and Chai at their table just inside the door.

"Wait here," ordered Chai as he followed the other officers

towards the left-hand side of the club. Most of the revellers had not noticed the line of police officers which was snaking its way through the maze of tables towards the VIP areas, but when they did, their gaze was transported from the podium dancers to the rare spectacle that was unfolding in the club.

Hobbs and Stirling watched as the officers neared the celebrating group, who had barely noticed the situation in their haze of alcohol and hostesses. Pawin and Tong showed their police IDs towards the group. The uniformed officers took this as a cue, brandishing their firearms and forming a tight arc with their weapons trained on the suspects. Party goers in the immediate vicinity slowly and deliberately got up from their seats and retreated to a safe distance. The members of the VIP group were strangely compliant, nonchalant even, and stayed seated. None of them raised their hands.

Stirling breathed a sigh of relief. In spite of all the planning and the confidence shown during the earlier briefing, she had still half-believed that the operation could have gone south with so many firearms and so many civilians involved. She watched as one of the party, presumably Brother Bear was hauled to his feet and handcuffs were placed on his wrists.

Just as she was about to suggest to Hobbs that they join the police, out of the corner of her eye she saw a series of small flashes emanate from the far end of the club, followed a split-second later by a series of staccato cracks which were half-lost in the hum of the music. As she turned her head, she watched as the group of police officers, staff and punters momentarily froze and then scattered before a volley of larger flashes and louder cracks echoed through the club, this time drowning out the music for a brief second.

It took Stirling a second or two to process what had

happened but Hobbs had been watching the entire time and had seen the desperate scene unfold before his very eyes.

Just as the suspect and his entourage had stood up and begun to follow the officers out of the club with Brother Bear in handcuffs, a young unidentified male had emerged from the bathrooms behind the VIP area. Seeing the group being led off by the police, the man had opened fire with a small calibre firearm, sending four rounds in the general direction of the police before his weapon seemed to jam. Before he could make his escape, the police had recovered their composure and sent a volley of larger calibre rounds in his direction. A good number of these rounds found their mark and thudded unceremoniously into the torso and legs of the surprise attacker and sent him slumping to the floor as his legs abandoned him, leaving streaks of dark blood descending down the bathroom door behind him. There he sat in a heap, as the colour drained from his face - his eyes wide in horror as he surveyed his own body in disbelief. Blood began to pool around him from his multiple wounds and his grey T-shirt and light coloured jeans very quickly turned a dark claret. He coughed and blood spluttered from his mouth. His leg twitched one last time in apparent futile protest as the life force drained from his helpless form.

The officers who had fired the shots lowered their weapons but began to survey the environment for any other threats. Hobbs and Stirling, following their initial shock, rose from their seats and moved quickly through the fracas towards the other side of the club. Frightened revellers scattered in all directions, their flight instinct kicking in. High tables and stools toppled and people vaulted over sofas, looking for their nearest exit.

CHAPTER 18

Hobbs scanned the dozens of faces that streamed towards him, anticipating that Brother Bear may have taken advantage of the unexpected diversion to make a mad dash for freedom. As Stirling made a mad dash to the other side of the club, Hobbs' head swivelled left and right. Most people seemed too young to be his man, but there were so many people flooding past him, his large frame like an island in a river estuary.

Finally, out of the corner of his eye, Hobbs spotted an older male. It was a split second and he couldn't be sure it was Brother Bear but he was sure he couldn't take the chance of him getting away, either. As the older male looked back over his shoulder in the direction he had come, Hobbs swung his sizeable arm in a long arc. His forearm connected squarely under the chin, sending the man's head snapping backwards and physically lifting him off his feet momentarily before he crashed to the floor in a semi-conscious heap. As soon as he had hit the floor, Hobbs was on him again, sprawling over the prone suspect, smothering him, preventing him from getting to his feet and making good on his escape. After a few seconds, more uniformed police joined him, placing knees in the small of the suspect's back and wrenching his arms behind him.

The uniformed officers worked together to flip the suspect onto his front and finally Hobbs was vindicated as he saw the face of the man he had seen on Chai's tablet, Brother Bear, laying dazed and confused on the floor of the nightclub he owned which was now empty other than the police and staff who were trying to make sense of the scene.

Hobbs rose slowly to his feet, rolling his arm in a circular motion. The blow he had delivered was accurate and well-timed, but it didn't stop it from hurting his ageing bones and joints.

Now that the suspect was subdued, Hobbs' thoughts turned immediately to his partner, Stirling, who had chosen to go directly towards the danger, rather than away. He saw her in the distance, on the far side of the club, crouched down next to someone who was laying on the ground, a small crowd of staff and police gathered around them.

Hobbs moved quickly across the centre of the club, stepping over toppled stools and pushing over tables that lay in his way. Hobbs faltered as he came upon the difficult scene that had transpired in the chaotic moments previous.

The person laying on the floor was a young girl, dressed in a toga of white with a wreath of golden leaves atop her curled dark locks. Her face was an ashen grey and drained of almost all colour. Her brilliant white toga now gradually turning a hideous shade of claret as blood spread in all directions through the fabric, emanating from a single gunshot wound in her abdomen.

Hobbs watched in horror as thick, dark blood bubbled from between the fingers of Stirling who attempted to put pressure on the wound while simultaneously trying to reassure the stricken hostess.

It was a delicate balancing act that nobody should ever have the responsibility of undertaking, but Stirling had experienced too many of these situations during her time in Iraq and appeared adept in conveying the graveness of the situation to the staff of the club while reassuring the wretched girl that she was going to be fine.

"Did someone call an ambulance?" she asked firmly, with one hand applying pressure to the wound and one gently stroking the hair from the girl's forehead. A male member of staff with a mobile phone glued to his ear nodded.

CHAPTER 18

"What's your name, Darling?" she asked the girl softly.

"Noon," replied the girl, breathlessly.

"You're going to be OK, Noon. Do you hear me? Just stay with me. The ambulance is on the way." One of the girl's colleagues, also in a brilliant white toga knelt beside her and appeared to be translating Stirling's speech.

The reality was that she probably wasn't fine. Far from it, in fact. She was bleeding out. She was dying - right there in front of their eyes while her friends and colleagues stood helplessly by.

"Where's that first aid kit?" she asked, trying hard to conceal the urgency in her voice.

After a few seconds, a manager appeared with a first aid kit. Hobbs took it from him and searched for a sterile pad and gauze as calmly as he could, picking up on Stirling's desire to keep the girl as calm as possible. He unwrapped them and passed them to Stirling who tore off a piece of gauze with her teeth.

"Noon, honey," she said firmly, taking the girl by her chin and looking into her eyes. "I'm not going to lie. This is going to hurt, but you'll be fine. Trust me, OK?" Before she could reply, Stirling had rolled up the gauze and shoved it roughly into the small hole as the girl squealed in agony. The onlooking female colleagues and friends of the injured girl wept openly, burying their faces in the chests of their male colleagues.

Stirling applied a sterile pad to the wound and lifted the girl up slightly to wind several lengths of gauze around the girl's waist to keep the dressing in place. The girl's breathing began to stabilise but became increasingly shallow.

"What do we do now?" asked Hobbs, helplessly, as he knelt

among the debris of scattered first aid packaging and smeared blood.

Stirling turned her head away from the girl, but still maintained a firm grip on her hand and replied, "We wait. Three minutes. If the bleeding hasn't slowed by then and the ambulance hasn't arrived…" She shook her head as if she didn't want to utter the inevitable.

Hobbs closed his eyes and breathed a long sigh, his eyes fixed on the dressing that Stirling had applied to the girl's abdomen - hoping, wishing, that his eyes weren't deceiving him and that the dressing wasn't becoming darker by the minute.

"Mae…mae," whispered the girl quietly as Stirling returned her attention. "Mae yoo nai?" she whispered again, this time more desperately.

"What's she saying?" asked Stirling to her friend who remained by her side, sobbing gently.

"She's asking for her mum," the friend replied before bursting into tears.

Hobbs checked his watch. "Where's that fucking ambulance?!" he bellowed, seeing no more reason to kid anyone about the gravity of the situation.

"Five minutes," replied the manager, desperately, who was looking more and more agitated, pacing back and forth rubbing his bald head over and over with the palm of his hand.

"Just hang on," said Stirling to the wounded girl. "Tell her, her mum is on the way and she'll be here soon," this time to the friend, who dutifully relayed the message between fits of teary sobs.

Hearing this, the girl nodded and a calm expression, that

CHAPTER 18

could almost have been a smile, appeared across her face. She closed her eyes.

Stirling gently slapped her cheek. "Noon…Noon, honey. Wake up. The ambulance is nearly here. You just hang on, OK?"

There was no response.

"Noon!" she shouted, slapping her more roughly this time. "Stay with me, Noon. Don't you fall asleep on me, Noon. Your mum is on her way. She's coming, OK?"

Hobbs watched on helplessly as the girl's friend, sobbing, relayed Stirling pleas.

Still no response.

Stirling raised two blood stained fingers to the girl's neck.

"No pulse," she remarked, lowering her ear to the girl's mouth and looking for a rise and fall of her chest. "She's not breathing, starting CPR." Stirling spoke matter-of-factly, like a pilot might when completing his pre-flight checks, as she knelt to the side of the girl, interlacing her fingers and plunging the heel of her hand deep into the girl's chest, over and over again, compressing the heart, artificially pushing blood around the body.

Every two compressions, Stirling blew two long, deep breaths into the mouth of the girl and watched as her chest rose and fell with each breath. She repeated this process over and over again, while Hobbs and the small crowd of staff and police officers watched impotently on.

After a minute or two, sirens began to fill the air and after another minute the club was filled with paramedics and other volunteers with the volunteer *Por Tech Teung* foundation. One female paramedic with short dark hair placed her hands gently on the shoulders and gestured that she would take over. Stirling, exhausted, acquiesced and rose gently from her knees to join the rest of the onlooking crowd. Hobbs went to Stirling and placed a comforting arm around her shoulders.

After what felt like an age, but was only a couple of minutes, the paramedic came to a stop and got slowly to her feet. Turning to Stirling and Hobbs, she shook her head sadly.

"I'm sorry," she said in English, placing a hand hand gently on Stirling's shoulder.

Stirling crumpled, her body folding in the middle and she dropped to her haunches with the physical and mental exhaustion. Hobbs dropped to one knee, still holding Stirling who stared morosely as two volunteers covered the girl's body with a dark red tablecloth from the VIP area.

A few minutes passed and the crowd of onlookers grew ever smaller as the emergency services wheeled the young girl's body away on a gurney.

"What are we doing here, Frank?" asked Stirling softly without averting her gaze.

"What do you mean, Debs?"

"I mean, what are we doing here?" replied Stirling, now looking sombrely into Hobbs' eyes. "We're Missing Persons, not Murder Squad. We should be in London tracking down teenaged runaways, not here in Bangkok, sticking our noses in where they don't belong."

"Woah, woah, woah," exclaimed Hobbs. "Where is this coming from? This isn't you. Who have you been talking to?"

"Nobody."

"Nobody, my arse. I know you, Debs, and I sure as shit know when you're not telling the truth."

"Alright, it's Harding. She E-Mailed earlier today. Told us

CHAPTER 18

to come back. Said our work here is done. It's not our job to solve murders in foreign countries."

"Did you reply?"

"Just briefly. I told her we were just tying up some loose ends. I didn't tell her about what we were going to be doing tonight."

"But, you agreed with her. You just wanted to go home and forget all this happened? Forget about Ella and her killers?"

"No. Of course not. Not until tonight. But, this changes things, Frank. If we weren't here, if we hadn't tracked down Win Nyan Bo and gone after this Brother Bear, that girl would still be alive. It's our fault she's dead, Frank."

Hobbs shook his head and pointed in the direction of the bathrooms. "No, no, no. Come on, Debs. You can't think like that. We didn't kill that girl, that little shit over there did. You can't blame yourself."

"But he opened fire because we were here to arrest his boss. If we weren't here, she would have finished her shift tonight and gone home to her mum."

"Listen, Debs. I don't know what the fuck is going on here, but what I do know is that I made a promise to my wife that I wouldn't come home until we've caught the bastard that killed our Ella. This thing is clearly bigger than Win or Brother Bear and I've got a feeling that if we crack this, we'll be helping a lot more people and saving a lot more lives."

Stirling shook her head sadly. "Maybe you're right, but I just can't handle this any more. I saw enough death and destruction in the army to last a lifetime. I thought joining Missing Persons would be my chance to do some good in the world; bring some kids back to their parents, for a change."

"And you've done that, Debs. Countless times. Look, I

know things didn't go down as we planned tonight but we got him. We got that bastard Brother Bear and if he isn't the one who wanted Ella dead, he sure as hell knows who did. We're getting close. I can feel it in my bones, Debs. We're going to solve this case and we're going to get home for Christmas, alright?"

Stirling sighed and wiped the tears from her eyes before rising slowly to her feet. "Alright, Frank," she replied. "I really hope you're right.""

Chapter 19

A small group of reporters crowded the entrance to Pahon Yothin Police Station as Chai pulled into the car park with Hobbs & Stirling. The debacle at Forum the evening before had made the local and national news but, thankfully, Hobbs and Stirling had not featured. They had both watched the morning news in the hotel lobby while waiting for Chai to pick them up, hoping that they had made their exit from the scene before anybody was able to get any video footage.

It would be impossible now, of course. As they exited the vehicle, the crowd of media personnel flung their equipment in their direction, in unison, like a hungry beast with limbs of cameras, sound booms and microphones bearing down on them. The beast's eyes flickered as flashbulbs went off, searing their image into digital files which would be on the news desks within the hour. Harding wasn't going to like this one bit but at least she wouldn't hear about it for seven hours, thanks to the time difference between the two countries.

Chai took the lead and barked orders at the baying crowd to move out of their way. Hobbs and Stirling followed swiftly, their heads bowed in a vain attempt at preserving their anonymity. Reaching the entrance, Chai ushered the detectives inside and slammed the swinging door shut with a reassuring thump. The reporters knew they weren't allowed inside but continued to press their lenses up against the glass to try and get a few more candid photographs of anyone who might have had something to do with the bloodbath at the nightclub the previous evening.

Brother Bear, thanks to Hobbs' intervention, had been apprehended and brought back to the station where he had spent the night in a holding cell before being formally charged the following morning. He was charged with suspected conspiracy to murder and resisting arrest. The former he would, presumably, vehemently deny but the latter was witnessed by several hundred people.

The trio made their way through to the incident room. The staff at Pahon Yothin were infinitely more accommodating than those at the station at Kanchanaburi. A junior staff member brought them all coffee as they met with the leaders of the task force from the night before. Pawin was at the helm, once again, but this time his confident swagger was absent, replaced with a more sheepish persona and a face which looked like it hadn't got many hours of sleep.

Pawin addressed the room in English, for the benefit of the visiting detectives, "Good morning, everyone. Please, excuse me. My English is not so well. As you know, last night we had some problem at the club. As team leader, I must apologise. Even we have success in catching the suspect, a member of the public was unfortunately killed." Pawin's English was not perfect, Stirling thought, but he was making the effort. Pawin continued, "I personally informed the victim's family last night and I will make a donation towards the funeral costs of the victim, Nong Noon." The members of the task force,

CHAPTER 19

as well as Hobbs and Stirling, all nodded sombrely.

"We would also like to make a donation, if that is appropriate," croaked Stirling, in a voice cracking with emotion."

"Yes, of course," replied Pawin, appreciatively. "Now, please excuse me, while I continue in Thai language. Constable Chai, if you could help the detectives."

Hobbs, Stirling and Chai moved to the back of the room so as not to disturb the rest of the team as Chai interpreted the information being relayed by Pawin. Pawin informed the team of the charges that had been filed against the suspect. The suspect had refused to make any comment at all the previous evening, demanding that his lawyer be present for any and all interviews. Pawin explained that the lawyer would be here shortly and an interview had been scheduled with the suspect for 10 that morning. Pawin would lead the interview with another senior officer present. Chai would also be allowed to attend in an observational capacity, to accommodate the visiting detectives. He also confirmed that the shooter had been identified as the first cousin of Phee Mhee and CCTV confirmed he fired the first shot, absolving the Thai officers of any blame by way of self-defence.

The other members of the team were delegated different duties and Pawin brought the briefing to a close with a *wai* which all in the room stood and returned before hurrying off to complete their designated duties.

Stirling finished making notes and placed her pen down beside her pad. "Looks like it's a waiting game for now," she said with a sigh.

"Maybe a bit of downtime is what we need," replied Hobbs, easing back into his chair. "It's been pretty full-on since we arrived. I'm not even sure what day it is, to be honest. Let's use this time to gather our thoughts and backtrack to anything we might have missed. We don't know what Brother Bear is going to say, if anything, so let's not waste our time."

"Right, let's focus on what we know and what we don't know," agreed Stirling, picking up her pen and leafing backwards through her trusty notebook. "First thing's first - we know that Ella's death wasn't an accident."

"Correct," agreed Hobbs. "Win has admitted to killing her, but claims he was paid by this Brother Bear character."

"Right, and how do we feel about that? Do we believe him?"

"Brother Bear is dodgy; look at him. Why would his cousin react like that without good reason, Debs?"

"I agree he seems dodgy but that doesn't necessarily mean he did this, right?"

"Right," conceded Hobbs, begrudgingly. "OK, what's next?"

"Ella's mother, Anchalee Jitpracharoen. What's the latest on her?"

"Oh, yeah. I forgot to tell you. Stella sent me a message. She said the mother would fly to London from Copenhagen when the body has arrived."

"When will that be, Chai? How long do these things normally take?"

"The autopsy is done and the body is already in Bangkok but there's always a lot of paperwork. It could be a couple of days," replied Chai.

"I'll contact Stella at the Embassy and see if they have any information on that," interjected Hobbs, making a note in his notebook. "What about the phone, Chai? Any news on that? I still find it odd that it hasn't been found yet."

"Nothing yet. I tried calling the station at Kanchanaburi, but they're not returning my calls."

CHAPTER 19

"They're not being very co-operative down there, are they? Especially that captain. What's his name?" asked Stirling, flicking backwards through her notepad.

"Anupong," replied Chai, quickly.

"Anupong. That's right. What do we know about him?" she asked to the room.

"We know he's a twat," replied Hobbs, flippantly.

"Thank you, Frank. I'm inclined to agree. But, what else?"

Chai replied, "From what I know, he's been at the station in Kanchanaburi for a long time - almost as long as Patterson has been Ambassador. He's worked himself up from Constable to Captain. He's not popular, but he has made some high-profile arrests which keeps the Police Chief happy."

"Why is he not popular?" asked Stirling, without looking up from her pad.

"Because he's a twat," replied Hobbs, for the second time.

Stirling looked up to glare at Hobbs. "Again," she replied tersely. "I'm aware the man is a twat, Frank. I was asking Chai."

"There's been a few things in the news about his finances. He's been photographed with some pretty expensive-looking watches and numerous luxury cars that would normally be too expensive for someone on his salary," Chai informed.

"Interesting," replied Stirling. "Can you look further into that, Chai?"

"Yes, of course. But why?"

Hobbs interjected, "That Captain Arsepong has been a thorn in our side since we arrived. Look at the co-operation here in Bangkok and then look at Kanchanaburi. Chalk and cheese. There's something that doesn't sit right with me out west and I think it's more than just having us stepping on their toes. You said about the money flowing up in the police here, right?"

"That's right."

"Well, let's find out if Anupong could afford those things on his salary and a few traffic bribes alone, or whether he might be into other stuff that he doesn't want us knowing about."

* * *

It was almost midday by the time Chai returned from the interview with Brother Bear. Hobbs and Stirling had waited patiently in the incident room and were understandably excited to see him return.

"Well, what did he say?" asked Hobbs, hopefully.

"He's denying everything, right now," replied Chai, with a somewhat dejected sigh.

"Everything?" posed Stirling.

"Everything," repeated Chai. "All he's admitted to is knowing Win and the karaoke bar owner Mama-San. He said they've got it in for him and they're trying to set him up. He says that he's had some problems with the Mama-San in the past. He's supplied her with girls from Buriram and Surin for her bar - all legal he says - but too dark-skinned for the Bangkok clubs. The Mama-San owes him a load of 'agent fees' and he thinks she wants him locked up so she doesn't have to pay."

"OK, well what about our boy, Win? What's he done to upset him?" asked Hobbs after taking a few notes.

"He said that Win owed him some money and he had threatened to tell his family about him working in the gay bars in Bangkok if he didn't pay up - that's the reason they

CHAPTER 19

want him locked up."

Stirling began to ask the questions. "So, who does he say killed Ella, then?"

"Win, he thinks. He says she must have rejected him on the train and he got angry and pushed her. He said he had seen Win get angry before, at the bar, when he asked for more interest on the loan that was late."

"Do you believe him?"

"I don't know. Win did only tell us 'the truth' when he realised what length of prison sentence he was going to get."

"That's true. His first instinct was to lie to try and get away with it."

"Do we have any evidence of money changing hands between Brother Bear and Win, Chai?" Hobbs asked.

"None. But he's too smart to leave a paper-trail, I'm sure."

"Win was popular among the girls at the camp, I remember," added Stirling. "It's possible that he could have thought Ella would be interested."

"Possibly," mused Hobbs. "But, what was he doing on the train? Selling snacks, wasn't he? Do we have any evidence of him selling snacks on that route before the day of Ella's murder?"

"The staff on the train said they had never seen him on that line before," replied Chai.

"So, it was either his first day on the line, or he was on the train specifically to kill Ella and the hawker gear was a prop."

"Right," agreed Stirling, tapping her ballpoint pen against her bottom-front teeth in a rhythmic fashion. "We need to find out more about our man, Win. Chai, could you arrange for some uniforms to do some digging around at his workplace - at the bar downtown? See if we can get some more background?"

"Of course," replied Chai. "But, it won't be until later this evening. The bar won't open until at least 7 P.M."

"No problem," replied Hobbs, closing his notebook and replacing the cap on his pen. "We have got plenty to be getting on with this afternoon, anyway."

"We have?" answered Stirling with a quizzical frown.

"We have. I thought that Brother Bear might clam up today and play the innocent, so I thought I would contact someone who might know a bit more about him or the kind of business he gets up to. Someone who speaks English and has got the low-down on all the ins and outs in Bangkok."

"Frank," started Stirling, glaring at her partner in realisation of who Hobbs had enlisted the help of. "Please don't tell me it's who I think it is?"

"And who might that be, young Debra?" Hobbs asked facetiously.

"That sweaty, loud-mouthed, obnoxious American reporter, by any chance?"

"Who? My ol' buddy, Larry?" asked Hobbs, with a terrible attempt at an American accent.

Stirling rolled her eyes and sat back in her chair with her arms folded. Chai and Hobbs looked at each other and chuckled.

"You must be some kind of detective," quipped Chai, getting in on the fun.

"Don't you start," she replied with a smirk. "It's bad enough with just him. So, we're going to Bangkok?"

Hobbs replied, "Yes, Sir-ee. It's time to saddle up."

CHAPTER 19

***

The meeting point that Larry Dean had chosen was a bar named Chequers, which he purported was just inside Soi 4 of the Sukhumvit Road which begins in the centre of Bangkok and stretches, remarkably, nearly 500 kilometres to the border with Cambodia. The primary portion of central Bangkok, regarded as the centre of the city, is home to many of the cities thriving tourist areas and red light districts. One such red light district loomed to the right of the taxi carrying Hobbs and Stirling down Soi 4 - the infamous Nana Plaza. Even in the early afternoon the 'entertainment plaza', as it was euphemistically named, thumped and throbbed with the sound from the beer-bars on the ground floor and the go-go bars which vied for attention on the upper floors. Hundreds of punters - many single, older, western men - sat drinking bottled local beers on high stools, engaging in Pidgin English conversations with a plethora of different scantily-clad Thai ladies who giggled and flirted as if their lives depended on it. At street level, groups of staff members held boards advertising the myriad of different bars, attempting to coax tourists and *sex-pats* into one of the waiting go-go bars, discos or ladyboy cabarets. Street vendors touted their wares to the never-ending throng of tourists and locals who snaked up and down the soi. Skewers of barbecued meats stood next to a cart selling every kind of deep-fried insect you could ever imagine.

It was all a bit much for Stirling who blew a deep sigh from her rosy cheeks and sat back into the seat of the taxi that Chai had arranged to take them to Bangkok, taking a break from the visceral assault on the senses which was Nana Plaza.

"Christ. It's only three in the afternoon," noted Stirling, looking at her watch. I dread to think what this place is like at 10 o'clock at night."

"Looks like it's always beer o'clock in Bangkok," replied Hobbs as he spied the black and white sign of Chequers and motioned for the taxi driver to stop.

Hobbs paid the driver, telling him to keep the change and they both made their way towards the bar. Hobbs smirked at a chalkboard sign that bore the message 'Dogs and well-behaved Americans welcome'.

"Hello, welcome!" chorused a small army of hostesses in matching black and white dresses.

Hobbs and Stirling nodded their appreciation. "We're looking for a friend," said Hobbs to the closest hostess whose name badge indicated she was named *Jane*. "He's a reporter with the Bangkok Post."

"American? Big fat guy?" she replied, matter-of-factly.

Stirling sniggered to herself, taken aback at the blunt nature of the girl. "Yes, that's him."

"Larry in the back," she replied, gesturing inside the bar. "He say he no like to sit at the front. Too many girl want to talk with he." she quipped in broken but endearing English. All the girls giggled at that and the two detectives made their way into the comparative darkness of the bar.

It turned out they needn't have asked where Larry was seated as the bar was a lot smaller than they had expected. The width of the place couldn't have been more than four metres and most of that was taken up by the bar, which ran almost the length of the establishment and the row of tall, black leather stools which accompanied it. The floor, unsurprisingly, was covered in a black and white chequer board pattern. Behind

CHAPTER 19

the bar, staff busied, opening bottles of beer and pouring drinks from the huge range of spirits which adorned the shelves on the right hand wall.

Larry Dean was seated at a table at the rear of the bar, close to the kitchen door. Stirling made a joke to herself that it was the perfect position for him, but decided not to say it out loud.

Larry rose from his seat as the detectives approached. He seemed genuinely happy to see them again and stuck out a pudgy paw to them both after wiping his hands on his trouser front.

"Frank, buddy, and the lovely Debra, it's great to see you guys again. Thanks for looking me up. I knew you couldn't stay away," he said with gusto, holding Stirling's hand just long enough for it to be awkward.

"Hi, Mr Dean. We're just here for some information, really..." replied Stirling, managing at last to free her hand from the reporter's clammy grasp.

Hobbs shot Stirling a glance. "...and we know you're the man to speak to, of course," he added quickly.

"Well, there's a saying around here, ya know?" Dean began. "If something happens in Thailand and Larry Dean doesn't know about it, it didn't happen."

There was a moment of uncomfortable silence which was eventually broken by Hobbs. "Who's up for a drink then? I'm gasping. These are on me, Larry, as a thank you for access to your fountain of knowledge."

"Why, thank you, good Sir," Dean replied in a feigned British accent and a strange motion that was evidently supposed to be a bow but ended up more of an awkward curtsy.

"Why the British pub, Larry?" asked Stirling.

"Well, I wanted to make sure you guys felt at home, of course. I know what it's like to experience that culture shock for the first time, especially with everything you guys have been through. I heard about what happened at the club. That must have shaken you up real good. Oh, and they do a great fish 'n' chips here. The Sunday lunch is pretty darn good, too….and the burger, the beef burger, of course, none of that chicken burger bullshit. It doesn't come close to a good ol' US burger, naturally, but…"

"Cheers!" interrupted Hobbs, right on queue, handing a bottle of Leo beer first to Dean and then to Stirling, stepping between them and creating some much-needed separation. Hobbs, Stirling thought, always managed to pick up on when Stirling was feeling awkward or uncomfortable and always used his size or humour to diffuse situations.

"How about we take a seat?" he asked, gesturing to the table.

Stirling moved quickly to the farthest possible seat at the table from where Dean had been sitting and Hobbs, instinctively plonked himself down between them.

"So, what is it you guys wanna know?" asked Dean, taking a long swig of his beer. "Lemme guess, you want to know more about this shady nightclub owner, right? What kind of other shit he's into."

Larry Dean, Stirling thought, may have been a slob and a creep, but he at least seemed to be decent at his job. Maybe the sayings were true, after all.

"Well, yes, that's right," conceded Stirling. We know he supplies girls from the countryside to different clubs and bars around Thailand…"

"…and Myanmar - Burma, to you Brits," Dean interrupted.

"Right. We just don't know what else he's into and whether

he's on a level that he would have anything to do with Ella's murder."

"Well, I did some digging, even before you guys contacted me. This *Brother Bear* as you call him, Pee Mhee, or whatever's real name is Udom Tongsomboon. He's from a pretty decent family."

Hobbs and Stirling exchanged a glance, both wondering how this foreign reporter in Bangkok knew the nickname for a suspect they had been using way out west in Kanchanaburi.

Dean caught the glance. "Look, I told you, I know everything there is to know, alright?"

"Do carry on, Larry. Don't mind us," said Hobbs, leaning forward in his chair and placing his elbows on the table.

"The guy is what you Brits might call 'dodgy'," he continued, the *o* in *dodgy* sounding much more like an *a* to their ears. "He's got a whole host of links to organised crime, but he's smart enough not to have anything come back on him personally. He uses middle-men, keeps his distance. As you know, he's pretty good at finding pretty girls for clubs and bars, here, there and everywhere. But, there's nothing illegal about that - as long as they're all of legal age."

"And are they?" Stirling chimed in.

Dean replied, "The ones in Bangkok? Probably. The ones in the provinces? Maybe. The boys in brown in the provinces are quite happy to turn a blind eye as long as they get their cut. But, again, the law is broken by the owners of the bars who employ them, not your friend Brother Bear."

"OK," began Hobbs. "So, morally reprehensible, definitely, but not illegal. What else is he connected to that is definitely not above board?"

"Well, this is where it gets interesting...and becomes

hearsay, of course, but I figured you'd wanna know. So, word on the street was that he is a reasonably big player in the trafficking of Rohingya refugees from Burma into Thailand and Malaysia. A few years ago, 2015, down in Songkhla province, authorities stumble upon an abandoned trafficking camp. They find the bodies of 30 people in shallow graves not far from the camp. The UN said the traffickers took them as far as the Malaysian border then demanded ransoms from their families before they would take them over the border. Most simply died of disease or starvation in the mean time."

"Jesus," swore Hobbs, shaking his head in disbelief. "Surely they have border police or rangers in the area that should be doing something about that?"

"Sure they do but, at best, they do nothing to help, and at worst, they're complicit."

Stirling took a long swig of her drink, trying to calm herself at the revelations, then said, "The more I learn about this country, the more I want to go home. How do these people sleep at night?"

Dean shook his head vigorously, half way through his own swig of lager. "Now, we're talking about a tiny minority of really bad dudes here, Debra. The vast majority of Thai people are kind, friendly, law-abiding folks. It's those assholes which give the place a bad name."

"Assholes like Brother Bear?" interjected Hobbs.

"Exactly right, Brother Frank. So, word is that your guy was pretty instrumental in getting those poor Rohingya folks down to Songkhla from the border with Kanchanaburi. Now, I have no idea if he had anything to do with the ransoms and ultimately their deaths, but he certainly didn't hand himself in after the fact, if you know what I mean?"

CHAPTER 19

"Well, he's certainly got some skeletons in the closet of some kind, if his minion was willing to shoot and kill police officers to help him get away," mused Hobbs, stroking his goatee beard in a pensive fashion.

"What about drugs?" asked Stirling, looking up from her notebook, which she had been furiously scribbling away in.

"Not a huge amount," Dean replied, shifting his weight uncomfortably in his seat. "But, ya know, if you're smuggling people across the border, you may as well smuggle some dope across at the same time."

"Dope? Marijuana?" Stirling quizzed.

"Marijuana, yaa-baa, opium; you name it, they smuggle it."

"Yaa-baa. That's what our misper had in her system. Right, Debs?" said Hobbs, looking over in her direction.

"Right. Could that be a possible link?"

"It could, but that shit is everywhere in Thailand. You don't need to be an international people trafficker to get your hands on it," replied Dean with an apologetic shrug. Hell, half of the girls in Nana Plaza down the street are on it.

Stirling sat back in her seat, deflated. Her opinion of Larry Dean had elevated somewhat with his seemingly limitless local knowledge and network of eyes and ears, but all she was hearing was hearsay and second-hand information. There was no direct link between Brother Bear and their supposed murder victim. If Brother Bear had been involved, he had been smart about it and not done the dirty work himself. She wondered what possible motive he might have had that would warrant killing a 15-year-old school girl, let alone an ambassador's daughter.

She took another swig of her drink before she posed her next question. "So, we're all in agreement that the guy's dodgy, but we're still without a link to our Ella. Let's say he did pay Win to kill Ella, what's the motive? 'Cause I can't think of one."

"If there is one, I haven't heard of it, Darlin'," replied Dean, dropping down a notch in Stirling's opinion once again. "There's a good chance he's a middle-man in all of this, or, of course, he may not have anything to do with it and your Win just knows he is dodgy and is saying anything he can to save his own skin."

"Well, that clears that up then," chirped Hobbs facetiously, taking a final long draw from his bottle. Stirling smiled at Hobbs' attempt to lighten the mood but the fact remained that they were no closer to the truth than they were before and they had travelled 150 kilometres for the privilege. Perhaps they could use their new found background knowledge about Brother Bear to lean on him a bit more, make him think they knew more than they were letting on. Maybe get a confession out of him.

She conceded that it wasn't a total loss, which she voiced to her companions. "Well, that definitely gives us something to go on and a bit of ammunition to try and get a confession if we get an interview with Brother Bear. Not that Captain Anupong will likely let us get a look in."

"Anupong? The captain over in Kanchanaburi?" interjected Dean, finishing off his own beer.

"Yep," replied Hobbs. "He's a right…"

"Yes, Larry," said Stirling, interrupting Hobbs mid-sentence. "What about him?"

"If you're talking about dodgy characters, he's one of the usual suspects. Large scale corruption, racketeering, money laundering; he's been accused of all of' em. Thing is, nothing seems to stick, unsurprisingly. He's got some powerful friends - some known, some unknown. The problem is that the money trickles up in Thailand, not down."

Hobbs and Stirling looked at each other knowingly. That wasn't the first time they had heard the expression and that time it was from a serving member of the Royal Thai Police.

Dean continued, "Just check out some news articles and you'll see him wearing a different gold watch each time. A *Rolex* one day, *Patek Phillipe* the next - he's not buying those on a police captain's salary, lemme tell ya."

"Our police liaison, Chai, said the same thing. He's looking into it for us now," replied Stirling while taking more notes in her pad.

"Then it sounds like you've found the only police officer in Thailand with a working moral compass. Cheers to that!" Dean raised his bottle but found it empty. "Hey, do you guys fancy another? I've got a while before I have to be back at the office." Dean was clearly using all his best Britishisms with them. Stirling had never heard any North American use the word 'fancy' in that context.

Hobbs was just about to politely decline when Stirling piped up. "Sure, Larry. Why not? You've been a big help and we appreciate your time."

Hobbs cocked his head to one side in surprise, but never one to turn down an ice cold beer, he signalled to the waitress to bring three more drinks. The trio chatted and drank for another hour. Larry Dean dominated the conversation with a long list of amusing anecdotes from his many years in the Land of Smiles. It was a welcome respite for the investigators from London who had, up until now, been subjected to a darker side of Thailand that they never would have guessed from the 'Amazing Thailand' commercials online. Stirling wondered if she had judged Larry Dean a little harshly. Maybe what she had seen as unwanted attention was just his way of being friendly. Maybe she had misjudged Thailand and its people. Maybe there *were* just a few bad eggs that ruin it for everyone else, just as in any country in the world.

"Debs?" said Hobbs, tapping her gently on the elbow.

Stirling woke from her daydream, slightly abashed.

"Time we were making a move?" asked Hobbs, looking concerned.

"Yeah, sorry. I was away with the fairies for a minute there. Haven't had a lot of sleep recently so have to do my dreaming during the day, apparently," she quipped. They all chuckled. Normally, it was Hobbs that was cracking the jokes. "Thanks again, Larry." We appreciate your time."

"Yeah. Cheers, Larry," agreed Hobbs.

"Hey, don't mention it," replied Dean, waving his hand dismissively. "*Mi casa, su casa*. If I hear anything else, I'll give you guys a call."

Stirling knew that certainly wasn't the correct usage but dismissed it with a grin.

"See you, Larry." she said as she quickly wrote down her contact number, tore it off her pad and handed it to Dean. He clasped the paper in his hand like a kid with his first lot of pocket money and his face lit up like a stained glass window.

Chapter 20

A slow and steady stream of Bangkok taxis of all different colours made its way past Hobbs and Stirling as they stood on the poor excuse for a footpath that ran down the side of Sukhumvit Soi 4. The surface was made up of concrete blocks which stuck up at dangerous angles all over. Roots of ancient trees also fought for space on the footpath, creating a perfect tripping hazard for a distracted tourist. As well as the uneven surface and gnarled tree roots, fire hydrants and gas meters peppered the walkway at random intervals. At some points, a road sign would completely block the footpath and one would have to duck underneath to continue one's journey.

"No wonder everyone rides motorcycles here," Hobbs remarked. "It's like a bloody obstacle course,"

"Let's get a cab then, shall we?" replied Stirling, raising her hand in the air to signal one of the multitude of cars for hire. One, then two, three, taxis drove past, their 'For Hire' signs shining a bright red on their dashboards. Stirling began to wave her arm in a more animated fashion, but still no taxis stopped for her fare. Hobbs watched as a young Thai woman emerged from the entrance to Nana Plaza and in what appeared to be one swift motion, managed to hail a cab, opened the door and was off down the soi before the door was even closed.

"What the…?" Stirling scoffed. "Do they not see me with my arm up? Are they blind or something?"

Hobbs, having paid more attention to the young woman, stepped in front of Stirling. "Let me show you how it's done, Debs. You're not in London now, you know?" he mocked.

Hobbs proceeded to wiggle his hand, gently, almost imperceptibly, down below his waist. Within seconds, the two-tone, green and yellow cab coming towards them flicked on its indicators and came to a stop in front of the duo.

"After you, m'Lady," Hobbs quipped as he opened the door for Stirling to enter the cab. Stirling stared at him in disbelief and Hobbs couldn't cover his smugness. Stirling scooted over to let Hobbs in and reached for her seatbelt. She poked around looking for a buckle but gave up, exasperated, when she realised there wasn't one.

"I don't think I'll ever understand this place," she exclaimed, blowing off a red frizzy lock of hair which had found a temporary home across her face. "I was waving my arms in the air like we were lost at sea and no bugger notices. You stroll up and give it the magic wiggle and they're all screeching to a halt."

Hobbs chuckled to himself as he too gave up trying to find a working seatbelt. "When in Rome, Debra. Do as the Romans do."

"Pai satanee rot fai Hua-lam-phong ka" said Stirling to the driver, in her best phrase-book Thai. Remarkably, the driver seemed to understand and flicked on the meter. "At least my Thai is better than yours, Frank."

"Well that's not difficult," he replied tersely.

CHAPTER 20

The conversation was interrupted by the ringing of Hobbs' mobile phone in the breast pocket of his white flannel shirt. Chai's name flashed up on the display.

"Hello, Chai mate," he answered.

"Hi, Frank. It's Chai. I just spoke to my colleague in Bangkok. He's going to check in at Win's bar tonight, when it opens - about 5 o'clock. He'll see if anyone there knows anything more about Win's personal life. Where are you?

"We just finished talking to Larry Dean, the reporter. He gave us some interesting background info' on Brother Bear, but nothing we could count on for evidence."

"Oh, that's a shame. You know, they were going to release him today. They said they didn't have enough evidence. Luckily, between us, we managed to dig up an old charge in Kanchanaburi - a fight in a bar - and now Bangkok are letting us move him down here. That should buy us some time."

"Great work, Chai. It might also give him a bit of a scare. Make sure they don't tell him why he's being moved, will you? We can make it seem like we have more than we do. "

"Roger that, Frank."

"OK. Debs and I are on the way to the train station, *Hua Lam* something. We thought it might be good to take the same journey that Ella did. Maybe it will jog something in our minds. We need all the help we can get."

"OK. Call me when you are close and I'll come pick you up."

Hobbs thanked Chai and hung up before relaying the gist of the conversation to Stirling.

"Well at least that's bought us some time," she replied. "Let's hope we get some decent intel' from Win's bar this evening - enough to lean on Brother Bear and get a bit closer to the truth. One of them is lying. Hopefully, it won't be too long until we find out who."

* * *

Hobbs & Stirling stood outside Hualamphong station on the edge of Bangkok's bustling China Town. They gazed up at the gigantic half-dome facade which was made of stained glass supported by a wrought-iron frame with a large analogue clock as its obligatory centrepiece. The clock was flanked by two towers, and stood resolutely above a balustraded balcony area upon which several Thai flags of red, white and blue flapped proudly next to the bright yellow flags of HM the King. Below that, a covered colonnade of pillars completed the grand front elevation and entrance to the station.

The station was designed in the Italian Neo-Renaissance style by a pair of Italian brothers more than one hundred years previous at the behest of the then King Rama V, who, upon falling in love with Frankfurt Central Station in Germany, decided that Bangkok must have a central station of similar opulence and grandeur.

The interior of the station was no less impressive; shaped like a mammoth half cylinder, the wrought-iron arches supported a high, vaulted ceiling not dissimilar to the ribs of a whale, while a long, clear skylight ran the entire length of the apex of the building like a shining backbone. The building hummed with a cacophony of voices and service announcements as thousands of would-be passengers rushed towards their platforms or sat lazily in the waiting areas fanning themselves and chatting in low tones with their travelling companions. All of this was lit in shafts of muted yellows and oranges by the semi-circular stained glass windows positioned at either end of the station.

Hobbs tried to imagine what this scene may have looked like a century ago when the station first opened. He imagined the engines pulling out of the station, their steam illuminated by the light of the giant windows, foreign and local travellers waving their tickets at busy conductors on their way north to Lampang, or north-east to Korat or Petchaburi.

The detectives found their platform with relative ease after buying their tickets from the ticket office; their one-way tickets from Bangkok to Kanchanaburi costing them a mere 25 Baht which Stirling calculated as being less than 60 pence. She wondered to herself what kind of luxury they could expect for less than one British pound.

Her wonderings were answered swiftly as they navigated a tall, iron step onto the ageing train carriage which would carry them west to Kanchanaburi. Hobbs shuddered momentarily as he surveyed the inside of the train carriage. The entire interior, bar the flooring, was painted in the very same duck-egg blue-green that he had seen in his dream-cum-premonition about the plane on his way to Thailand. Everything was the same: the iron seats padded in brown leather, the sash windows and metal grilled shutters to cover them, the long steel luggage racks that ran the length of the carriage, everything. Hobbs steadied himself against the first row of seats, apologising to an elderly lady with dyed black hair who had a grandchild perched happily on her knee.

"Are you alright, Frank?" asked Stirling.

"Yeah, I'm alright," replied Hobbs, wiping away a thin film of perspiration that had quickly formed on his forehead. "It's just, I've seen this place before. This train. I've been here. But, not really. In a dream, I mean. On the plane."

Stirling frowned and replied, "You're not making much sense, Frank. Come on, let's sit down."

There was no seat allocation and the train was rapidly filling with passengers, so they quickly found a vacant double seat, facing opposite the direction of travel and opposite a young family who also had children on their laps and between their knees. The couple smiled politely as Hobbs and Stirling sat down and the elder female child whispered something in her brother's ear. They both giggled and then went back to hanging precariously out of the window to wave at other passengers on the platform.

Stirling handed Hobbs a bottle of water she had bought earlier from a stand in the waiting area. "Are you sure you're OK, Frank? You look pale. What's all this about a dream?"

"It was on the plane, on the way over. I'd been going over Ella's files as I couldn't sleep and I must have been overthinking it, because as soon as I fell asleep, I had this awful dream. I guess you'd call it a type of premonition, after what's happened. I was in a train carriage, just like this one. I mean *exactly* like this one, but it was empty. There was this photograph of Ella - the one from the file - and it was blowing around in here, and I couldn't get it. No matter how hard I tried, it just kept slipping out of my hands. When I finally got hold of it, the picture was different. It was Ella, but she was dead. It was awful, she was in a skip, just like they found poor Ali."

Hobbs placed his head in his hands momentarily, for comfort. The couple opposite looked concerned but politely pretended to look away.

"Ali? The boxer you coached from before?" queried Stirling.

"Yeah. It was like the two situations merged together. You know what dreams are like. You must have had some similar ones with your work and your time with the army."

"Of course," Stirling replied. "but they're just dreams, Frank. Why didn't you tell me about it?"

"To be honest, I thought you might think I'm mental," Hobbs replied sheepishly having gathered his composure.

"You're joking, aren't you? How long have we worked together, Frank?" asked Stirling, placing a hand on her partner's shoulder.

"Too long," quipped Hobbs.

"Exactly. If we're going to catch the bastards that did this, we need to be in this together. 100%. That means we tell each other everything, any thought, any idea, any dream. Alright?"

Hobbs blew out his cheeks. "Alright. Thanks, Debs."

"Right, well, let's take a look at the back of the train, shall we?"

Hobbs and Stirling rose from their seats, asking the couple opposite if they would mind keeping their seats. They seemed to understand and the two kids jumped into the seats with beaming smiles. Stirling wondered if that was the first time they had had a seat to themselves. They walked cautiously down the aisle in the middle of the train, holding onto the backs of seats as they went as the train click-clacked down the tracks, swaying from left to right as it rounded the curves. Between the carriages they had to take large steps, holding onto long vertical handrails as they did. The ground rushed beneath them at an alarming speed and they both couldn't help but think of Ella, falling and meeting the rails, the gravel, the dirt and mud.

The train was busy with all manner of locals. Singles,

couples and families with young children all shared the space - a microcosm of the working class of Thailand. Most managed to find a seat, but some sat on worn and faded buckets in the areas by the doors. Younger and more-able people offered their seats to the elderly, pregnant or disabled. A team of food and drink hawkers plied their trade up and down the carriages, some with their wares in buckets, which also doubled as seats when they sold out, and some with trays, like the one they had seen Win dump in the CCTV footage from Kanchanaburi station.

After many an utterance of *excuse me* and *sorry,* they had threaded their way through the bustling train carriages and found themselves at the rear section of the train.

Looking out, they watched as the railway tracks stretched away across the Central Plains behind them to the horizon. As it had been where Ella's body was found, the railway was elevated atop a steep embankment and was surrounded on both sides by rice fields, plantations of tropical fruits and the occasional small settlement which ran alongside the tracks.

The area at the back of the train was small - just large enough for two people to stand side by side, leaning on the safety rail and admiring the view - just as Hobbs and Stirling were doing at that moment.

Stirling broke the silence. "Perfect place to clear your head after an argument with your dad, isn't it?"

"That it is, Debs," Hobbs replied with a sigh. "It would be nice and peaceful if we didn't know what had happened on a train just like this. Or, this train, even."

"Do you reckon it was this train?" asked Stirling.

"No idea, Debs. Could be, I suppose. Same time train as she took, but I don't know if they switch over the trains. They're probably all pretty similar though, I reckon." Hobbs gave the safety rail a couple of thumps. "This is pretty high, even for someone of my height. Would be difficult to go over it accidentally, I would have thought. What do you think?"

"Definitely. Even with some kind of disagreement between Ella and Win. It seems unlikely that she would have fallen over this barrier accidentally," Stirling agreed, noting where the barrier came up to on her own body.

"She'd have to be toppled over, or shoved under," Hobbs surmised, gesturing with his body what those two actions might look like. "Either way, it's a deliberate act."

"I agree. I wonder how easy it is to be seen or heard here, from inside the carriage," Stirling wondered out loud, pivoting to peer through the door and into the carriage.

"I would say only a heated argument would be heard over the noise from the train," opined Hobbs. "Especially if another train was coming the other way. What do you think, Debs?"

Stirling didn't answer. "Debs?" Hobbs asked again.

Stirling was focused on an area on the edge of the iron doorway to the back of the train. "Come here and take a look at this," she said without breaking her gaze. "Does that look like blood to you?"

Hobbs stepped towards the doorway and peered at the dark smear on the rusting iron door frame. "Certainly looks like it to me. Have you got any gloves on you?" he asked, wanting to touch the stain but erring on the side of his better judgement.

"I might have a pair in my bag," responded Stirling, fishing around a little frantically in her shoulder bag. After a moment, she pulled out a pair of gloves from a stash of two or three in a zip-lock bag. Stirling was nothing if not organised. She handed a pair to Hobbs, who struggled initially to get them over his oversized hands.

"Wait. Let me photograph it *in-situ* first," said Stirling, reaching for her mobile phone. Stirling snapped a few photos from different angles and at different distances, then took a short video clip of where they were on the train, for context.

Hobbs began to prod tentatively at the substance on the doorway. He checked his fingertip each time. Whatever it was wasn't in a liquid state any more. It had dried and no residue could be seen on the gloves. Hobbs began to gently scratch at the stain until a few flecks were deposited onto the fingertip of his glove. He continued until he had a few more. He raised his fingertip to his nose and took a deep inward sniff.

"Smells like blood, too," he said, taking another sniff. "Not that I'm an expert. What do you think?" Hobbs held out his finger for Stirling to sniff.

"I'm no expert, either," she confessed. "but, that definitely has the right smell to it. Get a few more flecks and seal them in the zip-lock bag with the glove. I'll get a video of you doing it."

Hobbs did as instructed. "I'm not sure the lab in Kanchanaburi will process this and I'm pretty sure it won't stand up as evidence in a court. But, it's definitely something we can use to lean on Brother Bear further," he said, taking off the remaining untainted glove and shoving it into his pocket.

Stirling agreed, "We can definitely paint a picture with this. If Win's advance was spurned and there had been an argument, it's highly unlikely she could have hit her head here and managed to fall over the railing…here," she said, taking two long, deliberate paces to the railing from the door.

"Here, let me film you doing that, as well," said Hobbs, taking

CHAPTER 20

his own phone from his pocket. Stirling repeated the action, this time for the benefit of the camera but made a point of making it as natural and realistic as possible. "We certainly haven't proved that Ella was deliberately killed, but I think we've got enough to sow some seeds of doubt in the mind of Brother Bear," he said smugly.

"I think we're done here, aren't we?" Stirling asked Hobbs, placing her things back into her bag. "Do you want to go back to our seats for the rest of the journey?"

"Nah," replied Hobbs leaning once more onto the railing with his forearms. "Let's let the kids have them for a while. I quite like it back here, even with everything that's happened. I feel like we're a bit closer to Ella, or her spirit, anyway. Maybe she'll throw us a bone and help us figure all of this out."

Stirling joined him at the railing and Hobbs lit a cigarette, which he held down low by his side to let the smoke be taken in the opposite direction of his partner. Neither of them spoke for a few minutes as the train wound its way through an urban area once more. Through the heat haze, a huge shape began to form and dominate the skyline to the side of the train. The shape appeared to be akin to a gigantic bell with a conical top that stretched skywards towards the heavens. In the dying light of the day, its terracotta colours began to glow a hue of soothing ochre.

"That must be the *Chedi* that the Ambassador was talking about," remarked Stirling quietly, as she leafed through her notebook for the name.

"The *Phra Pathom Chedi*," replied Hobbs, without taking his eyes off the monument which was growing steadily larger on the horizon.

"How did you remember that?" asked Stirling, genuinely

impressed.

Hobbs chuckled to himself. "You're not the only one with a good memory and an eye for detail, young Debra."

Stirling smiled. "It really is beautiful, isn't it? We'll have to come back and visit one day, when this is all over. Under better circumstances."

Hobbs took a long pull on his cigarette and replied, "Yeah, I think we will."

Chapter 21

It was late afternoon when Hobbs and Stirling's train came to a noisy stop at the platform of Kanchanaburi's central station. The sun once again hung low in the sky, radiating the once stifling heat that the two detectives were slowly getting used to. They moved quickly through the small crowd that was embarking and disembarking among the whistles of the train guards and the shouts of the platform hawkers who walked up and down beneath the open carriage windows plying their wares. Anonymous arms dangled from the windows exchanging handfuls of banknotes for small plastic bags of fresh fruits and various meat on skewers with sticky rice.

In front of the station, a colourful snake of tuk-tuks awaited them and Hobbs and Stirling jumped into the back of the one at the front of the queue. They stated their destination and the vehicle jerked to life, peeling away from the station and its manicured flowerbeds at record speed leaving behind a cloud of noxious exhaust gases for the waiting drivers behind.

Within a few minutes, they had arrived back at Pong Phen and within a further few minutes, they were both wallowing in the comparatively cool waters of the swimming pool. Stirling swam a few lengths while Hobbs generally relaxed in the shallow end of the pool, watching the sun lower itself down past the horizon and the river beyond the guest house.

A loud ringing began to emanate from the veranda of Hobbs' bungalow as his telephone rang from the pocket of his shirt that was draped haphazardly over one of the two chairs by the table. Hobbs hauled himself out in ungainly fashion, grabbing his towel from the pool side and drying his dripping body quickly in preparation for answering the phone call. Stirling, also hearing the ringing, paused her exercise and moved to the end of the pool to be within earshot. She knew that it was Hobbs' phone, rather than her own, because Hobbs always had a very traditional, very loud, *ring ring* tone on his telephone rather than a more modern, less jarring, musical tune.

Hobbs had managed to lumber over to his bungalow and retrieve his ringing telephone. Squinting at the call display, he saw that it was Chai.

"Hello, Chai mate," he answered in typical fashion.

"Frank, hi. It's Chai. I was just about to hang up."

"Sorry, mate. I was in the pool. It's been a long day. What's up? Did you hear back from your man at Win's bar?"

"Yes, that's why I am calling."

"Well, go on then, spit it out."

"OK, so, my colleague in Bangkok spoke to the staff at Win's bar. They all said that Win is openly gay and he's even married."

"Married?"

"Yes, apparently he married two or three years ago to a German guy named Stephan who works for the U.N."

"Interesting. Did they have a last name? Where is this Stephan now?"

"No last name. They said they had never met him, but

Win talked about him. They said they had been having some problems - financial problems which turned into marriage problems - and that's why he was back in the bar."

Stirling's curiosity had piqued and she now joined Hobbs on a chair on the veranda, towelling her wet hair.

"Debra's here too, Chai. I'm going to put you on speaker. There's nobody else here. Can you just repeat what you just said for her benefit?"

Chai dutifully repeated what he had been told.

"So, Brother Bear's theory about Win trying it on with Ella on the train looks increasingly unlikely then?" Stirling asked, rubbing her legs down with her towel.

"Yes, it looks that way," replied Chai on the phone speaker.

"What else did you find out?" asked Hobbs, this time.

"Staff said he had been behaving strangely in the past few months. They thought he may have been using drugs. Possibly yaa-baa."

"Well, that makes sense, considering we think that Ella was given yaa-baa by someone - probably Win - before she died," replied Stirling.

"Right," began Hobbs. "I feel like we definitely have enough to start leaning on Brother Bear. It shouldn't come as a surprise to him that Win is gay. In fact, I'm sure he knows but it might come as a surprise to him that we know he is."

"He was probably banking on us not looking any further into Win," remarked Stirling.

"So, what's the next step?" asked Chai.

"You said you had managed to get Brother Bear moved down from Bangkok?" asked Hobbs.

"Yes, on a different charge, though. A bar fight in Kanchanaburi a few weeks ago."

"Well, how are we going to get an interview with him about our murder? Anupong is not going to allow that."

"Anupong isn't going to know," replied Chai, with a hint of smugness. "He's not here. He's on a golf trip to Bangkok."

"You're joking," replied Hobbs, incredulous.

"No, I'm not. In fact, I'm sure he doesn't even know we have Brother Bear here out west. If he knew, I don't think he would be going golfing."

"Great work, Chai," complimented Stirling. "How did you manage that?"

"Let's just say, we're not the only ones who have had enough of Captain Anupong. We've got some friends on the force in Kanchanaburi at last."

"That's brilliant, Chai. Well done. Really well done."

"Thank you, Frank…and Debs," replied Chai with deference. Frank could almost see him bowing through the phone line.

"OK, let's get him in for interview as soon as possible tomorrow morning," said Hobbs, decisively. "Let's be in and out before Arsepong gets a sniff - no pun intended." Stirling couldn't help but smirk.

"We'll get our strategy sorted tonight and you just text us the time you'll pick us up. Is that OK, Chai?" asked Stirling, excited at the turn in the investigation.

"Yes, that's fine. See you tomorrow. Bye."

Chai hung up and the two detectives looked at each other.

"We're finally getting somewhere, Debs," said Hobbs, with an affirming nod.

"God, we needed a break," sighed Stirling, placing her now wet towel across her lap. "Hopefully, with Anupong out of the way for a while, we'll be able to make even more headway - thanks to our friends at the station."

CHAPTER 21

"Speaking of friends," began Hobbs. "Do you think we should be keeping the Ambassador up-to-date with what we have found out so far, or do you think it is too soon?"

"Well, last time we spoke to him, the consensus was that what happened to Ella was a terrible accident. Things have changed quite a lot since then but maybe we're better off with him thinking that until we have some strong evidence to suggest otherwise."

"True. Maybe we could speak to Stella, then. See what she thinks. She works very closely with him. Could send her a message?"

"That's a good idea."

"OK, well you send Stella a message and ask her if and when Patterson would like to talk to us. I'll get changed and then we'll get started on interview strategy for tomorrow."

"Can't think on an empty stomach, Debs."

Stirling laughed. "OK, Frankie. I'll go and grab us a couple of menus, shall I?"

Stirling tied her towel around her waist and wandered off towards the bar and restaurant in north-west corner of the guest house while Frank prodded away at the keys on his phone.

HI STELLA. SOME DEVELOPMENTS HERE IN KANCH. WE WONDERED IF RICHARD WOULD LIKE US TO FILL HIM IN. LET US KNOW. FRANK.

A few minutes later, Stirling returned from the bar with a couple of menus, a beer for Hobbs and some kind of garish cocktail, complete with miniature umbrella, for herself. They did a quick cheers and sipped at their drinks while they perused the menu for something to eat as the resident pipistrelle bats began their bombing runs over the swimming pool once again.

As Hobbs debated between fried rice or noodles, his phone chimed with an incoming message. Absent-mindedly he picked up his phone to see a reply from Stella Ismail.

HI, FRANK. THANKS FOR YOUR MESSAGE. WILL ASK HIM TOMORROW BUT DON'T EXPECT A QUICK REPLY AS HE IS AWAY FOR A COUPLE OF DAYS. WILL LET YOU KNOW A.S.A.P. TAKE CARE. S x

* * *

Debra Stirling slept fitfully that night, thinking through everything that had happened in the previous few days and what was to come the day after. She found herself staring at the ceiling of her hotel room, watching a small gecko go about his nocturnal business of catching the tiny flies and spiders which criss-crossed the ceiling above. Her wound from the attack a couple of nights earlier didn't bother her during the day, but at night, a gentle throb emanated from the back of her head like a nagging doubt that lingered uninvited in the periphery of her investigation. She touched the back of her head, feeling gingerly for the injury and checked her fingers to find a few specks of dried blood that persisted under her fingernails. She was healing well, at least on the surface, but laying there alone in her room she began to appreciate her own vulnerability and even mortality. She had been in

CHAPTER 21

dodgy situations before in London, especially on the council estates, but this time she had been targeted and whomever had ordered the attack was clearly capable of murder.

She thought again of the waitress who had died in the crossfire at the club in Bangkok. Nong Noon was her name and Stirling vowed that she would never forget it. She had become collateral in her investigation. It happened sometimes - she knew that - but she couldn't help but feel responsible, in some way, for the young girl's death. She tried to take Hobbs' advice and let the blame lay solely on the shoulders of the perpetrators but it wasn't easy. If they had kept their noses out, accepted the official line that Ella's death had been a tragic accident, Nong Noon would be alive right now and her family wouldn't be planning her funeral.

They had been in Thailand for six days. Their time was up and their boss, Yvonne Harding, would be calling them home soon. Stirling thought back to the first meeting with Harding back at Citadel Place in London. It seemed an age ago now, with all that had happened but she remembered the words she had said to them: *"You'll only be gone a week." "She might even be found by the time you get there."* Nobody, not even Yvonne Harding, with all her decades of experience in Missing Persons, could have predicted the chain of events that had befallen the two foreign detectives. They had gone down the proverbial rabbit hole and were still going. Every new piece of evidence, every hunch, every witness testimony was sending them deeper into the dark underbelly of this country.

It would be so easy, she thought to herself, as her eyelids finally began to droop and the resident geckos settled in for the night, to call it quits - to get on that plane tomorrow and head back to normality. They had done their job. Ella Patterson was no longer a missing person, that much was unfortunately certain. They had done what they could to support Richard Patterson with the loss of his daughter and now it was down to the local police to do their job and find those responsible for her death. The further they delved into this mystery, the more vulnerable they became. The closer they got to the truth, the more would be at stake for the person or persons who orchestrated the murder. They had gotten off easy when they were attacked a few evenings prior. It was a warning - they both knew that. The fact was that if someone wanted them dead, they would be dead already but they hadn't heeded that warning. They had been told to go home and they hadn't. They would have a chance tomorrow. They would take it, she thought. They would go home and no more young girls would have to die. The thought placated Stirling's busy and guilty mind and she, at last, let sleep take her.

Chapter 22

Stirling woke suddenly to the sound of knocking on her hotel room door. The loud thumps, she assumed, were coming from the fisted bear paws of her oversized partner, Hobbs.

"Wakey, wakey. Rise and shine," came a voice from the other side of the door. Stirling could see sunlight sneaking in from the small gap in the curtains. The sun was up, she thought. She must have slept better than she had thought.

Pulling on a robe, Stirling staggered sleepily towards the door and opened it to blinding sunshine and the silhouette of her partner holding out a cup of coffee and a small plate of freshly-cut tropical fruits.

"Shake a leg, Princess," he teased. "We've got an interview to do and we don't want to be sticking around for our friend Arsepong to get back. Chai will be here in a few minutes. I thought you would have set an alarm, or three. It's not like you to sleep in."

"I'm sorry, Frank. It's been a crazy few days and my head was giving me gyp last night. Give me a few minutes and I'll jump in the shower."

"Alright," replied Frank. "I'll be having a cigarette and another cup of coffee at reception. Don't take too long or yours will go cold."

"In this heat? I doubt it," joked Stirling closing the door and letting her robe drop messily to the floor. Looking in the mirror, she almost didn't recognise herself. Her hair was unkempt. Large bags had formed under her eyes and her trademark Celtic twinkle was nowhere to be seen. She noticed her hotel room was, uncharacteristically, a complete mess. Worn and unworn clothes were strewn roughly over the bed and floor. Chargers and other electricals formed a maelstrom of wires sticking out of her case. Half a dozen half-empty bottles of water stood discarded on her bedside table and on the floor next to it, along with empty plastic bags and snack wrappers from 7-11 and Family Mart.

She shook her head at herself. The highly organised, bordering on obsessive, Debra Stirling was fading away before her very eyes. In her place, an exhausted imposter, completely overwhelmed by the situation she found herself in, surviving on junk food and air-conditioning.

She took a very quick shower and brushed her teeth. She still hadn't got used to the taste of the water here and rarely completed her full two minutes as she did religiously back in the UK. She dried herself and tousled her hair roughly, hanging her towel up neatly this time. Throwing on the nearest clean clothes she could find and tying her hair, she quickly buzzed around the room, stuffing all the rubbish into discarded convenience store bags and placing her dirty clothes into a bag she had bought especially for the trip.

She looked at herself in the mirror once again. In a baggy sleeveless white shirt and khaki shorts with sandals, she certainly didn't embody her usual power-woman persona but it was a marked improvement on the shadow of her former self she had met just a few minutes earlier. She quickly grabbed her laptop and charger, stuffing them into a yellow, over-sized shoulder bag and made for the reception, making sure her room was locked securely after her.

Hobbs was waiting patiently on the edge of the reception-cum-bar area, smoking a cigarette and finishing off his second cup of coffee of the morning. With perfect timing, Stirling watched as the familiar sight of Chai's borrowed maroon Toyota Hilux pulled into the car park.

"You alright, Debs?" asked Hobbs, before taking a last drag on his cigarette and stubbing it out in a nearby ash tray. "I don't mean to be rude, but you looked like shit this morning."

"Why, thank you, Frank. Just what I needed to hear," Stirling replied. "You should have seen the state of my room."

"I did, it also looked like shit but also looked twice as clean as mine."

"Well at least that's some good news. I was beginning to get worried."

"I'm not worried about the state of my hotel room. They're supposed to be a mess. I *am* worried about you, though," stated Hobbs as they both walked across the car park towards the pick-up and the ever-faithful Chai.

"I'm fine, Frank. Don't worry. It's just been a whirlwind. That's all," replied Stirling, waving to Chai in the driver's seat.

"I *do* worry, though. That's the problem, Debs. You haven't looked yourself since you got bonked over the head. I bet you didn't even have your breakfast, did you?"

"No, you're right. I forgot. I just want to get this stuff over and done with, Frank. So we can go home. It's been nearly a week. We've got a flight tomorrow and I'm confident that Harding will want us on it. The strings to Johnny Taxpayer's purse are tighter than ever these days. To be honest, I would quite like to be on it, too."

Hobbs stopped, placing his hand on the door handle, but not opening it. "Do you mean that, Debs? We're closer than ever to nailing the bastards that killed our Ella. Surely, you're not giving up on her."

"Don't say thank, Frank. I'm not giving up on her. I'm just tired. Maybe Anupong is right. We're not murder squad. Maybe this isn't any of our business. We came here to find Ella, and we did. We didn't find her alive and I wish to God that we had, but she was dead before we even set foot in the country. I would love to find out who did this as much as you, Frank, but this isn't our fight any more. Maybe we should just leave it to the Thai police from now on."

Hobbs looked crestfallen. "You must be joking. The boys in brown? Apart from our Chai, all we've seen is their ineptitude at best and at worst systemic bloody corruption. They couldn't organise a piss up in a brewery and even if they could, they would find some way to rip off the punters.

"I know that, Frank, but what can we do? We can't do their job for them and we can't stay here forever. We've got people counting on us back home as well. We can actually make a difference for them. We might even save some lives. I just feel like the deeper we go into this, the more dangerous it becomes, and not just for us. That poor girl at the club. She'd still be alive if it wasn't for us."

Hobbs shook his head. "No, come on, Debs. We've talked about this. We didn't kill that girl. Some dickhead with a gun killed her because of some misplaced loyalty to his scumbag boss. We know who killed Nong Noon but we don't know who had our Ella killed. We can't give up now. We made a

CHAPTER 22

promise to her parents that we would find out who did this. I don't know about you, but I like to keep my promises."

Stirling sighed. She was happy that Hobbs also remembered Nong Noon's name but she didn't want to have another name to remember in the next few days.

"Of course, I want to find out and, of course, I want to keep my promise, too. It's just…"

Hobbs cut her off. "Listen, let's do this interview. If Brother Bear decides to clam up and say nothing then that will make our decision for us, won't it? If it comes to a dead-end, then we'll pack our bags and be on that flight home tomorrow."

"And if he does the opposite and gives us something tangible to go on?" asked Stirling, in earnest.

"Then we're all in. We're going headlong down that rabbit hole and we're not coming out until we're dragging that rabbit out by its sodding ears. Sod the boys in brown and sod Harding. We'll be here until the job's done. Deal?"

Stirling couldn't help but smile and reluctantly held out her hand to Hobbs. "Deal."

* * *

Hobbs, Stirling and Chai arrived at the police station and made their way first to the CCTV room. As they entered, a vivid memory entered Hobbs' head of the interview he had witnessed before of Win Nyan Bo and the blatant police brutality therein. He wondered if Brother Bear was going to get the same treatment or whether that was reserved for foreign nationals and/or stateless individuals.

The two detectives took their seats on two of the plastic seats that were anchored to the floor. Chai excused himself and went to speak to his colleagues to find out how things were going to happen. Hobbs and Stirling stared at grainy picture displayed on the ageing CCTV monitor. Before long, a door to the left opened and a uniformed officer appeared, holding the door open for another similarly-dressed officer who was ushering in a third person in civilian clothing whom Hobbs recognised as Brother Bear, the man he had clotheslined in the club in Bangkok earlier. He noticed he was not in the orange jump suit that Win had been wearing. He was not shackled and his face didn't bear any signs of abuse or maltreatment.

Hobbs shook his head. "Chalk and cheese," he muttered to nobody in particular.

"What's that, Frank?" asked Stirling, hearing him say something but not making it out.

"Chalk and cheese, Debs," he replied, pointing at the monitor. "Look how they treated Win during his interview and look how they're treating this slime bag."

Stirling frowned in agreement and replied, "I know what you mean. No cuffs, no shackles, no prison attire."

They both watched as Brother Bear took his seat and was offered a cigarette by one of the uniformed officers before he took his seat on the opposite side of the table.

"Bloody hell," scoffed Hobbs. Why don't they give him a spa voucher while they're at it."

"Maybe it's an interview technique," offered Stirling, but she didn't really believe that herself.

At that moment, Chai returned to the CCTV room and spent a few seconds standing watching the monitor before speaking to the detectives to fill them in. "Right, so the uniforms need to speak to Brother Bear about the actual charge we've got him in for first. Then, we can head in and question him about Ella's murder. He won't have to say anything, as this interview isn't official, but he doesn't know that."

Hobbs interjected with an idea, "And if it's not official then we don't need to be official either, right? We can bend the truth a little."

"Or a lot," offered Stirling. "We were talking last night, if we can put pressure on Brother Bear by threatening him with a heavy jail term, like the police did with Win, then he might start singing."

"You'll have to do that," replied Chai, visibly running through the situation in his mind. "I'll have to let the Thai detectives know, too. When it gets to that point, we just stay quiet and let you two do the talking."

"Exactly," replied Hobbs, standing up and patting Chai roughly on the shoulder.

"OK, they said they will signal to the camera when they are ready for us to come in."

For the next few minutes, they all sat and watched the monitor as the interview went on in the room down the hall. Stirling noted the suspect's body language. He appeared relaxed, almost nonchalant, as he had in the club in Bangkok. He sat with his legs open, his elbows on the table and his chin resting on his hands. He appeared bored by the interviewers' questions, aside from the odd smirk in response. He clearly thought he was untouchable by the police. He probably had at least one of them, possibly Anupong, in his pocket. She hoped he wasn't as untouchable as she thought or as clever as he looked.

As they watched on, the Thai officer in the foreground

turned and nodded deliberately to the camera in the corner of the room. At that, the three stood up and made their way down the hall to the interview room where Brother Bear was being questioned. After a swift knock, Chai entered the room first, striding confidently across the room to theatrically whisper in the ear of the interviewer. The theatrics continued with the feigned surprise by the interviewer as he ushered Hobbs and Stirling into the room and explained the situation to Brother Bear who, for the first time, began to look uncomfortable at the situation.

Chai slipped out of the room, leaving behind him an awkward silence which only served to increase the subject's discomfort. He reappeared a few moments later with two folding chairs which he set up on the opposite side of the table. The two Thai detectives stood and made way for Hobbs and Stirling who took the 'driving seats'.

"Good morning, Mr…Tongsomboon," began Hobbs, checking his notebook for the official name of the suspect they had dubbed Brother Bear and who went by his nickname Phee Mhee. "My name is Detective Frank Hobbs with the Metropolitan Police in the UK and this is my partner, Detective Debra Stirling. I'm told that you speak excellent English, so there shouldn't be any need for any interpretation by my Thai colleagues here, should there?"

Brother Bear smiled at the feigned compliment and replied, "Yes, of course I speak excellent English. It's essential in my line of work.

"What line of work would that be?" asked Hobbs.

"I'm a nightclub owner and promoter, Mr Hobbs. I seem to remember you frequented one of my clubs this week. Perhaps I should be offering you a job as my head of security with your

CHAPTER 22

particular skill set and penchant for violence."

The suspect indeed spoke English very well. His accent was almost that of a native speaker, with an almost antipodean twang at the end of his sentences.

"A penchant for violence, you say? Well, that brings me to my next question. I'm sure you're aware that my partner and I are in Thailand investigating the disappearance and subsequent murder of a British citizen, Ella Patterson."

"Yes, I heard about that in the news. The Ambassador's daughter. I heard it was a terrible accident, though."

"Unfortunately, not. The poor young thing was murdered. A murder for hire, we believe and we also believe that you had something to do with it. No, we know you had something to do with it."

"Well, unfortunately, *I* believe you are misinformed," the suspect retorted. Stirling noted that Brother Bear appeared to be purposefully using the same vocabulary as Hobbs; possibly in an attempt to appear a linguistic and intellectual equal. His English was undeniably good and he was evidently smart enough, or rich enough, to keep himself out of jail. But, Hobbs was smart, too.

Stirling cut in, "We have a suspect in custody who has confessed to the murder and has also told us who paid him to do it. That would be you, Mr. Tongsomboon."

"And who is this suspect?" asked Brother Bear, still appearing reasonably calm and confident, despite the situation he found himself in.

"Our suspect is a foreign national. Have you had any business dealings with any foreigners recently, Mr. Tongsomboon?"

Brother Bear feigned a look of puzzlement. "No, I don't

think I have."

"That's strange," replied Stirling, leafing through her notebook, "As we have witnesses that place you at a local karaoke bar talking to our suspect in the run-up to the murder."

"They must be mistaken," Brother Bear replied nonchalantly.

"No, no," interjected Hobbs. "We have our suspect, saying that you met there. We have the owner of the bar saying that you go there often and met with our suspect. We have at least one employee who also says that she saw you there."

Stirling noticed an almost imperceptible flush appear in the previously unfaltering exterior of the interviewee as he shifted slightly in his seat.

"So, you're going to take the word of a hooker, brothel owner and some Burmese migrant worker over a reputable local businessman?" asked Brother Bear feigning incredulity, once more.

Hobbs and Stirling looked at each other knowingly.

"Who said our suspect is Burmese?" asked Hobbs, a wry smile curling in the corners of his mouth.

A flash of panic dashed across the eyes of their suspect. It may not have been noticed by someone with an untrained eye, but Stirling was trained and she was looking for it.

"I mean, of course, he's Burmese. They all are around here in Kanchanaburi. You should work on your local knowledge, Detectives."

Brother Bear had recovered well, but the tell was there and Stirling knew they had their man.

"There are plenty of foreign tourists here in Kanchanaburi, Mr. Tongsomboon," began Hobbs again. "My partner and I saw dozens, perhaps hundreds, of them at the River Kwai

CHAPTER 22

Light and Sound Festival last weekend. But you happen to know our foreign suspect, don't you?"

"Look, even if I did. That's not enough evidence to make a case against me in a Thai court. It would be thrown out instantly. You are clutching at straws. Nobody here cares about your rich *farang* schoolgirl. This is Thailand, Detectives. You're not in merry old England now."

Hobbs new that he was right. He hated it. But, he was right. A couple of less-than dependable eye-witnesses wasn't going to cut it, but he couldn't let this guy sit there and deny all involvement. Hobbs knew he has one roll of the dice left. He hadn't discussed it with Stirling or Chai as a) he didn't know if it would work and b) he didn't even know if it was legal. It's too late for legal, he thought to himself. This entire interview isn't legal. This is just a means to an end. Brother Bear, no matter how big he thinks he is, is still a middle man in all of this. However, Hobbs knew that he was also the lynchpin. He was the key to finding out who had ordered the killing of Ella and all he needed to do was get this cretin to roll over and spill the beans. He decided to go for it and rolled the dice.

"A Thai court? Oh, no, Mr. Tongsomboon. We know what they are like and we know what your police force is like. We know how they let scumbags like you off the hook in exchange for bribes to supplement their measly salaries. No, no, Mr. Tongsomboon. We had a phone call from our superiors over in London today. Our boss, Detective Inspector Yvonne Harding, told us that we have the go-ahead to bring you back to London with us tomorrow. You'll stand trial in a *British* court, with a *British* judge and a jury made up of *British* people, who *all*, unfortunately for you, do care about our *rich farang schoolgirl*."

Stirling smiled inwardly as she watched the colour visibly drain from the face of their suspect. He, clearly, had not prepared for this eventuality and he, clearly, could not tell that Hobbs was bluffing. That was understandable, though, as Hobbs showed no sign of his deceit. He stared down his adversary, not breaking his gaze for a millisecond, waiting for a response.

The silence, as with the stare, continued, unbroken, as Brother Bear seemed to run through a plethora of scenarios and options in his head. The tension was palpable, the atmosphere tense. Chai sat motionless, also staring down Brother Bear, surprised by Hobbs' revelation, of which he himself did not know the veracity, waiting for the response of this suspect. The response which could make or break this case. Stirling also waited, her pen poised above her notebook, her inner voice screaming for Brother Bear to make a confession, right there and then.

"OK, look..." Brother Bear began. "I admit. I've been to the karaoke bar you're talking about. I do business with the mama-san there. She supplies me with good-looking Burmese girls for my clubs - all of age, of course - and she says that I haven't paid her a finder's fee for some of them. She's trying to fit me up. She told me if I didn't pay, she would tell the police that I had something to do with that missing girl. That's all there is to it. She's a washed-up, lying old hooker who wants to bring me down with her."

Hobbs swore inwardly but didn't let it show on his face. Brother Bear was still playing the innocent. This would be harder than he had thought. He was talking, though, and he was making some admissions.

"That may be, but that doesn't explain your meeting with

CHAPTER 22

our suspect, who has confessed to the murder of Ella and claims you paid him to do it."

"Yes, I met with that guy. I have some shares in some gay bars in Bangkok. I don't shout about it, but he works for one of them. He is one of the best boys I have there. Those European poofs love him. He's a good money maker for me. He contacts me and says he's going to quit. He's married now and his husband says he doesn't want him working there any more. So, I gave him a bit of a bonus, that's all; an incentive to stay. Well, he said it wasn't enough and if I didn't give him double, he would tell the police I had something to do with the missing girl. They must be working together. I didn't think they would actually do it."

Stirling flicked quickly back through her notes to the page from the gay bar in Bangkok. There, it was written, as she remembered, that Win and his husband were having marital problems. She seized the opportunity.

"Win's husband wanted him to stop working in the bar. Is that right?" she asked.

"That's right," replied Brother Bear.

"Well, that's the first lie of many," Stirling remarked. "Win and his husband, Stephan, are having financial problems. His husband wants him back in the bar. What else are you lying about, Mr. Tongsomboon?"

There was a long pause as Brother Bear again weighed up his options. The pause was broken by Hobbs as he leaned closer to the face of Brother Bear.

"Look, Mr. Tongsomboon, Mr. T, Phee Mhee, whatever your fucking name is. We know you're lying. We know you paid Win to kill Ella. We know that someone else paid you to pay Win to kill Ella. We also know that you're probably right.

You'll walk out of a Thai court with a slap on the wrist, a year or so jail time, at most. But, you're not going to a Thai court. You're coming with us. You're coming to London and there they are going to throw the fucking book at you. They don't know the full story and they certainly won't be getting it from us. They aren't going to be asking who paid you to pay Win. As far as they are concerned, you paid Win to kill our Ella. That's a murder charge; not accessory to murder...*murder*. That's a mandatory life sentence. A minimum of 25 years in prison before you even have the chance of parole; which you won't get because you're a child killer. Do you know what they do to child killers in prisons, mate? Do you know those nasty bastards do to pretty little Asian boys like you when they haven't got their end away for years?"

Hobbs paused at this point as the realisation of what he was saying appeared on the face of his suspect. Brother Bear's chin dropped to his chest and he covered his face with his hands as he attempted to process the enormity of what this detective had just laid out for him.

"Now, this isn't an inevitability, of course. You have options. You always have options. You can do the right thing. You can tell us who paid you to organise Ella's murder and we can keep you here in Thailand. We can make you out as simply the money man; a cog in the machine. Not a sadistic murderer but an ambitious businessman whose greed got the better of him. I'm sure the Thai courts would treat you quite favourably. Or, alternatively, you can carry on this pointless charade and you'll be on a one-way flight to Wormwood Scrubs, where you are going to be black and blue in places you didn't know you could be."

Hobbs sat back in his chair. Though he didn't show it,

CHAPTER 22

his body was on fire, every sinew of his being contorted in anticipation at what Brother Bear would say next. There were three scenarios. He would either: break, spilling the beans completely, remain obstinate and stick to his original story and hope for the best, or come up with another lie, a bigger lie, which might seem more believable to his tormentors.

Brother Bear motioned as if he were about to speak, then placed his head in his hands again. Hobbs and Stirling looked at each other and then at Chai before looking back again at the tormented soul in front of them.

All of a sudden, a sound emanated from Brother Bear, a frustrated, strangled scream, muffled by his hands now clamped tightly over his eyes. Hobbs and Stirling glanced at each other again.

Another tormented cry followed and then he looked up, fixing his gaze on Hobbs. "You lot have no fucking idea what they will do to me. You don't know who you are dealing with. And not just to me, but to my family. I know what they are capable of. I've seen what they do and that is to innocent people. What do you think they will do to me?"

"Who? Who are you talking about?" interjected Stirling.

"I can't. I just can't."

Hobbs waded in at this point, the suspect was about to clam up again through fear of reprisal. He couldn't let that happen. It was time for more half-truths and empty promises if the end should justify the means "Look, whoever it is. If you help us, we can protect you from them. We can get you to England. We have three seats booked tomorrow. We are supposed to take you there, to stand trial, but we can get you into a protection programme. They can't get to you there."

Stirling glared at Hobbs, though Brother Bear couldn't see,

his head was once again in his hands. She knew that Hobbs was making false promises. That wasn't the way she did things. She did things by the book. Fair and square. But, she also knew that Hobbs was so close to breaking the case. Hobbs' look that returned her glare told her that. She looked over at Brother Bear who was now almost convulsing with anxiety. He was either incredibly afraid or an incredibly good actor.

At last, Brother Bear became still. His shoulders slumped and he raised his head to meet Hobbs' gaze once more.

"OK. Here it is. All this time, the answer has been staring you in the face. You've been running all over this town, all over Bangkok looking for it. You should have been looking closer to home. You want to know who hired me? It was that fucking hua-nguu, snake head bastard, Richard Patterson, alright?"

The room fell deathly silent as the detectives tried to process what they had just heard.

"You wanna know what kind of people you're dealing with? The type of person who hires someone to kill their own daughter. That's who you're dealing with."

Suddenly, the door to the interview room burst open, revealing the unmistakeable silhouette of Captain Anupong, breathing heavily, dressed in ill-fitting golf attire, visibly seething at the scene he was witnessing take place under his nose. Two uniformed officers appeared and dragged Brother Bear out of the interview room by the scruff of his neck. Chai stood to attention as Anupong roared what sounded like a tirade of abuse in Thai, grabbing him roughly by the collar and shoving him out the door with the sole of his foot.

Anupong turned his gaze to Hobbs and Stirling who were stuck firmly in their seats, dumbfounded by the turn of events.

CHAPTER 22

Sweat dripped from the enraged captain's temples and rolled down his pudgy face while his eyes burned with rage.

"You fucking English," he began "have two minutes to get out of my station or I will have you both arrested. GO!"

Hobbs and Stirling gathered their things quickly and exited the interview room. As they hurried down the corridor, Stirling glanced back over her shoulder to see a figure who looked like Chai, sitting on the floor with his head between his knees, stripped of his police cap and shirt, covering his head as a barrage of savage blows rained down on him from above.

Chapter 23

It had been difficult to leave the station and Chai to his fate with the local police officers and Captain Anupong. Hobbs had to physically restrain Stirling from heading back down the corridor to his aid. Luckily, Hobbs was large enough to stop her and wise enough to talk her down once they got outside. They had hastily moved through the station and the public areas, receiving disapproving glares from the staff and bemused looks from the general public. Once outside, they both sat on the ground of the car park, their backs against each of the tyres of the maroon pickup that Chai had dutifully chauffeured them around in all week, waiting for him to emerge from the police station, half-wondering if he would emerge at all.

After around twenty minutes, Chai emerged from the station, hunched over slightly and carrying his cap under his arm, just as he had when they had first met. The Chai that stood before them now, though, was a shadow of his former self. Both eyes were swollen, his right more-so and beginning to close. He had a series of small lacerations across his scalp and, by the way he was walking, it appeared a broken rib, or two.

Hobbs and Stirling pushed themselves to their feet as he

approached.

"I'm so sorry, Chai," began Stirling, opening her arms, inviting Chai to embrace. "I wanted to go back for you, but…"

"It's OK, Debs. There was nothing you could do. You can't be getting arrested."

"That's what I told her, mate." interjected Hobbs. "As much as we both wanted to stop those bastards, I knew Anupong would have us locked up."

"It's fine, Frank. You did the right thing. I'm fine."

"You don't look it, mate. If I'm being honest, you look like shit." Hobbs replied, only half-joking.

Chai laughed and winced as he did so.

"Ribs?" asked Hobbs, knowingly. Chai nodded in a grimace. "Had a few of them in my time from the ring. Bloody painful. Do you want me to drive? The hospital isn't far away."

"Can't go to the hospital," replied Chai, matter-of-factly, as he clambered into the driver's seat of the pickup. "They'll ask too many questions. What do you guys say about a tin of worms?"

Hobbs smiled. "A can of worms, mate. Let's at least get you back to our hotel, then. We'll stop at the pharmacy and get some supplies. Debs can play nurse. Come on, hop it. I'm driving. You don't want that seatbelt across those ribs - trust me."

Chai did as he was told and made his way gingerly around the back of the truck to the passenger side. Stirling laid a hand on his shoulder before they both climbed into the passenger side of the truck.

They drove in silence to begin with before Stirling decided to say what was dwelling on her mind.

"We'll understand if you don't want to be involved with this any more, Chai," she began. "You wouldn't be in this mess if it weren't for us. You've obviously got a target on your back now. God knows what they'll do to you next time. Then what? Who are you going to go to? The police?"

"No, Debs. This is clearly bigger than any of us thought. Anupong has something big to hide and if we believe Brother Bear, then he's in on things with the Ambassador. We need to crack this. Other girls could be in danger, if we don't."

Hobbs said, "I admire your bravery, mate, but you can't put yourself in any more danger than you have already. They could have killed you in there -they might next time. You've been invaluable to us throughout our time here but we can't have you risking life and limb," stated Hobbs, still keeping his eyes on the road.

"It's not just for you, though. It's for Ella," replied Chai, earnestly. "We made a promise that we would get these bastards, didn't we? We all did. So I'm not going to quit. We're going to find out what they are hiding and we are going to bring them all down. It's about time."

"Fair enough, mate," replied Hobbs. "That's the end of that, then. We're all all-in."

* * *

Back at Pong Phen, Chai sat on one of the chairs on Stirling's veranda while she tended to his wounds with cotton wool and iodine they picked up at a pharmacy down the street. Hobbs paced back and forth as she worked, ideas and theories whizzed through his mind as he began to chain-smoke what was left of his pack of cigarettes in-between large glugs of neat whisky which he had purchased from the bar for all three

CHAPTER 23

of them. It was a little early for neat spirits, but this was not a normal day, or week.

"What do you think, Chai?" asked Hobbs, stopping his pacing momentarily. "He's one of your countrymen. Do you think Brother Bear is telling the truth about Patterson? That's one hell of an accusation to be making."

"I don't know, Frank," replied Chai, as Stirling wound a thin bandage around his head to keep on the small patches of gauze she had applied to his various cuts and bruises. "Patterson is one of your countrymen. Do you really think he would murder his own daughter?"

"Me, personally, as a father of daughters, I just can't imagine it. Brother Bear's desperate. He's gone for the big lie. Maybe he's hoping we'll spend so much time looking into it that we'll have to head home before the case is solved. What do you think, Debs? You're awfully quiet."

"I don't know, Frank. I'm normally pretty good at reading people. He seemed genuinely upset at the identification. He looked like a bona-fide grieving parent."

Chai replied, "Yes, but Brother Bear looked genuinely terrified when he was giving us the name, too."

"That's true," replied Stirling, finishing up her repair job.

"Oh, I forgot to tell you," said Chai, going to stand up but then reeling from a jolt of pain from his ribs. "As they were dragging him away, he was shouting, *She knew something she shouldn't! She knew too much!* something like that."

That piqued both their interests.

"What did he mean?" probed Stirling.

"What else did he say?" quizzed Hobbs.

"I don't know," Chai replied. "They dragged him away."

"Shit!" swore Hobbs, beginning to pace back and forth,

once again. "That Anupong has got a lot to answer for. Dirty crooked bastard. Whether Brother Bear is telling the truth, or not, that prick has got his chubby little fingers in someone's pie."

"That's about all we can say for sure," said Stirling, as she tidied up the rubbish from Chai's repairs. "We need to take stock, figure out what we know, what we don't know and what we think we know."

Hobbs nodded. "If we want to know more about the Ambassador, we need to talk to the person who knows him best - his ex-wife. Did we manage to track her down, Chai?"

"Yes, we have her Facebook account and I have added her as a friend, but I didn't contact her yet."

"Let's set that up for as soon as possible, then, please. Yeah?"

Chai reached for his phone. "It might be tricky with the time difference, they're quite a few hours behind us. I'll see what I can do."

"Thanks, Chai. We need to find out if this man is capable of what he is being accused of."

"The other thing we need to find out," interjected Stirling, "is what it might have been that Ella knew about that was bad enough to get her killed over. Again, if Brother Bear is to be believed. If she did find out something, who would she have reached out to? Obviously, not her father."

"What about her mother?" posed Chai.

"I think she would have contacted the authorities if that were the case," replied Hobbs. "What about the friend, that she was going to visit? What was her name?"

"Ploy," replied Stirling, instantly. Hobbs was always impressed at his partner's ability to recall tiny details from the cases she was working on."

CHAPTER 23

"That's right. Maybe she was on her way to confide in her. Maybe she called or messaged her before she left Bangkok."

"In that case, she could also be in danger," blurted Stirling, the realisation hitting her like a tonne of bricks. "Did anyone contact her at the beginning of the investigation?"

Chai gingerly reached into his back pocket and took out his wrinkled notebook. He flipped through a few pages before tapping roughly with his index finger on some information he had written.

"She was contacted early on, but there was no answer on her mobile telephone, or the telephone number registered at the condo they own at the golf course."

"And nobody went to check on her?!" Stirling asked, her eyes wide with incredulity.

"I don't know," replied Chai, sheepishly. "I passed the information onto my colleagues at Kanchanaburi station."

"Shit," swore Hobbs, again. "That's not good. Did they get back to you about it?"

"No, it doesn't look like it."

"Did you not think that was strange?" quizzed Stirling.

"No. I mean, I don't know," Chai stuttered. "There was a lot going on. We had just found the body. You got attacked. There was a lot going on."

Chai was beginning to defend himself as Stirling got more and more worked up at the prospect of another young girl in danger.

Hobbs came quickly to his aid. "Hey, Debs. Easy, yeah?? We're all on the same team. Chai is right. A lot has been going on and those dickheads at the station were either too incompetent to follow up or, more likely, purposely didn't get back to him."

"You're right," Stirling conceded. "I'm sorry, Chai. Do you have the address there?"

"Yes, I have it right here."

"Then, let's get over there and see if she is there. Come on. I've got a bad feeling about this."

"I'll drive," stated Hobbs.

Chai threw him the keys.

* * *

The traffic was thankfully light as Hobbs drove frantically out of town towards the golf resort. Chai hastily contacted his colleague at the station for the address of the condominium that Ella's friend Ploy's family owned. He scribbled it down quickly on a notepad on his lap as the pickup traversed over potholes and speed bumps. Chai gave Hobbs directions as he raced towards their destination, not dissimilar to the way a co-driver directs their driver in a rally-car. Stirling held on tight to the hand hold above the passenger door in the rear as her heart raced as quickly as the vehicle she was travelling in.

The roadway drastically improved as they reached the golf resort and turned into a well-paved drive. Hobbs came to a screeching stop in front of the main entrance, clambering out of the cab and almost throwing the keys at a bemused valet in a maroon-coloured tropical suit with no collar. The trio moved quickly to the foyer and Chai thrust the piece of paper across the reception desk, trying to relay the information as succinctly as possible.

Thankfully, the staff at reception understood the gravity of the situation and quickly rifled through a cabinet of spare keys to find the one they needed to unlock the door of the

CHAPTER 23

condominium in question. Following the receptionist - a pretty, young local girl with bright-red lipstick, immaculately slicked back hair and a purple orchid in her button-hole, the group raced out the main entrance and jumped into a waiting golf cart which travelled as fast as it could towards a separate block along a smooth concrete path flanked by palms and succulents.

Arriving in the foyer of the condo block, Hobbs hammered impatiently at the call button for the lift. "Come on, come on, come on," he muttered to himself until the doors finally opened on the 8th floor. "Which apartment, Chai?"

"Number 801, there," he replied quickly as he strode down the hall towards the door of the condominium. Chai smoothed down his uniform, presumably out of habit, before knocking stoutly at the door. Hobbs, Stirling and the receptionist waited patiently for an answer. No answer came from behind the door.

Stirling's heart sank. She stepped forward and knocked again - a sharp, repeated knock. Still nothing. "Open the door,"she said sharply to the receptionist.

"I'm sorry. Resort policy states that we must try to contact the owner by phone before using our key - to see if they are home."

"We called a few days ago," Hobbs butted in. "The police called. Many times. There was no answer."

"I will call again now," replied the receptionist, courteously, before scrolling through her phone to find the number.

It was another anxious wait as the group listened to the dial tone drone on and on from the receptionist's phone that she held flat in her palm, on speaker phone. Hobbs began to hammer on the door, so hard that it seemed it might break.

He continued hammering as the phone call timed out. The receptionist placed the phone back into her pocket and pulled out the small key from her breast pocket. Just as she was about to insert the key into the lock, the door swung unexpectedly open.

Standing in the doorway was a bleary-eyed teenaged girl with messy long dark hair, dressed in lounge wear and sporting a pair of fluffy white slippers.

A wave of relief flooded through Stirling as she took in the scene in front of her of a confused young girl being greeted by a police officer who looked like he had done twelve rounds with Mike Tyson and two foreign visitors.

"Ploy?" asked Stirling, beaming with relief."

"Yes," replied the befuddled girl, rubbing her eyes.

"Oh, thank God, exclaimed Stirling. "My name is Debra Stirling from the Missing Persons Unit in London and these are my colleagues Frank Hobbs and Constable Chai from the Thai police. We're here helping with the investigation into the disappearance of your friend, Ella Patterson. We were concerned for your safety. So, we're very happy to see you."

A look between panic and embarrassment crossed the young girl's face and she looked towards Chai and the receptionist.

"I sorry, I don't understand. My English is not very well," she replied.

Hobbs and Stirling looked at each other, visibly confused, both thinking the same thing. They were told Ploy was a classmate of Ella's at a prestigious boarding school in Bangkok - from a wealthy family. How was it that she didn't speak English?

Chai began to engage the girl in Thai. Hobbs and Stirling

CHAPTER 23

obviously didn't understand, but she appeared to be shaking her head a lot and still appeared confused. The expression on Chai's face changed as he finished questioning the girl.

"What's going on, Chai mate?" asked Hobbs. "Is she Ploy?"

"Her name is Ploy, but she's not the Ploy we're looking for," replied Chai. She goes to a private school here in Kanchanaburi, not in Bangkok.

Stirling's heart sunk once again. "What do you mean? I don't understand," she remarked, placing her hands on her hips in disbelief. "This is the correct address, isn't it?"

Chai took out his notebook and handed it to the receptionist to check.

"The address is correct, but the family name is not. This family, *Sityodtong*, they live in Block D. This is Block C.

"Ask her if her surname is Sityodtong," barked Hobbs.

The receptionist was taken aback, not fully understanding the gravity of the situation, but did as she was told.

The girl shook her head.

"Shit, we *have* got the wrong Ploy," swore Hobbs, turning on his heel and heading quickly towards the lifts once again. The remainder of the group quickly followed, leaving the bemused teenager standing in her doorway.

The lift up to the eighth floor of the adjacent condominium block seemed to take an age.

"I must have misheard by colleague when I wrote down the address," remarked Chai as they all watched the numbers ascending on the console of the lift.

"That doesn't explain why that girl is also named Ploy, though," replied Stirling.

"It's a very common nickname, I'm afraid.

Stirling could feel the bile rising in her stomach. Her

face was flushing hot and she couldn't shake the feeling of impending doom flooding her mind from the dark depths of her soul. As the lift doors opened, she watched, in slow-motion, Hobbs and Chai break into a run towards the apartment they now knew to belong to Ploy Sityodtong. They hoped to find her alive and well, like the Ploy they had just woken from her nap. Stirling knew from the feeling of dread that coursed through her that wouldn't be the case.

She watched as Hobbs used his brute strength to kick open the apartment door. She watched as the three people in front of her instinctively turned their heads to the side as the smell from the home entered their nostrils. As Stirling arrived at the door, her feelings of dread were ratified. She had been unfortunate enough in her career to smell this particular smell on more than one occasion and it was unmistakeable. It was that of a decomposing body.

* * *

An hour later, Stirling was sat on the floor in the corridor opposite the lifts. Various officials busied backwards and forwards out of the condominium. A few local residents stood in their doorways with solemn faces. A local reporter, clearly with a local police officer in his pocket, snapped photos frantically as a grey body bag was wheeled out on a trolley towards the lift. Stirling hung her head in profound sorrow at the sight of another young girl she believed she had failed to save.

The body of Ploy Sityongtong was found by Chai in the en-suite bathroom of her bedroom in her parents' condominium. She was naked, submerged in the shallow water of her bathtub.

CHAPTER 23

The wounds on her wrists had turned the water a most-grisly crimson red.

Following the body, Hobbs emerged from the dwelling and seeing Stirling sitting by herself in the corridor, plopped himself down next to her in his usual ungainly fashion.

"How long has she been there?" asked Stirling in a voice that was little more than a squeak.

"Around a week, they reckon," replied Hobbs staring straight ahead at the lift doors. The conversation was brief, solemn.

"Before we even arrived, then?"

"Maybe, yeah…Probably."

"Suicide, they're saying?"

"Of course."

"But we don't believe that."

"Of course not."

"You know what we need to do now?"

"I don't know. Go home?"

Stirling shook her head. "We need to find Ella's phone."

Chapter 24

After a quick debrief with Chai about their thoughts on the demise of yet another innocent victim. The trio made their way back to the golf club reception to pick up the keys to the pickup that had been dutifully parked by the original valet. Chai gave the valet a small tip and asked after the whereabouts of the poor receptionist who had accompanied them on their search for Ploy. The valet gestured across the space to where she was sitting in one of the comfy chairs in the foyer area, being comforted by her colleagues. The three made a point of thanking her and bidding her farewell which she reciprocated tearfully.

In the vehicle, Chai leafed through his notebook to earlier in the week where he had noted down the address of the family that had originally found Ella's body. It seemed such a long time ago and so much had happened since. Just watching Chai leaf so far back to the start of his notebook made Hobbs feel like they were going right back to square one in their investigation. He thought of the conversation he had earlier with Stirling. Maybe she was right, maybe it was time they called it a day. They had seen too much loss of life, too much bloodshed. He hoped that Ploy had been killed before they even arrived in Thailand. He hoped that their presence in

CHAPTER 24

the country had not directly or indirectly led to her death. He couldn't be sure. He caught a glimpse of his reflection in the wing mirror of the pickup. *I look like shit*, he thought to himself. He glanced backwards at his partner in the rear seat. She looked worse. He hated to see her like that. He had always admired her for her excellent work, her fastidious nature and her tenacious attitude. She really looked a shadow of her former self. Yes, maybe it was time to go home.

Hobbs' thoughts were interrupted by the ringtone of his mobile phone in his pocket. The country code +44 was displayed in front of the number.

"Looks like the office is calling," he remarked to Stirling via the rear-view mirror but she continued to stare morosely out of the window at the rows of palm trees that lined the roadside.

Hobbs answered the phone with a less-than-cheerful *hello*.

"Hi, Frank. Can you hear me? It's Yvonne. How are you?"

"I'm fine, Guv. Reading you loud and clear. What's up?"

"I was just seeing how you two are doing and making sure you're all set for your return flight tomorrow."

"Yes, we're OK, Guv. It's been an eventful week - a tough week, to be honest - we found another body today. A friend of Ella's."

"Oh, Gosh. How awful. It sounds like you will be glad to get home."

Hobbs hesitated.

"Yes, I think we will. I think it's about time we called it a day."

The telephone conversation was abruptly interrupted as Stirling, like a Jack-in-the box, sprung forward and swiped the phone from Hobbs' hand.

"Yvonne, it's Debra," she began, suddenly invigorated. "I need you to get Celia to change our flight. We can't come back yet. We're not done."

There was a palpable silence on the other end of the phone. It appeared the British Detective Inspector was in a similar state of shock to Hobbs.

Finally, Harding stammered her reply down the line. "Oh. Hi, Debra. I'm not so sure that's a good idea. I've spoken to the top brass here and they agree that you two have already gone above and beyond for Ella and the Ambassador. It appears they have spoken to the authorities there and the Ambassador about the accident. They feel that you have done more than enough and you may even be beginning to outstay your welcome."

"I'm not surprised they said that, Yvonne. We need to fill you in on what we have found out so far. Things have progressed quickly, so we haven't had a chance yet. We're also not sure who we can trust. This has to go no further for the minute. Can I trust you with this information, Yvonne?"

Harding seemed to be taken aback by the sudden role-reversal. Stirling was being unusually assertive; overly assertive, in fact."This is all highly abnormal, Debra, and to be honest, I'm not sure this is appropriate."

"Just listen, OK?" Chai shot Hobbs a look across from the driver's seat as he began to pull away from the car park of the golf resort. Hobbs acknowledged it with an awkward smile and wondered what had possessed his partner to speak to his superior in such a fashion.

"We have reason to believe that Ella's death was not an accident. We have a confession from Win Nyan Bo that he did indeed push Ella to her death and he was paid by a local

CHAPTER 24

man. This local man has confessed to arranging the murder at the behest of another individual."

"I see. And just who might that be?"

"Well, Ma'am, there is a possibility that it may have been Richard Patterson, the Ambassador, himself."

There was a silence from the other end of the phone though it was nothing to do with the physical distance between the two people engaged in the conversation.

Finally, Yvonne Harding broke said silence. "You can't be serious, Debra. That's one of the most ridiculous things I've heard in a long time."

"We're struggling to believe it ourselves, Ma'am. In fact, we don't know if it is true, at all. We haven't had the time to investigate the claim yet."

"Why would the man invite you all the way over there, knowing your calibre as detectives, to try and find out what happened to his daughter, only for you to name him as the killer? It just doesn't make sense, Debra."

"We know that, Ma'am. Believe me, we know that. We just need more time to figure this out. If the Ambassador is guilty, we'll find out why and if he isn't, we'll find out who is. Please, Ma'am. We just need more time."

There was another long pause on the other end of the phone as Harding tried to process the information she was hearing from the other side of the world. Hobbs looked expectedly at Stirling from the rear-view mirror, trying to gauge what was happening from the look on his partner's face.

"I'm sorry, Debra. It's just not doable from our end. It would be totally against protocol and those on-high will throw a fit. I'm going to have to ask you both to come back on your scheduled flight to London. Let the Thai police handle it from here. I'm sorry, Debra. It's just not possible."

Stirling shook her head in disappointment.

"Pass me the phone, Debs," said Hobbs, holding out his oversized paw behind him. Stirling shrugged and handed him the phone, slumping back in her seat, defeated. Hobbs put the call onto speaker phone for all to hear. "Yvonne? Hi, it's Frank. With all due respect, we're going to be a little late back to work. We've got unfinished business over here and, as much as I would like to be somewhere where I don't have to powder my balls every morning to stave off the chafe, we're going to stick around to finish it."

After a brief pause of incredulity, Harding replied, "Detective Hobbs. Never in all my years have I…"

"If this can't be official business," Hobbs interrupted, "then you'll have to suspend us, put us on desk duties, gardening leave, whatever you want to call it. Blame Debra's assault, if you want. Do whatever you need to do, Guv, 'coz we're not coming back 'til the job is done. We are Missing Persons. We find missing people and we bring them home. We couldn't bring Ella home, as much as it pains me to say it. But, we can find out what happened to her. We owe her that and that's what we're going to do. We're so close, Guv, honestly. We'll be back before you know it." Chai shot Stirling a glance over his shoulder that was a mixture of surprise and admiration.

On the other end of the phone, Yvonne Harding was inwardly seething, but she knew there was nothing she could do, other than having the two arrested, to get them on that plane back to London. "OK, Frank. I get it. I'm not happy about it, but I get it. I'll try and spin the line about Debra's assault and how she's not fit to fly; buy you some time, maybe a week. But after that, I'm going to have to suspend you. Call this fair warning, both of you."

"Roger that, Guv," replied Hobbs with a sigh of relief.

"Now, fill me in what you've got so far."

Hobbs, with the help of Stirling's timely interjections, spent the next few minutes reeling off all that had transpired in the days previous. Harding was brought up to speed on Win Nyan Bo's confession, Brother Bear's shocking accusation and the most recent body of another young girl who had been caught up in their sprawling mystery.

"So, that's where we are, Guv," Hobbs remarked as he brought his summary to a close. "We're currently on the way to speak to the local family who found Ella's body. It's imperative that we find Ella's phone. It's been missing so far, but it could be the key to all of this, especially seeing the probable murder of Ella's poor friend, Ploy."

"Right, well I better let you two get on with it, otherwise it'll be me that'll be sent off to a foreign country next," remarked Harding, only half-joking. "This is all off the books now. You understand that, don't you? You won't have the help of the local police and I'm sure they won't be happy with you sniffing around, either. I'll see if you can keep your assistant and translator, but I can't promise anything. He might have to head back to Bangkok sooner rather than later, so I would get a move on, if I were you."

"Yes, Ma'am. We'll keep you updated, Ma'am," chirped Stirling from the back seat.

"Be sure that you do," Harding replied. "But nothing by E-Mail, or text, please. I don't want any of this in black and white. Just call me when you've got something. Take care, both of you. I'll be in even more trouble if you end up coming back to London on a repatriation flight." And with that, Harding ended the call.

* * *

Hobbs pulled up the pickup in front of the house of the family who had found Ella's body a few days earlier. A cloud of white dust emanated from the gravel that covered the area in front of the very modest dwelling. It was a timber house, raised above the ground by concrete pilings which made the house effectively on stilts. Under the house was concreted roughly and furnished only with a large wooden piece of furniture which was somewhere between a table and a bench. Two ageing table-top fans with dust-covered blades whirred and oscillated in the afternoon heat. A threadbare hammock was strung up between two of the supporting pillars, upon which were tacked different yellowing pictures of the Thai royal family and what appeared to be fading calendars from years gone by. A set of rickety steps rose up to the main floor of the house where recycled promotional banners for KFC and DTAC mobile services acted as external curtains. A rusted blue Toyota pickup, which had seen better days, sat languishing under a lean-to shelter which was peppered with holes.

Chai stepped carefully out of the passenger side of the car, kicking out at the snout of a curious stray dog who had come to welcome the visitors. In the absence of a doorbell, and as is customary in Thailand, Chai shouted loudly to find out if anyone was home.

Hobbs and Stirling stepped out of vehicle and looked up at the house, shielding their eyes from the harsh sunlight and gravel dust which still hung in the still humid air. Sounds of

CHAPTER 24

bare feet on floorboards and hushed whispering signalled that there was indeed someone home, yet they seemed reluctant to greet their unannounced visitors.

After a minute or so, a man emerged from the house, padding quickly down the wooden stairs with his hands raised in the traditional *wai* greeting. Chai returned the greeting and the man's wife also emerged, following her husband down the stairs. After a perfunctory exchange of greetings, a school-aged girl exited the dwelling but chose to sit and spectate from the top of the stairs.

Neither of the homeowners spoke English, so Chai spoke in Thai and relayed the information to Hobbs and Stirling who were subtly edging towards an area of shade under an impressive mango tree at the corner of the house. Though they couldn't understand what was being said, it was clear that Chai was being rather curt and forward with his questioning. The couple were mostly quiet, with the husband doing the majority of the talking and the wife merely gesticulating towards their daughter at the top of the stairs and out across the rice fields towards the railway track.

"They have confirmed that they are the family that found the body - their daughter, in fact. I asked them whether they have since found Ella's bag, and in particular, her phone, but they still say that they haven't."

"Could you ask them if we could see their phones, please?" asked Stirling as politely as possible, while beads of sweat began to roll down her neck saturating the collar of her cotton shirt.

Chai relayed the request and the couple acquiesced, climbing the stairs to retrieve their devices. Chai took the opportunity to stretch out his aching body. He winced as he twisted his torso, left and right, feeling gingerly at his ribs.

"You need to get those ribs looked at, mate," remarked Hobbs, taking out his handkerchief and mopping his brow.

"I will. When this is all taken care of," Chai replied, as stoic as ever.

"What type of phone did Ella have, do we know?" asked Hobbs.

"An iPhone X, latest model," replied Stirling, as quick as a flash. "There were plenty of posts on her Instagram and Facebook, showing it off earlier in the year."

After a couple of minutes, the couple came down the stairs from the house, clutching their mobile devices. They handed them to Chai, who in turn handed them to Hobbs and Stirling while he continued to question them. Both phones appeared to be Android devices. One an almost obsolete Samsung and another a brand that neither of the detectives had heard of - Vivo. Both had cracks running through the screen protectors. The husband's phone sported a red and white Manchester United emblem as its background picture while the wife's showed a picture, presumably of their daughter, in a pretty white dress at what appeared to be a local wedding.

Stirling smiled at the picture and then at the mother who returned a nervous smile. Stirling was just about to return the phone, when she noticed something about the picture on the home screen. She squinted to get a better look.

"Hold this a second, Frank. Chai, tell her she needs to unlock the phone and get me the original picture of this home screen." The men did as they were told, while Stirling fumbled in her shoulder bag for her own phone. A few seconds, that felt like an age, later Stirling turned her own phone to Hobbs and Chai.

CHAPTER 24

"Take a look at the bracelet in this picture and tell me it doesn't match the bracelet that young lady is wearing in that picture," she remarked, triumphant.

Hobbs and Stirling squinted in the sun, angling both the screens to avoid the glare. The husband and wife team looked at each other, a look of pure fear flashed across their faces. They certainly didn't know what was going on, but they seemed to know they were in trouble.

"Debra Stirling does it again," exclaimed Hobbs. They must have found Ella's bag, after all, and I'm guessing her phone, too."

Chai turned the phones around to face the couple who were now resigned to their fate. The little girl at the top of the stairs was now conspicuous in her absence. Chai didn't have to say anything before the couple began to explain themselves.

"They said they're very sorry. They did find Ella's bag - not the day her body was found, but a day later. They were telling the truth that day but when they found it the next day and nobody had come back to ask for it, they decided to keep it. Wait for everything to, how do you say? *Blow over*? and then sell it, if they could."

Hobbs and Stirling looked over at the couple. A look of helplessness and guilt was etched across both of their faces.

"We sorry," said the woman in broken English. "We no have money. We sorry."

Hobbs shook his head. He couldn't help but feel sorry for the couple. It would have been a moral dilemma for anyone, but it had put them so far behind in their investigation.

"Where is the phone now?" he asked, putting aside his feelings, for a moment.

Chai asked the question and the mother called up in a

shriek to her daughter who appeared at the doorway looking very apprehensive. Her mother nodded in reassurance and a moment later, she trudged down the stairs and placed the phone in Chai's hand.

Chai said something in remonstration to the family which was met with a chorus of high *wais* before turning on his heel and heading back to the pickup. Hobbs and Stirling quickly followed suit, clambering into the vehicle and into the relative luxury of the air-conditioning.

"I assume it's got security on it," remarked Hobbs after struggling to fasten his seatbelt across his oversized frame.

"Of course," replied Chai, taking a couple of long-shot attempts at commonly-used PINs but not so many as to lock the phone. He had to assume that the family, or at least the daughter, had already tried at some point in the last week.

"Any way we can get past the security?" posed Stirling, from the back seat.

"There's always a way, but we're not welcome at the station here any more."

"What about your colleagues in Bangkok?"

"Yes, we could send it there, but it will take time and it will probably get back to Kanchanaburi one way or another, especially if we do it officially."

"What do you suggest then?"

"This is Thailand. If you have money, you can get anything. I know a guy. Drop me off in town and I'll see what I can do. It's not going to be cheap, though."

"Don't worry about that, Chai," Hobbs interjected. "We'll sort you out. I'll stick it on the expenses when we get home."

"Good luck with that," scoffed Stirling.

CHAPTER 24

* * *

After a quick stop at the ATM to withdraw the cash needed for their clandestine activities and a roadside stop for Chai to quickly change into civilian clothes, Hobbs dropped Chai off outside a nondescript building housing a few small mobile phone and computer repair shops. He waved a quick goodbye as he limped towards one of the shop fronts that was almost covered by a faded vinyl banner advertising the many mobile phone brands it catered for.

Stirling performed a graceful step-through to transition from the rear of the vehicle to the front, swiftly buckling her seatbelt in seemingly one motion.

"Oi! Debra Stirling. Watch the seats." rebuked Hobbs as he pulled away into the busy street.

"I think Chai has bigger things to worry about at the moment than a few footprints on his seat, Frank," Stirling replied, after blowing a rogue ringlet of red hair off her now darkly-freckled forehead. "Where to next?"

"Back to the hotel, I reckon - rest, regroup. Try and make some sense of all this. There's not a lot we can do until Chai manages to break the security on that phone and this stuff Brother Bear said about the Ambassador has been frying my noggin, to be honest."

"Me too, Frankie. I just don't get it. A father having his own daughter killed? It just doesn't make sense to me. What do you think? You're a father. A father to teenaged girls, too."

"I can't see it, either. It wouldn't matter what either of my two had done. I couldn't do that. That goes for any parent, doesn't it? Even the parents of serial killers still love their kids, don't they?"

"So you think Brother Bear is clutching at straws? He's desperate?"

"He could be. It's been known before. Christ, we've seen it, down on the estates. People who can see the writing on the wall will throw anyone under the bus to save their own skin, sometimes."

"What was it Chai said Brother Bear was shouting as they hauled him away? Something about Ella knowing too much?"

"Something like that. What do you reckon to that?"

Stirling shook her head and yawned a yawn so wide she felt like her face might turn inside-out. "I don't know, Frankie. I just don't know. What could possibly be so bad that he'd have his own daughter killed?"

Stirling's yawn was contagious and soon Hobbs was himself opening his mouth like a giant bear. He rubbed his face with a giant paw, opening his eyes wide to keep his attention on the busy road ahead of him.

"We'll be back at the hotel soon. Let's get a decent meal inside of us and a nap. I don't think we're solving any cases in our current state."

Stirling nodded. "Drive on, Driver," she said, grabbing Chai's police hat from the back seat and placing it on her own head, low enough to cover her eyes. She nestled herself back into the seat and folded her arms bracing herself against the cool chill of the air conditioning. "I'm going to have my nap now."

Hobbs feigned a two-fingered salute. "Yes, Ma'am."

Chapter 25

Hobbs was woken from his nap by a soft tapping on the door to his bungalow at Pong Phen guest house. Bleary-eyed and scratching at the coarse stubble that had grown around his new goatee, he lumbered over to the door. He opened the door to see Stirling silhouetted against the dying light of the day.

"Sorry, Frank. Did I wake you?" she asked.

"Nah, you're alright. Not sure I got to sleep really. All this stuff spinning around in my head. What's up?"

"Chai called. He said he messaged you, but you didn't reply. So, you must have got some sleep, after all."

Hobbs let out a long yawn. His head throbbed and he felt groggy from his nap.

"Did he manage to crack the phone?" he quizzed.

"Not yet. He's still working on it. In the meantime, he has set us up on a Skype call with Ella's mother in ten minutes."

"Oh, right, bugger. OK, I'll get myself sorted then," Hobbs remarked, running a hand through his thinning hair and noticing his state of semi-undress as he stood in the doorway in his vest and boxer shorts.

Stirling chuckled. "I'll set up my laptop on the veranda. Should be private enough. If not, we'll head inside."

"Rightio," replied Hobbs. "See you in a few."

It had taken a while to track down Ella's mother at her new home in Denmark. Stirling wondered if it had been an oversight by the local police, or another intended hurdle put in their way by the powers that be. Either way, she knew it was important to speak to her. If anyone knew whether Richard Patterson was capable of what Brother Bear had alleged, it would be Ella's mother.

Stirling checked back through her notes while she waited for Hobbs to freshen up. Ella's mother's full name was Anchalee Jitpracharoen but she thankfully went by the much easier-to-pronounce 'Anne'. Her notes stated that she and Patterson were divorced a few years previously and Ella had stayed in Thailand to finish her studies while her mother lived in Denmark with her new husband. She didn't have a name for him, she noticed.

Within a few minutes and right on time, for once, Hobbs appeared. Now fully clothed, he appeared in a greater state of readiness for the important call. Stirling checked the email address that Chai had sent after their call and added Ella's mother as a contact. Hobbs took his place on a seat next to Stirling and she hit the call button. After a few seconds, the call was answered. After the mandatory greetings and tech-check, Stirling cut straight to the chase.

"Hi, this is Debra Stirling and Frank Hobbs, calling you from Thailand. We've been looking into the disappearance and subsequent death of your daughter. Can we just say that we are so sorry about what's happened and we are doing all we can to find out who is responsible."

"Thank you. When I spoke to the Thai police man, Khun

CHAPTER 25

Chai. He said you've both been working hard. I'm sorry. I'm not sure what you mean by 'responsible'. We were told it was an accident."

Ella's mother's English seemed good; not fluent, by any means, and she spoke with the normal Thai accent but both detectives were getting more and more used to it the longer they spent in the Kingdom.

"That's what we originally believed, Ms. Jitpracharoen."

"Please, call me Anne, and it's Nilsson now. I remarried here in Denmark."

"Sorry, Anne. Yes. That's my mistake. During our investigations, we have had reason to believe that Ella's death was not an accident. We managed to track down and interrogate a Burmese national who has admitted pushing Ella from the train, causing her death. However, he maintains that he was paid by another man; a Thai national, to kill Ella."

There was a pause on the other end of the line.

"Anne, are you there?"

"Yes, I'm here. Sorry."

"No, I'm sorry. This is all so terribly impersonal. Perhaps it would be better if we turned on our video?"

"OK. Just a moment."

Stirling searched for the button to turn on her video. On the screen, Ella's mother's image appeared. It was clear that she had been crying. Her mascara appeared to be running and bags under her eyes hinted at many a recent sleepless night. Other than this, and despite her age, she was clearly a beautiful woman; with high, angled cheekbones, impossibly straight dark hair and beautifully smooth skin, bar a few crow's feet at the corners of her dark eyes. Stirling could see where Ella's beauty had come from and imagined how beautiful her mother must have been at her age. She felt a pang of sadness at the thought that Ella would never grow up to become a woman, a mother, a grandmother.

Ella's mother continued the conversation. "So, this man, this animal, that wanted her dead. Has he been caught?"

"He has, Anne. He has."

"And why? Did he say why? What could our poor little Elly Belly have done to deserve that?"

"Well, that's why we needed to talk to you, Anne. We have something to ask you and, well, it's highly unusual and, well, very hard to believe."

"OK."

Stirling glanced sideways at Hobbs, who took that as his cue to take over.

"Well, Anne," he began. "As my partner said, this isn't going to be a very nice thing to hear. So, I do want you to be prepared. Is your husband there? Someone who can support you once you've finished talking with us?"

"Umm, yes. He's in the garage at the moment, changing the tyres on the car."

"OK, so…during the process of our investigation. The man that Detective Stirling mentioned, he made quite an accusation. He alleges that he was also paid for his part in your daughter's murder."

"So he was a middle-man?"

"Yes, so he says."

"Did he say who it was that ordered him to…"

"Yes, he did. Now, this is the thing that is going to be difficult to hear, Anne. This man alleges that it was your ex-husband, Ella's father, Richard Patterson that paid him to organise the murder."

CHAPTER 25

The grieving mother on the other side of the world was suddenly and eerily still. It looked as though it could have been a technical glitch, a lag in the Internet, but as the curtains in the background swayed slowly, it was clear that the poor lady was in a deep state of shock. Hobbs paused a moment before continuing.

"Anne, are you OK? I know it's a lot to take in."

"Sorry, yes," she replied before her head bowed in a cascade of tears.

"I'm sorry to ask you this, and I don't want to keep you any longer than is necessary, but do you think your ex-husband, Richard Patterson, is capable, or has any reason to do something like this?"

Ella's mother was quiet once again. She shook her head.

"No, detectives. Richard is not a perfect man. I know that. There's a reason we're not married, but murder? No. And our Elly? I can't believe that."

Hobbs paused again, giving the grieving lady time to process what she had been told and time to scribble a quick note to his partner: 'Elly?' Stirling nodded and shrugged her shoulders, indicating that she, too, had noticed Ella's mother referring to her as 'Elly' rather than 'Ella'. Hobbs decided to ask the question.

"Forgive my curiosity, Anne, but I noticed that you seem to call your daughter Elly, where Mr Patterson calls her Ella."

"Oh, yes, sorry. She has always been Elly to us, to me and my husband Mads. Our little Elly Belly. Richard always called her Ella. He said Elly sounds silly. I'm not sure what she calls herself these days. We don't see her much. I guess you know that."

Stirling remembered Ella's Instagram handle:@ellybelly20

03, it hadn't occurred to her at the time that Ella might go by a slightly different name.

"I see. Well, Anne. As I said, we are doing everything we can to find out what happened to your daughter. If there's anything else you can think of, or if you change your mind about anything, anything at all. Please do let us know. You said your husband is there to support you?"

"Yes, he's here. He's just coming now."

From behind the computer in Denmark, a male figure appeared. Ella's mother ushered him over and he pulled up a chair beside her. He introduced himself as Mads Nilsson, from near Copenhagen in Denmark. Stirling couldn't help but notice he was a strikingly handsome man, despite his age. He still had most of his hair, though it was cropped short. He sported a fine stubble which was greying in parts and matched the salt and pepper grey flecks behind his temples. But the most striking thing was only revealed when he removed his glasses. Behind his thin, horn-rimmed spectacles hid a pair of dazzling hazel-green eyes.

Hobbs and Stirling exchanged another knowing glance. One of surprise, one of recognition, one of understanding. Hobbs raised his eyebrows and Stirling nodded back - a conversation held entirely in the body language of a two people who had worked together for a very long time.

Given the nod of confirmation, Hobbs posed his final question. "Just before we go, Mr and Mrs Nilsson, when were you going to tell us that Richard Patterson isn't Ella's father?"

There was a palpable pause in the conversation as the couple in Denmark seemingly recovered from the shock of the jarring question posed by Hobbs. He had not intended it to be so accusatory in tone, but he knew that he and Stirling were running out of time, and favour, with which to solve this case. He had seen it time and time again in his line of work; fear of shame resulting in reticence, particularly from those close to a missing person, to divulge the entire truth. Running an investigation based on half-truths and, at times, blatant lies, very rarely resulted in success.

Mads Nilsson spoke first. "I'm sorry, Detectives. We had decided between us that our daughter's paternity wasn't particularly relevant to your investigation. What, with it being deemed an accident in the first instance."

Nilsson's English was excellent, with only the hint of a Scandinavian accent. It reminded Stirling of the Danish and Norwegian detective series she habitually binged on Friday evenings with only her loyal cat and a bottle of Chilean red for company. She opted for a more conciliatory tone in her questioning, realising that the important thing was to get the information from this couple, rather than admonishment. "Well, the important thing is that it is out in the open now and we would appreciate *anything* you can tell us, whether you feel it pertinent, or not, that may assist us in our investigation."

The couple both breathed a visible sigh of relief. Stirling could tell it was a secret that they had harboured for more years than they should have and had become a burden.

"Yes, of course," replied Nilsson, replacing his spectacles and shifting for a more comfortable position in his chair. "Again, our apologies, Detectives. It has never been our intention to deceive anyone. We simply wanted what was best for Elly - sorry, Ella."

"You can call her Elly, Mr Nilsson. That's absolutely fine," replied Stirling, placatingly.

Hobbs, taking a back seat in a witness interview was somewhat of a rarity. It was normally his job to do the social smoothing, putting people at ease to try and squeeze as much information from them as possible. Now, he realised, Stirling had taken over the mantle and although the apparent role reversal had taken him by surprise, he was happy to see a new side to his partner and a new string to her bow as an investigator.

As he watched the grieving parents through the webcam from the other side of the world, he reflected inwardly. A missing persons investigation was just that - deeply personal. There are many reasons why a person may go missing, but the majority, if not all, are as a result of personal relationships breaking down - a teenager being kicked out by their parents, someone turning to drugs in an attempt to deal with a childhood trauma, a victim of domestic abuse finally having the courage to leave their partner and begin a healthier, happier life. Hobbs didn't yet know what had occurred in this particular case, but it was always prudent to delve deeper into the complex relationships of this particular family.

Hobbs was more than happy for Stirling to continue with her line of questioning. "One of the big questions is," Stirling continued "does Mr Patterson know that he isn't the father?"

"He does now, yes." Nilsson replied. "But only recently, Ms Stirling. When was it? Some weeks earlier, not more than two months?" He turned to his wife for confirmation. "Yes, six or seven weeks ago, possibly."

Hobbs made a note in his notebook while Stirling continued. "I see, and how did he take the news?"

"Not very well, unfortunately. We hadn't intended to tell him, it just sort of happened. He called Anne on the telephone.

CHAPTER 25

He was very anxious. He appeared to be quite drunk. He wasn't making much sense. He said that he wanted Ella to come to Denmark to finish her studies. He was very busy and didn't have time for her. It seemed he was under a lot of pressure, maybe from work."

"And what was your response?"

"Naturally, we were surprised. The plan had always been for Elly to finish her studies there in Bangkok. She was at a wonderful school. It was all paid for by the Embassy. Had she come here, she would have to transfer to a Danish state school. We just didn't see how that was good for Elly."

"I see, how did he react to this?"

"Well, he completely lost his mind. It was awful, especially for my wife. He launched into a tirade of abuse and insults towards her. I don't care to repeat them now for fear of upsetting her further but they pertained to her previous life and occupation. But Anne, well, she was very upset by this and began to get angry herself. There was a heated argument. Richard started to say that he had never wanted to have children and that Anne had tricked him into it. Well, that's when Anne really lost her cool and then, well, the secret was out."

Anne Nilsson began to sob quietly. Her husband placed a comforting arm around her shoulder and kissed her gently on the top of the head. He spoke something softly in Danish, which neither Hobbs nor Stirling could understand.

"Thank you, Mr Nilsson, for the information. I know it must be very difficult. The other thing we must ask is, did Ella - Elly - know that you were her father? Did you ever tell her?"

"No. We never told her. That's something I personally

regret now, more than ever, but we believed at the time it was the best thing for her. Richard had raised her well, provided for her, especially since Anne came here to Denmark to live. She was happy. We didn't want to potentially ruin that for her. We saw her in the summers and we had the most wonderful times. She loved me as her stepfather. That was enough for me."

A solitary tear rolled down Nilsson's cheek and he removed his glasses to wipe it, revealing to the camera once again his dazzling hazel-green eyes. Only this time, the eyes were tainted with sorrow and grief; grief for a daughter that never got to call him *Dad*. Stirling suddenly felt like she would be overcome by a wave of emotion. Tears began to well in her own eyes and she found herself wringing her hands under the table.

Hobbs, noticing this, decided it was his turn to continue the questioning. There was only really one more question that needed to be asked. "Do you think there was any way that Ella, sorry, Elly, could have found out about her paternity? A family friend letting the cat out of the bag? An online DNA test, perhaps?"

The couple both shook their heads. "No, definitely not from family friends," Nilsson responded confidently. "We never told a soul and nobody ever hinted to us that they might know. About the DNA test, I don't know. It's possible, I suppose. But, she never mentioned anything to us. I think she would have said something. Don't you, Anne?"

Anne Nilsson nodded her head and smiled a smile that was full of sorrow. "She always told us everything. We were very close. I know that sounds strange. She was in Thailand, we were in Denmark, but it's true. We were very close." She

CHAPTER 25

began to sob again and Nilsson wrapped his arms around her once more as she broke down.

Stirling nodded to Hobbs. It was time to leave the poor couple to their misery. They didn't need their grief to be beamed across the world to a pair of strangers.

Hobbs broke the awkward scene by saying, "Thank you, Mr and Mrs Nilsson. We have all the information we need for now."

The couple separated their embrace and Anne wiped the tears from both eyes with the backs of her hands. "Thank you, Detectives. Thank you for everything you are doing. We need to find out what happened to our baby," she replied with a snivel.

"We promise you. We'll do everything we can. We'll be in touch, here on Skype, if there is anything else we need to ask you. Take care now, both of you."

The couple thanked the detectives and Hobbs ended the call. In unison, they slumped back in their chairs and a duet of sighs echoed from their cheeks.

"That was a tough one," remarked Hobbs, turning to his partner.

Stirling closed the lid of her laptop, symbolically ending the interview and puffed, almost to herself, "There's never an easy one."

Chapter 26

Hobbs and Stirling had agreed that for a brief thirty minutes over dinner they wouldn't talk about the case. They had been there a week and, with all that had gone on, they were exhausted - not only physically, but mentally. Stirling picked away at a plate of *pad see-ew* - rice noodles stir-fried in soy sauce. Hobbs couldn't decide between rice and noodles, so ordered both. They sat and spoke about anything but the case they were working on: Brexit, of course, the drone debacle at Gatwick airport and the sacking of Manchester United boss, Jose Mourinho. For the latter, Stirling mostly just listened and nodded where she thought appropriate. She had never been much into sport.

Once their plates had been cleared away, they ordered drinks and retired to a more private end of the restaurant where they could converse without being overheard.

"So, where are we, Frankie?" Stirling asked, before taking the first swig of a large gin and tonic that had just arrived at their table.

"Well, my dear Debra. Let's take stock, shall we? Our Skype conversation this evening was very enlightening but still doesn't help me in figuring out whether Richard Patterson could have done what Brother Bear said he has done. What's

CHAPTER 26

your take on it?"

"I'm about as clueless as you. Anne doesn't seem to think him capable. She was pretty sure about that."

"She was. But, that stuff about the phone call, the argument. That was a bit weird, wasn't it? They said he was really wound up about something, really stressed out.What do you think that was about?"

"I don't know. But, it was enough for him to want to ship Ella back to Denmark."

Hobbs took a long draw from his bottle of Leo beer. "Must have had something on his mind to get drunk and call his ex-wife for a shouting match."

"Right. But, it wasn't the fact that he found out he wasn't Ella's father, because we've established he didn't know before that conversation. He was going off the deep end before receiving that bombshell."

"That's not enough of a motive for murder though, is it? If I found out one of my girls wasn't mine, I wouldn't take it out on them. The wife, though, that's a different story."

Stirling afforded him a wry smile. "So, what are we saying? Brother Bear is lying? I mean, they do say that if you're going to lie then make it a big one, but that's taking the biscuit."

"I don't know, Debs. We both said there was something off about his behaviour when we arrived."

"Yeah, we did. But, we both know that people process these things in different ways. We both said that, too."

Hobbs let out a hefty sigh and shook his head. "Yeah, we did. Jesus, Debs. We're going round in circles here. This is driving me nuts."

"Look. Let's forget about what we *think* happened and focus on the evidence, shall we? That's what investigations are built on, not hearsay and whodunnit hunches."

"Yeah, you're right. Chai will be back soon enough. He's a good man and he's invested. I don't think he's coming back without having cracked that phone. Did he tell you he's taking leave to stay down here and see this through?"

"He didn't say he was taking leave but he said he would be sticking around for a few days."

"Well, if I know Chai, he knows as well as we do that that phone could be the key to all of this. He won't rest until he cracks it. Let's just hope it doesn't fall into the hands of the local boys in brown before it gets to us."

"Cheers to that," replied Stirling raising her glass to Hobbs'. "I'm sure he'll be here any minute."

It transpired that Stirling had been a little too optimistic in her estimations of when Chai would arrive. Minutes turned into hours and the guest house began to wind down. The pool was empty, the car park full. Lights from inside the bungalows began to shut off, one-by-one, as the guests began to retire for the evening.

Hobbs and Stirling had been nursing the same drinks for over an hour when the waiting staff came and informed them that they too would be going to bed.

"I guess we should call it a night," remarked Stirling, stretching her arms to the ceiling in a long yawn.

"I guess so," replied Hobbs, checking his watch. It was nearly eleven; way past the bedtime of this sleepy tourist town on the banks of the Kwae River. As they rose from their seats, they noticed a pair of headlights coming down the small road that led to the guest house and a small cloud of dust being kicked up by the tyres of a police pick-up.

"Here he is," exclaimed Hobbs. "Right on time".

CHAPTER 26

The pair tucked in their chairs and quickly placed their empty glasses and bottles on the bar before hurrying over to the car park where Chai was parking up. Chai threw them both a quick *wai* before closing the car door behind him.

"Well?" Stirling asked in anticipation.

"We got it!" Chai announced in weary triumph.

Hobbs punched the air in celebration. "Yes! Chai, mate. We knew you could do it!" he exclaimed, putting a rough arm around Chai's shoulders. Chai winced in pain.

"Shit, sorry! I forgot all about your ribs, mate, you were gone so long."

"It's OK, Frank," Chai replied with a pained smile. "Here. I managed to crack it, but I haven't looked inside. I thought I would leave that to you two."

"Don't you want to know what's on it?" asked Stirling, amazed at his restraint.

Chai chuckled. "I do. But, what I want more right now is a shower, some paracetamol and a comfy bed. We can't do anything tonight and I'll only lose sleep if I know what's on it. Let me know the plan in the morning."

"Alright, mate," replied Hobbs, shaking Chai by the hand - gently this time. "Great work today. This could be the key to all of this, you know?"

"Let's hope so," Chai replied. "Good night, Debs. See you tomorrow."

Chai climbed slowly and purposely into the driver's seat before firing up the engine and making his way slowly down the road away from the guest house.

Clutching the mobile phone in both hands, Stirling powered on the phone and the Apple logo shone like a beacon through the dim of the car park. "Let's find somewhere to sit down, shall we?" she said, not taking her eyes off the boot screen. They shuffled together past the bar-restaurant and found themselves sitting on a pair of empty sun loungers at the side of the deserted pool. An eerie, shimmering glow emanated from the pool lights which were left on throughout the night. Ella's home screen appeared on the phone, with no security steps present. The picture was the very same one they had been given at the beginning of the investigation - the same image that had featured in Hobbs' nightmare at 30,000 feet en-route to their destination - a pretty teenaged girl, beaming from ear-to ear in her school uniform. A popular young lass with her whole life ahead of her - a life tragically cut short. Hobbs' felt a short but sharp pang of sadness at seeing the picture again.

"What's first? Messages, I suppose," said Stirling, almost to herself. It didn't feel right opening up someone else's messaging app, especially a teenaged girl, but now was not the time for respecting the privacy of others.

"Let's start with young Ploy, God rest her," replied Hobbs. "There's a reason she was killed and it's probably got something to do with messages on this phone."

Stirling opened up Ella's Whatsapp to a slew of unread messages; hundreds of them, from hundreds of different contacts. Judging from the message previews, it was a social media mausoleum. A horde of worried and grief-stricken friends, using online messaging as their way to express their concern and subsequent anguish at Ella's untimely demise. Stirling ploughed through the messages, scrolling down for what seemed like an eternity until she saw anything that remotely looked like Ploy's contact. Finally, she saw a contact name 'NuPloy555' and entered the chat. Hobbs leaned over to get a clearer look and the blue light from the display illuminated both their faces. There, in black and white was what they were looking for. The words seemed to jump out of the screen at them, like they had been waiting to be uncovered:

EllyBelly: Heyyy. This is going to sound weird. I saw some stuff on Dad's computer. I don't know who to talk to abt it. I'm coming to c u.

NuPloy555: Whaaaa? What r u talking abt? What kind of stuff??

NuPloy555: Elly? Ur scaring me.

EllyBelly: Can't talk here. I'll come to ur condo tmrw. afternoon. Send me the apt. number?

NuPloy555: Is this a joke?

EllyBelly: Trust me. Please

NuPloy555: Ok. Wait. C u tmrw. Love youu! xx

NuPloy555: Blue Mountain Golf Resort & Condominiums - Block D - 801

"That's it," remarked Stirling, passing the phone to Hobbs so he could get a better look. Hobbs scrolled up, disregarding the previous impertinent messages and then scrolled back to the bottom to the final messages exchanged between the two girls. Finally, he said,"Bloody hell, Debs. You know what this means?"

"Someone had access to this phone and the messages on it."

"Yep," Hobbs sighed. He pointed to the message at the top of the screen. "This is the one that got our Ella killed. And this," he said, pointing to the last message of the conversation. "This is the one that got her friend killed."

Stirling put her head in her hands as she struggled to process the information that she had just received. "Bloody hell is right, Frank. This puts the Ambassador square in the frame, doesn't it?"

"I'm no murder detective, but it definitely looks like it."

"Is it enough, though? I mean, it seems like a solid link. What do you think it was that she found? Couldn't have just been some dodgy porn, could it? Fetish stuff?"

"Whatever it was, it looks like it was enough to get these girls killed."

Stirling looked Hobbs in the eyes as the shimmering reflections from the pool lit up his weary face. "Jesus, Frank. I don't know how much more of this I can take. This is crazy."

Hobbs heaved a hefty sigh. "I know, Debs. It's bonkers. I can't believe it myself. It looks like our Brother Bear was telling the truth, after all."

"That's hard to believe in itself but how and why would someone be monitoring Ella's communications?"

"Remember what her parents said? When Patterson called he was highly stressed about something. So much so that he didn't want Ella around any more. Maybe this secret was getting too big to keep. Maybe he got paranoid and had her phone bugged."

"It's possible. Why would she be snooping around on his computer, though, to see what she saw? Maybe she had her doubts about her paternity, like they said?"

CHAPTER 26

"That would make sense. Let's see if there's anything on here that would suggest she knew about Nilsson being her father."

Stirling first scrolled up through the messages from Ploy to see if there was any mention of it. There wasn't. "Nothing in the messages to Ploy," she confirmed to Hobbs.

"What about in her E-Mails? A DNA test, maybe?" offered Hobbs.

Stirling opened up the Mail application, after a quick browse at her most recent E-Mails and finding nothing of interest, she moved to the search function, typing in the keywords *DNA*, *ancestry* and *heritage*. In the search results appeared four messages from the website *LivingDNA.com*. The earliest dated message confirmed a new account creation, another acknowledged the activation of a testing kit and the third was titled '*Full results available at Living DNA*' with a unique reference code. "There, Frank, look. I think we've got it," exclaimed Stirling, showing the screen to Hobbs. "She did do a DNA test. The results are right here."

"Go on, then. Let's see what we've got," replied Hobbs, excitedly.

"Gosh, it doesn't feel right though, does it? Messages and E-Mails are personal enough, but this is her DNA. It doesn't get more personal than that, does it?" Stirling replied.

"Come on, Debs. Believe me. I don't make a habit of going through my girls' personal stuff, but this is something we've got to do. If Ella realised, through this test, that Patterson wasn't her biological father, then it would give her cause to have a snoop around his computer, wouldn't it? This would tie everything together."

Stirling shook her head in concession. "I know. You're right.

Let's have a look, then."

The E-Mail contained a quick introduction which Stirling skimmed over and then a link titled *'Log in to your portal HERE to explore your ancestry'.* Clicking on the link took them to a slick looking dashboard, loaded with different tabs to explore a multitude of different aspects of Ella's DNA.

"I've not done one of these, have you?" asked Stirling, scanning the website and dashboard. "I don't know what I'm looking for."

"Nope, I've not either," replied Hobbs. "But, I heard they give you a percentage breakdown or something, don't they?"

Stirling scanned once more until her eyes fell on a tab entitled *'Your recent ancestry results'.* She clicked the link and the page that appeared showed the breakdown that Hobbs had mentioned just moments earlier. It contained detailed information about where Ella's unique genome markers were most commonly found across the world. Stirling read aloud, "Here we are. *East Asia: 48%.* That's broken down further. *Indonesia, Thailand, Cambodia and Myanmar: 40%, Southern China and Vietnam: 9%. Europe (North and West): 52%.* That's also broken down. *Denmark and Northern Germany (Jutland): 45%, Sweden: 6%, Finland: 1%.*"

"Definitely not British, then," remarked Hobbs.

"Definitely not. I'm sure Ella was smart enough to figure out who her biological father was, from those percentages."

"I'm sure she was. Christ. Poor girl. What a way to find out. Right. Let's take stock, here. Ella has suspicions Patterson may not be her real father, for whatever reason. I'm not sure it matters. This causes her to do a home DNA test, which confirms her suspicions. This causes her to do some more digging around and she finds something on Patterson's

CHAPTER 26

computer - something *weird,* as she puts it. Something dangerous, I think. Something dangerous enough to get her, and anyone else who might know about it, killed."

"Well, that's the next million-dollar question, isn't it, Frank? What was on that computer?"

"And how are we going to find out?" replied Hobbs.

Stirling sighed. "We're in well over our heads here, aren't we? This is starting to sound like one of those junk airport-bookshop thrillers that you read on your lunch breaks."

"Well, in one of those books, we would be looking to implant a device in Patterson's computer which downloads all his information. I don't even think they even exist, do they? You would know, with your time in the army - intelligence and all that."

"I didn't work for the Secret Service, Frank. My work was all pretty mundane - apart from the mortar attacks. I honestly don't know."

"Well, if they do exist, or something similar does, I bet I know someone who could get hold of one."

"No, Frank. Come on, not him again. You know how I feel about that guy. He creeps me out."

"Who? My mate Larry? Come on, he's been helpful so far and I thought you were starting to like him last time we met."

"Well, he wasn't quite so bad as the first time, but can we even trust him? He's a reporter."

"A reporter's job is to uncover the truth - not that dissimilar to ours."

"Look, Frank. Even if Larry were able to get us one of these devices, how would we get it into the Embassy? Would you even be comfortable doing that? It's completely illegal."

"So is having your own daughter killed, Debs. I think we're

past the point of debating legality. We're already *persona non grata,* and well on our way to becoming *excommunicado.* I think we're at the point where the end justifies the means, aren't we?"

"Gosh, I don't know, Frank. Hacking a dead teenager's phone for information is one thing, but we're talking about covertly bugging the computer of a senior diplomat. We're Missing Persons, not MI5."

"You mean MI6. MI5 deals with information regarding threats from within the UK and MI6 gathers intelligence from outside the UK - I learned that in one of those junk thrillers you mentioned."

Stirling shook her head. "Either way, Frank. Are we really thinking of doing this? I don't know how things work here, or at home for that matter, but wouldn't that information be useless if it was gained illegally?"

Hobbs shrugged. "Maybe. Probably. I don't know. What I do know is that Patterson is not just going to tell us if we ask nicely. We came here to find out the truth about Ella's disappearance and, as far as I can see, this is the only way."

"I know you're right but it just seems crazy. How would we even get this thing onto Patterson's computer? How would we even get into the Embassy? He's not going to let us in his office, is he? He must know we're onto him."

"What about Stella?"

"Stella? Do you think she would do it? She's been his deputy for ages, hasn't she? Do you think she's going to put her career on the line for this?"

"I don't know, Debs. I really don't know. I'm thinking out loud here. All I know is that I don't want to get on a plane and go home when we're this close to figuring this whole thing

CHAPTER 26

out. Let's just talk to Larry first, OK? If he can't help us, then the whole thing is null and void, anyway."

"OK. I suppose there's no harm in asking. Let's give him a call tomorrow. It's after 11 already."

"He strikes me as a night owl, Debs. I think I'll give him a buzz right now. My bet is he's in a bar somewhere."

Hobbs grabbed his phone from his breast pocket, where it always lived and cycled through his contacts to find Larry Dean's number. He placed the call and waited while the dial tone rang out.

Stirling looked on, counting in her head how many rings it had been. "Looks like he's turned in for the night," she remarked, unsurprised, given the lateness of the hour.

Just then, a cacophony of background noise emanated from the speaker of Hobbs' phone as it was answered.

"Y'ello?" came the unmistakable drawl of Larry Dean down the phone.

"Larry, it's Frank. Frank Hobbs, down in Kanchanaburi."

"Frank, Buddy! How are ya? Are you in town? Do you want to join us for a beer?"

"Sorry, Larry, no can do. Debs and I are still grinding away out here. We've got something we need to talk to you about, though,"

"Alright. Hang on, Buddy. Let me go outside a second."

The noise continued but then began to subside as Larry Dean evidently exited the drinking establishment into the relative quiet of the street outside.

"Hey, Frank. You still there?"

"I'm here, Larry."

"What can I do you for? Have you solved all that business down there? Hasn't been much information making its way up to Bangkok. You been holding out on me, Buddy?"

"Who me? Never, Larry. In fact, we wanted to fill you in on what we've found out and maybe ask a favour, if that's possible?"

"You know me, Frank. Anything for a juicy scoop. What have you got for me?"

"Well, as you can appreciate, it's a little sensitive. Do you think you'd be able to come and see us down here tomorrow morning? I know it's short notice."

"Not a problem, Buddy. I understand. Discretion is my middle name. I'll finish my drink here, make my apologies to the ladies and then head home for a little shut-eye. I'll see you in the restaurant for breakfast."

"Sounds good, Larry. Thanks. Say *hi* to the ladies from us."

"Will do, Buddy. I'll see you in the morning, Frank."

"Thanks, Larry. Bye."

Stirling was impressed by how easily Hobbs had got what he wanted from Larry Dean.

"He sure likes you, *Buddy*," she chirped in a terrible attempt at an American accent.

"He's an alright bloke, Debs. He's just American."

"*Very* American."

"OK, *very* American. But, he might just be able to help us solve this thing. I think it's worth getting a bit pally with him for that, isn't it?"

"Of course it is, Frank. I'm only pulling your leg. Anyway, I think it's time we both got some sleep. I'm exhausted. I don't know about you."

"Yeah, me too. Tomorrow's another day."

They both rose to their feet from their impromptu incident

CHAPTER 26

room by the side of the pool and shuffled back towards their bungalows.

"Night, Debs," said Hobbs, ruffling his partner's hair affectionately. "Today was a good day. We're going to solve this one. I can feel it."

"You feel it in those old bones of yours, do you?" replied Stirling, playfully.

"Yes, I do, actually, and they're not often wrong."

Chapter 27

Hobbs and Stirling were sitting drinking a much-needed cup of coffee, waiting for the arrival of Larry Dean from the comfort of the guest house restaurant. Neither had slept well and they were both sporting noticeable bags under their eyes from several sleepless nights ruminating over the details of the case.

Hobbs reached for his packet of cigarettes and was just about to get up when they heard the staccato *put-put* engine note of an approaching motor cycle. The pair both looked up to see the almost-comical sight of Larry Dean arriving into the car park on the back of a local motor cycle taxi. The driver, clad in his colourful, numbered vest, wrestled with the handlebars to keep the vehicle straight with the added weight of his western customer. As they approached the restaurant, the driver swerved to avoid a small pothole, almost sending Larry Dean tumbling to the ground as he had taken one hand off the grab handle to wave.

After coming to an ungainly halt, Larry swung his leg over the saddle, catching it slightly on a rear faring and had to do a small hop to keep his balance. He paid the driver and ran a chubby hand through his hair before entering the restaurant.

"Frank, Debs. Good morning," he exclaimed loudly, turning

CHAPTER 27

the heads of some of the other guests who were still enjoying their breakfasts. Hobbs and Stirling both rose from their seats to greet the reporter.

Stirling greeted him first. "Hi, Larry. Thanks for taking the time to come down and see us. We do appreciate it. It's been a very busy week."

"Are you kidding? I love Kanch'. I'd be down here every weekend, if I didn't have to work," replied Dean.

"Well, we're glad you could join us," said Hobbs. "I think we should go somewhere a little more private, if you don't mind? How about the patio down by the river? It's normally quiet down there."

"Of course. Let me just order some breakfast. I'll have them deliver it down there."

While Dean ordered his breakfast at the bar, Hobbs and Stirling gathered their things and they all walked down, past the pool and towards the river which flowed lazily past its banks, blissfully unaware, as always, of the relative chaos that unfolded around it.

The group found themselves a quiet spot upon a wrought iron table and chair set overlooking the river from the concrete promenade which had seen better days.

Larry Dean spoke first, after plopping himself down in one of the chairs, with his back to the river. "This is all a bit cloak-and-dagger, as you Brits might say. I'm assuming you've found something big, if you didn't want to talk over the phone," he began, in his matter-of-fact fashion, which Hobbs and Stirling had come to expect, appreciate and now reciprocate.

"Well, you're right there, Larry," said Hobbs. "It's been a whirlwind of a week and things have just gone from strange to downright incredible."

"Sounds like you've opened up a can of worms out here in the Wild West."

"I'm afraid so. Now, Larry, what we're about to tell you is honestly for your ears only, mate. In country, only myself, Debs - obviously, and our local guy, Chai, know. We have made Ella's parents aware of where we are in our investigation, but that's it. The boys in brown, as you call them, are otherwise unaware and we intend to keep it that way, for the time being."

"That's a good call, Buddy. Those guys are crooked as a dog's hind leg."

"That's what we've come to realise. So, without beating around the bush, Larry, we need your help. We've come to the point where we have a pretty good idea of what happened to Ella and who had her killed, but we don't yet know why. To understand that, we need access to a someone's laptop computer and the information off it."

"And you were hoping I would be able to get a hold of one of those cool USB gadgets that can copy the data from someone's computer?"

Stirling chimed in, "Well, yes, actually. That's exactly what we were hoping."

"Well, I'm flattered. You came to the right guy, that's for sure." Hobbs and Stirling hot each other a relieved smile. "There's only one problem, though. Those things don't exist. Well, not in the form that you see in the movies, that's for sure."

Hobbs' relief was short-lived. "What do you mean?"

Larry leaned in, and began to explain as if he were talking to a class of school kids. "Look, you've watched those movies,

CHAPTER 27

right? Where the dame sneaks into the office of the bad guy and plugs in this device. Automatically, a screen pops up with bright green lettering saying 'COPYING 5%', or something like that, right? And she's getting all shifty, watching the progress bar creep up to 100% in the hope that she won't get caught in the office and blow the whole thing, right?"

"Yes, that's kind of what we were thinking," replied Stirling sheepishly.

"Yeah. Those things don't exist."

"Bugger," exclaimed Hobbs. "Not even in the intelligence community?"

"Not like that, no. But, that's not to say that you can't crack a computer. It just takes longer - a lot longer - an hour, at least."

"But, it can be done? Do you know anyone who can do it?"

"That depends, Buddy. I hate to be *that* guy, but what you're talking about sounds very illegal, not that there's anything wrong with that. I wanna help, I do, but if I'm going out on a pretty shaky limb here, in this country, I've gotta ask, what's in it for me?"

"You've got the full scoop, Larry, alright? You'll have the info' before any news agency in the world. If this is what we think it is, it's going to be huge. This could be your big break and I'm not just blowing smoke up your arse, mate."

Dean chuckled. "You Brits certainly do have a way with words. OK, listen. If you can get me the computer, I *should* be able to get you what you need. There'll be a cost involved, not from me, of course - I'm only in it for the truth - but from the guy. This is Thailand, though. It won't be much. Do you want me to make the call?"

Hobbs looked over to Stirling. "Do we need to ask the other

person in this plan? Before we commit?"

"No, let's get the guy first. If we can't get a hold of the laptop. We'll just pay the guy anyway."

Hobbs nodded. "OK, Larry. You heard the lady. Make the call."

Larry Dean made a mock salute towards Hobbs and rose to his feet with some effort before walking over to the edge of the promenade to make his call. With perfect timing, a waitress arrived carrying their drinks and Larry's bumper breakfast, setting them down carefully on the table. Hobbs slipped her a green 20 Baht note, for her troubles, and she shuffled away towards the restaurant whence she came.

Larry Dean dramatically snapped shut his ageing flip phone before declaring triumphantly, "We're on."

Stirling breathed a sigh of relief. "Thanks, Larry. We owe you one. Breakfast is definitely on us."

"I am not a man to refuse a free breakfast, as you can see," Dean exclaimed, patting himself playfully on the stomach. I'll even see if I can get you a discount. Save you a few bucks. Might come in handy when all this is over."

"You can talk," scoffed Hobbs through a mouthful of coffee. "Have you seen the relic of a telephone you're using?"

"Oh, this?" asked Dean, picking up his flip phone, while shovelling a forkful of scrambled eggs into his mouth. "This is my burner. Do you really think I'm going to make the kind of call I just made on my personal phone?"

"OK, I'll give you that one, Larry. You're much better at this whole game than either of us," replied Hobbs, slightly abashed.

"I don't make a habit of this kind of thing, but this place is…different. You do what you have to do. This isn't America,

CHAPTER 27

or England. *T.I.T - This is Thailand,* ya know?"

"You're not the first person we've heard that from this week, Larry," replied Stirling.

Hobbs and Stirling sat and drank yet another cup of coffee while Larry Dean finished off his breakfast. Larry Dean may not be everyone's cup of tea, but they were pretty sure he could be trusted. He didn't appear to have anything to gain from derailing their investigation and, being so isolated in Thailand, they needed all the help they could get, even if that meant taking a chance on a relative stranger.

Dean finished his breakfast with a large wipe of his face with a napkin. "Hey, do you guys want to share a minivan back to Bangkok? I'm assuming you'll need to go there to meet with Stella Ismael."

Hobbs and Stirling were both taken aback momentarily. They hadn't mentioned their plan to Dean, yet he seemed to know the next step.

"Ummm, well.." spluttered Hobbs.

"Look, I may not be a detective, like you guys, but it's pretty obvious that she's the only person you know that would have access to Richard Patterson's computer. Now, you don't need to confirm nor deny any of my suspicions, but if I had to put money on it, I'd say there's something rotten in the state of Denver with that guy."

The two detectives looked at each other - one of the looks that they shared often, one of the looks where they needed to make a decision, there and then, but couldn't talk about it. They both nodded. It was settled.

"Do you know some things that we don't, Larry?" asked Stirling.

"No, Ma'am. I don't think I do. All I know is that I've been here long enough to know what that man is like - he's a god damn snake."

Stirling shrugged. "Well, that is our working theory, Larry, yes. We have reason to believe that Richard Patterson ordered the killing of Ella Patterson, or should I say, Elly Nilsson?"

Dean cocked his head to one side in an involuntary expression of surprise. He certainly didn't know everything. "Elly Nilsson?"

"Yes, from interviews with the family, we've found that Patterson is not Ella's biological father. Her real father is a Danish gentleman named Mads Nilsson - Ella's mother's new husband."

"The plot thickens," remarked Dean, sliding further down into his chair, the gears of his investigative brain clicking into gear.

"Indeed. We also know that Ella recently became privy to this information through a home DNA test. This, we assume, caused her to have a snoop on the Ambassador's computer, where she found something. Something big. Something big enough to get her killed, it seems."

Dean blew out his cheeks. "Holy shit. That is big. Big enough to get the other girl at the golf course killed, too. I assume they're connected."

Hobbs interjected, "I'm afraid so, Larry, and the attack on Debs. It's all connected."

"You guys are in deep, huh? Are you sure you wanna do this? What you're planning?"

"We've got no choice, Larry mate. If we don't, that bastard gets away with it. I've got teenage daughters myself. I'm not having that. *We're* not having that."

"I hear ya, Buddy. My daughters are all grown up. I

CHAPTER 27

don't see them much these days, with being over here, but I know exactly how you feel." Larry Dean paused, biting his lip, Stirling noticed, presumably at the memory of his girls growing up. "I'm all in with you guys. I'm mighty glad you've shown your hand here. It looks like you need all the help you can get to bring this bastard down. As it happens, you're in luck. There's an annual memorial going on down at the War Cemetery for the Death Railway - Patterson's grandfather was among the POWs who died building it. He tells the stories to just about anyone who will listen. There's a good chance he'll be in town. I think it's tomorrow."

"Tomorrow? Crikey," exclaimed Stirling, buoyed with excitement but simultaneously acutely aware of the time constraints they would be under.

"Can we get the guy down here, to Kanchanaburi?" asked Stirling, her voice a mixture of excitement and trepidation. "If we do what we're thinking of, we won't have a lot of time."

"I can ask. It shouldn't be a problem. Should just be a case of paying his expenses, assuming he is available. I'll see if they have a room here for him, on my way out. What is your plan, anyway?"

Stirling shrugged and looked over to Hobbs for inspiration. "We haven't really thought that far ahead, have we, Frank?"

"Well, it sounds like we're going to have to do *the old switcheroo* - switch out Patterson's computer for a similar one and hope he won't notice until your man has got us what we need. How long do you think he would need?" replied Hobbs.

"An hour, minimum. This guy is good, but it takes time."

"How long will this memorial go on for? Is Patterson speaking at it? Will he need his computer, for a script, or something?"

"That I don't know," replied Dean, shaking his head.

"Stella will know," replied Hobbs.

"But will she even go along with this? Can we do it without her? If she's loyal to the Ambassador and goes running to him, our plan, and entire investigation is out the window," Stirling thought out loud.

"And you better have an escape plan, if that's the case," remarked Dean. "In all seriousness."

There was a pregnant pause as the three appreciated the gravity of the situation. Whatever secrets were on that computer, they all had come to realise, were worth killing for. They had seen first hand what could happen - and that was just a warning. There was no telling the lengths these people would go.

Hobbs spoke first. "Patterson will be on edge. He will be wondering why we're still in country when our return flight has left. He's not a stupid man, that much is clear. He must assume that we have found something. He was probably hoping we didn't find Win Nyan Bo, let alone Brother Bear."

"Do you think he knows Brother Bear has rolled over on him?" asked Stirling.

"I don't know," replied Hobbs. "Brother Bear is still alive, which suggests he doesn't, but if Brother Bear was to suddenly pass away in police custody, that would be a pretty obvious sign of guilt on his part. Maybe he's hoping we don't believe Brother Bear's story. It is a pretty incredible one."

"I agree with Frank, here," offered Dean. "Patterson will be on guard. If someone is going to get close to him, it's gotta be someone he trusts. It's gonna be Stella, or no-one."

Larry Dean's declaration rang loud and true. Hobbs and

CHAPTER 27

Stirling looked at each other. Not even one of Hobbs' one-liners could defuse the tension of the situation they found themselves in. They both knew it was crunch time. Their conversation with Stella Ismael could go one of two ways: the former would get them one step closer to the truth. The latter, well, that didn't bear thinking about.

"What do you think, Debs?" asked Hobbs.

Stirling paused a moment. "We've come this far, Frank. Let's do it. For Ella."

Hobbs nodded. "It's settled then. For Ella."

Chapter 28

After dropping Larry Dean at the first BTS station on the outskirts of Bangkok, Hobbs and Stirling continued into the centre of the buzzing metropolis. Dean had said how much he hated the Bangkok traffic. He travelled by train or motorcycle taxi as much as possible and advised them to do the same. Sitting here, idling in the midday sun, they both were starting to wish they had taken his advice. Motorcycles weaved in and out of the gridlocked traffic, some of the riders physically leaned on the side of their van when they came to a spot impassable even for their narrow steeds.

Hobbs checked his watch. "I hope it's not too much further. We're supposed to meet Stella in five minutes."

Stirling had messaged Stella as soon as they had agreed to go ahead with the plan. Not wanting to give too much away, she had said that they were flying out that afternoon and would love to meet up and have a coffee before they left. Stella had agreed and sent them the location of a coffee shop which, thankfully, wasn't directly inside the building where the British Embassy was located. Stirling checked the time on her mobile phone and began rhythmically tapping her long nails on the screen. She looked back into the rear of the van at their suitcases which they had packed, ready for a quick exit.

"You alright, Debs?" asked Hobbs, sensing his partner's anxiety.

"Yeah. I'm alright. Just a few butterflies. That's normal, isn't it?" she replied, unconvincingly.

"I know this is big, Debs. But, we've been through some hairy situations before, haven't we? If she says no, we hotfoot it straight to the airport, right? We'll be fine if we just stick to our plan. There's a flight leaving for London and it's got seats." The pair were talking in hushed tones, even though they had ascertained that their driver had very limited English.

"I know, Frank. I'm just not used to all this, that's all. I just hope we can get Stella on board. Then, we can finish this, once and for all."

"I hope so, Debs, for everyone's sake."

After what felt like an eternity, the vehicles in front of them began to move, along with the long line of motorcycles that had accumulated on the other side of their van's windows. The driver made a right turn across traffic and within 30 metres or so, came to a stop outside a small strip mall that seemed to contain a mixture of cafes, restaurants and a small western-style supermarket.

"Arrive already," exclaimed the driver in broken but cheerful English before proceeding to the rear of the vehicle to help them with their bags. Stirling reached for her bag and paid the driver who thanked them and promptly disappeared into the relentless flow of traffic.

Stella Ismael was seated in the window of a medium-sized coffee shop, idly scrolling through her phone. Stirling recognised her instantly by her similar unruly mess of curls. Stella looked up and gave them a wave, pointing in the direction of the glass door which led out onto the street. The pair entered the coffee shop where they were greeted by Stella. A hug for Stirling and a friendly handshake for Hobbs. "How are you two doing? Can I get you a drink?" she asked, politely.

"That's kind of you, but we'll get them," replied Hobbs.

Stella shooed at them with her hands dismissively. "Nonsense, come on. I'll put it on the expenses."

They ordered their drinks and Stirling asked Stella if it was OK to sit in a quiet corner of the coffee shop, giving the excuse that they would be away from the heat of the opening and closing door. Stella agreed and they all flopped down into easy chairs in neutral colours, surrounded by tropical plants of various shapes and sizes.

"So, how has your investigation been going?" asked Stella, inquisitively. "It's a terrible business, isn't it? I'm not sure I could do what you two do."

"Well, this hasn't been a normal case for us, has it Debs?" replied Hobbs. Stirling nodded in agreement. "We're more used to finding people and reuniting them with their families." Hobbs decided to get straight to the point. "We're not used to our cases turning into murder enquiries."

Stella Ismael's eyes widened and her hand shot up to cover her mouth. "Murder?" she exclaimed, in a whisper. She was clearly used to exercising discretion. Hobbs wondered momentarily if that was a good thing or a bad thing. "But, Richard said that it was all a terrible accident."

"I'm afraid not," replied Hobbs, gravely, and then proceeded to fill Stella in on what they had uncovered, right up to the point where they had arrested Brother Bear in Bangkok.

At a very opportune moment, their drinks arrived. Stella sat back in her seat, visibly shaken by the information she had received. "Golly, well that's just unbelievable, Frank. It's like something out of a movie. Does the Ambassador know about all of this, yet?"

Hobbs turned to look at Stirling. 'Well, that's actually what we've come to talk to you about," Stirling replied, taking control of the conversation. She continued, discreetly, to inform Stella about what they had since uncovered from the conversations with Ella's parents and the information from her mobile phone. With every sentence that was uttered, Stella Ismael's face further drained of colour until, when Stirling had finished speaking, it was an ashen grey, held in place by her hands on either side of her face as she leaned forwards, placing her elbows on the table in front of her.

There was a long and uncomfortable silence as the three all looked at each other for a sliver of solace. There was none; the moment was only broken by Stella wiping away a single tear which had rolled quickly down her cheek.

"I don't believe it," she croaked. "This is a joke, isn't it? Why would you joke about something like that?"

"I wish it was," replied Stirling. "Believe me. I wish it was. But, this is where we are."

"But," Stella stammered. "Richard, he's...he's...he wouldn't do something like that. He's a bit of an oddball, but...surely, there's some kind of mistake?"

"Well, that's where we need your help, Stella," said Stirling, taking Stella's trembling hands in hers. "We need to find out what is on the Ambassador's computer. We need to find out the truth. We may find out that he is innocent, after all, or we may not. Either way, we need to find out why this all happened -provide some answers to the families of poor Ella, Ploy and Noon." Stirling was choosing her words very carefully, appealing to Stella's conscience and her feminity. "We know we are asking a lot. We do. But, you're the only person who can help us get access to that computer. We can blow this whole thing open and prevent any other women and girls coming to harm."

Stella covered her face with her hands, inhaling and exhaling heavily while she weighed the decision in her mind. Finally, she said, "What would you need me to do?"

"From what we understand, the Ambassador will be travelling again to Kanchanaburi for an event tomorrow," began Hobbs.

"Yes, that's right. The memorial. It's an annually reoccurring event on the calendar," Stella confirmed.

"All we would need is for you to switch the Ambassador's computer for an identical one, just for a while - an hour, two at most. We have someone ready to examine the computer and get us the information we need. All we need is the computer."

Stirling observed Stella Ismael as she tried to comprehend the information she was receiving. She could see from her body language and behaviour that she was a woman in turmoil. She clearly had loyalty to her superior - probably a good working relationship, even a good personal one. She had been at the Embassy long enough. She would also have had a personal relationship with Ella - watched her grow up into the beautiful young girl she became. The dilemma was weighing hard on her and she was squirming, being pulled inwardly from both sides.

Tears began to flow again from her eyes. As she leaned back and rested her head on the back of the easy chair. The tears came to rest upon her freckled nose and cheeks, waiting to roll one way or the other off her face. Hobbs sensed the

CHAPTER 28

decision was on a knife edge. "Will you help us, Stella? For Ella?"

Stella remained motionless for a moment before finally sitting forward. The tears, which were so perfectly balanced upon her high cheekbones just moments ago, finally cascaded down her face and onto her lap. She released a long outward breath, wiped her face with the heels of her hands and nodded tearfully. "I will."

* * *

It had taken a short while for Stella to regain her composure before they could go over the details of their hastily-devised plan. At regular intervals, Hobbs scanned the room to make sure their presence and conversations were going unnoticed. They spent the next 40 minutes going over every detail of the plan, so that it would go over without a hitch. Stella's first role was to get hold of the decoy computer and bag. Patterson would be travelling to Kanchanaburi by train, as was his preference. They assumed that he may want to use his computer at some point during the journey, so they couldn't make the switch until he arrived in Kanchanaburi. They devised that, as they boarded their taxi, Stella would create a diversion and Chai would make the switch. As a local, he would blend in much better than either Hobbs or Stirling, and especially Larry Dean. Chai would be dressed as a motorcycle taxi driver and, after switching the laptop bags, would race to hand over the computer to the hacker. They figured they would have enough time while Patterson attended the memorial to get the information they needed and they should be able to switch the bag back afterwards, with Patterson being none the wiser. That wasn't guaranteed, though-none of it was. There was plenty that could go wrong. They could all end up on a flight out of the Kingdom, or worse.

The plan was set. Stella knew her role. It was clear to the detectives that she wasn't happy about what they were doing, but something deep down must have told her that they were right. There must have been something in her interactions with Patterson that would make their story seem credible enough to go along with. That gave Stirling hope, for what they had was little more than hearsay and circumstantial evidence, at best. She wondered herself whether they were doing the right thing, but everything they had seen and learned so far had taken them down this path. It had been a non-stop, runaway-train ride since they had arrived, but she sensed the end of the line was fast approaching.

Stirling's musings were interrupted by Hobbs. "Well, I think that's it. I'll fill Chai in on the details. The rest is up to the Gods," he said.

"Gosh, I hope I'm doing the right thing," remarked Stella, sadly.

"I think it's our only option," replied Stirling. "Guilty, or not, we will find out soon enough."

Stella nodded her head. "I better be going, then. Get back to work before the Ambassador suspects anything."

"You'll be fine, Stella, but if there's anything you need, anything at all, you just give us a call, alright?" said Hobbs, reassuringly.

Stella Ismael nodded and made her way out of the coffee shop. She motioned a wave at Hobbs and Stirling as she passed the window.

CHAPTER 28

Stirling let out a long sigh. Relief flooding over her. "Christ, Frank. I didn't believe we could get her on side. We might make it back to London in one piece, after all."

"Yep. It looks like she's with us."

"Looks like? What do you mean? She agreed to do it, didn't she?"

"Well, yes. Ostensibly, it looks like she's in. But, if she wasn't, do you think she would tell us? There's always the chance that she just had us tell her the whole plan to bring down the Ambassador, and now she is off to tell him everything."

Stirling's face dropped. "But, wouldn't she have refused straight away, if she didn't want to do it?"

"She might, but that would prompt us to high-tail it out of here, wouldn't it? She saw our bags." Hobbs motioned over to their suitcases which were both stood neatly next to a tall potted plant. "If she's in cahoots with the Ambassador, she might want to keep us here while they figure out what to do with us."

"Well, how do we know if we really do have her on-side?"

"We don't. We'll just have to wait and see what she does tomorrow."

"Jesus, Frank," replied Stirling, clearly stunned by her partner's line of thought. "Either you've been reading too many of those airport bookshop thrillers or we are in this even deeper than I thought."

"I think it might be a bit of both, Debs," replied Hobbs, before finishing off the last remaining dregs of his coffee. "Come on, we better get out of here."

Chapter 29

The following day, Hobbs and Stirling were seated in a small restaurant with a reasonable view of the front of the main train station of Kanchanaburi. In contrast with the station itself, which was adorned with colourful tropical flower bushes and well-kept animal topiaries, the area opposite the main entrance to the station was dusty and barren, with only a large concrete waiting area that backed onto a landscaped park area with some kind of commemorative statue. There were no coffee shops, bars or restaurants immediately opposite for them to observe from, so this one, situated around forty metres away on a corner close by had to do.

To Hobbs' pleasure, the restaurant was basically open-air, bar an aged gazebo which protected the customers from the harsh tropical sun, so he was able to indulge in more than a few nervous cigarettes. Stirling sat nursing a now-warm bottle of orange Fanta, while her leg tapped unconsciously under the table. The restaurant served seafood and while it was a little late for lunch, they thought they should order something to blend in among the smattering of locals and western foreign tourists. Hobbs ordered a plate of breaded calamari but, unusually, it sat mostly uneaten on the table

CHAPTER 29

between them as they waited impatiently for the impending arrival of the train carrying Richard Patterson and Stella Ismael to Kanchanaburi.

There weren't many trains that came into the station, but when they did, they attracted a small horde of locals in their taxis, tuk-tuks and the local motorcycle taxi drivers in their coloured vests. It was the latter that Chai had been tasked to simulate. After renting a small Honda Wave semi-automatic motorcycle from one of the tourist rental shops on the main strip, Chai travelled to the other end of town where he paid a genuine motorcycle taxi driver 1000 Baht to borrow his coloured vest and full-face helmet for the afternoon. No questions were asked by the grateful driver who then happily retired to a gambling den for the afternoon.

The vest Chai had borrowed was the same colour as those worn by the drivers that were resident at the train station, but it would have been impossible to blend in fully with that group. The groups of drivers form a tight-knit community, spending their time between fares watching the world go by, reading newspapers or watching bouts of Thai boxing on ageing TV sets. These bands of motorcycle taxis were widely referred to as *human CCTV* in areas across Thailand where there is no genuine CCTV coverage. Sitting predominantly idly on busy corners, there is little that they collectively do not see. Despite the tinted full-face helmet, an out of place numbered vest or an unfamiliar bike would raise eyebrows and therefore suspicions. So, Chai would have to hold back until the last minute, watching intently from another corner, before he would swoop in and complete his part of the plan.

Hobbs checked his phone for the umpteenth time in the thirty minutes they had been sat at the observation point. They were pleased to see that Stella had messaged, as promised, when they boarded the train and were waiting for a final message to say that they were coming into Kanchanaburi.

"Anything?" asked Stirling.

"Not yet," replied Hobbs, placing the phone back onto the table, which was now wet from the condensation produced by their icy cold drinks getting slowly warm.

"Maybe she's had a change of heart."

"Maybe. She sent the first message, though. That's a good sign."

"God, I hate this, Frank. There's so much that could go wrong."

"It's a solid plan, Debs. If he notices, it'll look like a standard bag-grab by a meth-addled motorbike taxi. If he doesn't notice, even better."

"What about the taxi driver?"

"The same. It'll be fine, Debs."

Hobbs' phone buzzed on the table and he quickly grabbed it. Pulling his reading glasses from his pocket, he read the message:

JUST COMING INTO KANCHANABURI FOR A MEMORIAL SERVICE. WE HOPE YOU HAD A GOOD FLIGHT AND THANKS FOR ALL YOUR HELP. RICHARD REALLY APPRECIATES IT. BEST WISHES, S x

Hobbs handed the phone over to Stirling. "Keep your eyes peeled, Debs. We're on."

* * *

CHAPTER 29

The few minutes they needed to wait for the train to arrive felt like a lifetime. Finally, they thought they saw the silhouette of the Ambassador and his deputy emerge from the train station, both carrying briefcase-style computer bags in one hand and overnight bags in the other.

"There they are, Debs, whispered Hobbs. "Do you see them?"

Stirling simply nodded. They watched as Stella motioned to the driver of the taxi that was first-in-line and Patterson placed his overnight bag on the floor in order to mop his brow.

Hobbs looked for Chai on his motorcycle but saw nothing. Stirling seemed to be doing the same. "Where's Chai?" she asked, trying in vain to hide the panic in her voice.

"He'll be there. He hasn't let us down yet," replied Hobbs with more confidence than he genuinely felt.

Almost on queue, a motorcycle appeared from around the corner, the rider bearing the tall stature of Chai. A black bag hung from the luggage hook.

"There he is. Right on time," remarked Hobbs, breathing a sigh of relief. Patterson and Stella were at the taxi now with Chai making a beeline for them. Hobbs and Stirling watched as Patterson opened the taxi door, motioning for Stella to enter first.

"Shit," swore Hobbs. "He's got to get in first. Now's not the time for him to start being a gentleman."

There was a conversation but all they could see were gestures - Stella presumably insisting that Patterson board the vehicle first. Hobbs and Stirling stared, transfixed by the scene in front of them. Finally, they both breathed a sigh of relief as Patterson gave his overnight bag to Stella who moved to the rear of the vehicle to stow their luggage. This left Patterson to duck into the back of the taxi first, placing his computer bag into the footwell of the rear passenger seat.

What happened next occurred in the blink of an eye, but played out almost in slow motion for Hobbs and Stirling who sat helplessly observing from afar. As Stella closed the boot of the car and rounded the rear end, she stumbled and fell in a heap on the side of the dusty road. As planned, in a moment of gallantry, Patterson appeared from the back seat of the taxi, clumsily attempting to get Stella back to her feet. The taxi driver, fortuitously, followed suit. As Stella winced in pain and held her ankle in theatrics, Chai came to a stop next to the taxi and hopped off his bike, appearing to the casual observer as one of the many concerned citizens who were now forming a small crowd around the stricken foreigner.

Chai took his chance. Quickly, he opened the rear door of the taxi which faced the road, grabbed the computer bag from the footwell and replaced it with the decoy bag from his bike. The act seemed to go unnoticed and, boldly, after hanging Patterson's computer bag on his bike, Chai even rounded the rear of the vehicle to assist Patterson in helping Stella back to her feet and into the back of the taxi.

"Get back on the bike, you cheeky little bastard," muttered Hobbs under his breath.

Nonchalantly, Chai lifted the kickstand of his bike and kicked the engine into life before puttering off down the street, appearing to be in no hurry. After putting sufficient distance between himself and the station, Chai opened up the throttle and disappeared into the distance.

"We bloody got it, Debs," grinned Hobbs with delight. "Chai and Stella smashed it."

CHAPTER 29

Stirling smiled. "I guess we can safely say Stella is on side. What do we do now?"

"Now, we wait - hopefully, not too long. Larry's man needs to crack that computer before Patterson realises it's missing.

"And let us know what's on it."

"Exactly. We're nearly there, Debs. We're not out of the woods yet but there is light at the end of the tunnel."

Stirling chuckled. "You and your metaphors, Frank Hobbs. Are you going to eat that squid?"

Hobbs dragged the plate in front of him and held up a piece of the calamari. "Well, it's no bacon butty, that's for sure, but it would be a shame to waste it."

"Hurry up, then. We need to get back to the hotel where they have good Internet. This information coming will be crucial and we don't want to miss it."

* * *

Stirling and Chai sat nursing cups of coffee at the small table and chairs on Stirling's veranda outside her bungalow while Hobbs paced back and forth like a caged animal that happened to chain-smoke cigarettes.

"How long has it been?" asked Hobbs.

Stirling checked her watch again. "Almost an hour," she replied.

"I really hope this guy of Larry's is the business," said Hobbs, taking another long drag from his rapidly shortening cigarette. "If Patterson realises what's happened, we're screwed."

Chai interjected, "We've still got time. The memorial service will take a while and the Ambassador is unlikely to need his computer."

"In any case, I doubt he's going to make a connection to us right away, is he?" asked Stirling, rhetorically. "I know he might be on edge, but surely his first thought would be a simple theft."

"Simple thieves don't tend to swap out computers for identical ones," replied Hobbs. "It'll be Stella who takes the brunt, especially as she sourced the dummy laptop."

Chai continued to drag his finger from the top of his tablet screen at regular intervals to refresh the page of his burner E-Mail account inbox. The local man tasked with breaking the security of Richard Patterson's computer would be E-Mailing a secure link to the contents of any document files on the computer. The page refreshed. Nothing.

"What happens if we don't find anything?" asked Chai, refreshing the page once more, as he had been instructed.

"Well," began Hobbs between puffs. "I don't think we'll be able to return the computer to Patterson without him noticing. So, we'll probably have to just dump it near the train station. I grabbed a few bits from the hotel Lost Property box: a couple of old wallets, a set of keys. We can stick them all in a bag with the computer and dump it. That should be enough for the boys in brown to come to a false conclusion. No offence, Chai mate."

Chai nodded his head. "That's smart, Frank."

"They don't call me *Einstein* back in London, for nothing," replied Hobbs.

Chai looked over to Stirling who rolled her eyes and shook her head. Chai noticed himself that Hobbs always had a way of relieving the tension of stressful situations, even though he was probably feeling the stress himself - a skill of a good

CHAPTER 29

detective, he thought. Absent-mindedly, he slid his index finger once more from the top of the tablet's screen, fully expecting the same empty inbox he had encountered on the other fifty occasions. To his surprise, the word *Inbox* was now emboldened and the number one followed it in parentheses. He quickly clicked into his inbox.

"Got something," he blurted quickly and Hobbs and Stirling jumped out of their chairs to race around to the rear of Chai's chair, flanking him on either side, peering expectantly over each of his narrow shoulders.

The message was from a sender named *A.Non* and there was no subject. Chai quickly opened the message which contained nothing other than a link entitled *Files.* Clicking on the link started a process of unpacking seemingly hundreds of files to the small hard drive of the tablet computer in Chai's hands. The process seemed to take an age as they all willed the progress bar along until after 45 seconds or so, it reached 100% and a file folder opened automatically. On the screen was a folder containing a myriad of sub-folders from Richard Patterson's computer. Each of them scanned the filenames as Chai scrolled through the list.

"There's hundreds of them," remarked Hobbs, deflated. "This could take weeks. We don't even know what we're looking for."

Stirling paused a moment, deep in thought, before replying. "Well, we know from our conversation with Ella's parents that he appeared visibly stressed a couple of months ago and Ella was murdered around a week ago. So, we can do a search for any files created or received within that time frame, can't we, Chai?"

"Yes, I think so," replied Chai. "Let's see."

Chai moved to the search box and then used *Advanced Search* to change the parameters. To his relief, the hundreds of file folders turned into a much smaller list of folders and individual files - some images, some documents, some system files, but all created or modified within the time frame they had specified.

"What now?" asked Hobbs, betraying yet again his relative lack of experience with matters of information technology.

"What about messaging platforms? What do they use here, Chai? Whatsapp?"

"Mostly *Line* - it's like Whatsapp, but from Japan. I think Patterson would use Whatsapp, though - it's more secure."

"That's right. Even police forces can't get permission to break the encryption of suspected terrorist communications on Whatsapp," replied Stirling. "We had a terrible time with it in the Gulf."

"That would be on his phone anyway, wouldn't it?" asked Hobbs, the ash from his cigarette forming a precarious horizontal proboscis towards Chai's shoulder.

"Not necessarily," replied Stirling. "There is a Windows app as people use it on their computers, especially if they use it for business. If we're lucky, Richard Patterson is one of those people."

"We won't be able to see his messages though, will we?"

"No, probably not, but often people's Whatsapps are set up to automatically download any images that they receive in their chats. Can you look for a folder like that, Chai?"

Chai did as he was asked and the screen filled with a list of individual images, all presumably received through Whatsapp in the time frame they had stated.

"Nice one, Chai," remarked Hobbs, flicking his ash to the

CHAPTER 29

floor and trying to take a drag on his now already extinguished cigarette. "I guess we just have to go through them one-by-one, now. Looks like it might take a while. Here, let me have a crack, Chai."

Chai opened up the first image and then passed the tablet to Hobbs who slumped down in a chair and began to swipe through them. Chai and Stirling took up their positions over each of his shoulders. Hobbs continued, discounting any images which looked to be from Embassy functions or photos of shopping lists destined for Patterson's live-in maid. Any photos of documents were quickly skim-read to see if they potentially had any bearing to the case - none seemed to be. More photos swiped past their gaze: a picture of the Ambassador's car, a container lorry parked in a nondescript car park, a picture of an expensive-looking bottle of red wine.

"Stop," said Chai, gripping Hobbs roughly by the shoulder. "Go back. That truck. Lorry. Whatever you call it."

Hobbs swiped back to the picture of the truck. "This one?"

"Yes. It looks like it's got Burmese plates and that looks like the cargo terminal near the border at Phu Nam Ron." Chai grabbed the tablet from Hobbs and zoomed in. "Yes, look." Chai turned the screen to show the others.

"Doesn't mean anything to me, I'm afraid," replied Hobbs.

"Nor me," said Stirling.

Chai continued to swipe slowly through the next few pictures, then stopped dead in his tracks. A look appeared across his face that began as confusion, then morphed into shock and finally ended with what looked like profound sadness. He looked over to the two detectives who were waiting, wide-eyed, for some information on what the young Thai police officer had just seen. Chai clutched the tablet to his chest as if he was afraid the image would somehow escape from the screen. "I think we've found the secret that the Ambassador was hiding."

Slowly, he turned the tablet round to reveal the image and immediately the same look appeared etched across both of their faces - one of confusion, then shock and finally sadness.

It was a long time before any of them spoke. Their eyes traced over the image, trying in vain to understand, in a split-second, what they were seeing, the cause of it and who might be responsible.

Finally, Chai broke the silence. "I need to get over there and then call this in," he said, matter-of-factly. "We can't keep this a secret any more."

"Then, we'll come with you," replied Hobbs, tearing his gaze from the tablet to meet Chai's.

"No, you two need to find Patterson."

"He's right, Frank. When Chai calls this in, which he has to, there's going to be a circus down there. We don't know how Patterson is connected to this, so when he gets wind of it, there's no telling what he will do."

Hobbs sighed. "OK, fair enough. You know where you're going, Chai. You get down there and then call in the heavies. Let me get a photo of that image. As much as I don't want it on my phone, Patterson needs to see that we know what we know. Debs and I will get in touch with Stella and see where Patterson is. If we're lucky, we can get to him before it's too late."

Chapter 30

Chai pulled up alongside the container truck which was parked in an isolated corner of the cargo terminal. He did an initial walk-around of the vehicle, his right hand rested on his M1911 service pistol. It was nearing noon and the brutal midday sun was beating down on the bare concrete. Peering into the cab, there didn't seem to be anything of note. He tried the driver's door, but found it locked.

Walking around the front of the vehicle, he tried the passenger door, which swung open with a creak. He pulled on a pair of latex gloves that he had grabbed from his own glovebox and stepped up and into the cab. Whomever was driving the lorry had left in a hurry. An uneaten breakfast was moulding in the footwell of the passenger seat along with a half-finished can of Pepsi. He checked the ignition for the keys, but found none. He wondered if there may be a set stashed somewhere in the cab. Luckily, a quick search yielded a spare set and Chai alighted the vehicle, clutching them in his hand.

Walking to the rear of the vehicle, Chai took the time to check along the sides of the vehicle and underneath. Under the cab, a large pool of dark liquid sat staining the concrete.

Chai dropped to a prone position and reached under to test it with a finger tip. Motor oil, he thought to himself. The vehicle clearly had some kind of mechanical fault. The tyres, too, were in poor condition which, along with the rusted wheel nuts, said to Chai that this was a poorly maintained vehicle.

As he moved towards the rear of the vehicle, a moving picture was beginning to form in his mind as to what may have transpired to bring about what he knew was waiting for him. He rounded the rear of the vehicle to find the main rear door locked. He tried one of the keys in the door, which opened but not fully as an additional chain and padlock had been fitted. Chai wandered over to his own vehicle, grabbing a large pair of bolt cutters from the toolkit in the bed of his pickup. With some effort, he managed to cut the padlock and pull the chain out to free the container door. With a deep breath, he tugged on the door and it swung towards him with a long and foreboding creak.

Chai was prepared for what he was about to see, having seen the photographs in advance, but what he wasn't prepared for was the stench which hit him full in the nostrils without the door even being fully open. He wretched loudly, doubled over with tears forming in his eyes. Hands on his knees, he wretched hard again. He spat on the floor and wiped his mouth with his sleeve. Doing everything he could to delay the inevitable, even for a few seconds.

Regaining his composure, and with as deep a breath as he could muster, he swung the double doors open completely to reveal the desperate scene contained within.

Sunlight flooded into the container. Staring back at Chai were the lifeless eyes he had seen in the photographs. Dozens

CHAPTER 30

of pairs of lifeless eyes. Lifeless eyes belonging to dozens of greying lifeless bodies; most of them women, most of them young, many of them huddled together in a final embrace.

Chai turned away to break their gaze and walked a few steps to try and escape the stench of human waste and bodies in the early stages of decomposition. Turning back, Chai scanned the rest of the container. Discarded clothes, footwear and empty water bottles were scattered all over. Insulation, or rather sound-proofing covered the inside walls of the container. The inside of the container door was covered in scratches from the fingernails of the wretched people trapped inside.

Chai placed his hands on his head, interlacing his fingers and breathed heavily again, trying to make sense of what had happened to the people who lay expired in front of him. He counted the bodies.

There were 58.

Chai took out his mobile phone and made two phone calls: the first to Kanchanaburi Police Station to officially report what he had found and the second to Frank Hobbs.

Hobbs answered after only a couple of rings. "Hi, Chai. Can you hear me? How is it over there?"

"It's terrible, Frank. Really terrible. I'm glad you two aren't here to see it, to be honest."

"Shit, Chai. How many of them are there? Who are they? Burmese?"

"It looks like it. We'll have to check their IDs. There's 58, Frank."

"58? Jesus." Hobbs relayed the information to Stirling who was waiting anxiously. "I'm putting you on speaker, Chai. Don't worry, there's nobody around."

"It looks like they all suffocated. There's evidence of mechanical issues with the lorry. They must have broken down on the way for a substantial amount of time - a lot longer than planned - all their water is gone and most removed all their clothing to try and stay cool."

"It must have been like a furnace in there. Those poor bastards."

"Most of them are women; girls, really. I think I counted six males."

"Destined for the sex trade, I suppose. Even the underage ones?"

"I'm afraid so."

"Bloody hell. This is big, Chai. Did you call it in?"

"Yes, just before I called you. Did you call Stella?"

"We did. We explained what we found. She is pretty devastated, of course. She said the Ambassador is still at the cemetery, but she doesn't know for how long."

"OK. I need to stay here and wait for backup. Can you get to the cemetery?"

"Yeah, no worries. We'll get a tuk-tuk, or something. Did you find anything there that might tell us how Patterson is involved?"

"No, not yet. Did you find anything on his computer?"

"Not yet, but Debs is on the case. Her intelligence work should come in handy."

"What are you going to say to Patterson? We haven't really got any evidence he's involved."

"If he wasn't involved, he wouldn't have that picture. He's involved. We're just not sure to what extent yet. Hopefully, he will fold and tell all when we show him the picture."

"OK, call me and let me know what's going on. I have to go.

CHAPTER 30

The staff from the cargo terminal are coming."

"OK, Chai mate. Keep us posted, yeah? Bye."

"Bye, Frank."

Hobbs hung up the call. "We need to get a move on, Debs, before we lose Patterson," he said.

"This is insane, Frank," replied Stirling. "I just can't believe what's happened and that we are somehow at the centre of it all."

"I know, Debs, but it will all be over soon. We're on the final stretch. One last push and we will have all the answers we need - and closure for Ella's family. That's why we're here. That's why we're at the centre of all this. Let's not forget our why, yeah? Let's go get the bastard."

* * *

Less than fifteen minutes later, Hobbs and Stirling pulled up in their tuk-tuk to the entrance of the War Cemetery on the Saeng Chuto Road - the main thoroughfare through the centre of Kanchanaburi town. A grey stone entranceway with three arched walkways served as the entrance to the immaculately-kept graveyard. Hobbs and Stirling strode quickly through the central arch and were met with the sight of a huge turfed area covered on the left and right with rows upon rows of rectangular raised stone plinths, topped with a bronze plate dedicated to each of the nearly seven thousand servicemen who died as prisoners of war in the Japanese camps at Kanchanaburi. In the centre a wide channel of pristine turf ran towards the Cross of Sacrifice; a white stone monolithic cross that marked the very centre of the cemetery. Wreaths had been laid at the foot of the monument by the attendees of the memorial, for whom a host of folding chairs had been arranged.

As Hobbs and Stirling approached, they could see that the memorial service had ended. Attendees were shaking hands, embracing and slowly making their way back towards the entrance. They spotted Stella Ismael, easily distinguished by her mop of middle-eastern curls, sitting at the rear of the service and Richard Patterson, with his back to them, in the front row. They waited patiently at the back of the congregation with Stella for the attendees to slowly filter out.

When Richard Patterson had finished speaking with the last remnants, he turned to see them and was betrayed momentarily by the look of panic that flashed across his face. Recovering quickly, he strode confidently over to them. "Detective Hobbs, Detective Stirling. I was under the impression you were already winging your way back to London." He stretched out a hand for Hobbs to shake, who kept his hands firmly in his pockets.

"I wonder what gave you that idea, Mr Ambassador," Stirling replied, snidely.

"Gosh, gosh. I'm not so sure myself, actually. I've been ever so busy, as you can see. What is it that I can do for you? I was under the impression your business here was concluded and how grateful we all are for your assistance."

"Well," began Hobbs. "we didn't want to leave without filling you in on what we have concluded from our investigation."

"Of course, of course," replied the Ambassador, unconsciously wiping the sweat that had again begun to form on his brow. "I would very much like to be privy to any additional information that has come to light about the accident and its causes. For Ella's mother, you see. Being so far away, she's been very much in the dark about all of this."

"Haven't we all, Mr Ambassador?" replied Stirling, who was beginning to seethe inwardly at the audacity of the man stood in front of her.

Hobbs turned first to check that the remainder of the memorial attendees had left the site before pulling his phone from his pocket. "There was *this* piece of evidence that we found, Mr Patterson," Hobbs said. "We wondered if you could shed some light on it for us."

Hobbs turned the phone around to show the photograph of the gruesome scene that Chai had just witnessed at the cargo terminal. Upon laying eyes on the image, the blood visibly drained from the already pallid face of the Ambassador. He stared in silence for a moment before saying, "My Lord, you two have been very thorough, haven't you?"

"That we have, Mr Ambassador," replied Hobbs. "We don't know all the details yet, of course, but they will come out. The truth will come out."

Stirling tapped the screen of Hobbs' phone dramatically. "The truth that you had your own daughter killed in an attempt to keep your involvement in *this* covered up."

"That will be for the courts to decide, Ms Stirling. I very much doubt you have any legally-obtained evidence to support your case. While I admire your tenacious approach to the investigation, you never really had any jurisdiction here. In reality, you were just playing amateur sleuths in an exotic locale."

Stirling had had enough. "You really are a snake, Richard Patterson. Just like they all said." Her finger was pointed directly in the face of the diplomat now.

Hobbs thought it wise to intervene. "Now, you and I both

know we don't have the jurisdiction to arrest you right here, but I think you and I also both know that I could physically carry you to the station by the scruff of your neck. So, I would be grateful if you would come with us quietly, so as not to cause a scene. What do you think?"

"Certainly, certainly, Mr Hobbs, when you put it that way. I do just have one final request, if you don't mind. I'm sure Stella has told you that my grandfather is buried here - one of the fallen. I would very much like to pay my last respects to him. It may be a while before I next get the chance. His grave is just over there."

Hobbs looked over at Stirling who was stood with her arms folded, tears brimming at the edges of her eyes. She shrugged. Though she hated the thought of affording this monster any kind of fair treatment, she herself had lost friends in the military. She knew what it was like to stand at a graveside to pay your respects to someone who had lost their life in service. Reluctantly, she nodded her head.

Hobbs, Stirling and Stella Ismael followed Patterson over to the area where his grandfather's grave was located. Hanging back out of respect, they watched as Patterson sunk slowly to his knees on the green turf and began to speak in hushed tones. Reaching into his breast pocket, he took out a small, silver medal, which he placed gently in the grass in front of the grave marker.

The three watched as Patterson conducted the private ceremony so slowly and purposefully that he appeared to move in slow motion. When he reached into the inside pocket of his jacket, they assumed it was for another medal or other object of significance to honour his grandfather.

They saw the red mist appear behind his head before they

CHAPTER 30

heard the shot. They saw his body slump to the emerald turf before they could comprehend what had happened. They all stood frozen in time by the sound of the gunshot that echoed loudly among the thousands of graves which surrounded them; a look of shock and fear etched onto their faces as they ducked and sunk to their haunches.

By the time a look of realisation appeared across their faces, Richard Patterson was dead; his eyes rolled back in his head, slumped over the gravestone of his grandfather; a pool of crimson leaking slowly over its bronze engraved cross.

Epilogue

"Can you get that, love? I'm up to my elbows in giblets here," called Hobbs from the kitchen of their modest three-bedroom Victorian terrace. Eileen Hobbs tottered towards the front door, her high heels clattering rhythmically on the exposed wooden floorboards of the hall. She opened the door to see Debra Stirling, bundled up against the elements, clutching a bottle of white wine in one hand and a reusable carrier bag of gifts in another.

"Debra! Come in, Darlin'. It's freezing out there. Merry Christmas." They embraced and Eileen ushered Stirling into the warmth of the kitchen.

Hobbs looked up from the remains of the turkey that he was dutifully hacking to pieces on the kitchen counter. "Debs! You made it!" He dropped his knives and pulled his Santa apron over his head, wiping his hands roughly on it before balling it up and discarding it over the back of a chair.

"Of course, I made it. It's not often we both have Christmas off, is it?"

"That's because we're suspended, mate."

Stirling chuckled. "I think it's referred to as *Administrative Leave* these days."

"Well, I don't care what it's called if it means I get to spend

EPILOGUE

Christmas Day at home with my girls. Speaking of which, have you met Maddie and Millie?"

Stirling shook her head as she removed her winter coat and scarf. "Not yet. I should go and introduce myself."

"No need for that, love," replied Eileen, taking Stirling's coat and scarf from her. "They know all about you. Frank has been filling them in on what he can and they've been glued to the news since you two got back. They both think you're the bee's knees. Millie has already spent some of her Christmas money on this *true crime* book series and Maddie has been looking into joining Missing Persons after Uni."

"Debra Stirling - Feminist Icon," quipped Hobbs. "I guess it's better than her last career idea. What did she call it, babe?"

"Social Media FitFluencer," replied Eileen with a chuckle.

"Buggered if I know what that is," exclaimed Hobbs. "Can we get you something to drink, Debs? Glass of wine? Bucks Fizz?"

"Ooh, a Bucks Fizz would be lovely please, Frank,"

Hobbs grabbed an already-opened bottle of Cava from the fridge and poured Stirling half a flute, topping the rest up with orange juice from a jug on the side. "Didn't fancy Tenerife with your mum and dad for Christmas, then?" he asked, handing Stirling her glass.

"No, no. I told them I don't want to set foot in another tropical country for at least a year. Give me frigid South London any day."

Hobbs laughed. "Fair enough."

"I woke up to a message from Chai this morning, by the way," said Stirling off-handedly, after taking a sip of her drink.

"Ooh, I bet you did," teased Hobbs. "Business or *pleasure*?"

Stirling fought down a blush. "Mind your own business,

Frank,"

"That's the problem, Debs. I can't. It's my job not to mind my own business - and yours."

"Touché. Anyway, he said he'll give us a call later. He's quite a few hours ahead. He said he has some updates for us on the case."

"OK. I've seen some bits on the news but the girls have been filling me in, mostly. Chai will have the inside track, of course. We'll see after dinner, then. Come on, come and meet the girls properly. Eileen wasn't joking when she said they've been dying to meet you."

Maddie and Millie Hobbs were both curled up on the sofa in the living room scrolling through their Socials when Stirling poked her head around the door.

"Hi, Girls. Merry Christmas. I'm Debra; your dad's partner at work."

"Oh Em Gee!" they both squealed, dropping their phones instantly and racing across the living room, trapping Stirling in an enthusiastic double embrace.

"We've heard so much about you and what you did with dad out in Thailand. You were soooo brave," gushed Maddie, twirling the long blonde hair that she shared with her younger sister.

"And soooo smart," chirped Millie, not wanting to be left out. "Dad was telling us how you worked out how tall Win Nyan Bo would be, just from his stride. That's some real life *CSI: Miami*, stuff."

"Don't you mean, *CSI: Kanchanaburi*?" quipped Hobbs, garnering a groan and then a chuckle from the girls and Stirling.

"Come on, Girls. Let the poor woman sit down and relax,

EPILOGUE

won't you?" said Eileen, entering the room with the bottle of Cava.

"Yes, you can sit here with us," said Maddie, ushering Stirling towards a spot on the sofa.

"Yes, between us," Millie tweeted, patting the sofa and smiling from ear-to-ear.

For the next few hours, the Hobbs family and Stirling drank wine and orange juice, and feasted on Hobbs' famous turkey and all the trimmings. After dinner, they played party games and exchanged gifts. The call from Chai came fortuitously at the end of a long and drawn-out game of *Charades* wherein Hobbs just couldn't manage to muster up the answer of *Harry Potter and the Philosopher's Stone*.

"We'll take this in the kitchen, if you don't mind, babe?" said Hobbs to his wife, giving her a peck on the top of her head. "Won't be long."

"Sorry, Girls. "Duty calls." said Stirling, excusing herself and following Hobbs out of the living room and into the kitchen.

Stirling answered the call as she propped up her phone against an unopened bottle of wine on the breakfast bar in Frank's kitchen. "Hi, Chai. Merry Christmas!"

"Merry Christmas, Debs, and Frank," he replied with a wide smile. "Are you having a good day? I used to love Christmas when I was in the UK."

"Having a smashing day, mate," replied Hobbs. "We wish you were here - Debs, especially."

Stirling gave Hobbs a swift but playful jab in the ribs. "Yes, we're having a lovely time. Thanks, Chai. How are you?"

"I am fine. I just wanted to update you on what has been happening here. Not everything is in the news, you know?"

"Yes, mate. Fire away."

"OK. So, you know that the police were doing a proper forensic examination of Patterson's computer, right?" Hobbs nodded. "Well, you were right that he was involved. He was in deep with the trafficking ring. They found lists of names of senior and junior diplomats, police chiefs, CEOs of major companies from all over the region - not just Thailand but Laos, Vietnam, Cambodia, the Philippines, even Singapore."

"All places that Patterson had contacts," remarked Stirling.

"Right," continued Chai. "There was also evidence from his bank accounts of payments from these people into Patterson's personal offshore accounts. It appears he was finding wealthy clients for the traffickers who would supply them with the girls from Burma."

"How long has this been going on?" asked Hobbs.

"Years and years, there are records going back more than ten years."

"How did he get away with it for so long?" asked Stirling.

"Of course, he had the local police in his pocket."

"Anupong," blurted Hobbs, with venom.

"Yes, he was on the list - receiving regular money from Patterson, and the governor of Kanchanaburi, too. They were all involved, even the father of Ella's friend Ploy who was murdered. He maintains he didn't know about her murder, but who knows?"

"So what is going to happen to Captain Arsepong?" asked Hobbs with palpable distaste. "I hope he gets what's coming to him."

"He already did. He was murdered in a holding cell in Bangkok. He was stabbed. 58 times."

"Jesus. 58 times. That sounds personal," remarked Hobbs.

"One for every victim," replied Stirling, solemnly. "What

about the victims' families? Is there some kind of compensation coming from the Thai government?"

"There should be. It hasn't been confirmed but they're angry - of course."

"And rightly so. Is there going to be a memorial of any kind?" asked Hobbs.

"That's also what I wanted to talk to you about. Ella's parents, in Denmark, have been in contact with the families of the Burmese victims. They want to do a joint memorial in Kanchanaburi. Ella's parents wanted to plant a tree in memory of their daughter - a *leelawadee,* or *Frangipani* - it was Ella's favourite as it had the letters of her name in it. Patterson had arranged for it to be planted in the grounds of the British Club in Bangkok."

"Well that's entirely inappropriate," interjected Stirling.

"Exactly," said Chai, in agreement. "So Ella's family and the victim's families want it planted in Kanchanaburi. The new governor has offered for it to be planted in the park, opposite the train station to serve as a memorial for all the victims of human trafficking in the country."

"That's a nice idea," said Stirling. Hobbs nodded solemnly in agreement.

"There will be a memorial service in the new year, for the planting. Ella's parents are flying over from Denmark and they asked if you would attend."

Hobbs and Stirling looked at each other. "We would love to attend, Chai. Of course, we would," replied Hobbs. "It's just that we've only just got back and flights are expensive."

"That's all covered by the British Embassy in Bangkok. Flights, hotels, everything.

I spoke to the new Ambassador today. She confirmed it."

"She?" asked Stirling.

"Stella?" asked Hobbs, expectantly.

"She was one of the only senior diplomats not on Patterson's list. She's standing in at the moment, but everyone expects it to become official soon," replied Chai with a smile.

"In that case, I'll definitely be there," replied Hobbs, giving Chai a virtual thumbs up to the camera. "What do you think, Debs? Do you fancy another trip to the Land of Smiles?"

Stirling looked over at Hobbs and shrugged. "Why not? What's the worst that could happen?"

Author's Note

You would be forgiven, dear reader, for thinking that Thailand must be an abhorrent hive of scum and villainy, not unlike Tattooine's *Mos Eisley Cantina*. That is, of course, entirely my fault and the fault of some of the more nefarious characters in *Derailed*. Fortunately, the almost absolute opposite is true. Thailand is the most wonderful country and one that I spent some of the best years of my life. The people are, undoubtedly, some of the friendliest and kindest you could hope to find on your travels.

Of course, like any country, there are a few bad apples that can give a country a bad name but, thankfully, these type of people are just a tiny minority of the 65 million people who call the Kingdom of Thailand home. The vast majority (as mused by Stirling herself) are kind, wonderful human beings who would give you the shirt off their back even if they didn't have enough to buy a new one. The kindness and warmth I have been shown over the years by the Thai people, especially as a foreigner, will always stay with me and I hope resonates through the darker underbelly of this story.

The villains of this story are an amalgamation of many shady characters who hit the headlines over my nine-year stint of living full-time in Thailand. The events portrayed in this story are also an amalgamation of various news stories, *magpied* and modified to fit the plot of the story I wanted to tell.

Thailand, like many developing countries, has a long way to go in terms of human rights for all, and, in particular, for the stateless and refugee peoples who claim refuge within its borders. There will always be those who exploit others for their own personal gain, but I am hopeful with more progressive governance the situation for these people, especially the young women who often suffer the most, will improve.

This story had been lingering in the back of my mind for years. From the very first time the idea sprouted in my brain, it has caused me many a sleepless night. Too many times I found myself reaching for my phone after midnight to digitally scribble down my ideas before they were lost into the abyss of sleep. The credit for actually helping me putting pen to paper (or should I say, fingertips to keyboard?) on this project has to go to my good friends Emily and Hanif, who, on a visit to Chengdu in China's Sichuan province, gave me the confidence to make my dreams a reality (quite literally).

Thanks also have to go to my mother - my biggest fan and the first person to read the first few chapters of my first foray into the world of mystery fiction. She even said my writing reminded her of Robert Galbraith, better known as J.K. Rowling. She would say that - she's my mum.

Thanks also to my long-time *Habibi* of Bangkok, Chengdu and Guangzhou - Felipe, who was my earliest cheerleader, spurring me on with inspirational messages such as, "Where is my f***ing book?!" Sincere thanks to this special human and all the other special humans who took the time to read my incomplete ramblings in their infancy - Kent, Ben, et al.

Also spurring me on to finish this undertaking, Sam H of Brunei fame, who not only read my writing but managed to start, finish and get his own book on Amazon before mine was even half-done. Motivation indeed! Also from my Brunei chapter, special thanks must go to my good friend, Braaian Leadfoot, who helped to push me kicking and screaming over the finish line.

If you enjoyed this story, please consider leaving an honest review on Amazon or Goodreads. It would be greatly appreciated. Reviews help other readers to find stories they may enjoy and increase visibility and credibility for independent authors such as myself.

For updates on future works, you can follow me on Threads and Instagram: at **@a.m.riley_author** or visit my author website: **amrileyauthor.my.canva.site**

I'm off for a bacon butty.

Cheers.

A.M.R.

Printed in Great Britain
by Amazon